Keith Brooke & Eric Brown

WORMHOLE

ANGRY ROBOT

ANGRY ROBOT
An imprint of Watkins Media Ltd

Unit 11, Shepperton House
89 Shepperton Road
London N1 3DF
UK

angryrobotbooks.com
twitter.com/angryrobotbooks
They want it all

An Angry Robot paperback original, 2022

Cover by Kate Cromwell
Edited by Simon Spanton and Claire Rushbrook
Set in Meridien

ISBN 978 0 85766 996 4
Ebook ISBN 978 0 85766 998 8

Printed and bound in the United Kingdom by TJ Books Ltd.

9 8 7 6 5 4 3 2 1

To Alex Cannon,
with thanks

1

Cold Case

Kemp swivelled his recliner and stared through the narrow window of his office. Somewhere outside, he knew, the sun had come up over London. Snow had fallen during the night. On the rooftops it would be crisp and white, but down here in the shady alleyway to the rear of Homicide HQ all was grey slush and windblown litter. As Kemp peered up at the sliver of dawn sky, he caught the glare of a sub-orb rising like a slow firework from the Thames estuary hub fifty kilometres away, heading east to China.

Around Kemp, images of the dead shimmered in the unlighted office. He knew he owed it to these people – or rather to their loved ones and relatives – to turn his seat back to the console and engage with the database, but he was struck by a soul-sapping inertia that kept him staring through the window.

His imp bleeped and, reluctantly, he turned and signalled to take the call. He expected it to be Danni, telling him to shift himself and join her in the car. Either her or Commander Tsang with yet another case to add to the workload.

It was neither. The image of an overweight man in a crumpled suit resolved itself over his desk: Edouard Bryce. Kemp sat up. "Ed. It's been months."

A case had thrown Kemp and the lawyer together five years ago, and much to Kemp's surprise, the working liaison had developed into a friendship. They had a lot in common. They were both widowers – both in their late fifties – overweight and overworked, and they both liked dark, old-fashioned pubs where they could drink away their worries and gripe about their respective jobs.

"I'm sorry," Bryce said, "but Ma Holding died yesterday."

Kemp's automatic response was to glance immediately at the ghost image of Sophie Holding. "I knew she was ill."

"I saw her just before... She wanted to thank you for everything you'd done."

Kemp swore. "That was fuck all, Ed."

Bryce shrugged. "You could say that. Or you could say that you gave her hope. That was all she had to cling to. I saw her before those meetings you had with her, and I saw her afterwards. You were incredible. You gave her something to live for."

"For all the good it did."

"Nevertheless."

Kemp sighed. "I'm sorry. It's just..." He signalled, swung his hand around his head and the images of the dead processed around the room and lined up behind him so that Bryce could see the gallery.

"Look, Ed. Fifty-five of them. They're from nine years back to... to around twenty-five years ago. You know what they say on this job? The law of diminishing returns: the older a case is, the less chance there is of solving it. I worked my balls off on the Holding case and got nowhere. Dead end after dead end after..."

Bryce nodded, conciliatory. "I know, Gordon. But, you know, you do tend to dwell on the cases that remain unsolved. Don't forget all the ones you *do* resolve. Every time you do that, you allow entire families to move on, and you're damned good at what you do."

"*When* I crack the fuckers."

He waved again, killed the images – all but one. He dragged

it before him, so that the 3D portrait of the eighteen year-old Afro-Caribbean girl hung between him and Bryce, smiling out at him. He gestured, and the image started to cycle through a short recording of the girl laughing and talking to camera. He didn't have to unmute her to hear the soft tones of her voice in his head.

"Look at her, Bryce." Kemp shook his head. "You went to Ma Holding's place. You saw all the pix she had of Sophie. They were her way of coping, of keeping her only daughter alive and with her. And she trusted me to find her killer."

"As I said, you gave her hope."

"And there are fifty-four others. And their families and loved ones who *haven't* been able to move on. You know something?"

"Go on."

"Days like today, I feel like retiring."

Bryce smiled. "A little way to go yet, Gordon."

"Or requesting a transfer. Not that anywhere else would have me."

"Surely, with all your experience..."

"You know me, Ed. I don't fit anywhere else, and I can't take authority. Too bolshy by half – Tsang's own words."

Which wasn't the whole truth. Even Ed Bryce, who Kemp considered his best friend, didn't know why he'd been put out to pasture in the 'morgue' after twenty years in homicide.

"I called you about something else, other than Ma Holding," Bryce said.

"More bad news?"

"It's been a while since I had Martin look over your imp."

Kemp didn't trust his superiors – he wouldn't have been surprised if Commander Tsang turned out to be a Chinese mole – and his mistrust extended to the content of his annual implant upgrades. He didn't like the idea that every year Tsang had his techs download who-knew-what into his running system.

He'd once grumbled about this to Bryce over a beer, and the lawyer had said he knew just the man to run a few tests on Kemp's implant and ensure it was clean. Bryce knew a lot of people from every walk of life – and one of them was Martin Khalsa, a cyber-wizard whose definition of legality was elastic. The upshot was that after every department upgrade, Martin scanned Kemp's implant for spyware and whatever other nasties Tsang's team might have planted.

Now Kemp waved. "No need. Still running on the same program as last year. I'll be in touch when they call me in for an upgrade, okay?"

"In the meantime," Bryce said, "let's meet. You look like you could use a drink."

"I'm busy today, but maybe tomorrow."

"Tomorrow it is, then."

They chatted for another five minutes before Bryce was called away and cut the connection.

Kemp reinstated the gallery of the dead, pushed it back to the darkened walls, and once again turned to stare out at what passed for a view.

A month ago he'd gone to see Ma Holding in her bedsit by Hackney Lakes to give her what he euphemistically called a progress report. He visited her every once in a while, like a dutiful son, although it became harder on each occasion. This time he'd even considered lying about a new lead – anything to stoke her hope, particularly when her health was clearly failing. She'd gripped his hand and stared at him with her massive, yellowing eyes. "You'll find him for me, won't you, Gordon?"

He'd prised her fingers from his and promised that he'd find Sophie's killer if it were the last thing he did.

He willed himself to turn the seat, access the database and go through the Holding case yet again. He knew that for the next few days he'd be fired up, until frustration at not getting anywhere overcame him and he took up the freshest case on file, leaving Sophie's murder unsolved and Ma Holding's hope to die with her.

He looked up, seeing Danni in the doorway, leaning slantwise against the frame, and wondered how long she'd been there.

"You look, if you don't mind my saying, as if you've slept all night in that seat." Her voice was Home Counties, primly correct. Anyone less like a DI he'd never met. She wore a dark trouser suit like a uniform, with its side-fastening tunic and high collar, and her jet hair was long and straight. She looked like a high-flying executive up for an interview with a pan-global consortium.

"'My saying'," he mocked.

She was twenty-five years his junior, and even though they shared the same rank, she was his superior in charge of this unit. When she was instated over him in the morgue, he'd come in for relentless flak from colleagues. Kemp had shrugged and told them, truthfully, that he couldn't give a damn. In fact, he was glad of the company, and Danni Bellini turned out to be a decent kid who didn't rub his nose in the fact that she was a fast-tracked Cambridge graduate and he an ill-educated slob who'd risen, slowly, through the ranks.

"But no, I haven't been here all night. No more than an hour. Oh – I just had a call from Bryce. Ma Holding passed away yesterday."

"I heard." She entered the room, picked her way round discarded curry cartons and beer bulbs biodegrading on the floor, and sat down.

"So I'm setting a couple of things aside and going through the files again," he said.

She stared at him through the shadows, then shook her head. "Not today, Gordon."

"What?"

"I've just seen Tsang. You're not going to like this."

"Like what?"

She gestured around the office at the fifty-five dead people staring at them. "Tsang has just ordered us to put everything aside for a while."

"Everything? You're joking?"

"He wants us to look into something else. Priority. A single case. We've to give it our full attention."

Kemp grunted, "Fuck him."

"That's what I nearly said."

Kemp smiled at that. For all her middle-class primness, Danni could swear with the best of them. "So what's this case? Must be important." He had to admit, if only to himself, that his curiosity had been piqued.

"It is. A top research scientist, working at the cutting edge of suspension technology. Well-connected. A very high-profile case."

"Why haven't I heard of this before now? And since when has suspension technology been cutting edge?"

She combed a long strand of dark hair from her cheek and smiled at him. "Because this cold case is *really* cold," she said. "The victim was Sebastian White, and he was murdered eighty years ago."

Kemp blinked, processing her words. "That's not a cold case, Danni. That's an archaeological dig."

"I said something not dissimilar to Tsang."

"If we can't find Sophie's killer – and that happened fifteen years ago – then how the hell can we be expected to solve a case eighty years old?" He shook his head. "This doesn't make sense. The killer will be dead, any witnesses likewise. I mean, what the hell does it even *matter* after so long?"

"I know." She bit her lip. "There's something strange going on. Tsang was insistent. He wants us to devote everything to this. The odd thing is, he couldn't, or wouldn't, tell me who authorised the case."

"It's come down a long way?"

"From the very top," she said.

His first reaction was one of anger – anger that a pen-pusher like Tsang had ordered them to set aside more than fifty ongoing cases. Then he considered what Danni had told him, and his anger tempered into curiosity again.

"I'm intrigued. Look, I'll just grab a tea and we'll access the file."

"I squirted it to your desk as soon as I left Tsang," Danni said. "But let's go up to mine." She looked around the mess of his room.

They took the elevator to Danni's spacious office four floors up, with a view of snow-bound London on two sides. She made him a mug of English Breakfast tea while he accessed the file and brought a still image of the murder victim into the air before him.

They sat side by side, sipping tea, and Danni talked him through the case.

"Sebastian White," she said, indicating the floating image. "A British Euro national, fifty-four. He and his wife were two of the continent's leading scientists in the field of suspended animation."

The pix showed a thin-faced, hawk-nosed, balding man with a severe expression. "He graduated from Oxford in 2075," Danni said. "Spent ten years at MIT in the States, then was lured back by the European Space Organisation, who offered him a fabulous salary and a lab staffed by the best scientists and technicians from across Europe. For the last twenty-four years of his life, he worked in the ESO labs in Geneva."

"The name's familiar," he said. "Wasn't he related to Randolph White?"

Danni nodded. She moved a hand over the virtual keyboard and a second pix shimmered into life beside the first. This one showed a familiar head-and-shoulders image of Randolph White, the patrician statesman and the founding father of the United States of Europe. He was thin-faced and aquiline, with distinguished greying hair and smiling eyes.

"Randolph White was sixty when his younger brother was

murdered, and he took it badly, by all accounts. They were close. Randolph retired from public life soon after – some said he spiralled into depression after the murder. He died five years later, in 2114."

She waved a hand again and the image of Randolph vanished, to be replaced with a dozen scene-of-crime pix.

Kemp frowned. "These all we've got?"

"It's all Tsang came up with. He assumes interactives were shot, but if so, they were lost."

"Lost?"

"This was eighty years ago, Gordon. Officially, the case was closed five years later."

"What about interactives with the suspects?"

"Tsang has requested them from Geneva," she said.

Kemp studied the scene-of-crime pix.

Twenty years in Homicide had accustomed him to grisly images. By comparison with some, though, these were tame. There was a lot of blood, but the victim had suffered just a single stab wound.

Half a dozen images showed Sebastian White from different angles. He was lying on his back in a big, pristine kitchen, sunlight illuminating a face as pale as his old-fashioned white suit. The hilt of a knife emerged from the centre of his chest and the front of his suit was stained red.

"He died within seconds. Forensics have drawn up a profile of the killer. They think the culprit was taller than the victim, weighing between 70 and 90 kilos, either a man or a woman."

Kemp grunted. "That narrows it down. DNA?"

Danni shook her head. "None."

"What?"

"Not a trace."

"So it was a pro. An assassin. No one else could have got away without leaving some biological trace."

"Or it was someone with sufficient scientific know-how to be able to wipe the place clean."

"What about motive?"

"None apparent. He was, by all accounts, happily married to a fellow scientist, was well-liked and had plenty of friends. There was a rumour at the time that it might have been the Russians, attempting to slow down ESO's Mu Arae programme. But if that were so, they left it late in the day. I think we can discard that line of enquiry."

A government-backed assassin certainly fit the profile of someone who could cover their tracks so well, but Kemp knew the security services would have been all over that angle at the time and had clearly come up with nothing.

Danni waved again. The scene-of-crime images shrank to the periphery and the pix of a vast, bulky starship hovered above the desk. "The *Strasbourg*. You know what happened?"

"My father was obsessed," Kemp said. "He followed the mission when he was a kid, and while I was growing up, he watched the holos obsessively. It must have been a hell of a shock to those who'd lived through the mission at the time."

"You can say that again. The hope of Europe, if not the world, rested on the success of the *Strasbourg*."

Ninety years ago, ESO had discovered an Earth-like planet orbiting the star Mu Arae, fifty lightyears from Earth. Travelling at top speed, a ship would take almost eighty years to reach the planet – which pretty much ruled out a crewed expedition... until ESO announced a breakthrough in their research into suspended animation.

In 2110 the mission to Mu Arae II lighted out from the Earth orbital station with ninety-six technicians, scientists and assorted specialists aboard, all in suspended animation for the duration of the trip.

Danni stared at the image of the ship. "Hard to believe that they'd have arrived by now – this very year, in fact – if not for the blow-out." Seeing the spark in her eyes, Kemp was surprised; he'd never had her down as a space geek.

She waved, and the stilled image of the *Strasbourg* came to life, moving across a dusted starscape with stately grace. This was a computer-generated mock-up, of course, put together from facts gleaned from the telemetry that had reached Earth four months into the mission.

A tiny bloom of flame showed three quarters of the way down the colossal length of the *Strasbourg*, causing multiple internal explosions and a catastrophic rupture to the spine of the starship. With agonising slowness, over the course of ten long minutes, the ship broke up with the loss of all ninety-six scientists and technicians.

Danni said, "Sebastian White was one of the top scientists working on the suspended animation technology used aboard the *Strasbourg*."

She wiped the starship from above her desk and reinstated the scene-of-crime pix, staring at the image of the dead man. "For a time after White's murder, suspicion focused on three people."

"And these were?"

Danni waved, and three mugshots shimmered into life above the desk. "Lee Chan-Wu, White's deputy in the suspension lab at ESO. Motive: he wanted White's job. All very well, but Chan-Wu was at a conference in Paris at the time of the killing, with a comprehensive digital footprint and about a hundred witnesses. Then there was Ed Malroux, White's business partner. White had his fingers in a number of financial pies across the state, and not all of them were going well. Some sources suggest that there were 'differences of opinion' between the two men, leading to an argument."

"And I suppose Malroux had a cast-iron alibi too?"

She nodded. "He was in a business meeting with his financial adviser in Lucerne on the morning of White's death, all of which was confirmed by telemetry and digital mapping."

"They could always have hired a pro to do the job, of course," he pointed out. "Who's the woman?"

The third pix showed the smiling image of a dark-haired,

dark-skinned woman in her mid-thirties, attractive in a wide-jawed, broad-shouldered, athletic kind of way.

"Rima Cagnac, Sebastian White's wife. Parisian and a top researcher in the same field as her husband. They met working for ESO on the Mu Arae project. According to White's personal assistant, she'd been overheard arguing with her husband the day before the murder."

"But I take it that she had an alibi too?"

"She was in a one-to-one meeting with a Captain Xavier Fernandez, five kilometres away at the time of the murder. The digital trace isn't so comprehensive in Cagnac's case – she'd turned her comms off – but Fernandez was regarded as a solid witness."

Kemp frowned. "Now why is that name familiar?"

"He was the captain of the *Strasbourg*," Danni said.

"Why was Cagnac meeting him?"

"Rima Cagnac was heading the suspension team aboard the *Strasbourg*," Danni said. "Six days after her husband was killed, she left Earth for Mu Arae on the ill-fated ship."

Kemp looked at her. "That sounds... suspiciously convenient, not to mention cold-hearted, for her to leave at such a time."

Danni shrugged. "I'm not sure. She'd been training for the mission for years, remember. And we don't know how close she was to her husband."

He stared at the image of the smiling woman. "And four months after embarking on the mission, she died in the blow-out."

"Not that she would have suffered in the accident," she said. "The experts say that everyone aboard the ship perished instantly."

Kemp grunted. "It's to be hoped they're right."

"Such a tragic case in many ways," Danni said, staring at Cagnac. "I don't know... but she seems so – so confident and optimistic, there. She was at the top of her profession, about to travel to another star, then her husband is butchered and the *Strasbourg* explodes. Christ, no one knows what lies in wait."

"Either that or she was a stone-cold murderer," Kemp pointed out. "Cheer up. All this is long gone."

"Yes, but doesn't that make it all the more poignant? If the *Strasbourg* hadn't blown up, Cagnac would be alive and about to step onto the soil of another world."

"You love all this stuff, don't you, Danni? Starships and alien worlds. You're a real space geek."

She raised her cup to her mouth, hiding her smile. "Those movies were everywhere when I was growing up," she said. "Isn't it every child's dream to see new worlds?"

He shrugged. "So... where the hell do we start with this? The investigators' initial reports, I suppose."

She shook her head. "We start by interviewing someone who was around at the time."

He stared at her. "You're kidding? This was eighty years ago..."

"You've heard of Sir Alastair Fairleigh-White?"

"Wasn't he a politician?"

"A Tory cabinet minister. He was Sebastian White's son, from his first marriage."

"He must be a hell of an age by now."

"He's a hundred and twelve, and has just undergone his third rejuvenation treatment. According to Tsang, the process failed, spectacularly. An abortive telomerase snip disrupted neural functioning and dislodged some old memories."

"So this was why the case was reopened?"

"That's a possibility. I'm not exactly looking forward to this. Tsang asked how strong my stomach was."

Kemp raised an eyebrow.

"Apparently the man's little more than a cadaver. He's resident at some exclusive private hospital in Berkshire."

"Great," he said. "Are we taking your car? Mine's..."

"I've seen your car," she said. "It's not much better than your office."

Kemp smiled awkwardly. 'Not much better than his office' was putting it kindly.

2

Chromosomal Dysfunction

It took over an hour to motor through the fifty kilometres of urban sprawl from central London to rural Berkshire, but at least Danni's Zhongua was both spacious and immaculately clean.

They passed the ruins of the old sub-orbital station at Ealing, bombed by nationalist terrorists fifty years ago and left *in situ* – a surreal arrangement of twisted metal and blackened buildings – as an epitaph to the three thousand citizens killed in the attack. Around it, and on either side of the road leading out of London, gleaming state-of-the-art domes and minarets testified to massive Chinese investment. Kemp was old enough to accept the takeover as the inevitable consequence of a failing economy devoured by the expansionist tide of Cathay imperialism, though he recalled his father's animosity to all things Oriental. He'd died a bitter man, spouting the xenophobic tirades of his Tory heroes. His father would have given his right arm to have met Sir Alastair Fairleigh-White... though perhaps not in his current physical condition.

As the car eased itself from the slipway, the onboard narrated their route, interspersed with ads and a stream of mindless Shanghai popzak. The car slid between greenery dripping with deliquescing snow; wintry sunlight reflected in puddles on the tarmac ahead. Kemp found it oddly unsettling to be out of London.

He laughed.

"What?"

"I just realised, this must be the first time I've been out of the city in almost five years."

She stared at him. "Are you sure?"

"I think so. Can you recall a case that wasn't in London?"

"Okay, but you must have left the city at some point. Life isn't all about work."

"Why would I? I don't know anyone who lives outside the capital–"

"What about holidays?"

"You know I can't stand them. I'd rather spend my free time online."

She stared at him. "For someone who reads all that history stuff–"

"Says the space geek. Go on."

"You have a very limited... how shall I put this?"

"Knowledge? I know nothing, is what you mean. Well, I know a lot about life in the twentieth and twenty-first century, before the takeover."

She murmured, "For all the good that does you."

"We all have our interests. You're obsessed with spaceflight." He couldn't resist adding, "For all the good that does you."

"Touché."

He looked at her, surprised by her capitulation. Usually she would have argued with him – and won. There was something about her today. She seemed distant, distracted.

He changed the subject. "Anyway, what do you know about Sir Alastair Fairleigh-White, other than the fact that he was a Conservative cabinet minister back before you were born?"

He glanced at the windscreen readout, which told him they were five kilometres from their destination.

"He was on the far right of the party," Danni said, "anti-Europe and virulently anti-Chinese."

"A Little Englander, in other words." He thought back to the bombed-out ruins they had passed in Ealing, relic of a bitterly nationalistic period.

She frowned. "I haven't heard that expression."

"Ah... you should read more history," he said. "It's a mid-twentieth term to denote a prevalent political insularity amongst those of the right at the time."

"His pro-British stance put him out of step with his uncle, Randolph White. They had little time for each other, and Alastair ploughed a lone political furrow."

"What were the politics of his father, Sebastian?"

"Sebastian and his brother Randolph were both pro-European Unionists."

The car took a turning off the main road and decreased speed along a leafy lane between vast fields of gnarled grapevines. "How old was Alastair when his father was murdered? Hold on, you said he's a hundred and twelve now, and Sebastian was killed eighty years ago... Thirty-two, right?"

Danni laughed. "My God, Gordon, you're a mathematician, too."

Kemp tipped an imaginary hat. "I wonder what memories the rejuve process has dislodged? Do you know where he was when his father was murdered?"

"According to the investigator's reports, he was a junior minister at the time, attending a committee meeting in Westminster."

"Probably trying his best to scupper the Chinese buyout of Birmingham. That was around that time, wasn't it?"

"Pass."

"Eighty years ago..." Kemp said. "Join the cold case team and visit the past."

The onboard carolled, "We approach our destination. Please prepare for arrival."

Kemp straightened in his seat as they progressed along a lane between ancient oak trees. In the distance, standing on a slight rise, was the foursquare Georgian monolith of Carstairs

Hall. They came to a perimeter wall and the car slowed to a halt before an iron gate. Danni touched her wristcom and murmured her name.

The gates swung slowly open and the car eased up a gravelled drive towards the house.

They were met on a grand sweep of steps of the Hall by a tall young man in an impeccably cut black suit who introduced himself as Peter Conway, the business manager at Carstairs Hall.

"Commander Tsang informed me you were on your way. If you'd care to follow me..." He led them into a vast marble hallway, then gestured along a corridor. Despite the manor house exterior of the Hall, its interior was decorated in generic Chinoiserie style: geometrical wooden furniture, folding screens decorated with red and gold brushstroke dragons and pagodas, planters of orchids and porcelain foo dogs. "This way. I'll introduce you to Sir Alastair's personal clinician."

They proceeded along the corridor to the building's west wing, then through an archway and along another corridor. The young man paused before a door, knocked, and stood back as it opened and a small, birdlike man in a grey suit stepped out into the corridor, pulling the door shut behind him.

Conway introduced them to Dr Radzinski, who gave the impression that he could have done without the interruption.

He dismissed Conway with a tetchy wave and said, as he watched the young man retreat, "This is highly irregular, Inspector Bellini. My patient is far from well."

"We'll be as quick as we possibly can, Doctor. We wouldn't be here if it wasn't absolutely–"

"Very well," Radzinski said irritably.

"We understand that your patient's rejuvenation process wasn't one hundred percent successful," Kemp said, and relished the doctor's uneasy wince.

"Sir Alastair was undergoing a tertiary telomerase procedure – not in itself a challenging process. However, his age, and the fact that it was his third..."

"What happened?" Danni asked.

"In layman's terms, the procedure sequentially splits open the telomeres in order to splice in new sequences and prolong chromosomal lifespan. In this case the telomeres had suffered considerable wear and tear in the earlier operations and so the splicing stage proceeded incompletely."

"You pulled a thread and couldn't put it all back together again?" Kemp said, gratified once more by the doctor's wincing response.

"There's nothing you can do to save him?" Danni asked.

"His condition is terminal," Radzinski replied. "He is currently experiencing a brief period of boosted neural activity, after which..."

"How long is he expected to live?" Kemp asked.

"A matter of days. Perhaps, if he is unfortunate, a week or two."

"And this brief period of neural activity is what's released some long-buried memories?" Kemp asked.

Radzinski nodded. "I told Commander Tsang that you should prepare yourself for a shock. Patients at this stage of rejuvenation corruption do not present a pretty sight."

"I spent twenty years in Homicide," Kemp said. "I've seen lots of ugly sights."

"This way," the doctor said, opening the door.

Kemp glanced at Danni and gestured for her to precede him into the room. He expected to enter a regulation bedroom, decorated in the same Chinoiserie style as the rest of Carstairs Hall, and to see the patient stretched out in bed. Instead, the room's décor was a facsimile of how these rooms might have looked when the hall had been a stately home, with a Chippendale dresser, a plush chaise longue by the window, and a deep carpet. Presumably the room had been fitted out in this way so its inhabitant was not reminded that he was in anything but an idyllic and very English setting.

Instead of a bed, though, Sir Alastair Fairleigh-White

was contained in a diaphanous rejuve pod the like of which Kemp had only ever seen before in interactives: a transparent carapace plugged into monitors and life-support systems, with a clear screen flipped back so that its occupant could peer out at them without hindrance.

No words of warning could have prepared Kemp for the sight of the body, its papery skin stretched over protuberant bones. The pod stood at a forty-five-degree angle, with sulphurous fluid bubbling in its bottom half and swirling around the patient's skeletal legs. A dozen catheters were jacked into veins across his chest and arms, but it was the man's head that Kemp found most shocking. The skin was almost translucent, with seemingly no flesh or musculature beneath – as if a layer of tissue had been soaked in clarified butter and stretched like papier-mâché across his skull.

Bright blue eyes rolled in the direction of the visitors.

Kemp noted the flutter of Danni's eyes as she blinked the command for her imp to record what followed.

Dr Radzinski murmured, "He can hear only with an embedded amplifier, and any replies he might make will be sub-vocal and computer-aided." He brushed his fingers across a virtual keyboard beside the pod, then looked at his watch. "Five minutes only," he said, and left the room.

Danni glanced at Kemp, who gestured for her to begin. Unsurely, she introduced herself and Kemp, then said, "Thank you for agreeing to see us, Sir Alastair. We're investigating the murder of your father. We understand you have information relevant to the case."

Kemp found himself staring at the man's bright blue eyes. He wondered at the level of mentation functioning behind them, wondered if the remains of the centenarian were aware of the horrible irony of paying for treatment to renew his life only to have it go so terribly wrong.

He expected Fairleigh-White to croak a reply, then recalled that any words he might utter would be computer-assisted.

His reply, when it came, was loaded with yet more irony: the old nationalist's last words on Earth would be replicated in the lilting cadence of Chinese English. "My father... so long ago... murdered..."

Danni licked her lips. "That's right. I'm so sorry. The memory must be painful."

"Memory... memories. My father... dead now, dead so long ago. Murdered... stabbed to death. We... we never saw eye to eye, but I loved him... loved him. My mother... she died young... I never knew her... My father brought me up... so long ago."

Danni said, "We understand that you might be able to aid our investigation into who murdered your father. You have information...?"

Kemp stared at the face. The flesh might have been dead, as no flicker of expression moved across its surface. The mouth sagged, revealing buttery nubbins of teeth and a cataract of saliva.

"The killer... I know... I know who killed my father."

Danni stepped forward and asked, softly, "Who was it, Sir Alastair?"

"My uncle knew who did it, you see... One day I was in... in Paris... at his house. This was some years after the murder. Randolph was... I overheard him talking to his secretary... My uncle, Randolph... he heard me outside the door, called me in... He... he told me not to repeat what I'd heard."

Danni glanced at Kemp, then asked, "Sir Alastair, please tell me who killed your father."

Kemp stared at the eyes as they rolled slackly from him to Danni. The masculine Chinese contralto carolled, "My uncle told me... he knew who it was... She saw Randolph before she... before she left, confessed to him..."

"Who?" Danni persisted.

"She confessed... She stabbed him to death... his own wife, Rima... Rima Cagnac."

Danni shook her head. "But she was kilometres away across Geneva. She was meeting the captain of the *Strasbourg*."

Fairleigh-White said, "The captain... he and Rima... They were lovers. Randolph told me. The captain... he provided her with an alibi. And six days later... six days later she left the planet, forever... for all the good it did her."

Danni said, "Did she kill him herself, Sir Alastair – or did she hire someone to...?"

"She did it herself! Stabbed him... stabbed my father!"

"But why didn't you inform the authorities at the time?" Danni asked.

"Because... because it didn't matter. Randolph told me that Rima was responsible four years after she did it, and by then... she had been dead those four years, along... along with all the other poor bastards in the starship. And my uncle... he didn't want the scandal... All swept under the carpet... Silence. Best for all concerned, he said."

Danni nodded. "Best for all concerned," she whispered.

"Radzinski..." the com-assisted voice sang out, "Dr Radzinski... Tell Radzinski to come here! I want my treatment! I paid good money... good money for..." He raised a skeletally thin arm. "I want to go out... Do you hear me? I want fresh air, a walk around the grounds... Do you hear me? I want to get out of here!"

Danni looked at Kemp, then turned back to Fairleigh-White. "Tell me, Sir Alastair: why would Rima Cagnac kill her husband?"

It was a second before he responded. "Why...? She was leaving aboard the *Strasbourg*, but he clung to her... He resented her going, wanted her to stay..." He stopped, then called out, "I want my treatment! Fetch Dr Radzinski!"

"But why would she do something as stupid as killing her husband when she was leaving him anyway in a matter of days?" Danni persisted.

"Dr Radzinski!" Fairleigh-White cried. "Doctor!"

The door opened and Radzinski rushed in. Kemp and Danni

backed off while the doctor tapped at the virtual keyboard, his actions subduing the patient.

Radzinski joined them at the door and ushered them into the corridor. "In cases like this, to be honest, I'm all in favour of euthanasia. But in this instance, Sir Alastair has the law on his side, despite the wishes of his family. All I can do is sedate him."

Danni thanked him and they took their leave. As they were crossing the hall, Peter Conway appeared from a side room and signalled to Danni that he would like a word. She crossed to him, and Kemp stepped from the building and stared out across the snow-covered grounds.

Danni joined him a minute later. "What did he want?" Kemp asked.

"He asked if he'd see me again. I think he likes me."

He stared at her. "And what did you say?"

"I told him the truth," she said, "that I prefer older men."

They walked to the car, Kemp thinking about her comment. For a second, he wondered if it was a come-on, before dismissing the idea. A woman as attractive as Danni wouldn't be interested in him, someone in his late fifties with a paunch.

"You're right," he said. "This case doesn't hang together. Why would Cagnac kill her husband when she was leaving on the starship?" He gestured back to the hall. "Or perhaps that was just the raving of a dying man? Memories unlocked after so long are always going to be jumbled, confused."

"We need a motive," Danni said. "Let's get back and trawl through the files, see if we can come up with anything to corroborate his claim."

Kemp squeezed himself back into Danni's car and tried to ignore the popzak as they drove away from Carstairs Hall.

3

Quantum Lattice

They sat in Danni's office, making their way methodically through the case files. At this rate, Kemp estimated they'd need another week of working twelve hours a day to sift through all the information.

They accessed the initial police interview with the suspension scientist, Rima Cagnac, conducted by two Genovese Homicide inspectors a day after her husband's murder and just five days before she was due to leave Earth. Apparently still in a state of shock, Cagnac answered all the questions factually, stating that she'd been in a meeting with Captain Xavier Fernandez at the time of the killing. The interview was in French, auto-translated for Kemp's benefit, although he knew Danni understood the original. When asked about the state of her relationship with her late husband, Kemp noticed that Cagnac blinked and hesitated fractionally before replying, ambiguously, that after five years of marriage they remained good friends.

"And how did your husband feel about the fact that you were about to leave him forever?"

"We both knew that from the day we first met."

"But you still married?"

She eyed the detective coldly and said with barely concealed sarcasm, "Evidently."

"You didn't have second thoughts about going on the mission?"

"None at all."

"So... would it be true to say that scientific enquiry triumphed over... emotional considerations?"

"I don't care for such a crass dichotomy, and anyway I'd question your assumption that scientific enquiry, as you put it, is divorced from 'emotional considerations'."

The second inspector took up the interrogation. "We have a witness report that you argued with your husband during the last week of his life. That hardly accords with your statement that you were still good friends."

She shook her head. "I don't think the two are mutually exclusive, gentlemen. Of course we argued. Have you never argued with a loved one?"

A little later she interrupted a question to say, glancing at her wristcom, "I have been here for two hours, gentlemen, and would like to take advantage of my statutory right to a ten-minute break."

The detectives granted her the break with ill grace and left the interview room.

Kemp froze the image. "What do you think?"

"Bright woman. She tied them in knots, and she knew her rights, for someone never involved with a police investigation before."

"You think she was prepared for the interview?" Kemp stretched. "I don't know about you, but I'm famished. We could break for thirty minutes and I'll call out for noodles?"

Danni pulled an expression and placed a hand on her flat stomach. "Fine," she said, "but I'll pass on the food, if you don't mind. Feeling a bit gippy."

He was about to place his usual order for hongshao niurou mian with the Happy Valley when a screen showing Tsang's head and shoulders materialised over Danni's desk. "I've just watched your interview with Fairleigh-White. I want to see you both up here immediately."

He cut the connection before Danni had time to reply.

"Even more surly than usual," she said. "Do you think he didn't like the way we conducted the interview? Not deferential enough?"

Kemp hauled himself out of the recliner. "Just his usual sweet self, I'd say. So much for lunch."

"You'll enjoy dinner all the more. How about we go to Rossi's later and have some decent food?"

"Sounds good to me."

They took the lift up to Tsang's penthouse office. Commander Tsang, up in the gods, enjoyed a dome with a superb three-hundred-and-sixty-degree view over central London.

They stepped through the sliding door and approached the kidney-shaped desk. Winter sunlight was melting the cap of snow that had settled on the dome, creating shifting shadows that slid over the desk and the two men facing them.

Tsang, a bulky, silver-haired martinet in his sixties introduced a slight, dark-suited man in his late forties, thin-faced and expressionless. "Bellini, Kemp, this is Major Gellner of European Security."

Kemp took a seat, nodding to the major. He noticed a jet-black device as long as his forefinger positioned on the desk before Tsang. The commander leaned forward, touched the object, and said, "Twelve-fifty, Tuesday the 9th of February, 2190. Interview conducted with Inspectors Bellini and Kemp, in the presence of Major Gellner of the European Security Agency."

Kemp glanced at Danni, wondering what the hell was going on. The device on the desk was purely for show: he could have had the meeting recorded surreptitiously.

He sat back, trying to make himself comfortable on the hard chair.

Tsang said, "What passes between the four of us today is confidential. Not a word of our conversation – or indeed the fact that this meeting ever took place – is to be mentioned beyond these four walls."

Kemp smiled to himself, but refrained from pointing out that they were inhabiting a dome. He glanced at Danni, his expression saying, *What the hell is this?*

Tsang went on, "To ensure your cooperation on this matter – though I hasten to add that I don't doubt your integrity for one second – I ask you to consent to having your imps slaved to Surveillance. In effect, your every movement, word and e-transactions will be monitored while in this room."

Involuntarily, Kemp found his fingers straying to the tiny implant at his temple.

"If you don't agree to this, you are free to leave now and you'll be replaced on this case."

Kemp shot Danni a quick glance, and remained seated.

"Good," Tsang said. "Now, to signify your agreement, if you'd kindly apply your print to the..." He gestured to the jet-black device before him.

Kemp gestured for Danni to go first, then leaned forward and thumbed the data-store after her. He glanced at Major Gellner. The security man watched him inscrutably, his silence intimidating.

Tsang leaned back in his seat and smiled. "Very well. I'm glad to have you aboard. Needless to say, the case is extremely sensitive, politically, as you will soon find out." He gestured, and in the air to Kemp's left shimmered the emaciated image of Sir Alastair Fairleigh-White in his rejuvenation pod.

"We have examined your interview with Fairleigh-White–"

Danni interrupted, smiling, "But learned nothing that you didn't already know?"

Tsang turned a conciliatory hand. "Dr Radzinski reported Fairleigh-White's claims yesterday. I wanted you to follow up the matter."

Kemp leaned forward, but Danni was there before him. "Why?" she asked. "What's happening here? All this about Cagnac being responsible for her husband's murder..." She shook her head. "I don't get it. Why does it matter any more?

She died in the starship blow-out nearly eighty years ago. So… I can see from a technical point of view why we need to clear up who killed Sebastian White, but I don't see the need for all this hush-hush malarkey."

Suppressing a smile, Commander Tsang turned to Gellner. "Major…?"

The security officer turned his gaze from Danni to Kemp, and back again, not once allowing his face the luxury of expression.

"What do you know about the *Strasbourg* mission, inspectors?" the major said in accentless English.

Kemp glanced at Danni, giving her the floor. She shrugged. "Just what everyone else knows. A multi-trillion-euro project wiped out four months into the voyage by some kind of catastrophic blow-out."

Major Gellner leaned forward. "There *was* a blow-out aboard the *Strasbourg*. However…" he paused, as if for dramatic emphasis, "the explosion was not fatal. In fact, it was minor, and soon repaired by the ship's onboard systems."

Kemp sat back, stunned. He recalled his father's fascination with the disaster, his constant viewings of the computer-generated mock-up of the accident.

Danni was the first to recover. "I don't understand. If it wasn't fatal… then why the lie?"

Major Gellner inclined his head, as if acceding that this was a reasonable question. "There was a leak when the telemetry came in. At first it was assumed by the press that the explosion had destroyed the *Strasbourg*. Within minutes it was all over the world – news of the loss of Europe's greatest scientific project in the nation's history… As you can well imagine, China was delighted with the failure…"

"So why was the story not stamped on when the true facts were known?" Kemp asked.

"There were two factions of opinion among those few in the know," Gellner said. "Some wanted to come clean, tell the word that the *Strasbourg* had risen phoenix-like from the ashes of its misreported destruction. But another, more powerful faction, led by Randolph White, saw value in allowing the world to continue thinking that the ship was lost."

Danni shook her head. "But why? I don't understand."

Major Gellner sighed and glanced at Tsang. "To be honest, inspectors, neither do we. Randolph White was a cunning politician, as well as a multi-billionaire. All we know is that he had his own, private reasons, he and his political affiliates. He played, as the saying goes, his cards close to his chest. But we think his decision to perpetuate the lie was in some way due to what the *Strasbourg* was carrying."

Kemp leaned forward, his heart racing. "And what was that, Major?"

"For twenty years before the *Strasbourg* blasted out of Earth orbit bound for Mu Arae," Gellner said, "Randolph had headed a project to develop wormhole technology. He seconded a team of top physicists from CERN, expanded the orbital station, and built a quantum lattice out in orbit at L5."

"A quantum lattice," Danni repeated in awe. "But... but that still doesn't answer Gordon's question. What was the *Strasbourg* carrying?"

Kemp guessed what was coming, and he knew that Danni must know, too. She was always a step ahead of him.

Gellner said, "The *Strasbourg* was loaded with the reception nexus of the quantum lattice."

A ringing silence seemed to fill the dome. Kemp felt a hot flush rise from his chest and engulf his face in a dizzying wave. He had a tenuous intimation – like a future move glimpsed in a complex game of chess – of where all this was heading.

Danni said, slowly, "So... if the *Strasbourg* didn't blow up, if it continued on its mission... then it must be reaching Mu Arae around about now, right?"

Smiling indulgently like a teacher whose star pupil has at

last worked out a knotty problem, Gellner said, "That's right, Inspector."

"And if it's carrying the reception nexus of the quantum lattice," Danni went on, "then... then..." She shook her head at the enormity of the notion.

Gellner finished for her, "Then very soon a wormhole should give instantaneous access from Earth to Mu Arae. Is that what you wanted to say, Inspector Bellini?"

She could only nod mutely.

Gellner said, "Do you recall the sub-orb accident a week ago, the explosion way beyond the troposphere? Or so it was reported at the time..."

Kemp had seen the explosion while driving home to his flat in Bermondsey. The silver-blue flash had illuminated the night sky above the northern hemisphere for about a minute, fuelling all manner of speculation until the ESO announced the loss of an unmanned supply shuttle.

Kemp turned to Danni and watched the slow dawning of wonder on the woman's face; it was a sight he would treasure for a long, long time.

She whispered, "It was the wormhole to Mu Arae, opening?"

Gellner nodded. "A test run, the engineers aboard the *Strasbourg* sending a drone through with the message that they'd arrived at the target planet, Mu Arae II."

Danni sat back in her seat, tilted her head to stare through the snow-streaked dome, and laughed aloud.

Kemp, his heart hammering, stared at Gellner and asked, "And the reason you've told us all this?"

Tsang replied. "Rima Cagnac is the prime suspect in the murder of her husband, Sebastian White. Right now, she is orbiting Mu Arae II, supervising the resuscitation of the exploration team from suspension. A dangerous woman in a highly critical role."

"In two days from now," Gellner said, "ESO will open the quantum lattice at this end, facilitating the passage of a ship from Earth to the first extra-solar planet to be explored by humankind." He paused, and then continued, "The ship will be carrying supplies, and a security team. Also, you, Inspector Bellini, will be aboard that ship. You will arrest Rima Cagnac and bring her back to Earth for questioning."

"And me?" Kemp asked.

"You will coordinate things here in London," Tsang told him. "And you will prepare the case files for Cagnac's subsequent prosecution."

Kemp looked across at Danni, expecting to see her features flushed with excited anticipation that she would, quite unexpectedly, get to fulfil a lifelong ambition not only to go into space, but to travel to another star. Instead, her expression was clouded, unreadable – perhaps scared by the sudden reality.

Tsang finished. "Dismissed. We'll meet again in a couple of hours, to discuss the logistics of the mission." He smiled. "I suspect you might have a few questions you want answering, which I'll be happy to do after lunch."

Kemp followed Danni from the room in a daze. In the elevator to Danni's office, he leaned against the wall and murmured, "Jesus Christ..."

Danni stared at him, shaking her head. "I don't get it," she said.

"Don't get what?"

The doors slid open and they made their way along the corridor to her office. "There's something that doesn't add up. I mean... I don't buy it that Gellner doesn't know why Randolph White insisted on perpetuating the starship blow-out story," she said. "And that trip to Carstairs Hall this morning. They knew all along what he was going to say."

She slumped into her recliner and watched Kemp as he strode to the window and stared out.

She said, "We're being manipulated, Gordon. We're being set up. I don't like it."

He watched a scintillating sub-orb rise slowly on a pillar

of flame and twinkle away into the heaviside layer. "Face it, Danni. We're lowly homicide cops. We've got no idea what the authorities are up to." He refrained from saying that, maybe, she was being paranoid.

"Granted. But I still don't like it."

He turned from the window. "How do you feel about the idea of travelling to another star?" So far, she hadn't even mentioned that aspect, when he'd have expected her to be bursting with excitement. "It's okay to feel a little daunted by it all, you know." He told himself he was being nice to her, trying to reassure her, when in truth his overwhelming emotion was relief that Tsang had not chosen him to be the one to go through the quantum lattice. Whereas others might feel slighted to be relegated to staying behind and dealing with the admin, Kemp was happy to accept his role. He certainly didn't want the honour of being among the first human beings to set foot on an extra-solar world.

The idea filled him with an irrational fear.

Danni had that look on her face again, the one he couldn't quite work out.

"Really, Gordon? You call yourself a detective, but..."

She sat with her eyebrows raised, a hand on her belly – and then finally he understood. The strange mood she'd been in recently, the distractedness, the queasiness when he'd suggested noodles...

"You can't go, can you?"

She shook her head. "They'd never send a pregnant woman through a wormhole, would they?"

"So who will they send instead?" Kemp asked.

Again, that look on her face, the one he now understood, which said he was missing the blindingly obvious.

4

First Woman

Rima Cagnac woke, only to learn that she had come close to dying almost eight decades earlier.

The cover of the suspension pod scrolled back. She sat up and felt a rush of dizziness, her vision darkening. She gripped the rim of the pod to stop herself floating out of control across the suspension suite. When her vision cleared, she saw a wall that should have been a flawless off-white and smooth, now blackened with smut marks, bulging inwards in ugly blisters.

She knew that almost eighty years had passed, but in her perception she'd been in suspension for barely more than the blink of an eye. When she had entered her pod, the suite had not been like this.

The damaged wall flickered, and a face appeared – the anonymised, genderless features of the ship's smartcore. "Doctor Cagnac," it said, its tone as anonymous as its features. "The *Strasbourg* is currently approaching parking orbit around Carrasco, Mu Arae II. All systems are functioning adequately. You–"

"But what's wrong?" Rima interrupted.

"Nothing is wrong, Doctor Cagnac."

"Then what *was* wrong?"

"Seventy-nine years, eight months and seven days ago the *Strasbourg*'s cooling systems failed, generating concomitant combustion incidents–"

"There was a *fire?*"

Rima stared at the damaged wall around the smartcore's projected talking head. Her first thoughts were of what disaster she had woken up to, and only then did her rational side kick in and suggest that as they had arrived at their destination, it could not be so bad. Indeed, that she had woken at all should tell her there was no need to worry.

Seventy-nine years ago? That meant the ship hadn't even left the solar system when the fires occurred, and must have completed the entire interstellar journey in this state.

"All systems are functioning adequately," the ship repeated. "The *Strasbourg* is currently approaching parking orbit around Carrasco, Mu Arae II."

Rima pushed herself free of the suspension pod and drifted towards the door. Back in training she'd spent weeks in orbit, so freefall was familiar, yet still it felt wrong.

She grabbed at a grip and gestured at the door to open.

Out in the corridor she saw what hell she had somehow survived. Every surface was blackened and warped, blistered from the heat of the explosion.

She gestured again and the smartcore's talking head appeared on a nearby wall, its features pebbled by the fire damage.

"Is everything really working okay?" Rima asked. "No substantial damage?"

"The fire was triggered by a miscalibration of cooling systems under acceleration," the ship told her. "Damage was either superficial or was repaired en route. All systems are functioning adequately."

"Show me where we are," Rima said, as if she didn't believe the onboard. "Show me Carrasco."

The talking head was replaced by the image of a planet. Blues, greens, and the white of icecaps and swirling cloud systems. It might easily have been Earth, but the shapes of the continents were different, mostly bunched around the equator as if thrown there by centrifugal force.

The view was familiar to her from the enhanced imagery from the deep-space telescopes that had identified this as the most Earth-like of known extrasolar planets, and yet... there was new detail, definition to the outlines of the continents, the patterns of the weather systems. This was a real-time view of the planet as the *Strasbourg* approached.

They were really here, in the Mu Arae system, orbiting the planet that had been named Carrasco.

And Rima Cagnac was the only woman – the only fully functioning, conscious human being! – beyond the solar system, viewing the planet of an alien star.

She did not consider herself to be the bold, adventurous type, so to be the first conscious human in another star system felt bizarre. It went with the role, though: she was the mission's suspension specialist, the first to be awoken so she could monitor the resuscitation of the others.

She should be doing that right now, not floating here staring at the new planet. Daydreaming.

That was when the image of the planet morphed, acquiring human features – dark brown skin, braided hair, hooked nose. Rima laughed, just as the image of Jayne Waterford winked, then smiled.

"Come on, my lovely," said the image. "Time to get your arse into gear. Chop chop, and be done with all that daydreaming. You've had enough Rima-time!"

It was a recording that Jayne must have planted in the system before departure, all those years ago. Jayne's specialty was exotic ecology, but she doubled as a comms tech, hence her access to onboard comms channels like the one that had been showing Rima the approaching planet. And she knew Rima better than almost anyone on this mission: back on Earth they had been training buddies, two souls that had clicked the moment they met.

Jayne had *known* Rima would take some time out, revel in that short period of absolute isolation before setting to work.

"*Strasbourg*," Rima said. "Self-check readouts."

Figures, graphs, and a simplified schematic representation of Rima's body, with overlays for different measurements, came into focus on the fire-scarred wall before her. Instantly, Rima was back in professional mode, reading her own physical data, looking for anomalies.

"*Tres bien, tres bien*," she murmured as she worked. For someone who had been asleep for close to eighty years, she wasn't in bad shape.

She put a hand to her head, recalling the myth that the hair and nails of cadavers continued to grow after death – they didn't. The same was true of those in suspension: Rima's nails were short; the sides and back of her scalp were smooth as if freshly shaved, the short hair on the top of her head still a crisp flat-top.

She had specialised in suspension biology for much of her professional life, and had supervised the resuscitation of individuals who had been suspended for weeks, months, as long as four years. But she was now the only person in human history who had been successfully revived after almost eight decades' suspension.

And she felt good.

"Okay, *Strasbourg*," she said. "Let's do it. Let's start waking folk up."

The suspension suite in which Rima had woken was eight metres by three by five, with two entire walls composed of suspension pods, forty-eight to a side, each set into the wall like body drawers in a morgue. There was space for an entire row of pods to slide out of the wall, with Rima floating over them, monitoring vitals.

First to be roused were mission commander Sander Hertzberger, the *Strasbourg*'s captain Xavier Fernandez, the commander's deputy Sylvie Wilson, and the captain's deputy Luis Vignol.

For a couple of minutes, the scene really did resemble a morgue, the four bodies deathly still, not even breathing, their faces pale and waxen.

Data represented by numbers, graphs and schematics flowed across the blistered wall. No damage, no deterioration, all organs in good shape.

She gestured at Hertzberger, and immediately the resuscitation algorithms pushed stimuli his way. His body twitched, his chest lifted and fell, and soon that pallor started to dissipate.

Rima had witnessed this hundreds of times, and yet it still appeared to her as magic. A body that had been so utterly empty and lifeless, now... breathing, blood pumping colour back under the skin, muscles twitching involuntarily... Hertzberger gave a soft sigh, a grunt, and his grey eyes opened. He was fifty-three, but with the honed physique of someone twenty years younger. His hair was a distinguished silver that had once been black, and he had the manner of one in control, even as his brain was quite clearly still confused, fighting its way up from an eighty-year sleep.

He sat, the motion making him lift clumsily from the pod. Rima reached down, nudged him gently until he gripped the rim. "Take it easy, *Mijnheer* Hertzberger."

"Cagnac," he said, then he paused as his eyes took in the damaged walls around the chamber's door.

"All is fine, Mijnheer. The *Strasbourg* assures me the damage is superficial, from a fire near the start of our voyage. We are now approaching orbit of Mu Arae II, exactly as planned."

Hertzberger cursed, pushing himself away from the pod and barrelling clumsily into Rima. He gestured the door to open and drifted out, barking a string of commands to the ship's onboard before glancing back at Rima. "Continue with the resus as planned, Cagnac. Get Fernandez and Vignol out here immediately."

Rima bit down on any kneejerk response. She hadn't had

time to complete her checks on Hertzberger, and she knew the importance of a carefully managed emergence from suspension – particularly the longest suspension on record, by many decades – but also she knew Hertzberger would not listen to her objections. He was in crisis mode, and hadn't yet adjusted to the simple fact of the situation: the crisis had occurred almost eighty years ago, and had been dealt with.

And now they were here, approaching an alien planet exactly as planned...

She rolled one-eighty and then stopped herself with a spread of the arms so she hung facing her charges. She was getting used to freefall again.

She took a deep breath, reminding herself that Hertzberger spoke to everyone that way: he didn't suffer fools gladly, and he considered everyone around him a fool. It still jarred, though, to be spoken to in such a way after a career as one of the world's leading experts in her field.

The world. She smiled. She was going to have to reassess the very language she used. The world... *which* world?

She gestured at Fernandez, Vignol and Wilson in turn, triggering the resus routines. She wouldn't run more than one at a time under normal circumstances, preferring to give her full attention to each patient's stats, but these were clearly not normal circumstances.

Fernandez was the first to stir, that familiar pattern of chest starting to rise and fall, colour returning, a couple of muscle twitches and then a sigh, a grunt.

His eyes opened, a brown that was almost black. A wink. "Long time no see, Rima," he said, and she had to suppress a smile at his easy humour, remembering the strains between them.

And that was all it took for the memories to come flooding back, memories she had been suppressing in the rush of all that was new. Oh, Sebastian...

She swallowed, forced a smile. Already Fernandez was

moving to push himself away from the pod and towards her. She wagged a finger and said, *"Non.* I must check your readings."

But by then, Vignol and Wilson to either side of Fernandez had begun to stir. Rima was trying to multitask, read their data while the ship's captain registered the state of the fire-blistered wall.

Now he would not be stopped. He pushed clear of the pod, snaked expertly around Rima – an old pro in freefall, unlike the mission chief Hertzberger – and a second later passed out of sight down the corridor.

Rima rolled in midair to face Vignol and Wilson, hands palm outwards to silence their questions. "It's all fine," she said. "We've arrived at Mu Arae. The ship suffered some minor damage along the way, but it's all fine. *Ça va?"*

Rima's assistant, the mission's medical officer Jimmy Ranatunga, was among the next batch to be resuscitated, and once he was awake the process became easier to manage, and the explanation for the damage to the ship became routine for both of them as they oriented the revivees.

Soon, the corridor beyond the suspension suite was full of the buzz of conversation, and Rima felt almost claustrophobic. It was hard to recall the spell of almost Zen calm when she had been the only functioning person within fifty lightyears. She tried to shut it all out and concentrate on her tasks.

"You weren't tempted just to let us all sleep a little longer?" Jayne Waterford said, sitting upright in her suspension pod, one of the last to be awoken. It was as if she were reading Rima's thoughts – or at least the wistfulness of her expression amidst the chaos of resus. No matter how thoroughly they had trained and rehearsed this process, the reality of reviving close to a hundred people en masse – particularly when there were such visible signs that the journey had not gone smoothly –

was both exhilarating and exhausting. They had certainly underestimated the psychological and emotional impact of resuscitation beyond the solar system.

"It's just weird," Rima said, "seeing so many people again, after–"

"After so long?"

Rima laughed at the absurdity of it all. It was eighty years since she'd seen or spoken to another human being, but in subjective experience almost no time had passed at all. How could she feel the weight of those years so intensely?

Eighty years.

She'd had no one when she left Earth. Those close to her were dead, and she had no children to continue her line. There had been a couple of nieces on her mother's side, but who knew what had become of them in the chaos of a climate-devastated West Africa? Those nieces might have had children and grandchildren by now, but then again, their line of descent might have died out.

She thought of Sebastian again, but clamped down on that thought. Too raw, too painful. Too much confused guilt...

Before leaving Earth she'd done all she could to suppress those memories. She'd even taken illicit substances to do so, the pain too great. They hadn't worked at the time, but now she found her thoughts muddled and had difficulty focusing. She wondered if this strange distancing from a past that should still be recent to her was a result of eighty years in suspension, an indirect side-effect of those illicit substances, or maybe simply the consequence of grief. She suspected she was still suffering from shock.

She should monitor this, she knew, but she should do so discreetly. It had been a close call whether she would be allowed to come on the mission, after what had happened in Geneva. At the time, she had argued that members of the exploratory team had been selected not only for their specialisms but on the basis of the strengths shown in their psychological profiling:

by definition, she had already been selected as emotionally resilient, so they could not drop her on those grounds because of what had happened to Sebastian. Now, though, she knew she must not show any signs of weakness, any signs that shock and grief were clouding her abilities.

She returned to her work, reading Jayne's stats in the air between them, looking for any sign that she was not the only one suffering disjoint between this world and the one they had left behind.

Alone now in the suspension suite, her immediate duties accomplished, Rima gripped a handhold on the bulkhead and took a deep breath.

The smartcore's talking head appeared before her. "Doctor Cagnac."

"I know. It's such a relief. Everyone resuscitated and no casualties."

"Not everyone has been revived, Doctor Cagnac."

Rima blinked. "I assure you—"

"Follow me, please."

The anonymised head sequenced across the wall, leading her from the suite and along the corridor. Rima pushed off and floated in pursuit. "Just what the hell…?"

They came to a sliding door, which opened to reveal a small chamber equipped with six suspension pods.

The talking head said, "Enter, please, Doctor Cagnac."

She pushed herself from the corridor and floated into the chamber, the door sliding shut behind her.

"Now, please resuscitate the engineers."

"Engineers? But…" Rima shook her head. "These people weren't on the manifest."

"A late addition to the crew," the talking head informed her. "Revive them, please, before Commander Hertzberger's briefing begins in thirty minutes."

Late addition? This chamber was clearly part of the design of the ship: it had not been constructed at the last minute...

She set to work bringing these six strangers back to life: it should have been routine, but a combination of fatigue and unease – the notion that something was going on here that was not quite right – slowed her down.

The six, three men and three women, wore red coveralls without nametags, which again she found odd. They floated silently in the chamber when awoken, not venturing out into the corridor and showing no curiosity.

Before she quit the chamber, Rima floated before them. "I'm Dr Cagnac," she said. "Chief resus medic, and you are...?"

The six exchanged glances amongst themselves but remained silent.

"The smartcore informed me that you're engineers, a late addition to the crew."

A big, blond-haired man said, "Which is all you need to know, Dr Cagnac."

"Look, we're all in this together," she snapped.

"Commander Hertzberger will explain our presence in due course," the man said.

Rima stared at him, unable to find a reply, then pushed herself towards the sliding door and retreated down the corridor.

Hertzberger called a briefing, once everyone had been revived and assessed, and he and Captain Fernandez had had time for a full consultation with the *Strasbourg*'s smartcore.

Designed for the efficiencies of interstellar travel and transport of essential equipment and supplies, rather than anything more than the basic comforts, the ship did not have a space large enough for the entire team to gather in one place, so instead they grouped together for the briefing in sleeping chambers, corridors, and even the small kitchen space.

Rima tagged along with Fernandez, uncomfortable to be close to him, but telling herself that the confines of an interstellar ship orbiting an alien planet was not the place to be getting precious about such matters. She considered asking him if he knew anything about the six engineers but thought better of it: she really wanted as little to do with the man as possible.

She found herself in a group of a dozen men and women in the *Strasbourg*'s control room. Sander Hertzberger hung before them in the flesh, looking far calmer than he had when she'd last seen him. A wall to his left showed imagery from around the ship, scientists and crew gathered to hear what their chief had to say.

"We are here..." he told them, and with a wave of his right hand he cast that image of Carrasco onto the wall behind him. She wondered how many times he'd rehearsed this scene, or even had it scripted for him: his *One small step* moment. The words *We are here* conveyed so much.

Rima stared at the weather systems, the shape of the continents. She would never tire of this view.

"But as I'm sure you all realise by now, our journey was not without its difficulties. The ship has briefed Captain Fernandez and me, and I am satisfied that we have everything in place for a complete and successful mission. Yes, there was a fire onboard, but that was almost eighty years ago. The fault has been traced to a stray decimal point in the algorithm controlling the *Strasbourg*'s cooling systems, specifically those under full load when the ship is at maximum acceleration. Our smartcore has had almost eighty years to identify and analyse that fault, to correct it, and to repeatedly search its systems for any other comparable error, of which none were found."

He clearly meant that to be reassuring, but Rima could see from the looks on some of the faces that others had had the same thought as her: if that stray decimal point had been missed in all the rigorous preparation for this mission, and only appeared under specific circumstances, then who was to say there might not be more?

"I can assure you," Hertzberger continued, "that even if we had not identified the fault, it was one that would only ever recur at full acceleration. And now you are wondering why that is reassuring, for surely at the end point of our mission, in ten years' time, we will return to suspension and initiate the return journey?

"I can now tell you that that is not the case, for on board the *Strasbourg* we are carrying a new technology that will make our ship's propulsion unit close to redundant. We have brought with us the reception nexus for a quantum lattice, the root element of which is in orbit around Earth. So when our work here is complete, the *Strasbourg* will enter the lattice – one end of a quantum wormhole – and emerge in Earth orbit. Near-instantaneous interstellar travel."

Rima looked around her at the men and women floating in the room, and saw her own amazement mirrored in their faces – and in the reaction of those in other areas of the ship. She heard exclamations, and someone called out to the commander: "What the hell... Why weren't we told?" The question was taken up by others, and for a few minutes, chaos reigned in the chamber.

Hertzberger hung before them, his presence dominating as he raised both hands to quell the dissent.

"I'll explain everything, in detail, but not now. I'd like to do it face to face, in small groups. I assure you that I'll answer all your questions then, ladies and gentlemen."

The engineers, Rima thought. Well, this explained their clandestine, last-minute addition to the crew. They would be the men and women tasked with opening the quantum lattice in the heavens above Carrasco.

A quantum lattice... It was far outside Rima's areas of expertise, and in her mind it was like cold fusion: a technology theoretically possible but never achieved. Her brother-in-law,

Randolph White, had poured vast quantities of his wealth into researching the technology, but she'd had no idea that the work had borne fruit.

A navigable wormhole between Earth and Mu Arae!

Dizzy, she tried to work out the implications of Hertzberger's revelation.

It fundamentally changed the nature of this exploratory mission, of course. No longer here for a ten-year haul, followed by an eighty-year return journey; would they now be able to come and go at will? She suspected it would not be as simple as that: the energy costs alone of maintaining a viable wormhole must be huge, perhaps limiting its use.

Soon, there would be passage between Mu Arae and the planet – with all its messy complications – she had left behind, and she did not know how she felt about that.

5

Upgrade

Kemp sat in the semi-darkness of his office, staring at the on-screen notes he'd collated on the Sebastian White/Rima Cagnac case and trying not to dwell on the possibility that soon he would be shunted fifty lightyears through space. It wasn't, as yet, a cut and dried certainty. Last night Danni had informed Commander Tsang of her condition; an hour later she'd been pulled from the mission.

Now she was having it out with Tsang, arguing her case to be allowed to go.

It made sense that she should, Kemp thought, even if she was pregnant. She was younger than him, physically fitter and, if he were brutally honest with himself, the better detective.

He stopped that line of thought when he realised that he was doing nothing more than trying to cover for his fear. The notion of travelling through space, even into Earth orbit, scared him to death. If he were honest, even the prospect of air flight left him feeling nauseous. But to be pushed lightyears through space, at the mercy of a new technology… The idea brought him out in a cold sweat.

And why did they need someone from their department to bring back Rima Cagnac, anyway? Why couldn't a security agent from the European Space Organisation do the dirty work?

He looked up as the door slid open and Danni walked in.

He could tell from her silence that she'd been unsuccessful. She lowered herself into a swivel seat and moved it to and fro, staring across the room at the wall.

"What did he say?"

She shrugged. "Last night, when I told him I was four months pregnant... You should have seen his face. He'd simmered down a bit by this morning."

"Did you manage to convince him?"

She sighed. "I said that I'd take all responsibility. I'd even sign a waiver to that effect – but he wasn't having it."

"So... you can't go?"

"He said he couldn't take the risk. They weren't equipped to maintain a medical back-up aboard the shuttle in the event of an emergency. And his trump card was that the lead medical officer on Carrasco is... yes, Rima Cagnac. There was nothing I could argue against that." She shrugged. "So there we are."

"Did they say who...?" he trailed off, dreading her reply.

"Tsang wants to see you, pronto."

"The bastard can wait," he said, feeling a little sick. "Jesus."

Danni looked across at him. "You don't want to go, do you?"

"Like hell I do." He laughed. "I don't even like leaving London. Also..."

"Go on."

"What you said yesterday, about our being set up–"

She smiled at him, wickedly. "'Our being'...?"

"Touché," he said. "But I agree with you. There's something they aren't telling us. Tsang could easily get onto ESO security and have Cagnac brought back as a matter of course. So why are they sending one of us?"

With her right foot, Danni pushed herself back and forth, staring at him. "Well, Gordon, you're the one who might find out, sooner rather than later. You'll be standing on the soil of an alien world in a day or so."

She stopped, her expression drawn into an angry scowl.

"Christ!" she said a second later. "You know something? On the way down, in the elevator, it crossed my mind to…" She fell silent.

"Go on."

She bit her lip, as if considering whether to tell him. "I seriously considered, for about three seconds, having a termination. Going back up to Tsang and telling him. And demanding he reinstate me on the mission."

Kemp swallowed, feeling a quick hit of guilt at the thought that *that* would solve his problem…

"But?"

"I didn't plan for this pregnancy. In fact, when I found out, I was *furious* about it. Furious with myself at my own stupidity. But…" She put a hand on her belly as she paused. "Well… I'm having a baby, Gordon. How damned strange is that?"

He smiled. "I didn't even guess you were…" He gestured to her stomach.

"I was going to tell you, when the time was right."

"Who's the father?"

She shrugged. "That hardly matters."

"I don't suppose congratulations are in order?"

"In the circumstances, Gordon, perhaps not."

He looked away from her dark, staring eyes, trying to find the appropriate words.

"Well," he said at last, slapping his thighs with both hands, "if Tsang wants to see me…"

He climbed to his feet, then stopped on the way to the door. "I could always refuse point blank to go. I mean, they couldn't demote me any further, could they?"

Danni laughed, without humour. "No, but they could fire you, Gordon. You'd lose your pension."

He paused by the door. "Can you think of anything, anything at all, that might get me off the job?"

"To be honest, no. And anyway, you have to go. I want to

hear all about Carrasco when you get back, you see. In minute detail, okay?"

He swore at her and stepped from the office.

He rode the elevator to the penthouse suite and stepped into Tsang's dome.

The commander sat behind his desk, pointedly gesturing for the time to flash up on an old-fashioned analogue clockface in the air between them. Major Gellner sat beside him, as bereft of discernible emotion as he had been at their last meeting.

"So pleased you could join us, at last," Tsang said.

"Had a file to clear up..." Kemp muttered as he slipped into a seat across the desk from the pair.

"You're probably aware of what this is about, Inspector?"

Kemp stared at his boss. "Let me guess – you're promoting me?"

His sarcasm was lost on Tsang. "In a way, you could say that, yes. Due to unforeseen circumstances, Inspector Bellini is no longer available for the mission we discussed yesterday."

"So she told me," Kemp said.

"In her place, we are sending you to Carrasco."

Keeping his expression neutral, he stared at the two men. "That's all very well but, having given the matter some thought, I'd rather not–"

"The choice is not yours to make, Kemp," Tsang said in a voice like a steel whip. "You're going."

Kemp sat back in his seat and stared up at the curve of the dome. Snow was falling over London and flakes had settled on the dome's membrane, melting and flowing like tears.

He considered his response. "And if I hand in my resignation–?"

Tsang had his reply ready: "Then it would take effect from the completion of your work on Carrasco."

Kemp nodded. He looked from Tsang to Gellner. "You really think I'm the best man you can find for the job?"

Gellner leaned forward, and spoke for the first time that morning. "Commander Tsang insists on a European police presence in the operation, and your profile fits the required criteria."

Tsang said, "You will accompany Major Gellner to the squad clinic where you will undergo a thorough medical check-up, followed by an upgrade."

Kemp repeated the word, uneasy.

"… An upgrade of your implant tech. You must be fully prepared for this assignment. That will be all." Tsang turned in his swivel chair and busied himself accessing a screen hovering above his desk.

Major Gellner stood and gestured to the door. "After you, Inspector Kemp."

They rode the elevator to the second floor and Gellner led him down a long corridor. The major was determinedly silent, his manner habitually cold, distant. They passed through a room busy with detectives seated before floating screens. Kemp had worked here before his demotion. Little had changed, barring the high resolution of the screens and some of the personnel.

They passed down another corridor to the clinic, then paused before a locked door as it scanned their identities.

As they waited, Kemp said, "Why me, Major?"

Gellner flicked him a glance. "Because your colleague, Inspector Bellini, dropped the bombshell last night that she was pregnant."

"I meant why *either* of us? Why send a lowly cold-case cop to another world to retrieve a suspect? I would have thought it'd be much easier to have someone from ESO security do the job."

The door clicked and sighed open. As they stepped through, Gellner said, "It's a cold case, Inspector. The very definition of one." He smiled to himself, and Kemp wondered if that line was his idea of humour. "And anyway, Commander Tsang wanted to keep the case in-house, as it were. Why rely on ESO when you're perfectly capable of handling the situation yourselves?"

They pulled bucket seats out from the wall and sat side by side in an aseptic corridor outside a door marked 'Dr Singh'. Kemp wondered at the reason for Gellner's presence. He felt as if he were under arrest, or surveillance. But if that were the case, they could do so with far more subtlety. No, it seemed pretty clear they *wanted* him to know he was being watched.

The door opened and a woman in her forties said, "Ah, Inspector Kemp. This way, please. We shouldn't take too long."

For the next half hour he underwent a series of examinations familiar from his annual check-ups. Singh inserted a probe into his wristcom, and he told himself that he could feel the cold rush of the nano-bots as they coursed through his system and reported his condition, while Dr Singh scanned a screen floating before her.

"For someone of your age and weight," she said, "you're in fair condition. Cut down on the sugars, okay? You need to lose ten kilos."

He nodded his compliance, wondering if they had tangyuan on Carrasco.

When he was released with a clean bill of health a little later, he was surprised to see Gellner still seated in the corridor. "This way," the major said.

They took the elevator up a couple of levels and passed through another pair of security doors into the tech-lab where Kemp had last been two years ago, when he'd had his most recent implant upgrade.

A young woman who looked as if she'd just left high school told him to remove his jacket and shirt and lie on a padded bunk before an array of diagnostic hardware. Across the room, a grey-haired tech spoke to Major Gellner in hushed tones, both men glancing at Kemp from time to time.

Uneasy, he did as he was told and lay down, aware of his flabby gut as the young woman – with the swift impersonality of a robot – slapped diagnostic tags onto his arms and torso. She jacked a lead into his wristcom, then glanced up at the grey-haired tech. He nodded.

She waved a hand, and Kemp passed out.

He came to his senses and immediately registered alarm. At his last upgrade session, he'd remained fully conscious throughout the procedure.

Oddly, now, he felt neither groggy nor disoriented, as he would after coming round from anaesthetic. He felt as alert as he had been a subjective second ago, when unconsciousness claimed him. Instinctively he called up the time and was surprised to see that almost an hour had elapsed.

"Routine," the young woman said. "Nothing to worry about. Things get obsolete so fast these days, and you've been putting off your upgrades for too long. You've just had a major firmware overhaul, with much better security and functionality."

"Which means what, exactly?"

"Major Gellner will fill you in on the details, Inspector. If you'd care to go through to the lounge, where you can help yourself to tea or coffee, the major will be with you presently."

Kemp pulled on his shirt and jacket and stepped through a sliding door into a plush lounge. Unlike the severely functional clinic, this room was hung with Chinese satin prints and dotted with fake Han dynasty vases. Guzheng music played softly in the background.

He grabbed a bulb of coffee from the dispenser and crossed to the window, sipping the surprisingly good brew and staring out across the snow-laden rooftops of central London.

To the east, a shuttle rose on a pillar of flame, describing a slow parabola through the milky-grey sky. Soon he'd be aboard an orbital flight heading for the waiting spacecraft that would take him through the wormhole... The very idea made him dizzy.

He considered the wormhole, and what little Gellner had told him and Danni yesterday about Randolph White's motives in covering up the fact that the *Strasbourg* had survived the blow-out.

The sliding door sighed open behind him, interrupting his line of thought.

Gellner helped himself to a tea and joined Kemp before the window.

"How are you feeling, Inspector?"

Kemp shrugged. "I'm fine. Something you said yesterday..." he went on before the major could interrupt, "about Randolph White and his motives in perpetuating the idea that the *Strasbourg* was destroyed in the blow-out..."

Gellner hesitated. "What about it, Inspector?"

"You said you didn't know the reason for why White 'saw value in allowing the world to continue thinking that the ship was lost'."

"That's correct."

"But you went on to say that you thought it might have something to do with what the ship was carrying – the wormhole tech." Kemp shrugged. "Call me slow, but I don't get it. So the ship was loaded with tech that would make star-travel well-nigh instantaneous, eighty years down the line." He glanced at Gellner as he went on, "But I don't see why this would motivate White to cover-up the survival of the ship – or why *you* thought it might be connected."

Gellner turned to him and smiled, suavely. "Who can second-guess the motivations of wily politicians, Inspector?"

Kemp took a mouthful of coffee. "You said he was playing his cards close to his chest. So, was he playing the long game, perhaps in the hope that the *Strasbourg*'s secret would in some way assist political affiliates, way down the line? *Now*, in fact."

Gellner smiled. "Perhaps he was, Inspector. But the fact is

that we shall never know what motivated Randolph White. He took his secret with him to the grave."

Kemp stared out at the falling snow. In the distance, a megascreen hung low over the rooftops and garish Big-5 Chinese hieroglyphs burned through the mist, flashing red and yellow.

He gestured back towards the clinic. "I was unconscious in there for an hour. That didn't happen last time. What exactly did you load me with, Major?"

"Your imp was getting old, slow. You're going to be operating alone out there, so you need to be equipped with the very best tech. You had a complete reinstallation. You'll find that it's more... interactive."

"Meaning?"

"Technology moves quickly, Inspector, and much as you might deny it, so must you. Your upgraded imp is faster, smarter, a genuine virtual assistant inside your head that learns as you do, so that eventually it will be anticipating your needs, feeding you the information you need before you even know you need it, assessing environmental inputs for risk and opportunity. It will keep you safe, protected. Consider it a guardian angel, riding your consciousness."

Kemp stared at the major. "It can contact me, unbidden?"

Startling him, a voice sounded in his head. *"That is correct, Gordon, although I will rapidly learn your preferences. You have the ability to choose to recalibrate my tone, of course. Knowing you as I do, I elected to use a feminine contralto based on the received pronunciation of a BBC presenter, circa 1950."*

Despite himself, he smiled at the prim tone of voice in his head. It certainly beat the maddening high-energy prattle that most applications were loaded with these days.

Not that he liked the idea that his imp could now interrupt his thoughts.

He turned to Gellner. "And if I don't want the voice in my head?"

"You have the facility to switch your imp's communications to retinal script, if you so wish. And you can adjust the notification thresholds so that your imp is less, shall we say, pushy."

Kemp nodded. "And what else have you loaded me with?"

The major shrugged easily, draining his tea in one go. "No more surprises, I assure you. Your imp is simply more powerful and effective, which is exactly what you will need when you're out there on your own."

"Speaking of which—"

Gellner anticipated the question. "You will be aboard the shuttle leaving at sixteen hundred hours tomorrow, Inspector. Commander Tsang will be in touch in due course with all the details. Now, if you'd excuse me."

Kemp stood before the window for another two minutes when Gellner had quit the lounge, staring out across frozen London and going over what the major had told him.

He finished his coffee, lobbed the bulb into the compost chute, and took the elevator down to his basement office. In the reassuring, familiar twilight chaos of litter and floating headshots, he sat back in his recliner and sub-vocced, "Imp. Contact Danni."

Normally, a screen would flash up a couple of seconds later, showing Danni's image. Now it appeared in the air instantly, startling him.

"Gordon, how did it go?" Danni asked, chewing on something.

She was at home in her Highgate apartment, the wall behind her plastered with images of manga heroines. She caught his glance and explained, "I'm on my way to Berkshire, so as I was passing, I stopped to grab a samosa – and a thicker coat. It's freezing out there."

"Berkshire?"

"I'm going over things in the Cagnac case, for when you return—"

"But we interviewed Fairleigh-White yesterday."

"I thought I'd tidy up one or two things," she said. She leaned forward suddenly, so that her face filled the screen, and pressed a finger to her lips.

He got the message and nodded.

Breezily, she asked, "So when are you leaving, Gordon? I'd like to see you before you go."

He told her when he was scheduled to leave. "We could meet for breakfast?"

"My place at eight?" she said. "I'll do you beef noodles, okay?"

"And I'll tell you all about the upgrade."

She waved fingers at him, popped the last of the samosa into her mouth, and cut the connection.

Kemp sat back in his recliner, rocking, and wondered at the reason for Danni's secrecy – and the reason she wanted to interview Fairleigh-White again.

He was about to sub-voc his imp to contact Edouard Bryce, but stopped himself. Instead, he waved for a floating keyboard screen and typed the solicitor's address, then the message: *Ed, we need to meet? Are you free now? Utmost discretion.*

Seconds later, a line of script appeared in the air above the keyboard. *You're a mind reader, Gordon. A beer at the* Cockerel *in an hour?*

Kemp smiled and typed: *See you there.*

He grabbed his coat on the way out. He'd get there early and have a drink or two while he waited. As he climbed the steps from his basement office, into the teeth of the freezing wind slicing down the alleyway, he told himself that he had to make the most of his last few hours on Earth.

And how better than to spend the time enjoying a drink with a friend?

6

We've Only Gone and Done it, Darling

The *Strasbourg* was a hive of activity, and for the first time in her professional life Rima Cagnac felt redundant – a point that was only reinforced when she spoke to Captain Xavier Fernandez a few hours after revival.

She'd left Jimmy Ranatunga at the medical station, running through the ship's summary reports of one hundred and two people spending close to eighty years in suspension. The only data-points of interest were from the period four months into the voyage when Captain Fernandez and four of his crew had been prepared for emergency resus in case real people were required to do anything in the aftermath of the fire. The ship had averted the emergency, though, and no resuscitation had been initiated.

And so Rima and Jimmy had time on their hands, with nobody sick and no anomalies detected. She recalled something she'd once been told about warfare, that the action was only ever fleeting and nothing much happened for most of the time. This was her war.

After leaving the medical station, she'd drifted through the ship's corridors before pausing before a clean wall and calling up more visuals of the planet. Soon they would have drones down there, scouting out the proposed landing site. She felt a thrill of anticipation: the drones would reach the planetary

59

surface in a matter of hours, and then people would start landing within forty-eight hours.

Xavier Fernandez almost barged into her, barrelling down the corridor, face like an Atlantic storm.

"Trouble?" she asked.

He visibly forced himself to relax as he reached for a grip, bringing his flight to a halt. "Oh, just Hertzberger," he said. "You know how he is at the best of times, and…"

The mission chief had been disturbed by news of the fire, even though it was almost eighty years behind them. Rima suspected it had brought home to him the realities of being fifty lightyears from home, with no back-up. In the few hours since resus, Hertzberger had been making life hell for everyone around him.

"How about you?" Fernandez said.

"We really are lucky," she told him. "A hundred and two people revived without issue, from the longest suspension by many decades."

"Should luck have been involved?" he snapped, a flash of anger, or perhaps merely irritation, in his dark eyes. Rima tried not to read too much into it, because he had clearly been having a hard time of it all.

"It was a figure of speech," she said. "There are always unknowns."

Fernandez nodded, then smiled. "Sorry," he said. "A lot on my mind, you know?"

"Everything is okay, *oui?*"

"The fire did remarkably little harm, and the ship's self-repair mechanisms fixed all but the most superficial damage. We really were–"

"Lucky?" she said.

They laughed.

"And now all this…" Rima gestured around them – Fernandez would know her gesture encompassed more than just the corridor, but the ship in its entirety. "No longer needed, no?"

Fernandez said nothing.

"The wormhole. With near-instantaneous travel between Earth and Mu Arae, there will be no need for ships like this, *non?* Your job is done." It was only as she spoke the words aloud that she realised how fundamentally the wormhole would change things for them all, and for Xavier Fernandez in particular.

"Not me alone," he told her. "But for you, too. Your work, your life... It got us here, but now? Who needs to go into suspension when we have the wormhole?"

It was true. She had been under the impression that when the mission was complete, they would return in the *Strasbourg*, in suspension again, but now there was no need. Her entire professional discipline was eighty years redundant.

"Why the secrecy?" she asked. "Why weren't we told about the wormhole? Did *you* even know?"

"The wormhole technology is commercially sensitive," Fernandez said, clearly avoiding the last question. "It was kept under the utmost secrecy back on Earth to prevent word reaching our commercial rivals."

"China."

"China. The Pacific Treaty group. New California. Any of a number of global corporations."

Could the European Space Organisation really do that? Morally, at least? Commit almost a hundred researchers to a mission that would throw them eighty years into the future, and not even tell them that the nature of that mission would fundamentally change because of technological developments?

"When we set out, the nature of the wormhole technology was uncertain," Fernandez went on. "The *Strasbourg*'s smartcore has been running simulations for the duration of the voyage to test and refine the systems that govern the wormhole. It has, quite literally, taken us this long to be confident it will work. And it was only upon entering the Mu Arae system that the *Strasbourg* could confirm that the local spacetime fabric would not be dangerously disrupted by the quantum lattice."

"But now we know," Rima said. "It will work, and everything about our mission changes."

"The mission remains the same," Fernandez corrected her. "We prepare to land on Carrasco, leaving only a small team of technicians in orbit to establish the wormhole. We study the planet's biome and geology. We do our science. All that has changed is the roles of people like you and me. I am no longer a starship captain. Soon I'll be just a shuttle pilot, ferrying personnel and supplies from the wormhole to Carrasco. And you are no longer a suspension specialist."

They had both become redundant. Rima almost felt sympathy for him, but then... His dark eyes met hers as he reached out, put a hand on her arm.

She didn't know what the gesture meant, whether it even meant anything at all other than simply being the unthinking response of a man who spoke seven languages but understood the word *no* in none of them.

Rima flinched, twisting away from the touch, and for an embarrassing few seconds found herself flailing in freefall as a result of the sudden movement.

When she met his look again, his expression was laced with contempt, and she wondered how she could ever have considered him a friend. He had always been angling for more, and when he didn't get it...

"I should never have done it," he said. "I should never have lied for you back in Geneva. You should not be here, Rima. You know that."

She stared at him, stung both by the utter injustice of his words but also by the truth they contained. For if Xavier Fernandez had not confirmed that he had been in a private meeting with her on that fateful day, then she would never have been able to fight her corner and convince the *Strasbourg*'s supervisory board that they should honour her place on the mission.

Without Fernandez's lies, she would have been left on Earth, leading a life that no longer had meaning, facing the consequences of events beyond her control.

"But what will it really be *like?*"

Rima knew she was bugging Jayne Waterford, but she also knew her friend quite liked that. Jayne always said she worked best surrounded by chaos and noise. Rima was doing her a service, really.

Jayne was at a workstation in a small area just off the control room. Five others shared the space, two of them hanging in what was, to Rima, an upside down position, although orientation meant little in freefall. The air of the room was full of numbers and imagery, each set oriented so only the principal user saw them with clarity, but to others appearing like shimmering dust motes drifting on the air.

Hanging at Jayne's shoulder, Rima could see her friend's data flows more clearly. The main imagery showed three perspectives on a clearing in a jungle that, at first glance, might have been any jungle on Earth. Studied more closely, the vegetation had a predominantly turquoise, metallic sheen, and tree limbs and climbers grew in great tangled twists rather than clearly defined trunks and branches.

They were looking at a jungle growing on an alien planet.

"You want to know what's it like?" Jayne said. "It'll stink like high hell. Methane, sulphur, hydrogen sulphide. Rotten eggs. But we always knew that, right from the first analyses of the atmosphere's chemical signature."

Rima knew this. Deep space telescopy had advanced so far in the years before the launch of the *Strasbourg* that not only had Earth-type planets been detected around many dozens of stars, but their atmospheres had been spectrographically analysed and their chemical make-up determined. Mu Arae II had an atmospheric fingerprint rich in oxygen, held so far out of chemical equilibrium that only an active biome could maintain it at such levels: it was a living planet, with a biochemical homeostasis similar to that of Earth. And the levels of biological activity were such that it was also an atmosphere rich in the products of life; the media back home had joked that the scientists had discovered a new Eden, but it was an Eden that stank of old socks and flatulence.

"But what will it really be *like?*"

"Hot and sweaty. It's not only the planet that's going to stink, once we're down there." Jayne waved a hand through a flow of figures, dismissing them.

"I wonder what that means for novel illnesses, allergies…" It had always been the plan that after resuscitation Rima's role would shift to becoming the mission's chief medical officer, and she and Jimmy Ranatunga had extensive experience and training in all the kinds of emergencies and routine work that might be needed during the mission. Allergies, heart attack, emergency surgery and broken limbs, pregnancy, even. But as the onboard fire had shown, no matter how well prepared, there was always room for the unexpected.

One possibility that had received much discussion and scenario-planning had been the possibility that lifeforms on Carrasco might prove so closely compatible with human biology that pathogens might rush to colonise the new, human hosts. Another was that any agriculture the explorers established might provide transitional hosts for pathogens that would in turn infect humans.

"We all know the risks of pathogens finding new hosts," Jayne agreed. "Rapid mutation of variants, rapid spread… An epidemic among such a small community would be disastrous. We need to maintain biohazard discipline. That's key."

The media portrayal of Carrasco as an Eden that smelt bad was misleading. No matter how idyllic the planet appeared – and those images hanging before Rima and Jayne certainly looked idyllic – the exploratory team wouldn't know for a long time whether it was Heaven they had entered, or Hell.

***

Work, for most, came to a halt on the *Strasbourg* when the first shuttle made planetfall on Carrasco. Gathered in groups, Rima and the others watched live coverage of the landing projected onto any available surface.

In the forty-eight hours that drones had been exploring the landing site, no hazards had been identified, no warning indicators that might delay the planned landings.

As the shuttle descended, the drones surveying the local environment turned their cameras skywards. The shuttle appeared first as a speck of light in the delicate turquoise of the morning sky, burning steadily brighter until the cameras had darkened the sky to black to compensate.

Slowly, the shuttle descended the last hundred metres, coming to land on ground burned clear to bedrock by the lander's descent burners.

The gathering in the crowded control room of the *Strasbourg* had fallen silent, as if taking a collective deep breath. Then someone whooped, someone else started to clap, and suddenly the place was full of sound.

Rima was hugging Jayne; she had no idea who had instigated the embrace, had not even fully comprehended the tension they had all felt until now, as it was released.

"We've only gone and done it, darling," Jayne said. "We've only gone and landed on another world, haven't we?"

One of the projected feeds switched to a bodycam view of the interior of the lander's airlock, the suited back of Lieutenant James Harvey. On cue, Harvey turned and gave a thumbs up sign, just as the door lifted and the airlock was flooded with harsh light.

"We really are here," he said, echoing Chief Hertzberger's *We are here.*

Whatever the first words spoken on another planet, Rima suspected they would have felt forced. Best to keep it simple, like this, let the moment and its importance speak for itself.

Without further ado, Lieutenant Harvey stepped forward, out of the shuttle. One of the projected views continued to show the perspective of his colleague, still in the airlock. Other views came from the drones gathered outside, watching what looked like a remarkably small figure step out from the lock, pause on the top tier of the steps, and then take a step down, another, and another, until he paused again, one step from the bedrock of a new planet.

The most powerful view of all came from Harvey's own suitcam as he stepped down, his legs adjusting to alien gravity after a couple of days in freefall. That final pause, a twist at the hips as he took in the view in a slow panning motion.

And then one more step, feet landing on rock, pausing again, panning around.

Standing on another planet.

We really are here – although for posterity, Rima preferred Jayne's *We've only gone and done it, darling.*

7

Outside

Life on another planet took some getting used to.

Life on another planet... Rima Cagnac had to pinch herself every time she thought in terms like this. She suspected everyone felt the same, constantly pulling themselves up in wonderment and awe at this extraordinary undertaking.

Life on another planet...

Rima had been in the fourth shuttle landing, one day after they had witnessed James Harvey's first steps on Carrasco's surface.

Fully suited, she had stepped down onto the bare rock of the landing pad, stopped, and looked around. She'd realised that what she had taken for an affectation – the way Harvey had turned at the waist so that his bodycam slowly panned – was more an automatic reaction, the slow appreciation of the surrounding wonder.

The gravity, at ninety percent Earth-norm, had felt strange, but that was probably because she'd spent a few days in freefall. She suspected the difference from Earth was actually barely perceptible, and would only manifest in a few subtle misjudgements and some clumsiness.

The landing site had been selected at least partly because it was a natural clearing where thin soil over bedrock had led to a thinning of the jungle. Even so, an area of vegetation had been cleared so that the research base's domes could erect themselves without hindrance.

Vegetation... They had been lectured early on in the project about the importance of labelling. The plants here were not plants, the trees were not trees, the living, breathing creatures skimming around the canopy of the jungle were neither bats nor birds. Using Earth-centric labels for the planet's lifeforms led to assumptions and oversights, where in truth all had derived from entirely different evolutionary maps, with different physical structures, different organs, different mechanisms for reading and passing on hereditary information.

Rima understood this, and at a stretch she could bring herself to talk of the flying creatures as flyers, not birds, and the smaller creatures simply as bugs until they had been classified and given their own names, not insects, or flies, or worms. But for some reason she found it harder to stop herself thinking of trees and plants, and the surrounding habitat as jungle.

The research base established itself in a clearing in the jungle, against a backdrop of trees and creepers beneath a sky whose turquoise tints were a blue turned green by layers of floating algae-like microorganisms drifting high in the atmosphere. Above the dark green horizon hung the bloated orange sun, Mu Arae; observed through suitable solar filters, it was possible to see the passage of the innermost planet, Dulcinea, across the primary's face.

Rima was careful to observe the tightest biohazard discipline. On the two occasions in the first week when she emerged from the complex of domes, she wore full bodysuit, and upon re-entering the base she passed through two sets of airlocks and a thorough decontamination.

The rest of the time, she remained inside, establishing the base's medical centre and monitoring every single report that came in for any indication of medical hazard.

In all that time, the most serious condition she treated was a broken wrist, when Chief Hertzberger's deputy, Sylvie Wilson, either through natural distraction or clumsiness, or as a result of one of those marginal misjudgements due to Carrasco's ninety-percent Earth gravity, missed her footing in the jungle and landed badly on one hand, fracturing a scaphoid.

It seemed that those early media reports had been accurate. Carrasco was, to all appearances, a new Eden, and if it stank of bad farts then no one had yet found out because the air they breathed, in suit and dome, was filtered, perfumed, untarnished.

"You really think it'll be safe to go out without suits before long?" Rima asked Jayne. This was where their two disciplines overlapped: exotic ecology, and the impact it had on the human body.

The two sat with cool drinks before a window that looked out into the jungle. The vegetation thinned here, gaps in the tangles through which flyers darted. The creatures were so fast they were hard to make out, but Rima had seen specimens up close in Jayne's lab. The closest comparison she could think of was that the creatures looked like stingrays, cutting through the air on kite-like wings.

"I do," Jayne told her. "There are some who are arguing it's safe right now, although I'd still err on the side of caution. But for how long?"

Rima saw no sense in rushing things. Just because they had been testing under lab conditions and had identified no immediate hazards, it didn't mean there were none.

"How long is it since you've set foot outside the domes?" Jayne asked. "You should come out with me. We're on *another planet*, darling! Come on, let's go out now. You never know, you might choose to stay."

They'd talked about that a couple of times. Rima's first assumption, when they'd learned of the new wormhole technology, was that the ten-year cycle of the original project was no longer relevant. New personnel would arrive, and the original team members would no longer be bound to remain here for the full ten-year stretch; they would be able to leave early, or even take vacation time on Earth before returning to Carrasco.

The prospect of returning to Earth held nothing for Rima.

She had not, though, considered the alternative possibility: that if the research base was able to expand on Carrasco, then there might be opportunity to remain beyond the initial ten years. That held obvious appeal for hardcore researchers like Jayne, whose careers had built up to this point, to working on Carrasco, and returning to Earth would mark the end of active professional lives. But also, for Rima, too, the prospect was tantalising. As Xavier Fernandez had so crudely pointed out, her professional discipline of suspension research had become a dead-end eighty years ago, so now she might have the choice between returning to Earth to a mundane medical practice or, worse, an even more monotonous retirement; or remaining here, establishing herself as the foremost expert in exo-medicine and the particular quirks and ailments of life on Carrasco.

"Come on, let's go for an amble."

Before she knew it, Rima was following Jayne to the nearest airlock, getting suited up and then exchanging checks on each other's suits before cycling the lock and setting foot outside under that turquoise, alien sky.

Outside.

For the first time, this was starting to feel real. It was a strange sensation. Most of Rima's time on Carrasco had been spent within the domes. The planet, from that perspective, was at a remove: seen through viewing panels or through real-times displayed on walls. Even on the two occasions she had ventured out, on formal site tours organised for team members like Rima whose roles kept them inside the domes, everything had felt structured, controlled – literally like being on an excursion – and somehow it had felt more as if she was viewing than participating.

Perhaps it was the discussion with Jayne. The very real possibility that this research base would continue beyond its original ten-year plan and become a permanent scientific outpost, and as such would require infrastructure, support staff – there would clearly be a role for an experienced medical director like Rima, if that was what she chose.

So now she saw things differently. She stood in a cleared space between the main dome and the first of a cluster of agri-domes, and she saw this place as something that might one day be home.

Rima's visor was misting. At first she thought it was on the inside, but the green tinge reminded her that the atmosphere was loaded with the microorganisms that gave the sky its turquoise tint. She commanded her suit to spray the visor, and her view cleared.

What would it be like to feel this alien air on bare skin? She knew about the smell – analyses had confirmed the heavy biological load in the air, the stench of flatulence and decay. But would something as simple as these floating microorganisms cause problems? A constant film of slime gathering on the skin... She suspected, though, that it would simply be something you got used to, like the smell.

A flyer swooped down, passing so close she felt the downdraft from its broad wings against the thin membrane of her suit. Was that curiosity it showed, or simply some form of behaviour programmed by evolution, passing by larger animals in anticipation of prey disturbed?

"Aren't they simply terrific?" Jayne was grinning through her visor.

Rima felt a flash of pure envy then, that this was the absolute peak of her friend's career while for Rima it was a time of regrouping and starting afresh.

"Come and see the nest," Jayne said.

Jayne had told her about the flyer colony, but words were no preparation for actually seeing it. They followed a path cut through the dense jungle. A few minutes from the base the path opened out into an area of bare rock, a craggy outcropping above a ravine.

Following her friend's lead, Rima dropped to her knees at the edge of the crag, then lay full stretch so she could peer over, down into the drop. About thirty metres below, white rapids surged through this crack in the planet's surface. As Rima's sight adjusted to the gloom of the ravine, she made out a bulge in the rock-face about halfway down, then saw that the bulge moved, its surface seething and pulsing. She realised that the bulge comprised hundreds of flyers, the outer layer with wings spread like a protective membrane encapsulating the nest.

As she watched, another flyer swooped in, landed, and a gap opened in the mass into which it squirmed until it was lost to sight.

"I estimate there are over a thousand individuals in that nest. We've scanned the mass with ultrasound, and we think there are either eggs or cocoons of some sort at the centre. But we've no idea why they swarm like this, or why flyers come and go, pushing through to the centre and remaining for several hours before emerging again."

Rima wiped her visor with the back of a gloved hand. "What's the equivalent on Earth?" she asked. "An ants' nest? A beehive?" She still found it easier to think in terms of what she knew.

"There doesn't have to be an equivalent. We're on an alien planet. This is all new. We leave all assumptions behind. As far as we understand, it's a protective thing, shielding eggs or young from danger."

Jayne rolled over onto her back, staring up at the sky.

Rima turned onto her side, studying her friend. "You're never going back, are you?"

Jayne shook her head. "They'd have to drag me away, kicking and screaming. You?"

"I... I don't know. I have nothing back on Earth."

She rolled onto her front again, accidentally dislodging a small stone from the crag. She gasped, seeing exactly what was happening. The stone bounced off a rock, then struck the seething nest of flyers. Instantly a mad skittering sound echoed around the ravine and, almost in slow motion, the outer layer of flyers peeled away from the mass, tumbling into flight, swooping around in a chaotic mid-air ballet that would disorient any predator.

"It's okay," Jayne said. "Watch."

The layer of flyers newly exposed seethed and pulsed so that Rima thought the whole mass was falling apart, but then they stabilised, wings spread again in a protective membrane, as one by one the disturbed flyers returned to the nest and formed themselves around it again as a shield.

"I should be getting back," Rima said, after a time.

"Just in case some other clumsy arse has taken a tumble in the jungle? I'm sure Jimmy can cope with that, and you'll be summoned if he can't."

Still, more than a week into the mission, Sylvie Wilson's scaphoid fracture was the most serious condition Rima had treated.

As they walked back through the jungle, Rima felt a sudden weight on her shoulder, disturbingly wet and jelly-like through the hypersensitive membrane of her protective suit. She jumped and slapped at her shoulder, and a polyp the size of her fist fell to the ground, then slithered slug-like away.

"It's okay!" Jayne assured her, clearly struggling to suppress a laugh. "We get that all the time. They're drawn to heat, but they don't like our suits so they don't stick. They're harmless."

Sure enough, a moment later another polyp dropped from the vegetation and adhered briefly to the ecologist's chest before falling away.

For the next fifty metres before they emerged into the base's clearing, Rima had to force herself not to walk as fast as she possibly could.

And there, as if mention of her broken wrist had summoned her, Rima saw a group of four people, one of them Deputy Chief Sylvie Wilson.

"For Chrissake!" Rima said, staring at the women.

"What?" Jayne asked.

Without pausing to think, Rima strode across to them, cut through their babble of conversation with a single gesture of her hand, and said, "You. *Bon sang!* Inside now. What on earth do you think you're doing?"

She didn't care that she was talking to the second most senior person on the project in such a way. She didn't care that the deputy chief was out and about only days after a serious injury when she really should be giving the healer-mesh more of a chance to do its thing.

Wilson was in full protective gear: body suit, visor, breather, heavy boots. But what should have been a flawless hermetic seal between her and the outside world was rendered useless by the fact she had declined to fit the glove to her right hand, and the suit was pushed up to mid forearm.

Even now, Wilson didn't seem to get it. She held her right arm up, displaying the flexicast fitted mitt-like over the wrist and part of the hand, there for support and to hold the healer-mesh in place. "You try putting a glove over this," she said.

Rima bit down on her anger, only muttering "*Imbécile*" under her breath. "I told you," she said, forcing calmness into her words, "if you really must venture outside there are special adaptations available to the suit: a protective glove that fits around the cast could have been printed in seconds. But instead…"

She couldn't believe it. That anyone, let alone someone in such a position of authority, should be so ignorant of biohazard protocol was beyond understanding.

"Inside," she said. "And straight to the infirmary."

Wilson was about to object, but then someone in her small group – Lieutenant Harvey, Rima realised – put a hand on her arm and murmured something. The deputy chief's expression changed, as she realised, perhaps, how irresponsible she had been.

They carried out tests for far longer than was really necessary. So long that Rima had run out of tests to do, but she persisted for the principle of it. Screening for all known toxins, and for the body's known reactions to toxins; temperature, antibody and lymph response; constant measuring of vitals, and comparing them to Wilson's history, to look for any deviation from the expected.

Before allowing Wilson back through the airlock and into the dome, Rima had stripped her out of her suit, run a full decontamination, then put her into another suit, trying not to be *too* rough when she eased the glove over the deputy chief's injured hand.

Now, in the medical unit, Wilson was in complete isolation. Even if Rima was the only person on this damned planet who understood biohazard risk, she was going to stick to the protocols to the absolute letter.

Rima sat at a workstation, running through Wilson's data once again. They had been here three hours, and the deputy chief's attitude had gradually shifted from embarrassed acknowledgement of her own stupidity, through growing frustration, and now to the point where she was starting to throw her weight about.

"What's to stop me just walking out of here right now?" Wilson demanded. "You've run your tests, I've been decontaminated to within an inch of my life... I'm *clean*, damn it."

"Do you know how long it can take before you display the

effects of biohazard contamination from just those toxins we know about from the local environment, let alone those we don't?"

"No," Wilson responded, grudgingly.

"And neither do I," Rima told her, and watched the anger instantly deflate, as Wilson's frame visibly slumped.

"You understand the importance of the biohazard protocols," Rima continued. "And in particular, you should understand how vital it is that everyone else *sees* that those protocols are observed, because there are people among us who expose themselves to far greater possible risk than merely flashing a forearm for a few minutes outside the dome."

"How long?"

"Twenty-four hours in complete quarantine with no statistically significant deviation from your historical biomed norms, followed by further close monitoring for ten days, and reduced but still additional monitoring for a further thirty."

Wilson knew the rules. Along with Hertzberger, she'd signed them off.

A few days later, and Sylvie Wilson had followed Rima's instructions to the letter. After twenty-four hours in quarantine, she was back in circulation, subject to close monitoring and a daily routine that minimised contact with those around her.

"Thank you," she said, sitting in Rima's consulting room, pushing the sleeve of her tunic back down to the wrist that was fully healed now. The new healing mesh did wonders for bone injuries, as well as the soft tissue injuries for which it had originally been developed.

New... Yet again, Rima pulled herself up on the language she used. Healing mesh had been new technology eighty years ago, and while it remained a novelty to Rima, back on Earth they must regard it as a medical relic, akin to leeches and herbal poultices.

"Why thank me?" Rima asked.

"For being the bitch who put me in my place and made me do the right thing. It was stupid of me to take such a risk, and you were right."

Rima nodded, but said nothing. Of course she was right, but for all the good it had done she might as well have turned a blind eye. The change in attitudes around the base when Wilson emerged from quarantine had been subtle, but clear. Rima had stopped counting the number of times she'd observed someone outside with suit fastenings only loosely applied, and the number of jokey references to the stink of the planet – references that could only have been made by someone who had breathed the air, unencumbered by masks and breathing units.

People were starting to relax, and perhaps that was no bad thing.

"I went outside this morning," Rima said. She'd become quite close to Wilson over the past week: two strangers thrown together, who had nothing better to do than to talk.

"Outside?" Wilson was studying her closely, and Rima could tell she had made the connection.

Rima looked away, then back up to meet that look. "The air," she said. "It really is bad, isn't it?"

"You get used to it, so I've been told."

This morning she'd gone out to the ravine with Jayne, but the flyers' nest had dispersed since their last visit. The two had lain on the rocks, face up to the turquoise sky, both still meticulously suited up. "You think it's safe?" Jayne had said. "You're the doctor, after all."

"Do *you* think it's safe? You're the ecologist."

Rima hadn't even noticed at first that Jayne had pushed her visor up while they had been lying there, removed the breather clip from her nose. She lay there, face exposed to the elements.

Rima had fought off her initial shock, making herself

remember the *old* Rima, from before things had become so
messy back on Earth. The Rima who had always urged those
around her to seize the moment, to live as if there were no
tomorrow.

And so she had reached up, pushed her visor up, felt the
first touch of alien air on her face. The heat of the sun. When
she removed the breather from her nose, the air really did
stink like rotten eggs.

"Do you think we should ease the biohazard protocols?"
Sylvie Wilson asked now.

"That's a strategic choice, I think. Would you rather have
people increasingly ignoring the requirements, steadily
undermining authority in other areas, too, or would you prefer
to lift those requirements so people are still doing what they
are supposed to do? There's a big psychological difference."

"Which avoids the question, doesn't it, Rima? Do *you* think
we should ease the protocols?"

"The science suggests so," said Rima cautiously. "With
careful monitoring, of course."

Wilson nodded. "I'll consult with Mijnheer Hertzberger."

Three days later, Sylvie Wilson was the first to die.

8

Faraday Cage

The *Cockerel* was a narrow, ancient building wedged between two ugly concrete monoliths, one housing the Beijing-London Bank, the other a baijiu bar. The interior of the pub had changed little in the thirty years that Kemp had been drinking there, a refuge of buttoned leather banquettes, beaten-copper tabletops, and polished mahogany wall-panels. He'd often daydreamed of finishing a drink and stepping out of the pub to find himself miraculously transported back in time twenty, thirty, forty years to the era of the cold cases he was now investigating. Then he'd be able to interview suspects, witnesses and relatives who were still living, not dead or vanished for decades and thus reduced to holographic images and old case notes.

Today was the first time he'd noticed the addition of a few fake customers projected around the tables near the entrance to give the impression that the pub was popular even at quiet times like this. He hoped that wasn't a sign of imminent decline. He was on his third beer and trying to ignore the popzak oozing from the speakers, when the door swung open to admit a blast of cold air and the shambling, ursine form of Edouard Bryce.

The big man indicated the half-litre glasses on the tabletop. "A refill? What is it?"

"Fuller's-Tsing-Tao."

"How is it?" Bryce asked.

Kemp drained the dregs of his third beer. "Much as ever – too sweet since the take-over. And too bloody cold."

Bryce returned from the bar with two tall glasses and sat down across the table from Kemp.

They sat in silence for a short time, then Bryce raised his eyebrows and mouthed the single word *Discretion*. Kemp had hoped he'd pick that up from his message.

"So what's all this about?" Bryce asked, clearly choosing his words carefully.

"I might be over-reacting–"

"I detect a but coming."

"… But I've just had an–" he gestured vaguely at his temple, hoping Bryce would understand "–upgrade and it's making me uneasy."

Bryce pulled a face, then stood and gestured for Kemp to follow.

A short time later they were sitting in a booth at the rear of the pub. "We can talk more freely now," Bryce said. "I often meet clients here. The landlord assured me that these booths are screened from prying ears, if you catch my drift. So…?"

Kemp took another sip of his beer. He knew how paranoid he was going to sound. "First, some background," he said. "But you won't believe a word of this."

"Try me." The solicitor tipped half the glass down his throat.

"Tomorrow I'm leaving planet Earth and heading for the stars."

Bryce pointed to the empty glasses at the table they'd vacated. "One, two, three… and how many more has little Lucy cleared away? You're drunk, man."

Kemp gave the solicitor a stripped-down resume of the Rima Cagnac case, and the revelation about the starship and what it was carrying. Bryce nodded, phlegmatic; nothing could faze the big man, not even the miraculous fact of near-instantaneous travel to the stars.

"So I'm going through the wormhole tomorrow, and I can't help feeling I'm being set up as some kind of fall guy."

"How so?"

"Wouldn't it be far simpler to send some ESO security heavies in to grab Cagnac and return her to Earth? Why me? And this thing in my head..." He tapped his temple.

"You mentioned the imp upgrade. You said it was making you uneasy. Why's that?"

Kemp wiped his lips with the back of his hand and thought about it. "The upgrade... It wasn't like last time. I was out cold for an hour. That seems pretty drastic, don't you think? Tell me: it's possible that my imp's been loaded with spyware, right? Stuff that reports everything I experience – Christ, everything I think – right back to whoever's in control?"

Bryce rocked his big head. "Well, I don't know about everything you *think* – I don't think such refined neural interfacing has been developed, yet. But the other stuff – yes, of course."

"That's what I thought, and it's understandable. I'm being sent on a mission to the stars to bring back a murder suspect, so of course my controllers want to keep tabs on me..." The idea made him very, very uneasy. "So, how will I be monitored?"

"Do you mean, how will they go about sifting the wheat from the chaff of your experience? Well, when they can monitor you in real time, they will, but this booth is screened – it's wired like a Faraday cage – so we're okay for now. But your imp will probably be recording your input and storing anything of value for later study. I suspect your imp will rely on some kind of AI smartware primed to listen for keywords – like the names of the people involved, the starship, that kind of thing. Maybe some facial recognition for when you encounter anyone flagged up as significant. Anything like this will be sorted and stored for later retrieval. So we're safe for now, given that this booth is screened, but..."

"But as soon as we set foot outside the *Cockerel*, chances are this conversation will be screened, flagged as significant, and relayed in its entirety to Tsang – is that right?"

Bryce nodded.

"So I was hoping, now that I've unburdened myself to you, that you might call your tame tech-wizard and get him to take a look at what they upgraded me with."

"And while he's at it, perhaps delete any record of this conversation from your imp before it gets the chance to relay it to Tsang?"

"Is that the kind of thing he could do?" Kemp asked. "Because otherwise, well, we're a bit screwed, aren't we?"

Bryce downed the second half of his drink and signalled to Lucy for two refills. "I'm sure my man will be more than amenable," he told Kemp. "Just let me get away from this screening so I can give him a buzz. Bear with me."

Bryce lumbered to his feet and eased his way through the lunchtime crowd starting to fill the taproom.

Kemp smiled as Lucy came over, set two full glasses on the table before him and gathered the empties. She'd worked at the *Cockerel* for years, and Kemp always admired her facility for dispensing flagons, dazzling smiles, and razor-sharp quips with equal grace. These days he found himself regarding female beauty with an appreciation wholly divorced from desire. It was over five years since he'd last attempted a relationship with a member of the opposite sex, and that had been a short-lived disaster.

Bryce returned and nodded as he took his seat. "We're in luck. Martin can see us in an hour. I'm afraid we'll have to remain in the *Cockerel*, though, because the moment we're unscreened your imp will be up to its mischief."

"You mean... another hour stuck in a pub on my last day on Earth? You've twisted my arm."

They drank their beer as the taproom gradually filled up around them, and Bryce followed the direction of Kemp's gaze.

"And thinking of divine beauty, Gordon, how is the gorgeous Ms Bellini these days?"

"Pregnant," Kemp said.

Bryce lowered his glass. He looked surprised. "Who's the lucky man?"

"She isn't saying. She lives for her work, and has little time to socialise, so I wouldn't be surprised if it's donated." He thought about it. "Come to that, I'm not even sure if she prefers men."

Smiling to himself, Bryce raised his eyebrows. "How long have you worked with her?"

"Three years now."

"And you don't even know her sexual preferences? Call yourself a detective?"

Kemp shrugged. "I once got a bit prickly with her when she asked when I'd lasted dated, so who am I to ask about *her* love-life? Anyway," he went on, "talking about women...?"

Bryce shook his head, his jowls wobbling. "I'm almost sixty, twice married, and work from eight till seven, six days a week." He hoisted his glass. "This is about as entertaining as it gets. And do you know something, Gordon? I'm not complaining."

When the hour was nearly up, a turbaned boy who could barely have been fifteen shuffled into the bar and looked around, as if searching for someone. His skinny frame was emphasised by his outfit of kilt and t-shirt, swamped by a big quilted jacket. As soon as he saw Bryce and Kemp, he came across to their booth. Kemp guessed he'd IDed them with the help of some smartware in the dark glasses he wore.

Without ceremony, the boy unslung a bag from his shoulder, extracted a hooded jacket and dumped it on the table. "Martin-ji says wear this, hood up."

Kemp complied. He felt some kind of wiring concealed in the fabric of the hood as he pulled it over his head – screening, he presumed, to prevent his imp from contacting its controllers when they left the safety of the *Cockerel*.

He'd never felt so paranoid in all his life.

"You follow me, yah?" And without further comment, the kid turned and made for the door.

Kemp and Bryce finished their beers and shuffled out into the freezing wind.

The boy had an electric rickshaw and they squeezed in

behind him. A little later they crossed the bridge over the frozen Thames, packed with traffic because of the ferry closures. Bryce indicated the river's gunmetal-grey ice. "There was a time when the Thames never got like this, can you believe that, Gordon?"

Kemp turned his collar up against the cutting wind, wishing their under-age chauffeur owned a covered rickshaw. "Up until the nineteenth century the river used to freeze over regularly," he said. "It was only the couple of centuries after that when it became infrequent." These days, the river froze most winters, alternating with intense droughts in the summer months, when water supplies in the city were rationed and even the lakes in the great parks dried up.

The snow came down in huge wet flakes now, settling on Bryce's bald pate, melting, and flowing down his face like tears. The streets were thronged with citizens on bikes and power scooters zigzagging in and out between larger vehicles, municipal buses and hydrogen tankers.

It was a relief when they left central London in their wake and came to the once leafy residential avenues of Southwark. Now the plane trees stood dead and dying along the side of the road – those not felled by locals in desperate need of winter fuel.

The rickshaw pulled up outside a fruit and veg shop, above which Martin Khalsa lived and worked. "Here now," the boy said. He indicated a narrow flight of stairs to the side of the shop. "Up there. Martin-ji, he's expecting you, acha?"

At the top of the stairs they came to a steel plate door. It was opened instantly by a tall, twitchy Sikh in Bermuda shorts and a Free Mongolia t-shirt. The temperature inside the cramped room was sweltering, more like a hothouse than a suburban sitting room, though there was not a single plant in sight. Amid the debris of old com-consoles, headphones, and miscellaneous techno-junk, Kemp made out a lone battered armchair. Air-screens displaying a dizzying range of images flitted through the air like giant, polychromatic butterflies.

"Ed, Mr Kemp... sorry about the mess. I had to leave the last place pretty damned quick when some government thugs were looking for me."

Although he was sweating hard in the room's heat, Kemp resisted the temptation to remove the hooded jacket.

Martin was constantly on the move, darting around the room, attending to screens and airborne keypads. When he paused for a second, it was only to crack his knuckles and jerk his head back and forth like a sufferer from Tourette's without the verbals.

Kemp had wondered, at their first meeting, if Martin had been on some kind of chemical high, but Bryce assured him that he was clean. His illegal activity of choice involved hacking the government datasphere and disabling corporate virtual infrastructure. Martin's nervous energy was the result of continually keeping one step ahead of the authorities, both here in London and in Beijing.

Kemp looked around the room as he recalled Martin's last residence: a bedsit in Hackney filled with identical junk, though even smaller than this place. "You're going up in the world, Martin."

"I do my best, Mr Kemp."

"You do realise I could be up on a disciplinary charge just for being here and not trying to arrest you, don't you?"

Martin gave a grin and an involuntary head-jerk. "And that's exactly why you're here, isn't it? I'm that good."

Bryce said, "We're safe?"

Martin nodded. "As always," he said. "You can take off the coat, Mr Kemp."

Kemp did so, then loosened his collar. The light in the room was wholly artificial. The single window was covered with the same steel plate as the door. A mesh of silver gauze, like chain mail, covered the ceiling, walls and floor like an avant garde work of art. The room was, in effect, a giant Faraday cage.

Bryce pointed to Kemp. "Gordon's just been upgraded. He's

afraid they've loaded spyware, and everything he's doing will be beamed back to his bosses. If you could be a good chap and check it out, Martin."

"Only too glad to assist."

Martin indicated the armchair and Kemp sat down. Bryce lowered his bulk to the floor and sat back against the door, watching Kemp over his knees.

What happened over the course of the next thirty minutes Kemp would have been unable to describe in any coherent detail. Martin waved his hands, spoke into floating mics, and accessed on-screen text – a magician performing arcane rites.

At one point he said, "You were out cold when they downloaded the upgrade, right?"

"For an hour, yes. How do you know?"

"An hour. Shit, that was some download." Martin indicated a screen full of code, as if that explained anything. "Conscious, you would've been blitzed and hallucinating like a gash-junkie. They had to put you under to stop you after-flashing for months."

"What did they download?"

"What *didn't* they?" Martin stared at a screen floating before him, his bloodshot eyes shuttling back and forth. "Geltabs, cell-mimics, nano-info-flechettes… you name it."

"What the hell," Kemp said, feeling sick, "are those?"

"In a word, spyware."

Bryce said, "So you were well within your rights to be paranoid, Gordon."

"Okay…" Kemp breathed out. "So… what you've done now won't be detectable by my bosses?"

Martin shook his head. "Of course not. I pride myself on discretion, Mr Kemp."

"Martin," Bryce said from his position against the door, "if you could explain just what they uploaded in simple words that we might understand – and the consequences of the upload – we'd be more than grateful."

"Very well," Martin said. "It's like this. Your imp is now military-grade AI-ware, and your body has been hardwired as a multiply redundant data warehouse. Your imp uses storage throughout your body at the molecular level: billions of cells carrying processing algorithms, data storage. Your imp is no longer just an implant, riding your occipital lobe: it's *you*. Throughout you. You're your own little ecosystem of data-processing. You really are quite something, Mr Kemp. I've never seen anything like it," he finished.

"Very well," Bryce said, "but why have they done this?"

The Sikh sucked his lips. "My guess is that it's mainly spyware, lots of processing of input going on before it relays everything back to a main source – or stores it until it can do so at some point in the near future. Are you going anywhere off-grid soon, where this system might have to operate in isolation?"

Kemp exchanged a look with Bryce, and they both laughed. "You could say that, yes," Kemp said.

"So what can we do?" Bryce said. "Is there any way that Gordon might be able to disable what they've installed at some point? Perhaps even remove it?"

"Disable? Remove?" Martin grimaced. "You heard the part where I said the imp has been integrated somatically, right? There's no way you can just whip something like that out of someone. I'll tell you something else, too." He held his hands up in the air, as if surrendering. "Some of this stuff is way beyond the kind of things I work with. I've infiltrated some high-grade military shit in my time." He glanced almost apologetically at Kemp as he said this. "But this stuff is *new*. There's something in there that's encrypted behind so many fail-safes it'd take a me a decade to work it out."

"Encrypted?"

"There are layers I can't get to. Things they don't want anyone finding out about, and that's for sure."

Kemp stared at the screens revolving through the air. If

the veiled motives of his superiors were not enough to deal with, the thought of being host to inimical spyware made him uneasy in his own skin. Until now, his imp had been merely an adjunct, a useful resource to call upon in times of need. Now it was a treacherous alter ego, an ineradicable spy – not only riding in his head, but hijacking his entire body.

Martin was silent for a few seconds, then nodded and said, "There is one thing…"

Bryce looked up. "Go on."

"I couldn't write a routine to disable the encrypted area without your bosses knowing about it – chances are if I added anything at all my code might trigger alarms and everyone would know you've been messing with your gelware. No, that'd be too dangerous."

"But?" Kemp asked, staring at the pensive Sikh.

"I could write a killfile and store it somewhere, say on a datapin, which you could insert when necessary. This would blitz the system, wipe it completely. Not subtle, but effective – and I could code it in such a way that your bosses wouldn't be able to trace the source: it'd just look like some random, catastrophic software malfunction. Trouble is…"

"Out with it," Bryce barked from the door.

"With your body so fully integrated into the AIware, I'm not sure of the physiological consequences of such a blitz. I can't make any guarantees that you'd emerge unscathed in the event of you triggering the killfile."

"Unscathed?"

"I'm no neurosurgeon, Mr Kemp, but I can tell you that if you fry a bunch of neurones, then chances are there's going to be some collateral damage. Disability, cognitive functioning, who knows?"

Bryce looked across at Kemp. "What do you think, Gordon?"

Kemp stared at his fingers on the arm of the chair, drumming an uneasy tattoo. "The choice would be mine, wouldn't it?

Whether to use the pin or not. It might be useful, as a last resort." He nodded. "Go ahead, Martin. Write it."

The Sikh nodded, called up a screen, and ran a frantic arpeggio across an airborne keyboard, his expression one of intense absorption.

"Do you have anything to drink in here, Martin?" Bryce said, climbing to his feet.

Dreamily, lost in his realm of abstruse code, Martin said, "You know I don't touch alcohol, Ed."

Bryce grunted. "Something cold, then? Do you have a dispenser round here?"

Martin pointed to a mound of tech in one corner.

Bryce dialled himself a ginseng energy drink, but Kemp waved that he was fine. He was keyed up enough already without taking an artificial stimulant. Bryce crossed the room, side-stepping through an obstacle course of hardware, and sat down on the arm of Kemp's chair.

"So, why you, Gordon?" he said, taking a swig of ginseng. "And why all this business with your imp? Any ideas?"

Kemp gestured. "Beats me. I had it down as an open and shut case. Go on my little journey, find the suspect, and bring her back. I don't see all the need for what they've done to me."

Bryce looked thoughtful. "My suspicion is that it's linked," he said at last.

Kemp looked up. "What is?"

"What they've done to you, and... all the malarkey with what's aboard the ship – the quantum lattice, and why they kept it quiet."

Kemp grunted a laugh. "I just want to get this over with. Then I can get back to Earth and hope that by then our resident tech-genius will have had time to work out how to have all the implants wiped, so I can retire. I've had enough."

It was, he thought, a spur of the moment thing. After what Martin had disclosed, he'd reached a tipping-point. He wanted his future to be his own, no longer play the lackey of people he couldn't trust.

"There," Martin said a little later. He pulled something from a stack of hardware and held it up before his eyes. The silver needle caught the light from a nearby floating screen, two centimetres long and scintillating.

"One moment," Martin said, and crossed the room to an ancient filing cabinet. He found a fine silver chain, slipped the pin into the head of a small figurine, and passed it to Kemp.

"I don't usually go for personal jewellery, Martin," Kemp said, turning over the Buddha figure in his hand.

"A modesty that Siddhartha would approve of," Martin laughed. "Keep it in your pocket, then – but don't lose it, okay? That's some expensive hardware."

Kemp smiled, pocketing the Buddha. "How much do I owe you?"

"To you, five hundred New Euros."

Bryce said, "Put it on my tab, Martin," and to Kemp, "You can settle with me when you get back, okay?"

Martin said, "There's something else…"

Kemp looked up. "Go on."

Martin glanced from Kemp to Bryce. "Something that isn't right," he went on, frowning. "I said your bosses have loaded you with all kinds of extras… But there's something they *haven't* installed."

"Which is?" Kemp asked.

"This was developed in the Shanghai labs about three months back, and released in the East a month or so ago once all the glitches had been sorted. I hacked a copy a couple of weeks back. Ever heard of lieware?"

Frowning, Bryce repeated, "Lieware?"

"It's a sophisticated suite of algorithms that collates and intuits from a subject's physical reactions to questions. In a word, it detects when a subject is lying, or telling the truth. I've heard from friends in the business that high-ups in Whitehall have had them installed, and a few people in Government security."

Kemp said, "You said you had a copy?"

"It doesn't come cheap."

"But you could install it without my new implant finding out and informing my bosses? I thought you said you couldn't install anything new without giving the game away?"

"This isn't new, though. It's already configured in your latest upgrade: I just need to enable it."

He nodded. "Do it," he said, sitting back in the armchair and feeling, for the first time that day, that he was doing something to get back at Commander Tsang. "How much more do we owe you for that?"

"Consider it my gift. I have a feeling you're going to need all the help you can get." Martin turned to a screen and tapped a floating keyboard. Bryce removed himself from the arm of the chair and stood by the door, chugging on his ginseng.

Two minutes later Martin said, "All done."

"How does it work?"

"You initiate the routine with a left-right eyeblink. This will bring up a retinal overlay at the bottom left of your vision. Go on."

Kemp blinked rapidly, left-right.

Instantly, a sliding scale vector appeared at the bottom left of his vision, with a bar located at midpoint.

"It's a line-of-sight routine," Martin said. "The indicator moves to the left when the subject is telling the truth, and to the right when he or she is lying."

As Martin spoke, the slide moved left.

"Now, if I were to lie..." He pulled a face. "Okay, how about this: I like going out for long walks in the park..."

The sliding indicator in Kemp's vision moved rapidly to the right.

Kemp smiled. "I like it, Martin. If only I'd had this years ago..."

"It's accurate to within three percentiles," Martin said. "And it learns on the job, so it should become more accurate as time goes by. To end the program, reverse the initial command and blink right-left."

Kemp did so, and the sliding scale vanished.

As they were about to leave, Kemp said, "If I use the Buddha pin, then presumably it would scrub my record facility, right?"

Martin nodded. "Is that a problem?"

"I'd like to have my own record of whatever happens on Carrasco," he said.

"Okay," Martin said. "There is a way round that, Mr Kemp. I could copy the record program and re-install it on a separate system, which the killfile wouldn't affect."

"Do it."

It took Martin another fifteen minutes to make the adaptation and install it, by which time Kemp was more than ready to quit the hothouse atmosphere of the bedsit.

Martin said, "One last thing. The spyware doesn't appear to be active now, so you're not being monitored. But all it will take is a command from its controllers and it will kick into action. You'd better take this." Martin handed him the hooded jacket, and Kemp slipped it on.

Back on the street, the east wind cut to the bone. Bryce called up a rickshaw – a covered one this time – and they headed back across the Thames to central London.

They parted outside Bryce's run-down office building, a Victorian pile in Holborn that had seen better days. "When you get back," Bryce said before they went their separate ways, "let's meet up and you can tell me all about it."

Kemp watched the big man shamble through the sliding doors, then stood in the street, buffeted by pedestrians and the icy wind as he wondered how to fill the rest of the day. It was four o'clock, and the last thing he wanted to do was to go back to his basement office.

He took a rickshaw north to his bedsit in Finsbury Park, but rather than spend long hours alone in the cold, bleak room, he dropped by his favourite noodle bar and ordered pan mee and a beer. He sat at the bar by the window and stared out at the crowded street, at the endless flow of pedestrians huddled in padded jackets against the February cold.

He'd almost finished the noodles when his implant pinged. The woman's voice, old-fashioned BBC and oddly seductive, said, *"Commander Tsang, Gordon."*

Was Tsang suspicious that he couldn't monitor Kemp's implant, due to the hooded jacket?

Alarmed that Tsang might be on to him, he said, "Allow."

The image of Tsang's overfed face floated in his vision in the air before the window.

"Commander," Kemp said, taking a swallow of beer to cover his nervousness.

"Inspector Kemp," Tsang said, and something about the immobility of the man's features increased Kemp's unease – before he realised that his commander appeared no more stern than usual. "I'll see you in the morning, at ten, for a final briefing before your departure. All ready, I take it?"

"As I'll ever be," Kemp said, relieved.

"Very good. Until tomorrow, Inspector."

The face vanished, and Kemp was left staring out at the busy street.

He supposed he'd better go home and prepare – but what exactly did you pack for a trip to an extra-solar planet? The very idea of filling a suitcase with clothing in this situation seemed absurd.

So instead of taking the short walk to his bedsit, he ordered another bowl of pan mee and a beer.

9

Green Rain

"We must reinstate the biohazard protocols, *tout de suite*," Rima insisted. She stood with Mijnheer Hertzberger and one of his strategy advisers, the geologist Cherie Martinez, outside Sylvie Wilson's isolation room.

She'd argued this point with the commander yesterday, too, the day after Sylvie Wilson had gone down with an illness yet to be identified. Now Sylvie lay in an infirmary bed, under strict quarantine. She was running a fever of a little over thirty-nine degrees, her body wracked with pains and intense muscle cramps. She was delirious, too, lost in a world of hallucination and what appeared to be some kind of mental regression, reliving jumbled up episodes from her past, her childhood even. Three others lay in isolation units elsewhere in the base, showing a similar range of symptoms.

"Have we pinpointed the source of the condition?" Martinez asked.

"We're working on it."

"Then we do not know for certain that it is a biohazard, do we? I suggest we refrain from jumping to convenient conclusions in an attempt to evade responsibility."

Martinez was not subtle in her attempts to make Rima feel responsible, and Hertzberger was lapping it up.

"Responsibility? What are you saying?" Rima snapped.

"What if Doctor Wilson's condition is a consequence of

eighty years in suspension?" Martinez said. "Something you overlooked, perhaps?"

Rima took a step towards Martinez, then forced herself to stop. She didn't know what she'd been about to do. She was exhausted from monitoring Sylvie around the clock, and she didn't need some second-rate adviser like Cherie Martinez scoring points by putting her down.

In any case, Rima felt bad enough as it was. She'd allowed herself to be swayed by hope. She'd seen Sylvie exposed to the air of Carrasco, monitored her closely, and seen no sign that anything was wrong. She'd seen others, encouraged by Sylvie's experience, start to ease their guards.

She'd eased her guard, too. Felt the air on her skin, the heat of Mu Arae shining down. Smelt the bad-egg odour of the planet's air.

They'd eased precautions far too soon, ignoring all training and preparation. Sylvie's experience should have been a warning to them, not an excuse to relax.

"We have an exploratory team more than a hundred klicks to the west," Hertzberger said. "Do you propose that I recall them?"

"Yes. Or at least warn them to follow strict protocols."

"You think I have not done the latter already?"

"We were lucky once," Rima said. "We cannot rely on luck every time." She remembered the commander's reaction when he'd emerged from the suspension pod on the *Strasbourg*: the shock when he saw the fire-damage on the ship's interior walls.

"We continue to impose strict quarantine on those who have fallen ill," Hertzberger told her, "and you will report to me on every single development. Other than that, we all have work to do."

The research base went under full biohazard protocols twenty-four hours later, within an hour of Sylvie Wilson's death.

Rima sat with her for the last hour, separated by the microfilm sheeting of the quarantine shield. She had run out of things to try. The infirmary's smart systems were keeping Sylvie's heart pumping, feeding oxygen into her blood, replacing the functions of failed liver and kidneys. For that hour, the deputy chief drifted in and out of delirious consciousness.

"Monique? Monique? *Toi aussi?*" Until Sylvie's regression, Rima had not even realised her native tongue was French. Monique was Sylvie's sister, who had died in her teens, although Rima did not know the cause, or why Sylvie was saying, *You too?*

Rima knew much more about Sylvie now than she ever had before, particularly her early years. Back on Earth, Rima had been indirectly involved in research on rejuvenation therapies, and there had been issues where some of these treatments had triggered similar regression, patients reliving episodes from their youth as the chemistry of their brains unravelled. Rima's involvement had come about because there had been the suggestion that suspension might trigger a similar process; the possibility had been discounted, but it was just another reason she'd felt guilty when Cherie Martinez suggested the illness might be the result of suspension rather than anything environmental.

"*Je ne suis pas Monique.*"

"Monique?"

That was the last thing Sylvie Wilson said. Her mouth remained open, her eyes staring, but the life had finally departed.

Rima sat back. "Jimmy? How are the others? We've just lost Sylvie."

Her assistant's face appeared projected onto the quarantine shield in front of her. "James Harvey and Rachel Grant are stable. Anders Willan isn't doing so good."

They both knew this was going to get a whole lot worse before there was any chance of it getting better.

Jimmy looked exhausted, and Rima was sure she looked no better. She couldn't remember the last time she'd slept, other than slumped in a chair in the infirmary.

"I'm heading over to Lucia's lab, see how she's getting on."

The survivors had been divided into three mini-communities, each quarantined in its own dome. The cold calculation was that if the illness that had taken Wilson and looked like taking Harvey, Grant and Willan was transmissible in any way, then isolation into three communities might just limit an outbreak to only a third of the population.

There was still limited movement, though. Hertzberger had sat with Wilson for a time, and Rima knew he had visited Jimmy's patients in the reserve infirmary in the main accommodation dome. His reasoning must be that strict biohazard discipline combined with important person status gave him some kind of protection. Whatever attributes Hertzberger brought to his role, they did not include a balanced understanding of the sciences.

Rima and Jimmy had been approved to move between domes too, because Rima had argued there was no substitute for full consultation with patients, and such observations might be the difference between life and death for the research colony as a whole.

Now Rima suited up in an airlock, under the expressionless gaze of her security minder. She didn't even know the man's name, even though he accompanied her everywhere she went.

She knew it was all about intimidation, a constant reminder that they must follow the rules, and she hated it. In theory, the security unit was here to protect the researchers against hazards from outside, but in practice it felt as if it had become some kind of police squad, now that rules needed enforcing.

Rima wriggled into the suit and let it seal around her, then pulled the visor down. Disinfectant mists descended. She didn't say it out loud, for fear of undermining the very protocols upon which she had insisted, but she couldn't help feeling that this was as much ritual as science. More than three days into this crisis and they still did not know the cause or vector for the illness, let alone that the disinfectant mixture they used could counter it.

It was the best they could do, though.

She stepped outside, tipped her head up to the sky and saw flyers circling high on a thermal.

Shadowed by her minder, she made her way across the clearing to the main airlock for the dome they'd nicknamed Lab Central. A short time later, decontaminated once more, Rima emerged into the main work area, only to find that Sander Hertzberger was already there.

Lucia Barnard saw Rima immediately and met her look with an almost imperceptible roll of the eyes. "Rima," she said, "I was just bringing Mijnheer Hertzberger up to date with our work."

"The polyp theory," Rima said, and Lucia nodded. "The creatures appear to be drawn to body heat, and adhere to any exposed flesh." ·

Rima had spoken to a number of people who had experienced this. Their descriptions of a slug-like sensation on the skin – an intense suckering followed by a pins and needles sensation as the polyps appeared to be tasting the new substrate – reminded her uneasily of her own fleeting contact with a polyp when she had been outside with Jayne Waterford.

"Doctor Barnard has posited a novel neurochemical transfer when a polyp adheres," Hertzberger said. "Something that might migrate to the brain and trigger the symptoms we are witnessing."

Lucia said, "We won't know, of course, until we can sample the affected tissues, and we're all praying it doesn't come to that–"

She registered Rima's expression and stopped.

"I'm sorry," Rima said. "But we've lost Sylvie. The infirmary's diagnostic engine is performing an autopsy right now."

She'd expected Hertzberger to at least exhibit some degree of shock and sadness at the news of his deputy's death, but instead there was something else in his expression. Hope, even?

"If we can narrow this down," he said, "then we might be able to move out of this limbo."

"I don't understand," Rima said.

"Don't you see? If the autopsy confirms Doctor Barnard's polyp theory, then we have a manageable hazard. A containable one."

"Manageable? It might be ambitious to hope for a treatment so soon after identifying a cause," Lucia said.

"Treatment would be good," Hertzberger said. "But there are other options. We wiped out smallpox and rabies. We pretty much eradicated the Anopheles mosquito."

Rima was aghast. "Our first response cannot be to try to 'wipe out' the first potentially hazardous alien species we encounter."

"Our first response, and any subsequent response, is whatever is necessary to ensure the success of this venture. This planet is even closer to Earth-norm than we had dared dream. And if we can manage the risks, the possibilities are endless."

"Possibilities?"

Hertzberger stared at her. "You've seen the mess we've made of our own planet. Here we have the chance of a fresh start, a Plan B for humankind. And if that requires a bit of localised adaptation, the eradication of a few threats, environmental intervention and management on whatever scale necessary, then that is what we are here to do. We need to establish a viable colony here. And we will not let anything, or anyone, stand in the way of that."

The chief's glance towards the watching security guard and then back to Rima was neither subtle nor necessary.

"What if it's not the polyps?" Rima said. "Sylvie was only

exposed to the air for a short time. She didn't encounter a polyp during that period. I was there."

"Can you be sure of that? Can you be sure she didn't expose herself at other times?"

The chief was desperate for it to be true, to turn this crisis into something he could understand and defeat.

"What if it's something else, more insidious?" Rima persisted.

"Then we will confront that in whatever way is necessary."

Rima was right. It wasn't the polyps.

She sat in her workspace, with a view out over the main clearing. The planet out there really did look Eden-like, the turquoise tint of the sky now so familiar that she struggled to remember skies of pure blue.

A tint that was deadly poisonous.

A talking head of Lucia Barnard was projected onto the window, beside one of Jimmy Ranatunga, so that the two appeared as ghosts, the jungle backdrop showing through their translucent features.

"Extensive neurochemical disruption. Synapse malformation caused by the presence of exotic proteins in the synaptic vesicles."

"But not from the polyps?" Rima asked.

"No," Barnard confirmed. "The signature of those exotic proteins is distinctive, and the only two sites where we have identified it are in the brain and in the lungs."

It wasn't just Sylvie Wilson now. In the two days since her death they had lost Anders Willan and now James Harvey too – the first man to set foot on Carrasco, and one of the first to die. That gave them the results of three autopsies to work on, and all three had exhibited the same pattern of neurochemical disruption, synapse malformation and exotic proteins in the synapses and in the lungs.

"It's in the air," Rima said. For some reason this prompted

thoughts of that nest of flyers, deep in the ravine a few minutes' walk from base. Thousands of flyers wrapped in a ball, forming a multi-layered protective suit around vulnerable eggs or young. They weren't protecting their offspring from predators, as Jayne Waterford had suggested; they were shielding them from the air itself, until such time as juvenile immune systems matured.

"So why have only seven succumbed?" Jimmy asked.

Three more had fallen ill as the crisis continued, far fewer than Rima had feared, although she kept reminding herself that they didn't know the length of incubation for this disease.

Lucia Barnard was shaking her head. "Give us a chance," she said. "Back home it can take hundreds of researchers years to get this far. We've done all this with a team of eight, inside a week!"

"But why?" Rima asked, only half-teasing. It was the question they all wanted answered. All *needed* answered, because she suspected there was not a single person in this expedition who had not been exposed to the air of the planet to some degree or another.

"Natural immunity?" Lucia suggested. "That's what the great Mijnheer wants. Natural immunity is something that can be analysed, extracted, synthesised in a lab and shared around to everyone."

"And your theory?"

"Sheer, god-damned luck, good and bad. Look out of that window of yours, Rima. You, Jimmy–" Rima's assistant's workspace was deep in the accommodation dome "–head out to one of the viewing areas and look out. Look up at the sky, that weird-as-shit colour of it. Without the biotic load, that sky would be blue, except when the clouds come over. Just as it is on Earth. But it *isn't* without that biotic load. It's stuffed full of microorganisms we haven't even come close to identifying and cataloguing, let alone understanding. The clouds are seething Petri dishes packed with bugs. There must be millions, billions, of species, and every time we set foot outside a dome we're subjected to a constant rainfall of exotic biology."

"And not all of them are toxic," Rima said.

"I'd guess almost none of them are," Lucia agreed. "So most of the time we're fine to expose ourselves to the biological stew. Most of the people who've done so have suffered no more than a bit of slime on the skin and maybe a mild allergic response. *Most* of them..."

"You've told Hertzberger?"

"His security mob are monitoring everything we do. He knew before you do. I spoke to him an hour ago, and his first question was about how we 'clean up the atmosphere', to use his phrase."

"You're stressing, darling," Jayne Waterford told her. "It's not healthy."

The two were fully suited and outside again, following a trail through the jungle to gather samples from Jayne's network of trapping stations. Restrictions had been eased since Lucia Barnard had confirmed the theory that Sylvie's disease had been caused by airborne vectors and did not appear to be transmissible from person to person. This had allowed Jayne to resume her forays into the jungle, and she was clearly happier out here than back at the base.

"Have we learnt nothing?" Rima said. "Nobody ever said establishing a research outpost on another planet would be easy and safe. Yet Hertzberger's first response is that we should wipe out anything that stands in our way. We should be trying to understand Carrasco, not change it. You're an ecologist: surely you agree?"

"I'm a scientist. I develop hypotheses and test them."

"And what is your current hypothesis?"

"That you need a change of scene, and you should volunteer yourself for my expedition to Base West One. The first team out there came across all sorts of, to say the very least, *intriguing* findings. Some of their results are firewalled, but what I do know is that Gianfranco Marcosi is on the roster for the follow-up expedition."

"Hertzberger will never let me go. I'm chief medical officer and we're just emerging from a medical crisis that we're still only starting to understand."

"In young Jimmy Ranatunga you have a capable deputy, and he's not the kind of confrontational pain in the proverbial who challenges our chief at every turn. Hertzberger will be glad to see the back of you for a week or two. I'd say that *particularly* given our recent medical crisis, having an experienced doctor with the team at West One is a proposition that has a lot to commend it."

Only then did something Jayne had said start to sink in. "Gianfranco? Well that makes sense," Rima said tentatively. "There'll be lots of ecological sampling to do." Every specialist on the *Strasbourg* had also been trained in at least one extra discipline. Jayne had picked up communications in addition to her primary speciality of exotic ecology, because she had a background in journalism. Gianfranco was unusual in that since landing, he'd been occupied entirely in his secondary role, mainly helping Jayne in trapping and sampling activities. The reason for this was that his principal role had become a running joke as the discipline least likely to be called upon, for Gianfranco Marcosi was a specialist in exo-culture: the sociology of sentient aliens.

Behind the visor, Jayne had a strange look on her face.

"You don't think...?" Rima said.

"I think young Franco is going to spend a lot of time checking traps and running the quadrats, and not a lot else, is what I think, but you never know, do you?"

Rima agreed with that assessment. It made perfect sense to utilise the most under-used specialist on the mission running the ecology team's scut work and doing anything else that might make him at least halfway useful.

But what if there were more to it than simple expediency?

Rima found herself both intrigued and slightly aghast, because discovering even a hint of sentient life on Carrasco – either contemporary or in historical or archaeological remnants – would prove a major obstacle to Commander Hertzberger's hell-bent pursuit of turning the planet into a Plan B for humanity at any cost.

And his first response to any threat to this plan had been: *How do we wipe it out?*

"You're tempted, aren't you, darling?"

How could she not be? For she suspected strongly that whatever the mission to Base West One discovered, it might be pivotal to whatever came next on Carrasco.

10

Mismatch

The outer door to Danni's Highgate apartment recognised his facial features and signature mannerisms and swung open. Kemp climbed the stairs to the second floor, out of breath before he reached the landing. He shrugged off the protective coat Martin had given him, crossed to her door and stood still, staring at the micro-lens of the security system. A second later the door opened and he entered the plush hallway.

Danni stepped from the bathroom, a long bath-towel wrapped loosely around her. He caught a flash of long, tanned legs and bare shoulders before looking away. "Be right with you, Gordon. Help yourself to coffee. The noodles are almost ready."

He moved through to the lounge, a long room tastefully furnished: Japanese minimalism and ukiyo-e prints. Music played softly, again Japanese: traditional Shōmyō chanting. Danni went through phases, immersing herself in various cultures before tiring of them and moving on. Last year it had been South American Aztec, soon followed by Maori. Kemp wondered if her global eclecticism was a subconscious reaction to the spread of Chinese imperialism.

He entered the kitchen and poured himself a coffee with soya milk. On the worktop, a bowl of noodles heated itself.

He moved back to the lounge and lowered himself, gingerly, onto a futon. It was far too close to the ground for comfort;

he stretched his legs across the biscuit-coloured tatami mat, balancing the coffee bulb on his stomach.

Danni entered the room, dressed now in a two-piece navy-blue trouser suit, her long hair a shade darker than her outfit.

"Hungry?" she asked, moving to the kitchen.

"Famished."

She appeared with a bowl of beef noodles for him and a plate of samosas for her. She sat cross-legged on the floor before him and bit the corner off a samosa.

"Before we go any further..." Kemp said, wondering how to go about telling her what had occurred yesterday at Martin's apartment, and what the tech-genius had discovered. Martin had told him the spyware was yet to be activated, but how would he know when that happened? He could hardly wear that shielded coat everywhere he went. Throwing caution to the wind, he said, "Tsang had my implant upgraded, and I had one of Bryce's people take a look."

She nodded, chewing. "And?"

He tried to recall exactly the terminology Martin had employed yesterday, and failed. Instead he told Danni, in layman's terms, that Tsang had had him installed with spyware and much more, some of which was encrypted. He couldn't help but be paranoid now. He knew he could trust Danni, but what if *she* were somehow being spied upon?

"I think we're okay for now. I don't think my life in London before the trip is interesting enough for them to monitor, but at some point, it will be turned on."

"I get the picture," Danni said. "We're going to have to be careful what we say. Wasn't there any way your man could... I don't know... subvert the new implant?"

"Not without the possibility of doing me physical harm," he said. He took out the Buddha necklace and dangled it on its chain, then told her about the datapin Martin had programmed to scrub the entirety of the installation in the event of an emergency.

"There's more," he said, returning the Buddha to his pocket. "Martin was surprised with what Tsang *hadn't* had me installed with."

"Which was?"

"Ever heard of lieware?"

"Rumours, nothing more."

"It exists. Spooks in Whitehall and government security are rigged with the systems. Martin says it's going to become standard issue – he said it's installed in my upgrade. The odd thing is, you'd think Tsang would have it enabled. I'm being sent on a potentially dangerous mission to capture a fugitive, so you'd think me knowing whether she was lying or not would ease things along a little, wouldn't you? And she'll almost certainly have established bonds with people who might wish to protect her. I need to be able to see through all that."

Danni nodded, her samosa forgotten. "Which would lead one to believe," she mused, "that there are people on Carrasco who the authorities don't want you to question too closely, in case you uncover lies – or the truth."

They stared at each other. "Exactly. However..." Kemp let the word hang, smiling at her as she took another bite from her samosa.

She read his expression and said, "Don't tell me – Bryce's man enabled your upgrade? You're loaded with lieware."

Kemp nodded.

Wide-eyed again, Danni stared at him. "Holy shit, Gordon. And... how was it? I take it you've tried it out. This could revolutionise how we work."

"I tested it on Martin himself."

She grinned at him. "So, give me a demonstration, okay? I'll say a few things and you pick out the lies."

"You're like a child with a new gizmo, Danni."

"You know I'm a sucker for the latest tech."

He blinked the lieware into life and the sliding scale appeared. "Go ahead."

She leaned forward, frowning as she considered what to say – like a performer in a game of charades. "Okay... When I was seven, I fell down the stairs at school and broke my leg."

The indicator slid to the left on the sliding scale.

"That's true."

She nodded. "Right. Okay, next... My first boyfriend was called Bukayo and I was sixteen."

"True again."

"When I was twenty, I decided I'd had enough of roughing it around Europe, came home and worked on the harvest at my father's vineyard in Devon."

As she spoke, he tried to match his own skills to those of the lieware: he saw the brief break in eye contact as Danni glanced away to the left, and he registered that perhaps she was trying too hard to fill her statement with specific detail.

The sigil slid to the right. "A lie," he said.

She nodded, "Impressive. Yes, I came back to England, but the last thing I wanted to do was work in yet another vineyard. So I applied to Cambridge. Okay, ask me any question."

He nodded towards her stomach and said, "Who...?" and stopped himself. "I'm sorry," he said, colouring.

"No, that's fine. That's okay. Ask away."

He said, "Who's the father of your child, Danni?"

"Albert Einstein."

For a split second Kemp paused, then he laughed. "I'm calling that one as a lie," he said.

Danni laughed. "Fun and games aside... We've established that the damn thing works."

"It'll make my job out there all the easier–"

She stared at him, screwing her rouged lips to one side. "And potentially, all the more dangerous – if Tsang's people find out what you're packing."

He stared down at his noodles, contemplating the thought.

"Take care out there, you hear?" Danni murmured.

Kemp nodded, and forked noodles for a time in silence.

He set the bowl aside. "How did it go with Fairleigh-White yesterday?"

"It didn't – go, that is. It went nowhere. I got as far as the front door, and Dr Radzinski wouldn't allow me any further. He said his patient was extremely ill and any excitement might prove fatal, etcetera." She pointed the remains of a third samosa at him. "However, resourceful being my middle name, I'm not going to let that stop me. I'm going back there today."

"Why are you so keen to talk to him again? You saw the state he was in. He was probably talking gibberish when he said what he said."

Danni stared at him in silence for a while, until he said, "What?"

"Gordon, I went through the recording I made at the clinic the other day. And I noticed something."

She stood in one graceful movement and sat next to him on the futon. She gestured and a screen expanded in the air before them. Then she lifted a slim hand, tipped with crimson lacquered nails, and fingered a virtual keypad.

"Watch."

She expanded the screen so that it was fully two metres square. Fairleigh-White hung in the air before them, almost life-sized in his rejuvenation pod. She waved a hand, and the image was accompanied by the soundtrack.

Fairleigh-White was saying, his feeble voice rendered into lilting tones, *"My uncle knew who did it, you see... One day I was in... in Paris... at his house. This was some years after the murder."*

Danni glanced at Kemp. "Notice anything odd?"

He stared at the man's ancient skull, his trembling lips. "No. Tell me."

"Watch the lips."

On the screen, Fairleigh-White said, *"My uncle told me... he knew who it was... She saw Randolph before she... before she left, confessed to him... She confessed... She stabbed him to death... his own wife, Rima... Rima Cagnac."*

Danni waved a hand and the image of the old man's head froze.

"Rewind," she said.

The image backed up until Danni commanded it to play again. "Now watch his lips *very* closely when he speaks."

"*My uncle told me…*" Fairleigh-White said, "*he knew who it was…*"

"The movement of his lips and the words don't match up," Danni said. "I didn't notice it at the time. Only when I reviewed the recording last night… I saw the mismatch, then."

"But he was sub-voccing and his support systems were picking that up and converting it into smooth speech. That wasn't his voice we heard. Wouldn't you expect a mismatch?"

"I've watched that recording over and over," Danni told him. "There's really very little correspondence between what he was trying to say and what we heard."

"Play it again. Let's see if he was lying."

Kemp watched in silence. It was true that there was little correspondence between the movement of the old man's lips and the words rendered, but there could be any number of explanations.

"Was he lying?" Danni asked.

"I don't know," he said. The lieware marker had been wavering all over the scale as he watched. "He's old, confused. His brain is fried. But he does appear to believe that what he's telling us is the truth."

"Which doesn't, of course, confirm either way whether the truth he spoke matched the words we heard."

"So you think…?"

"Well, it's a possibility, isn't it? What we thought we heard that day wasn't Fairleigh-White speaking, but something programmed and spoken by his voice-assist com."

"Telling us what *someone* wants us to believe," he said. "That Rima Cagnac killed her husband, all those years ago?"

On the screen, the skeletal ancient said, "*She did it herself! Stabbed him… stabbed my father!*"

Danni stilled the image, and the screen collapsed.

In the resulting silence, they stared at each other.

"Do you know something, Gordon?"

"Go on."

"For all *I* wanted to go to... out there, on this mission... For all I cursed my luck, and cursed *you*, when I learned I couldn't go... Well, I'm damned glad it's not me who's going, now." She shook her head, her eyes wide. "Is that selfish of me, Gordon?"

He tried to reassure her. "No," he said. "No, not at all."

She reached out and squeezed his hand. "Take care out there, you hear? Take care."

11

Into the Jungle

Right from the outset, the expedition to Base West One did not go as Rima had anticipated.

Once Jayne Waterford had made the suggestion, Rima found herself increasingly keen to see more of the new world. She recognised that this seed of curiosity was something that had been missing since she'd realised her hard-earned specialism had become redundant.

That spirit of enthusiastic scientific curiosity was something she shared with Jayne right up to the evening before they were due to set out.

But then Jayne had fallen ill.

They were sitting by a window in Lab Central, looking out over the main clearing as the shadows of the surrounding jungle grew long across the exposed rock. It would be dark soon, a sudden nightfall on Carrasco, like the flip of a switch.

Jayne had been quiet this evening, and now she had fallen silent altogether.

Something was clearly wrong.

"What's up?"

"Nothing. I'm fine, darling."

"Then why, *ma chérie*, do you sit that way, with your arms across your abdomen, and why do you narrow your eyes against the light?"

Jayne looked away. Outside, the flyers were swooping low, a distraction for a moment.

"Just a headache," she said. When pressed, she admitted that the headache was an intense, stabbing one, and she was sitting awkwardly because she had stomach cramps.

"You have a fever, I think, also." There was a sheen to the skin of Jayne's forehead and cheeks.

"Infirmary: a scan for Doctor Waterford." Remote systems kicked into action, reading Jayne's vitals from sensors built into the smart structure of the dome, and from her wristcom. As well as confirming a slight fever, the summary report flagged up raised blood pressure and a white cell profile typical of the early stages of a body's response to infection.

"It's just a headache. I'm fine," Jayne said, but they both knew that this was a pattern of symptoms familiar from other cases.

"It's nothing," the ecologist insisted, which was also familiar: more often than not, it was, indeed, nothing. But as they were still to develop a definitive test for what had come to be known as cloud fever, the only way to be sure if it was just a headache or something more sinister was isolation and observation.

Overnight, Jayne's condition remained stable, and by the time the team was ready to depart in the morning her main symptom was a general air of being pissed off to be in an isolation bubble and not leading the way.

Rima was fully suited and riding shotgun in an open-topped, balloon-tyred ATV alongside Franco Marcosi, trying her best not to be irritated by his puppy-dog enthusiasm for absolutely everything, and trying to resist the urge to continually check back in with Jimmy Ranatunga on the condition of her friend.

The others on this expedition were field geologist Harrie Spier and microbiologist Annika Muller, riding the lead ATV. The second vehicle was larger, an all-terrain truck carrying supplies and equipment. Its driver was Lars Anderson, an ecologist specialising in inter-species dynamics, accompanied by Stephan Taylor, a meteorologist who would work with Muller to assess airborne biohazards out here. The final member of the team was Abdul Cole, one of Hertzberger's security men, here to protect the team from any hazards big enough to be taken down with any of the weaponry he carried.

The jungle here grew patchily, separated by the areas of bare bedrock across which they drove. Now Franco pointed at one of the clumps of jungle, a tangled mass of fibres heaped high and glistening with a film of slime. It looked as if it were deliquescing. Animals moved within, their shapes impossible to make out clearly through the slimy film. "Do you think it's dying, or growing?" he asked.

He was right. What Rima had taken for putrescent decay might easily be jungle growths taking new form, jungle giving birth to itself rather than dying back and decaying.

"Doctor Waterford will be fine," Franco said a short time later, and Rima wished he'd keep his eyes ahead rather than turning to her when he spoke. She'd been checking the comms panel on the back of her glove again for any messages from the base. Then, with characteristic bluntness, he added, "And if she is not, there's nothing you can do about it."

"Have you been out beyond the base before?" Rima asked him to make conversation. She already knew the answer.

"Never more than a few kilometres. I'm buzzing with it. This place… Just, *incredible*, don't you think? Everywhere you look there's something new to take in. Fauna no human has ever set eyes on before, vegetation no one has ever catalogued…"

"And do you think… you know?" Rima didn't understand why it was so difficult to put into words: *Do you think there's really sentient life out there?*

Once she'd been enrolled in this small expedition team, Rima had seen the firewalled reports, but they were far more ambiguous than she'd expected. There had been no dramatic encounter, not even a sighting of any form of advanced fauna. Indeed, the only clue buried away in the reports had been mention of tunnels excavated through the jungle.

"It's the most logical extrapolation, isn't it?" Franco said. "That there is other sentient life, I mean. You have to believe there's something out there. If not here, then on the next planet we find, or the next."

"But here, on Carrasco? Tunnels in the jungle... it's hardly archaeological remains, is it? Back on Earth, animals leave tunnels through the vegetation just by passing through on a regular basis."

"There's a difference between a tunnel formed by passage, and one that's been crafted," Franco told her.

It still struck Rima as tenuous, to say the least, but she didn't press the point.

"Just give it a few more minutes," Franco said, "and I'll show you what I mean."

They had been passing through an open landscape matted with heather-like vegetation, but a short time later they came to a halt before what appeared to be a solid wall of green, rising high before them.

"What now?" Rima asked. They still had fifty kilometres to go, with only a few hours of remaining daylight. Now that they had paused, she could see that what she had taken to be heather-like vegetation was, in fact, a seething mass of life: plant-like tendrils twisted together with what looked like silken webs, glistening worm-like creatures, black and brown bugs forming shifting clusters and crusts that were constantly changing.

The green wall of the jungle before them was a similar melange of lifeforms, as if woven together in three dimensions. Its texture reminded her of loofah or wire wool, and it looked both unscalable and impenetrable. And everywhere she looked, something wriggled or scuttled or writhed.

"Now?" Franco said, beaming through his visor at her. "Now we ascend."

Ahead, the other two ATVs were already moving out. At first, Rima thought they were driving directly into the tangled undergrowth, then the first vehicle tipped up at an angle, so that it appeared to be doing a slow-motion wheelie, and then it started to ascend the green wall. Within seconds it was lost to sight.

Rima swallowed. A last-minute addition to the expedition, she didn't feel fully briefed, and had little idea what to expect. Now she felt vulnerable and a long way out of her depth.

At her side, Franco Marcosi whooped as their ATV's balloon-like front tyres took purchase on the vegetation and the vehicle started to climb. Close up, the jungle wall was not vertical, but canted at about forty-five degrees – still a vertiginous angle. Rima's knuckles, as she gripped the ATV's grab rail for all she was worth, would have been white if she could see them through the gloves of her suit.

"Look at the sides," Franco said. "*Capisce?* See what I mean?" He was loving it: the alienness of their surroundings, the adrenaline rush of the drive.

The walls of vegetation were sheer on either side, rising four or five metres above a track that had clearly been carved into the jungle, reducing the angle of the incline to something the ATVs could manage.

"This is it?" Rima asked. "Aliens made this?" The roadway was clearly an artefact of a culture that used tools and was able to plan.

Franco laughed again – he seemed to laugh at almost anything.

"No, *we* made this. Or rather the first expedition did. They couldn't pass through the jungle here, so they cut a road up to the canopy. But you see what I mean? One look and you can just *tell* that the roadway has been crafted by sentience. There's a difference, and that's what I'll be investigating when we reach Base West One."

A short time later, the track levelled out, the roadway's

walls fell away to either side and they joined the other two ATVs on a vast, tangled plain of greenery. They were on top of the jungle.

The vehicles came to a halt and Franco climbed from the ATV.

When Rima stepped out, the surface was springy, like a mattress, and she watched every footfall carefully for fear of plunging through.

"It's fine," Harrie called across to her. "Really. You're not going to fall through. The canopy surface is elastic, but secure."

Was she that obvious?

On Earth, she knew that in the last few remaining slivers of equatorial jungle it was the canopy that was remote and inaccessible. Here... She stood on the canopy, perhaps a hundred metres above ground level, and what lay below was an impenetrable mystery.

As they paused atop the canopy, first Harrie Spier and then Stephan Taylor started to jump, until they were springing a couple of metres into the air like kids on a trampoline.

"Do you really think...?" Rima said to Franco as they watched. She didn't like to spoil the fun, but even walking across this springy surface, so high above ground, made her feel vertiginous. Their security guard, Abdul Cole, looked on disapprovingly, too. He appeared comfortable with the prospect of protecting his charges from wild animal attack, but wouldn't have a clue what to do if someone plunged a hundred metres through the jungle canopy, no matter how unlikely that may be.

Standing still was little better, though. When Rima looked down, she saw worms writhing in the densely matted vegetation, other tiny creatures crawling; where her feet rested, they made hollows in the canopy and a jelly-like substance oozed out as if to heal the dent, flowing around her boots and then, as if defying gravity, starting to flow up over her boots.

Reflexively, Rima pulled her feet clear, kicking them in the air to remove any residue.

The closest environment to this that Rima had experienced before was some of the remnant forest she'd seen on her last family visit to Senegal. By that time, just a year before the departure of the *Strasbourg*, much of equatorial Africa had become a no-go zone, torn apart by desertification and the resultant migration and resource wars. Rima had tagged along on a UNICEF conference, hoping to track down her surviving cousins in Dakar and Tambacounda, but when she got there she realised she had little chance of success. The country's infrastructure and administration were almost non-existent, and the settlements she recalled from previous trips had become no more than ruined ghost-towns.

Much of the interior had been swallowed by the Sahel, and great swathes of coast lost to the Atlantic. The only fertile land remaining had been ribbons of remnant forest along the flooded basins of the great rivers – the Gambie, the Senegal, the Casamance. On one trip south out of Tambacounda she had entered a landscape of sudden fecundity, striking after passing through the decay of a dying landscape. Where the African jungle lived on, it did so with astounding vigour, and that was why her subconscious had drawn comparisons between that trip and the landscape of Carrasco.

They drove on in silence for a time, even Franco's enthusiasm dampened by passing through a landscape so alien. Then he turned to her, that big kid's grin plastered over his features again, and he said, "Incredible…"

Mu Arae had dipped close to the horizon now, their progress much slower than they'd aimed for. Sunset tones of pink and mauve were spreading across the sky, painting rainbow highlights across the jungle canopy ahead. It was a breathtaking sight.

A few minutes later Harrie Spier's face scrolled up on the ATV's windscreen. "Hey all," he said. "Looks like it's going to be dark by the time we reach Base West One, so I'm making the call that we stop and break out camp here, and then aim to get there in the morning. I don't want to be driving over this terrain in darkness."

Already the other two ATVs had come to a halt, and now Franco pulled up next to them.

"Have you made contact with West One?" Rima asked Harrie as they climbed out and stretched. Thankfully the canopy had formed a dry crust here, no goo flowing up around her boots.

"I spoke to Liza Staffel a couple of hours ago," Harrie said. "I warned her we're running late. No response when I tried again just now, but I've left a message so they know we won't be there until morning."

Rima tethered her overnight sac to the ATV, then left it to inflate and walked away from the group. The silence was good, after a long journey with Gianfranco. She checked her glove and saw that she'd missed a call from Jayne. She played the recording on the inside of her visor. Jayne looked like a ghost, but she was smiling, trying to be bright. She was still stable, she said, and then insisted it was probably no more than a cold, even though ESO had been careful to ensure no stray viruses had left with the *Strasbourg* eighty years ago.

Back at the camp, Rima let her suit seal itself to the sac, then squirmed through. The sac was not big, somewhere between a one-person tent and a cocoon, but it was good to be free of the suit. She sucked at a tube of nondescript dinner, then rolled over onto her back.

She could feel the texture of the forest canopy through the groundsheet – wiry tendrils, scale-like crusts, things that moved… She would never sleep tonight.

It was hard not to be overcome by panic at the thought of waking to find that her sac had been absorbed by the canopy, scabbed over, healed into the jungle's interior.

Her comms pinged. The others were in their sacs, isolated yet calling up talking heads on the sac walls to chat. Rima ignored hers, turned over, and went to sleep in seconds.

She woke to turquoise light glowing through the overnight sac's membrane. When she wriggled into her suit and stood, she surveyed the camp and saw that none of the sacs or vehicles had been absorbed overnight by the jungle. She was the last to emerge, all survivors of their first night wild-camping on Carrasco.

Then she saw the way they stood, the look on Harrie's face behind his visor.

"What is it?" she said. "What's wrong?"

"Nothing," the geologist said. "We hope."

"It's Base West One," Franco explained. "Liza Staffel never replied last night, and no one is responding this morning."

Staffel was the leader of the team that had established the western research camp, and there were five other scientists based there.

"Nothing at all?" Rima asked. No one needed to reply.

"Time to hit the road," Harrie said. "Stephan has sent a couple of drones ahead to check out the base. We should be there in an hour. I've sent a report back to Hertzberger, too, but the atmospherics are terrible today – too much interference for a consultation."

"So we just plough on and hope for the best?" Rima said. She realised it sounded as if she was being negative, when in fact all she was doing was thinking out loud. Of course they should head on to the base. It was almost certainly the case that nothing was wrong, that it was a simple comms glitch due to those bad atmospherics.

And if there *was* something wrong? Far better to find out soon, than have some other new disaster sneak up and surprise them later.

12

Read My Lips

Danni Bellini sat back in her recliner and considered the meeting with Alastair Fairleigh-White. She still thought she was right, despite Kemp's dismissal of her suspicions; there was little correspondence between the old man's lip movements and the subsequent com-generated vocalisations. That, of course, *might* be explained by the fact that Fairleigh-White had been sub-vocalising, and the program had inferred his intended meaning and rendered it in a voice that was not his own. Or, as Danni suspected, what they had heard that day had been what someone had wanted them to hear.

She stood and crossed to the office window. It was still snowing. To the north, a megascreen floated over the city, relaying its usual bland fare of rolling world news, corporate propaganda, and sporting events from around the globe. She wondered why the hell anyone in London should have the slightest interest in how many medals some muscle-bound, pharmaceutically trained Chinese power-skater was winning in the Asian games.

She turned and leaned against the windowsill, calling up the image of Sir Alastair Fairleigh-White. It hung in the air before her, showing his emaciated, skeletal form plugged in to the life-support pod.

"Imp," she sub-vocced, "run a lip-reading routine on the

subject from" ... she peered at the timer at the bottom-left of the image... "1.42 onwards."

She watched the old man's lips move minimally, the voice-over rendering his words in an incongruous Chinese accent: "*Memory... memories. My father... dead now, dead so long ago. Murdered... stabbed to death. We... we never saw eye to eye, but I loved him... loved him. My mother... she died young... I never knew her... My father... my father brought me up... so long ago.*"

At the foot of the image, her imp's lip-reading program ran its text translation: "Memory... memories. My father... dead now, dead so long ago. [Unreadable...] My father... my father brought me up... so long ago."

It went on like this for the next seven minutes of the interview, with perhaps two thirds of what the old man said rendered untranslatable.

She swore, crossed the room and gestured for a black tea. Back in her recliner, she stared out at the falling snow and considered what to do next.

Her imp said, "*Incoming, Danni, from Edouard Bryce.*"

"Message him that I'm busy."

"*And will return the call?*"

"Just tell him I'm working, okay?"

She sipped her tea, wishing Bryce would drop it. That was the tenth time he'd tried to get through to her in under a day.

"What did he want?"

"*Shall I run the call?*"

"Go ahead."

Instantly the image of Edouard Bryce, seated behind a desk in a gloomy office, appeared in the air beside that of Fairleigh-White.

"Danni, hi. I was wondering... I know you're busy, but it would be nice to meet up again. I'm free any time. Give me a call? Bye."

Danni killed the image, feeling a twinge of guilt. "From now on," she sub-vocced, "bounce him an unavailable message when he calls."

"Knock-knock."

The voice startled her. She swivelled her recliner so she was facing the door. Commander Tsang leaned against the frame, studying her. She wondered why he'd bothered to come down here in person, then how long he'd been standing there, watching her.

"Busy?" he asked.

She indicated Fairleigh-White's stilled image hanging in mid-air.

The features of Tsang's slab face moved to display an exaggerated frown. "Fairleigh-White?"

"I was going over the interview. I take it you'll be wanting a report, right?"

He pursed his lips and rocked his head, thinking it over. "Don't bother yourself with it, Inspector Bellini. It would only be a waste of time, when you have so many other cases to work on."

"Very well…" She took a sip of tea.

Tsang said, mistaking her reaction, "You're still upset at being passed over? You would rather be in Kemp's position, out there?"

"I'll get over it."

"That's the spirit. We could hardly have sent you, could we, in your condition?"

"I said I'll get over it."

He moved from the door, crossed the room and stood staring out through the window, hands clasped behind his back. "The dangers involved, on an unexplored alien world… Who knows what one might encounter out there? No," he said with a sense of finality, "all in all, you're safer here with us on Earth."

"Your solicitude, Commander, is endearing."

He nodded, and as ever she was amazed by his inability to pick up on her sarcasm.

He remained standing with his back to her, staring out across frozen London. Just *go*, she thought.

He turned and gestured to the old man's image. "As I said, drop the case, Danni. Work on existing investigations, okay?"

"My pleasure."

He nodded again, staring at her as if trying to work out her sincerity, then moved from the window and left the room. She heard the elevator door sigh open along the corridor, then close.

"Fuck you," she said.

She drained her tea, came to a decision, and said, "Imp, contact Maria Pellegrini."

Seconds later the image of a middle-aged blonde woman hung in the air before her, smiling out. "Danni. It's been a while. How are you keeping?"

"I'm well, thanks. Listen, are you busy? I could use a favour. Professionally."

"I can make some time," she said. "Professional, you say? I'm not cheap, Danni."

"I'll buy you a meal? My department won't be paying for this one."

"You're on."

"Thanks, Maria. It's not a big job. I'll send you the file now. It's just a simple reading..." She went on to explain her suspicion that the programmed voice-over was masking Fairleigh-White's intended vocalisations, and would like Maria to lip-read the sequence.

"Should be simple enough," Pellegrini said. "I'll get back to you before noon."

"You're a star." She ordered her imp to send the Fairleigh-White file, then thanked Maria and cut the connection.

She summoned another tea, then slid open a drawer and took out a tray of cold samosas and began eating. She placed a hand over her stomach; she wasn't showing yet – she was less than three months gone – but already her eating habits were affected and she was experiencing odd mood swings. She was addicted to Indian food, and found herself becoming irate at the slightest provocation... Or was that more to do with the Rima Cagnac case, and whatever the hell had happened in Geneva eighty years ago?

In five months from now she'd take maternity leave, and six months after she gave birth she'd be back at her desk. But she'd come to the decision, over the course of the past couple of days, that she was through with full-time work. When she was a mother, she'd scale back her hours and work part-time. *Who would have thought it?* she mused – and her a fast-track career woman destined for great things.

Who would have thought, come to that, that she would be so excited at the prospect of bringing a child into this godforsaken world?

Her imp said, *"Call from Maria Pellegrini, Danni."*

"Put her through."

Pellegrini's image hung in the air before Danni, smiling out at her.

"Quick work," Danni said.

"There wasn't much I could make out. Lip movement was minimal, and often slurred, and it was really hard to make out consecutive phrases. I think he must have had a stroke at some point, too, which often makes mouth movements harder to decipher. I'd say that the voice-over was faithful perhaps fifty per cent of the time–"

Danni leaned forward. "And in the other fifty per cent?"

Pellegrini shrugged. "Impossible to tell. His mouth movements were so slurred it was hard to even guess at what he was saying."

"What about the passage where he accused Rima of stabbing her husband?"

Pellegrini frowned. "Minimal lip movement there, unfortunately. I couldn't read a single word."

"So the voice-over *might* have been manipulated to relay something other than what he said?"

"It's impossible to say, Danni. I wouldn't stick my neck out so far as to agree…"

"Okay…"

"There was one thing that struck me as odd, though," Pellegrini went on.

"Go on."

"At one point, his lips were moving but there was no voice-over translation. What he actually said was, 'Rima… she was one beautiful black woman I really wanted to…' You can fill in the next four-letter word yourself, Danni." She hesitated. "You see the contradiction?"

Danni smiled, vindicated. "I do. That's hardly something you'd say, or even think, about the woman you were accusing of murdering your father, is it?"

"It certainly isn't, Danni. I thought I'd better mention it."

"I'm glad you did. Great. Thanks for this."

"Any time. And you owe me one."

"I know an excellent Italian in Islington. I'll be in touch."

"*Ciao*, Danni."

Danni thanked her again, cut the connection, and sat back in her recliner.

Smiling to herself, she considered her next move. Then she instructed her imp to contact Peter Conway at Carstairs Hall.

Danni tapped override to take control of the car, pulled onto the hard-shoulder and braked. Traffic thundered past, a train of linked automated juggernauts loaded with containers covered in Big-5 hieroglyphs. Far behind her in the midday January gloom, the lights of London lit up a haze above the capital, interspersed with flashing neons and floating megascreens. To her left, the hillside rose in a series of serried vines. It was the sight of the vineyard, and the memories it provoked, that had made her pull up.

She climbed out and walked across to the verge, turning her collar up against the biting east wind. She stared up the hillside at the bare, blackened vines – and she was ten again, on her father's vineyard in Devon, helping him mulch the vines at the onset of winter.

"Imp, my father, please."

Instantly he appeared before her, just three metres away. As ever, she gave an involuntary gasp at the fidelity of his image. He was fifty once more, grey-haired but upright and smiling: she had taken this towards the end of the good times, when her father was still happy, the family business doing well.

"*Sound, Danni?*" her imp asked.

Sound would be too painful. "No, just the visuals."

The image that overlaid the winter landscape showed her father on his vineyard in high summer, walking amongst the vines, turning occasionally to smile and speak to a younger Danni. The contrast between the searing summer of twenty years ago and the present winter was stark, laid one on top of the other.

He turned now and smiled at her, radiant with happiness.

"Pause," she commanded, and his image froze, the smile of yesteryear fixed in place.

She touched her stomach through her winter coat. He had been good with children; he would have made a wonderful grandfather.

She gave the command for her imp to cease the projection, and stared across the uniform hectares of the vineyard. It was yet another of the vast concerns that covered so much of the home counties, industrial vineyards growing supergene merlot-grenache hybrids for the undiscerning *nouveau riches* of Asia.

Ten years ago, the Chinese had moved into the production of wine in a big way, buying up many of the distinguished vineyards in the West Country and turning them into great automated concerns. They'd made an offer for her father's land but, bloody-minded and proud of the organic zinfandel grapes he produced – and the award-winning biodynamic wine that was the result – he refused. Danni had seen what was coming and advised him to take the offer and move to the Midlands, buy a smaller vineyard and start again. He'd told her, correctly, that wherever he went, he would fail: how could he compete against the big Beijing conglomerates which produced wines that sold at a third of the price of his own? Stubborn to the very end, he'd rejected the offer.

Just three years later, he was declared bankrupt, and his vineyard was bought up by Shenju Industries, his workers sacked to be replaced by robots, his organic tilth adulterated with sulphates.

Danni climbed back into the car and told it to resume the journey.

Fifteen minutes later, she turned into the driveway at Carstairs Hall and drew up before the imposing Georgian building.

Peter Conway stood at the top of the steps, smiling as she climbed from the car and crunched across the gravel.

"How lovely to see you again," he said as she climbed the steps.

"Mr Conway," she said, giving him her best smile. "I'd like to see Sir Alastair again, if he's up to it this time?"

"Please, call me Peter. And you're in luck. Dr Radzinski is mired in admin and won't be looking in on the old man for another hour." He hesitated, then said, "And afterwards, if you'd care for coffee…?"

"Why not?" she said. "I could do with something to warm me up."

She followed Conway into the hall and along the corridor towards Fairleigh-White's room.

She hesitated outside the door. "How's the patient today?"

"I suspect much as ever. He has his lucid moments. If you'd limit your stay to half an hour…? I'll be in my office off the entrance hall."

He opened the door for her and she stepped inside.

She looked across at the skeletal old man, canted at an angle in his life-support pod. The contrast between the hi-tech apparatus that was keeping him alive, and the old-fashioned furnishings that filled the room, struck her anew.

"Young woman?"

The lilting, computer-generated voice caught her off guard. Fairleigh-White was staring at her, his bright blue eyes seemingly the only living things in his long, immobile face.

"Hello, Sir Alastair."

"Young woman? Lost your way...? Or have they finally given me a doctor worth looking at?"

She stepped forward. "I've come to see you." She stood beside the life-support machine, trying not to wince at the combined odour of chemicals and stale urine that rose in waves from the old man.

"See me...? Who are you?" He seemed brighter today, more alive. His lips moved, even though the sound that issued from his throat had to be assisted by the computer program.

She found a scat and pulled it up to the pod. "I came to see you the other day. I'm Detective Inspector Bellini."

"See me? I don't recall..."

"Perhaps you weren't having a good day?"

"Days? All alike..." He stared at her. "What do you want?"

"To talk," she said. "I'd like to ask you some questions, if that's all right?"

The man chuckled, the noise rendered as a ghastly choking sound by the program. "Questions? Ask away. I'm a hundred... a hundred and... I've forgotten more than you've ever known!"

She smiled. "You probably have," she said. "I'd like to ask you about Rima Cagnac."

He blinked. He appeared to be considering the name. "Rima..." he said at last.

"That's right, Rima – your stepmother."

"But of course," he said. "Such a striking woman. Ah, perhaps I shouldn't..."

She leaned forward. "Shouldn't what?"

"Say such things... about one's stepmother. Not the form, eh? But she *was* a beauty, and a lovely woman."

"I wanted to ask about your father–"

"He was murdered... all those years ago. In Geneva. Killed... Such an awful time."

Danni said, "Your uncle, Randolph, he told you who killed your father–"

The blue eyes widened. "He did? Randolph? He knew who...? No. No, no, no... That can't be right."

"Can't it?" She leaned forward, watching for any reaction on the lifeless face as she went on. "He told you that Rima killed her husband."

He blinked rapidly as if in confusion. "Rima? My uncle told me that? No! No, Rima wouldn't..."

Danni swallowed, aware of her heartbeat as she said, "But you said to me, the other day, that Randolph told you Rima had killed your father."

"I said that? No! That can't be... You're lying! Rima, kill my father? Preposterous!"

His skeletal arms twitched, his fingers scrabbling on the plastic sheet that covered his lap. He stared up at her, his bright blue eyes pooled with unshed tears.

"I'm sorry," she said.

He closed his eyes, muttering something that even the voice-recognition failed to pick up.

She wished that Kemp were with her now, to share this, to discuss the very real possibility that what Fairleigh-White had told them, three days ago, had been no more than a lie fabricated by whoever was behind overriding the voice-recognition program.

She considered Kemp, being prepared to embark on a

trumped-up mission to arrest a woman framed for the murder of her husband eighty years ago...

Now Fairleigh-White appeared to be unconscious, though his hands still twitched on the plastic counterpane.

"Sir Alastair?"

His eyes still closed, he murmured something inaudible.

"Can you recall if you had any visitors last week, before I saw you? Sir Alastair?"

He made no response.

Danni looked around the room, at the array of photographs and interactives on top of a cabinet beside the life-support pod.

She stood and moved closer, her attention caught by a framed picture showing a group of men with drinks in hand, one of whom was a much younger Alastair Fairleigh-White, and next to him a grey-haired figure she recognised as his uncle, the tycoon Randolph White.

It was neither man, however, who interested her so much as the figure standing between them. He was tall and dark-haired, with a hatchet face and an emotionless, gimlet stare. He bore a distinct resemblance to the man she'd met just the other day, Major Gellner.

"Imp, record and archive the photograph."

She turned back to the bed, wanting to ask Fairleigh-White about the picture and specifically the identity of the dark-haired man. Could it be Major Gellner's father, she wondered? The picture was taken over eighty years ago, so the man was more likely to be Gellner's grandfather.

Fairleigh-White lay very still, his hands no longer twitching, with only the shallow rise and fall of his chest indicating that he was still alive.

Danni slipped from the room and crossed the hallway towards Peter Conway's office.

For the next half an hour, Conway chatted about his duties at the Hall – he described himself self-deprecatingly as a glorified office boy – and then asked about Danni's job. She gave him the short-hand version she had ready for the curious at parties: that it comprised periods of fruitless footslogging with even more tedious admin. She omitted to mention the tiny percentile of satisfaction that came from successfully completing a case.

She finished her coffee. "I suppose I'd better slip away before Radzinski makes his rounds."

Conway smiled. "Hardly rounds. Fairleigh-White is the doctor's only patient."

She stared at the fair-haired young man. "But I thought Carstairs Hall was a nursing home?"

"I suppose you could, at a stretch, call it that – for one patient. But no, it's the administrative headquarters of the White Foundation."

She repeated the name. "Would that be associated with Sebastian White, or Randolph – or both?"

"Randolph. He established the Foundation just before his death, to pull together all the many strands of his business empire."

"Which must be worth a small fortune."

"The Foundation's combined gross annual turnover exceeds fifty billion euros."

She stood up, then said, "While I remember, do you know who this might be?"

She sub-vocced a command to her imp, and the image of the three men in the photograph appeared in the air before her. She pointed to the central figure. "This man, with the rather glacial stare?"

Conway nodded. "I think it's some relation to Major Gellner, the Foundation's security chief. His grandfather, I think it must be."

Danni stared at him. "Major Gellner works for the Foundation?" Commander Tsang had introduced him as someone from the European Security Agency.

"That's right. He was here just a few days ago. If you'd like me to arrange a meeting…"

She opened her mouth to reply, considering her words. This was a twist she wished she could talk over with Kemp. "I… No, that's okay. The major and I are in touch."

Conway opened his mouth to say something, but then hesitated.

"Yes?" Danni prompted.

"I was just wondering," he said. "If it's not too presumptuous. Would you consider joining me for dinner one evening this week?"

She gave him her most dazzling smile. "Would it be okay if I got back to you on that, Peter?"

She thanked him for the coffee, said goodbye, and hurried from the Hall.

13

Transit

After breakfast at Danni's, Kemp took a rickshaw to the police headquarters, then rode the elevator to Commander Tsang's dome. Due to iced roads at Charing Cross, he was ten minutes late for the briefing. It afforded him a small pleasure to imagine Tsang seated in his office, impatiently waiting as the minutes ticked by.

He wondered what form the briefing might take, and how long Tsang would detain him. He didn't like his commanding officer – he found the man's aloof demeanour supercilious and demeaning – and normally would have resented wasting time with a face-to-face meeting. Now, however, he might be able to use the meeting to his own advantage.

As the door slid open and Kemp entered the dome, he blinked his lieware into life. After the relative gloom of the corridor, the brightness of the dome dazzled him and rendered the seated figure in stark silhouette.

"Sit down, Inspector. This shouldn't take long."

Kemp set his valise on the floor and took a seat.

Tsang frowned. "And that is?" he asked.

"A few things." He shrugged. "I didn't know what to bring."

Tsang smiled, managing in that quick expression a degree of condescension that riled Kemp. "You won't be taking anything with you, Inspector," Tsang said. "Everything you need will be supplied. We can't risk contamination of a pristine new planet with…" He nodded towards the case, not even attempting to hide the sneer.

Kemp nodded. "I'll leave it in my office."

Tsang waved a hand, and Kemp's wristcom pinged with an incoming message. "That's the accreditation you'll need to see you through the security check at the port, plus the authorisation you'll present to one Commander Hertzberger, who's running the show on Carrasco. You will have his full cooperation."

Tsang went on, "The shuttle from Earth will take you through the wormhole to dock with the orbiting *Strasbourg*. From there, another shuttle will ferry you down to the planet."

"How long will I be on Carrasco?"

"I don't envisage the mission lasting more than a couple of days, Inspector. Time to land, locate Rima Cagnac, and arrest her."

Kemp was surprised to see that the slider edged to the right. Tsang was lying, evidently, though whether about the length of the mission or if he simply had no idea how long the mission might take, it was impossible to say.

"And Cagnac herself?" Kemp asked.

"What about her?"

"Will she be expecting to be arrested?"

Tsang considered the question, moving a forefinger back and forth across his lips. "She will have no reason to suspect that her part in the murder of her husband has become known," he said. The slider moved to the left; he was telling the truth.

"I take it she won't be armed?"

Tsang smiled. "They're exploring an alien planet, subject to unknown risks, so weapons will be easily available. However, Cagnac is a cryogenic specialist and medic, so she would have no reason to carry weapons while performing her duties around the main base."

"And should I question her as to her part in the murder, try to learn–?"

"That won't be necessary. Any interrogation prior to her return runs the risk of compromising a successful prosecution. I have a team primed and waiting here for her."

That, Kemp noted with alarm, was a lie: the commander didn't have a team awaiting Cagnac's arrival. Kemp was trying to work out what this might mean when Tsang went on, "Your brief is simply to land on Carrasco, arrest Cagnac, and return to Earth. I foresee no difficulties that might arise, and look forward to your return."

More lies. Obviously Tsang didn't look forward to Kemp's return, but did he also foresee difficulties?

Taking this as a dismissal, Kemp climbed to his feet.

"There is one more thing," Tsang went on. "You'll be accompanied to Carrasco by Major Gellner, who will provide security and facilitate your duties. If you would report to his office immediately..."

Kemp nodded, trying not to show his annoyance that Gellner, of all people, should be the one chosen to hold his hand on the mission to Carrasco.

He climbed from the chair and made for the door.

"Good luck, Inspector," Tsang said. "Oh – and don't forget your luggage."

Colouring, Kemp returned to the desk, picked up his valise, and hurried from the dome.

Kemp and Gellner stood side by side as they waited to be processed through the security check at the Thames estuary spaceport. Ahead of them, a dozen men in civilian clothing passed through the scanner. They had the brusque, no-nonsense, non-committal manner of a security squad, and Kemp wondered what their brief was on Carrasco. They were led by a short, bullet-headed thug Gellner had introduced as Lieutenant Connery, and from the latter's deferential manner towards Gellner, it was clear that the major was running the show. Aside from the security detachment, they were accompanied by six men and women Gellner had explained were scientists who would be replacing their opposite numbers on Carrasco.

"Replacing?" Kemp asked with a raised eyebrow.

"A consequence of natural wastage," the major said.

"What on earth does that mean?"

Instead of replying, Gellner said, "Have you ever taken a shuttle into orbit before, Inspector Kemp?"

"Never," Kemp said.

"In that case, I suggest you take the option of being sedated for the duration, until we reach the quantum lattice itself. The effects of g-force at take-off can be quite unpleasant."

Kemp wasn't exactly looking forward to the ride into orbit, and was secretly relieved at the option of sedation. "I'll do that."

They passed through the scanner and into a long, white corridor, the security team leading the way.

"What about when we go through the wormhole itself? Will we be offered sedation then?" Kemp asked.

"I understand that the transition is almost unnoticeable," Gellner said. "So sedation will not be necessary."

They passed through a sliding door and entered a changing room. Immediately Gellner and his security retinue started to remove their clothing. Slightly more reticent, the scientists followed suit and entered a shower area.

Kemp slipped out of his jacket and began to unbutton his shirt. He watched Gellner step into the shower, then took the opportunity to palm the small Buddha figure from his pocket and conceal it in his fist.

He joined the others in the shower, intensely aware of his paunch and his sagging chest. He could barely remember the last time he had been naked before another person, let alone been comfortable with it.

After a few minutes, the water cut out and hot air blasted

him, while the light turned violet and harsh, so that he had to squint his watering eyes.

When the blasting air ceased, Kemp followed a small Chinese woman out through an irising door at the far end of the shower chamber. They entered another changing room hung with light-blue coveralls. Gellner, wearing a black suit similar to the one he had worn on the other side, instructed Kemp and the scientists to change into the coveralls.

On Gellner's blindside, Kemp slipped the Buddha figure into the coverall's pouch.

He felt not only uncomfortable but slightly ridiculous in the coverall. He never liked wearing new clothing anyway, and the garment's clinging stretch fabric did nothing to conceal his bulging stomach.

One of the scientists, a tall middle-aged woman, caught his eye and pulled a pained expression. Kemp smiled in return.

A port official passed among them handing out drink bulbs. When she came to Kemp he raised his eyebrows in question. "You've cleaned the outside," she told him. "Now clean the inside."

Kemp took the bulb and downed its sweet contents in a single gulp.

Finally, Gellner ushered them from the changing room and along a sloping umbilical into the shuttle itself. The dozen security men were already strapped into the first three rows of bulky padded seats.

Kemp sat down behind them, next to Gellner, and fastened himself in with broad cross-straps as the head support adjusted itself around skull and neck. The scientists seated themselves behind them.

The port official offered sedatives; Gellner and the security men declined, and Kemp was pleased to see that, like him, all the scientists elected to be sedated.

He watched as the official placed the nozzle of the hypoject to the upper arm of the scientist across the aisle from him, and pressed the stud. The man's features relaxed as he slipped into unconsciousness.

Kemp offered his arm and a second later felt a blissful lassitude ease him into oblivion.

He opened his eyes and was instantly aware of a curious light-headedness that he suspected was the effect of weightlessness, and the dull droning of the shuttle's drive.

The scientists were coming round, rubbing their faces and stretching as if after a period of sleep.

Beside him, Gellner asked, "How are you feeling, Inspector?"

Kemp nodded. "I'm fine."

He was about to ask Gellner something about Carrasco when a voice filled the chamber. "Lieutenant Harper here, your pilot. We're approaching L5 and the quantum lattice. I'm patching through visual now. Enjoy the transit, ladies and gentlemen."

Instantly, an image appeared in the air before the forward bulkhead: it showed an expanse of space, a scattering of distant stars, and in the foreground six scintillating silver points of light forming the outer edge of a hexagon.

Kemp glanced across at the security men. One or two watched the screen; the rest affected a bored indifference that he suspected was part of their practised professional élan.

Unbidden, the rarefied BBC tones of his new implant sounded in Kemp's inner ear. "What you see on the screen are the fulcrum lodes of the quantum lattice arranged in a configuration measuring precisely one kilometre in diameter. Once activated, they will power and define the limits of the wormhole. Stated simply, the lattice distorts the space-time continuum in such a way as to create a passage from here to there, from where we are now to a point thirty kilometres above the surface of Carrasco."

The points of silver light were linked by a frame of lapis lazuli light forming a vast hexagon. The light from the vectors expanded to fill the hexagonal space, shading from the deepest blue at the edges to a roiling, cloudy sky blue towards the centre.

"The quantum lattice is now operative," his implant said. *"The continuum has been annihilated in two far distant loci."*

The pilot said, "Initiating approach run. Transition in five, four, three..."

"The act of transition–" his imp began.

Kemp sub-vocced, "Mute imp."

He gripped the handholds to either side of the seat, sweating. The shuttle's engines vibrated and the image – the cloudy light within the brilliant blue vectors – expanded to fill the screen.

Kemp held his breath as the shuttle raced towards the wormhole – and then they were through, without the slightest jolt to suggest that in a fraction of a second, they had jumped fifty lightyears through space.

The shuttle's drives commenced a gradual diminuendo, and the screen no longer showed the quantum lattice but a scene of sable space glinting with distant stars. The elongated bulk of the *Strasbourg* hung to the left, and in the midground was the blue and white immensity of the extra-solar planet, Carrasco.

"Transition successfully accomplished," the disembodied voice of Lieutenant Harper announced.

Gellner turned a patronising glance towards Kemp. "There, Inspector. Nothing to fear, was there?"

Kemp was still gripping the handholds and sweating inordinately. He must have presented a pathetic sight to the annoyingly nonchalant major. Up front, two of the security men were staring back at him and smiling to themselves. He fixed his gaze on the screen as the shuttle approached the excoriated exterior of the *Strasbourg*.

Thirty minutes later they docked with the starship. Gellner unstrapped himself and, with practised movements that surprised Kemp, pushed himself across the chamber and spoke to Connery. The bullet-head security man nodded, then turned to his men and issued orders that Kemp didn't catch.

The security detail floated one by one from the chamber into a blindingly white corridor. Gellner and the scientists followed, gripping a series of handholds ranged along the umbilical's 'ceiling'. Last to leave the safety of his seat, Kemp eased himself into the air, but even that small push-off was misjudged and he was abruptly careening across the aisle until he grabbed a handhold to stop himself.

Ahead, Gellner and some of the others were peering back at him, and Kemp felt his skin burning with embarrassment at his own clumsiness. Cautiously, he reached for another handhold and started to work his way along the aisle towards the disembarkation lock.

They were met by half a dozen floating figures in red coveralls. As Kemp looked on, Connery pushed himself towards the six and they conferred. The spacers moved to one side and watched in silence as the security detail passed by, followed by Gellner, Kemp and the scientists.

They moved along the corridor towards a circular hatch which irised, giving access to a cramped area fitted with workspaces bolted to the walls and cross-hatched with handling straps. Kemp didn't know what he'd expected, but certainly not the sense of claustrophobia he felt now.

The spacers entered the communal space after them and hung together, watching the new arrivals with what might have been suspicion.

Kemp, hanging uneasily from a cross-strap, was still struggling to get his head around the way people hung with different orientations to each other, with no sense of up or down. He returned the spacers' stares as it came to him, suddenly, that these people – four men and two women in their late twenties and early thirties – had been born more than a century ago. The notion was oddly unsettling.

He thought he understood their suspicion as they regarded the new arrivals, men and women who had suddenly appeared before them from an unknown future age.

Gellner said, "The shuttle will ferry us to the surface in a little under one hour. Right now, we'll pick up our life-packs, proceed to the shuttle, and spend a little time familiarising ourselves with safety protocols to be observed during our stay on Carrasco." He waved, and Kemp's wristcom pinged with an incoming data flow.

A spacer detached herself from the floating group and acted as a guide, leading Gellner and the others from the communal area and along another corridor. On the way, they halted outside a storage unit to collect the life-packs, small rucksacks that had the odd, indefinable appearance of relics from an earlier age.

They processed along an umbilical and into the chamber of another shuttle. Again, Kemp was assailed with the odd sensation of an encounter with the past, as if the interior of the shuttle was an exhibit in a museum. As he buckled himself into his seat, and a heavy door swung into place behind him, he noticed the chunky, clunky design of the seats themselves, the worn carbon fibre bulkheads and halogen lighting arrays. All of this had been manufactured long before he had been born.

Gellner settled himself beside Kemp again, and the scientists slotted in behind them, just as on the previous journey.

"Is there a comms channel back to London I can use?" Kemp asked. He felt the need to let Danni and Bryce know he had survived the jump.

Gellner laughed. "No direct comms through the wormhole," he said. "It's not physically possible. But every time a shuttle passes through it carries reports and other communications. Anything you want to send will have to go by that route – just ask anyone on my team."

Kemp should have realised Gellner would have taken as much control as possible – including, it appeared, all comms channels between Earth and Carrasco.

"We have some time before we embark," Gellner said, "so

my advice is that we spend the time listening to what our imps have to say about the prevailing conditions on Carrasco..."

Kemp closed his eyes and sub-vocced, "Imp, tell me about the planet Carrasco."

For the next twenty minutes, he listened as the velvety tones of his implant told him about the atmospheric conditions, the incidence of airborne pathogens, and what visitors must do to ensure they did not become contaminated.

The bottom line was that he should listen to the edicts of the medical officers at all times.

Then his imp launched a more detailed analysis of conditions on Carrasco, sounding like a treatise on abstruse exo-biology, and Kemp sub-vocced the sound to the threshold of audibility.

He was almost asleep when Connery snapped, "Kemp! You with us? I asked if you'll be wanting sedation this time?"

The scientists seated across the aisle from Kemp were already dead to the world, and the other scientists were also being sedated. Kemp proffered his arm. When he next came to his senses, he would be on the surface of another world.

Seconds later he was unconscious.

14

Beneath the Canopy

Base West One consisted of a single small dome anchored to the jungle canopy and a smaller dome where they stored equipment and ATVs. The place was deserted.

Harrie Spier returned to the small group, shaking his head. "Still nothing. I just hope it's a signals failure."

"They wouldn't have *all* left the base, surely?" Franco said.

Spier stared at him. "Well, evidently they have – there's no one here, is there?" Rima's group explored cautiously. The canopy surface here was undulating, with metre-deep folds that made her think of crevices in an ice floe, or the surface of a brain. At every footfall, some small creature scuttled or writhed away.

The air was misted thick with green, so that Rima had to wipe repeatedly at her visor as she walked. They still had no rapid test to determine whether airborne microorganisms were benign or deadly, but the mist was a constant reminder of just how subtly dangerous this planet could be.

She couldn't help wondering if Liza Staffel and her team had succumbed to a version of cloud fever, despite all the precautions everyone was now taking.

"So what do you make of it?" The tone of Harrie Spier's questioning was brusque, impatient.

"I... *Non lo so*. I don't know." Gianfranco Marcosi's body language was clear, despite the suit. Franco had been in the background for weeks; now Harrie was suddenly making him the centre of attention, and he didn't know how to handle it.

"They can't just vanish." Harrie turned away, shaking his head, making no effort to hide his frustrations with Franco. The young Italian was hard to handle at the best of times, and Harrie was out of his depth too. They all were.

"I work with theoretical models of alien culture," Franco said, regaining some of his confidence. "I'm not a detective. I can't look at an empty camp and tell you whether or not aliens have abducted our colleagues. I–"

"It's okay, Franco." Rima put a hand on his arm, turning him away. "We're all stressed right now. All scared. Harrie's just trying to work it out." There was no official hierarchy on this team, but Harrie had assumed the role of leader, for now.

Annika Muller and Lars Anderson had entered the main dome, and now they emerged from the airlock. "Nothing," Annika told them. "Or at least, it all looks perfectly normal. Nothing to indicate why they're not here."

A short distance away, Abdul Cole watched them, an automatic weapon slung from one shoulder and another across his back. Behind him, a new dome was assembling itself from a pack they had brought on the ATV truck: a safe space for Rima's team, so they could stay separate from the area that had been occupied by Staffel's team.

"Stephan?" Harrie called across to the meteorologist, who was squatting by a pile of crates they'd unloaded from the truck.

Stephan Taylor gestured at the side of the truck, casting images from three drones onto the smooth surface. One showed a high aerial view in which the only distinguishable features were the domes and the smaller shapes of the ATVs. Another panned slowly, the horizon dividing the view in two. A third was lower, swooping over the tangled canopy, following what appeared to be a groove through the surface.

Rima glanced at Franco, saw that he was staring at that last drone's imagery.

"What do you think?" Harrie asked him.

"I..." Franco clearly didn't want to commit himself, even though he was unable to take his eyes off what appeared to be a straight track which the drone still followed.

"You don't know, I get it." Again, Harrie didn't even try to hide his frustration with the young alien cultures specialist. He wanted answers, not sensible academic caution.

They paired up and set off, each with a drone monitoring their progress from a safe height. Harrie and Annika, Lars and Stephan, Rima and Franco. Abdul Cole remained at the research outpost, monitoring the feeds and ready to come to anyone's assistance.

Harrie and Annika took what they were referring to as the highway, much to Franco's irritation. He wanted to get out there, get a firsthand view of the channels through the canopy that Liza Staffel's team had identified as possible signs of intelligent activity. It was why he was here.

Rima said nothing. She understood Harrie's decision completely: their priority now was locating Staffel's team. If Franco had been allocated the highway, looking for Staffel would be the last thing on his mind.

"Come on," she said, holding onto a grab rail so she could stand on the ATV's footplate. "You drive. You know the terrain far better than I do."

He flashed her a resentful look, but said nothing.

They headed south, Rima switching her attention between their drone's coverage and her own view of the terrain all around. She felt powerless. Despite all the training for the mission, nothing had prepared her for this. She didn't even know what she was looking for, beyond the obvious: a cheery group hiking through the wilderness, or bodies...

Eventually, they came to a halt. "You drive," Franco snapped at her, all his puppy-dog enthusiasm for this new world long-vanished. "You've got to be good for something."

Rima stared. She considered letting it pass, filed under tensions of the moment, but… "What do you mean? Good for something?" She hadn't realised he had such a dim view of her.

He met her look, visibly shrinking back as he realised he'd spoken out loud what he'd been bottling up inside. No going back now. "I've worked for this my whole career," he said, struggling to measure his words. "I've fought to become one of the world's leading specialists in a field that studies something we've never even encountered. And then when I get here, I'm consigned to checking traps for the ecologists, taking measurements… all the dogsbody work the *real* ecologists can delegate. And now, finally, when my discipline is called for, I don't even get to explore the highway where I can use my skills. I end up paired up with someone who doesn't even deserve to be here."

He stopped. He'd said too much.

Doesn't even deserve to be here.

Rima took a deep breath, opened her mouth to speak, and then was interrupted.

Harrie Spier's face pinged up on the side of the ATV. "Hey, everyone. Rendezvous back at West One. We've found them safe and well."

"Where the hell were they?" she asked.

"On a little jaunt beneath the canopy, is all," he laughed.

Rima spent the next few hours giving Liza Staffel and her team a full medical work over, and also taking the opportunity to bring them up to speed on developments in the understanding of cloud fever.

"The mist here, is it always so thick?" Rima asked Liza. "Any indications of toxicity?"

"It varies," Liza told her. "And we've been scrupulously

careful. No contamination, so we can't comment on toxicity. All I can tell you is it's a constant battle to keep exterior surfaces clean of the green muck."

Liza's readings were comfortably within the normal range on her medical records. She was the last of the six to be checked by Rima. All were healthy, and Liza assured her there had been no biohazard lapses, so the two teams would be allowed to mingle in the outpost's main dome.

"What's it like down there?" Rima asked, as Liza pulled on a t-shirt.

Liza had led a team of four under the jungle canopy yesterday, with every intention of returning to base in time to greet Harrie and the other new arrivals. Then one of the two left behind had seen the message to say the convoy was delayed, and they'd headed down to join them, so that all six scientists were below the canopy, pushing deeper into the tunnels than ever before.

"We lost track of time," Liza admitted. "You get just a short distance down one of those tunnels and all daylight is gone. Some of the undergrowth has a kind of bioluminescence, so your eyes adjust and, you know... We had no signal, too. A lot of that blue tint to the vegetation is from compounds of copper, which plays havoc with communications, so we never saw Harrie's messages."

They'd spent the night camping out in self-inflating sacs just as Rima and her convoy had done up on the canopy.

"We could have come back last night," Liza said. "But while we had dim light from the bioluminescence down there, we knew that once we hit the surface it'd be dark, and the nights out here are pitch black under those green clouds. So we took the safe option and waited until morning."

Rima had the distinct sense that there was an element of last night of the school holidays about the little adventure: Liza's team had established this outpost alone, and operated under their own rules, and they knew that as soon as Harrie and the others arrived, they would be back under central rule – a sentiment reinforced by the presence of Abdul Cole among them now. Indeed, Rima suspected that the night camping out might have been far more deliberate than Liza's version of events implied.

"But what was it *like?*" Rima pressed.

Liza Staffel smiled. "The jury's out," she said. "Those tunnels: they look deliberate. Planned. But..."

Rima raised her eyebrows, waited.

"Have you seen the incredible structures of a coral reef?" Liza asked. "Or termite towers that can be metres high?"

As far as Rima knew, coral reefs had been extinct for a hundred years, although she was familiar with termites' high mud towers.

"Nature makes incredible structures," Liza went on. "And these tunnels..."

"You think the jungle just grows that way?"

Liza shrugged. "It's not my speciality," she admitted. "But I haven't seen anything yet that sways me from the most likely explanation, and that's that, yes, the jungle just grows that way."

Gianfranco Marcosi didn't think the jungle just grew that way. That much was obvious from how long he spent out there investigating the tunnels.

Rima found him the next day, hanging from a rope under the lip of one of the tunnel entrances, where it dropped away from the flank of the long surface track they called the highway.

"Do you think it grows, or was it made?" Rima called up to him.

He peered down. "The tunnels?" he said. "The walls show signs of being cut, although they also seem to grow that way, as if trained. But then..." He still didn't want to commit an opinion.

Slowly, he lowered himself, so he could stand with her.

"Look, I'm sorry," he said. "Yesterday. I was stressed. I..."

"I know. We all were." But Franco had been the only one throwing accusations around. Then, Rima asked: "What did you mean? You said I shouldn't be here."

"It's not me. I didn't... It's just talk."

She waited for him to go on, which eventually he did.

He looked away as he said, "People say that anyone else would have been dropped from the mission."

Rima took a breath, so tempted to leave it at that. She'd known there would be gossip. This was nothing new. She didn't want to talk about all that now, because talk would prompt memories, memories she'd tried so hard to suppress. It was all, still, so raw and painful.

"Why?" she asked, unable to just turn away.

Franco studied her carefully, clearly trying to work out what trap he was walking into.

"You were at the heart of the investigation into the murder of... a prominent person," he said.

A prominent person. Sebastian White. Her husband.

"People assume strings were pulled to allow you to retain your place on the Carrasco mission. You're a White. Married into the family."

"Really?" she said. "Is that the best people can do? Can't they see that Randolph White would have done everything in his power to get me pulled from the *Strasbourg* if he'd thought I killed his brother?"

No pain could ever surpass that she had felt when she heard of Sebastian's fate, but saying those words out loud came close.

"And did you?"

Rima looked away, again. Her marriage with Sebastian had been struggling. They would have separated even if Rima had not been confirmed on the Mu Arae mission. But they had never ceased to be the closest of friends – a bond deeper in many ways than one clouded by sex and notions of romantic love. They had always known their relationship would be finite, and perhaps it was all the more intense because of that.

She met Franco's look again.

"No," she said. "I did not kill my husband. I don't know who did. And I did not rely on family connections to secure my place on this mission. I did the same as you and Liza and all the others – I earned my place on merit, and then when things got tough I had to fight my corner, convince the most senior figures at ESO that it would be worse to drop me at the last minute than to back me. And so they backed me. They brought in lawyers to advise me, to coach me on what to expect and how to handle the police interviews, and make sure that Earth-side complications didn't interfere with my role on the *Strasbourg*."

"That's not exactly a convincing argument that strings weren't pulled on your behalf."

"They were different strings, Franco. Not the strings of family connection and influence, but ESO strings – the kind of protection any one of us on this mission would have received in a comparable situation."

She saw Franco's jaw flex, a retort bitten off.

"What?"

"There are other strings too," he said. "Other connections." He swallowed. "Like Captain Fernandez."

"Is that more gossip, or just you joining the dots?"

"I don't care," he said. "Really, I don't care who you sleep with and what it gets you. It's why I do this." He waved a hand to indicate the rope hanging nearby, the sides of the tunnel. "I work with imaginary aliens, not people. I don't understand people. It's too... too *messy*."

He'd taken a step away from Rima and now he took another. His whole body was shaking.

"It's okay," Rima said. She hadn't understood Franco until now, and probably still didn't. The hyper-enthusiasm, the surface veneer he hid behind. His lack of filters and clumsiness with people – which clearly frustrated Harrie Spier and others – and the way he would swing from the extremes of avoiding saying what needed to be said to blurting out things most people would never say aloud.

She'd worked with the neurally diverse at various times over the years – she really should have read Franco better than she had.

"It's okay, Franco," she said again, and a moment of what she took to be understanding passed between them. She'd seen through his layers and he knew it, and somehow they needed to move on from this point.

"I'll leave you to it," she said. "But if you need anything… Remember how the ecologists relied on you for the legwork back at the main base? Well, that's my role now, and you're the specialist, so if there's anything I can do."

He smiled at that, and she smiled back, then turned and left him to his work of studying aliens that probably weren't there at all.

They settled into a camp routine. Liza Staffel stayed on, while the five members of her team returned to base. Now Harrie took over the running of Base West One and Liza returned to her primary specialism as lead ecologist, taking the role Jayne Waterford would have adopted if she'd been able to make this trip. Rima, nominally the outpost's medic, but not called on once since checking over Liza's team on their return from their night-time adventure, took over what had been Franco's secondary role: the ecology team's gofer, checking traps, carrying equipment, and assisting in whatever other ways she could.

Franco had clearly come to resent that role, but Rima quite liked it. She felt useful, and she got to know the people around her. Also, she found it reassuring, for despite Franco's talk of rumours and gossip, no one else here seemed to have any issue with Rima's presence, or her usefulness.

She kept an eye on Franco, too, concerned for him now that she had come to at least a crude understanding of why he didn't seem to fit in to any team or social arrangement.

Two days into the expedition, Rima joined Franco for his first venture deep into the jungle tunnels. He'd surprised her by his restraint: his first reaction to not being allowed to check out the tunnels straight away had been frustration, and she would have expected him to plunge right in. Instead, once he was allowed to start his work, he was methodical, painstakingly studying the three-kilometre-long highway before even venturing more than a few tens of metres into the tunnels.

Rima had learned not to press him for conclusions, or even early impressions, so she'd been surprised when he'd turned to her this morning and said, "I'm going into the alien tunnels today. Are you free to assist?"

Abdul Cole was an unanticipated addition to the little expedition. Somehow he'd learned of Franco's plans and announced that he was joining them. Rima was unable to fathom the man. He kept himself aloof and said little. He seemed if anything clumsy in his movements, and yet she knew he was a military veteran, trained in special ops – someone never to be underestimated.

Now, as the three paused before the dark, circular mouth of a tunnel, Abdul stepped forward, and all Rima could think of was a mother duck, venturing out protectively before her ducklings on their first venture onto the water.

The tunnel was maybe three metres in diameter, its walls a dense fibroid tangle of vegetal matter. Rima's glove readout told her the atmosphere was becoming more oxygen- and methane-rich as they walked in. The bad fart smell would be intense, if it were not for their suits and breathing apparatus.

About half a metre above Franco's shoulder, a drone recorded everything, and the young Italian gave a running commentary of his observations. Rima found herself impressed by the breadth of the skillset required by his discipline: he recorded ecological data and observations, but also commented on physical structure with the knowledge of an architect, on the fabric of the walls with the expertise of a civil engineer. She knew also that he had an in-depth knowledge of human cultures, and theoretical models for alien cultures, of mammalian and insect social structures, of religion and linguistics, and much more.

People like Harrie Spier saw Franco as the most frivolous expert to be on this expedition, but now Rima saw him as perhaps the most broad-ranging and accomplished.

They came to a split in the tunnel, and in response to a command from Franco the drone cleaved itself in two, one of which took the left fork while the other stayed with the humans.

"I spoke to Jayne Waterford this morning," Rima said, although she knew Franco had little interest in conversation, except when he used it to fill uncomfortable silences. "She says she's well, although I'm not so sure."

Franco continued his commentary uninterrupted.

They worked steadily deeper. Rima's glove readout told her they'd come five hundred metres from the tunnel entrance. Now, she understood Liza's comment about the timelessness of the place: there was no hint of daylight, and the place was lit only by a dim greenish glow from the vegetal walls. They'd turned their own lights off almost immediately, because Franco wanted to see the tunnels as the putative aliens did.

They came to a point where the tunnel opened into a chamber maybe ten metres across, and paused.

"Earlier," Rima said, "you told me you were going into the alien tunnels. Why did you call them that?"

It was impossible to read Franco's expression in the low light. "Everyone else calls them that," he said, "so I thought I'd see how it sounded."

"And how did it sound?"

"Right."

She could tell he wasn't giving her the full answer, but she couldn't work out if he was deliberately teasing her or simply being obtuse.

A short time later, Franco stopped so abruptly that Rima walked into his back.

"What is it?"

The tunnel had become narrower again, no room to pass, and now Franco was squatting, gloved hand scrabbling at the floor as if trying to part the tightly knit tendrils.

He twisted to look up at Rima then. "We have to get back," he told her. "Right now. We need to consult Mijnheer Hertzberger."

"What? Why?" Rima peered at the floor, but could see nothing different about it.

Franco stood, then twisted sideways and squeezed past Rima, heading back the way they'd come. The drone remained where it was, left here as a lone observer.

"Come on!"

"Wait, Franco. What have you found?"

He glanced back, but kept walking. "They've been here. Recently. We have to report back."

"What do you mean, Franco? Who's been here? How do you know?"

Abdul had squeezed past them in the confines of the tunnel and was now ahead of them on point, moving with the agility of a predator, an automatic gun cradled across his chest.

Franco stopped abruptly again and pointed at the ground.

Rima peered, and for a moment her eyes failed to adjust, but then she saw it. An indent in the densely packed fabric of the tunnel's lining. A long, narrow groove. Something had passed this way, heavy enough or frequently enough to leave that imprint.

Something with wheels?

"Come on," Abdul snapped, from up ahead. "Pronto!"

Rima still didn't quite understand the urgency. It was as if their guard had picked up on the change in Franco, and now *his* greater urgency was winding up Franco even further.

Rima reached for Franco as they half-walked, half-jogged, and put a calming hand on his arm. "Let's just pace ourselves, okay?" she said.

"No," Franco replied, simply. "Abdul is right. We should hurry." He paused, then added, "We should hurry because they're coming."

He gestured, casting imagery onto the inside of Rima's visor. Footage from the drone he had instructed to remain behind.

At first Rima saw only the dimly lit interior of the tunnel they had vacated mere minutes before, but then she saw it.

Them.

Grey shapes, here and then gone in the blink of an eye so that she had no real idea of their number, or even what they looked like.

Humanoid, with skinny, wisp-like figures. Moving with a cat-like litheness and no hesitation – clearly accustomed to moving fast in the tunnels. Rima assumed they must either see well in the gloom, or rely on some mix of other senses to negotiate the space.

She started to run, her brain racing with clumsy calculation as she tried to work out how long ago they had left that drone, how far they had come.

The aliens were moving fast. They must only have seconds.

Rima was sprinting, the breath burning in her lungs as her breather struggled to keep up. All she could see was the dim glow of the walls and the dark shape of the tunnel, disrupted by the running figure of Franco ahead of her.

"Go! Go!" Abdul had stopped, pressing himself to the tunnel wall so they could run past. Now, as Rima passed him, he turned to cover their retreat from behind.

For a moment then, Rima allowed herself to wonder at their kneejerk response: run, prepare to defend – and feel pathetically grateful that they were being protected by a military vet with a powerful automatic weapon. All they'd seen were a few fleeting figures. They had no reason to believe their lives were at risk. And she hated that it made her feel like Hertzberger: at the first hint of threat their response – the default human response – was to wipe out that threat.

She tripped. Her feet hit something both hard and soft, and the upper half of her body kept going even as her legs went from under her.

She hit the ground face-first, and for a panicked moment thought her suit must be compromised, her visor split or dislodged, but all was okay. She was just lying in a heap on the ground, the breath knocked from her lungs.

She twisted, peered back, and saw that Franco was sprawling too. He must have caught his foot on something, and it was his collapsed figure she had tripped over.

She forced herself to her hands and knees, straightened, reached for Franco. "Come on, Franco, *c'est ça.*"

"Mayday, mayday." Abdul Cole's voice echoed in the confines of her helmet. "Confronted by hostiles. They came from nowhere. I took out three, but–"

Just as Franco took Rima's outstretched hand, she heard another sound, from deeper into the tunnel. A deep grunt, a meaty thud.

And then, agonisingly, a sharp, piercing scream.

Abdul Cole, screaming like a skewered animal and then stopping, cut off, cut silent.

Rima grabbed for Franco and drew him to her, despite his feeble struggles. She embraced him and rolled over to the side until they pressed against the tunnel wall. The vegetation eased, parted a little, allowed them to press further into the mass. Rima fought down a surge of claustrophobia as the growth closed around them.

She heard sounds again, the thump of running feet, although the rhythm was irregular.

She held her breath, willed herself not to move and prayed that Franco would have the sense to do likewise.

The sounds passed them, retreated, went silent.

Somehow the creatures – the aliens – had missed them. Which only left the fact that now the aliens were between them and the outside world.

"Okay, Franco," Rima murmured, close to his helmet. "You're the expert. You've studied this all your life. First contact. All the scenarios. All the models for an event like this. So what do we do next?"

"I... I really don't know."

There were many reasons why Franco's default response was to say he did not know. Lack of confidence. A rigid adherence to academic caution, where answers were never clear-cut, and more data was almost always required. Perhaps perceptual differences where he simply failed to understand that sometimes people just wanted certainty and reassurance, even when the answer was not clear.

And, sometimes, he simply did not know.

Rima tried to push away from him so that she could stand, but something held her.

"Let go, Franco. I need to stand up."

"I... I'm not holding you," he said, panic in his voice.

She pushed away from him again, but couldn't move.

Panic started to tug at her awareness, then. An ancient, claustrophobic terror.

She pushed harder, tried to kick her legs free, but nothing would budge.

Now Franco was struggling, too, but to no avail. They were stuck. Where they'd pushed themselves against the tunnel wall so they might hide, the vegetation had folded around them and knitted itself closed.

She tried to push more gently, repeating the kind of pressure they'd used to secrete themselves here, but it was no good.

"I... I think we're stuck."

No, not stuck. Worse than that. Now that she had stopped struggling, Rima could feel the almost imperceptible movements of their cocoon, closing tighter around them.

More than that, she sensed motion, too, a dragging sensation, a tipping so that the blood started to rush to her head, as the alien jungle closed around them, drew them in, drew them deeper, swallowing them into its depths.

15

An Older Man

On returning to the office two days ago, after learning that Major Gellner worked for the White Foundation as a security chief, Danni had done some discreet digging on the police intelligence system. She was not in the least surprised that she'd come up with nothing.

Now, as the snow sifted down outside and she bit into her third samosa of the morning, she used a cloaked data-mining agent to search files from eighty-plus years ago for anything that correlated *Gellner* and *Randolph White* and came up with a list of three hundred entries: mostly news reports, gossip feeds, and corporate minutes. Many were firewalled and barred her entry. Others gave her scant details: Marius Gellner had been born in 2060 in the principality of Germany, United States of Europe. Through his twenties and thirties, he'd worked his way up the ranks of the European Army, retiring at the age of forty and joining one of Randolph White's subsidiary companies: his role was unspecified, but going by his career history Danni suspected that it was along the lines of security – like grandfather, like grandson, she thought.

When she tried to find out whether Marius Gellner had had any children, she drew a blank. After 2100, when he joined forces with Randolph White, there was very little information available on the man.

She turned her attention to the person she suspected was

his grandson, Major Gellner, and drew a big fat blank. Which she supposed made sense. Commander Tsang had introduced him last week as someone in European security, failing to mention the fact that Gellner was moonlighting for the White Foundation. In either capacity, she reckoned it was in his interest to minimise his digital footprint.

Her imp said, *"A call from Commander Tsang, Danni."*

She started guiltily and blanked her private screen.

"Put him through."

A screen expanded in the air before her, showing a head-and-shoulders shot of her boss.

"Inspector Bellini," he began, and his formality made her pulse race, "I understand you visited Carstairs Hall on Tuesday?"

She nodded, brushing pastry crumbs from the front of her blouse. She wondered how he'd found out. Either Peter Conway was not to be trusted, or Tsang had run a check on her movements.

"I distinctly recall telling you to drop the Fairleigh White case."

"You know me, Commander. I'm thorough. There was something I wanted to check before I moved on..."

"Which was?"

"Just something Fairleigh-White said about what his uncle had told him concerning Rima Cagnac's killing her husband. I wanted to see if he recalled anything further from the meeting."

"And?"

Danni shrugged. "He was comatose. He didn't say a word." The ease of the lie surprised her.

Tsang nodded. He let a second or two elapse, then said, "Your other cases are backing up, Inspector. And I have a long list of cold cases awaiting review. So... if you could leave the ongoing Cagnac investigation in the capable hands of Inspector Kemp, I'd be most grateful."

She nodded again, keeping her expression neutral.

Tsang cut the connection and his floating mugshot vanished. Seconds later her desk smartcore pinged with incoming files: queries relating to existing cases and case files for other investigations. It would take her a week just to review it all.

She pushed her swivel chair away from the desk and turned, staring out through the window at the slate grey sky.

If Gordon were here, they'd sneak off to some quiet cafe and over coffee try to work out just what the hell was going on, what Commander Tsang was trying to hide, and why someone wanted to pin the blame for an eighty-year-old murder on a potentially innocent woman.

She reached down, unconsciously, and smoothed the material over her stomach.

She felt oddly alone, isolated, which was not a condition that would normally concern her. She prided herself on her independence, her resourcefulness under stress. But now she was unaccountably anxious, afraid she was getting into something too big to handle alone. The fact was, she was missing Gordon. She cursed herself, blaming her hormones, and sub-vocced, "Imp, has Edouard Bryce attempted contact recently?"

"Twice last night and once this morning. You instructed me to send him unavailable notices."

"But he still called... Christ!" She frowned, biting her lip as she considered what to do next. "Okay, look, give him a call. Say I need to talk."

"Calling now."

A screen expanded before her. Edouard Bryce peered out, looking wary. "Danni... hello."

"Hi, there, Ed. Look..."

He held up a pudgy hand. "I apologise. I know I've been bombarding you. It won't happen again, Danni. I'll stop. It's just... well, I thought it would be good if we met up again, talked about–"

"That would be good, yes."

He appeared surprised. "Are you free for lunch?"

She nodded.

"Yin's noodle bar, Holborn?"

"How about Ricci's, just along the street? You know how much I hate noodles."

"Ricci's it is. I'll meet you at the Thunberg Monument at one, okay?"

"See you there," she said, and cut the connection.

At twelve-thirty she took the elevator to the foyer and stepped out into a sub-zero wind. She hailed a covered rickshaw and sat back as it puttered east through the crowded streets to Holborn. The driver tried to engage her in conversation, grinning over his shoulder and saying something about the weather, but Danni ignored him. She was too busy thinking about Edouard, and their upcoming meeting, to listen to platitudes. Not that she could hear much, anyway, above the banal blare of Mandarin popzac blasting from baijiu bars along the street, and a floating megascreen exhorting citizens to try their luck in the daily state lottery. She smiled at that: a couple of days ago one of these large screens had been hacked by pranksters, and started showing infographics illustrating just whose pockets the lottery income lined – that was the most interesting the feeds had been in a long time.

She was five minutes early when she stepped from the rickshaw beneath the monument at Holborn. She paced back and forth, her collar turned up against the cold.

Danni saw Bryce as he hurried along the street towards her; he caught her eye and smiled. He reached out and took her frozen hand. "Danni? You look as if you've seen a ghost."

She pulled her hand away. "I... for a second back there, you reminded me of my father."

"I'll take that as a compliment." He pointed across the street to the restaurant. "Shall we?"

He took her elbow to assist her across the crowded road, the old-fashioned gesture verging on the patronising. As ever,

Danni was conflicted: part of her resented his chauvinism, while another put it down as an example of Edouard Bryce's innate old-world charm.

"I took the precaution of booking a booth," he said as they sat down in the warmth of the restaurant. "And I'm glad I did. Everywhere's so busy these days."

She nodded, feigning interest in the menu that hung in the air between them.

He said, "You never mentioned your father."

She shrugged. She'd never mentioned a lot of things.

"What did he do?"

"Viniculture. He ran a place down in Devon."

He pulled a face. "Ouch. Let me guess. The Shenju buy-out?"

She nodded. "Filed for bankruptcy in '82."

"Is he still…?"

She shook her head. "He died a year later."

"I'm sorry."

She swallowed, avoiding his eyes. "He took his own life."

"Ah… I'm sorry."

His hand reached across the table, covered hers. She wanted to pull it away, but she let it remain, her fingers dwarfed by his, big and warm.

"Danni, about the calls. I'm sorry–"

"You're using that word a lot, Edouard."

He shivered and mimed turning up his collar. "Brrr… cold out there, *and* in here."

Now it was her turn to apologise, and she nearly did so, but stopped herself.

"I just wanted to see you again," he said at last, staring down at his hand on hers, "to tell you that I understand."

She swallowed, nodded. "What do you understand?" she asked quietly.

"How you feel about what happened, about us." He stopped. "I just wanted to say that it's okay. I'm no catch, and what

happened between us was just a fling. So I can live with that...
But it'd be nice if we could still be friends, okay?"

She found herself nodding mechanically while thinking that
he understood nothing, nothing at all.

They selected their meals – risotto for Danni, three cheese
tagliatelle for Bryce – and he said, "A drink? Beer?"

"I... No, no alcohol – too cold out there. Coffee, please."

He tapped for a long black and a beer. He glanced at her, as
if about to ask a question.

When their drinks arrived, he sipped his beer and murmured,
"I'd value that friendship more than anything. I'd like to be
part of your life."

She swallowed, nodding. She withdrew her hand to pick up
and sip her coffee.

"As you say," she said, "there's no reason why we can't still
be friends."

He smiled, nodded. "Good, that's good. So, how's work?"

She resented the part of her that wanted nothing more than
to take his hand and shout out that she needed his help, that
she was into something over her head and needed his calm
wisdom and reassurance.

Christ, her hormones *were* traitorous today.

She said, "I went back to Carstairs Hall a couple of days ago."

Bryce nodded. "Gordon said you'd interviewed Alastair
Fairleigh-White last week."

Their dishes arrived and they ate. Even the risotto reminded
her of her father; he'd considered himself something of a chef,
and risotto with porcini mushrooms had been his signature
dish.

"Go on," he prompted. "I can see something's concerning
you."

She smiled. Bryce had always been able to empathise with
her, to second-guess her emotions, her concerns.

"There are a few things that worry me."

She told him about her second meeting with Fairleigh-

White, and how the old man had had no recollection of telling her and Kemp about his uncle's revelation that it had been Rima Cagnac who'd murdered her husband.

Bryce pointed at her with his fork. "You're talking about an old, old man here, whose third telomerase procedure had gone pear-shaped. He's just suffered a neurological firestorm – you can't rely on his memory to be perfect, Danni."

"I know that: on my second visit he couldn't even remember I'd been there before. But there was something else." She told him about her lip-reader friend's analysis. "You see, Fairleigh-White said something along the lines that he'd found Cagnac, his stepmother, sexually attractive, and he reiterated that when I questioned him again. Now that's not something you'd say about the woman who'd killed your father, is it?"

He nodded. "Okay, so what do you think accounts for the inconsistencies in his account?"

"I think it wasn't entirely his own words we heard, that first time, but something programmed into his voice-recognition software that took what he said and twisted and embellished it."

He looked sceptical. "By whom?"

"A security high-up, Major Gellner, works for both Commander Tsang and the White Foundation. He was at the Hall a few days before Gordon and I were sent there by Tsang. And Gellner's grandfather also worked for Randolph White. There are family ties going back generations."

"How do you know this?"

She told him about her contact at the Hall, Peter Conway.

Bryce sat back, his lips pursed. "Okay…"

She forked another mouthful of risotto; it was nothing like her father's – risotto should not be so thick you could cut it with a knife. "Also, this morning Tsang warned me off the case, then dumped another load of cold-case files in my 'core to occupy me. There's something going on, Ed."

"So it would seem."

"One," she said, "why do they want to pin the blame for Sebastian White's killing on Cagnac? Two, why send Gordon to Carrasco to arrest her when they could have just as easily tasked someone from ESO security with the job? Three, who is Major Gellner – is he just a bit-part player in all this, or is he working on behalf of the White Foundation and pulling Commander's Tsang's strings?"

Bryce said, "Then there's the question Gordon wanted answering before he left for the stars: why was ESO content to let the world believe the *Strasbourg* had been destroyed en route to Mu Arae, and why was it kept secret that the ship was carrying technology capable of opening up wormhole travel between Earth and Carrasco? Who benefited from that secrecy?"

"You think they're all connected?"

He pursed his lips and rocked his head. "Well, it would be too much of a coincidence if they weren't – Rima Cagnac was part of the White dynasty, after all, if only by marriage. This Gellner character interests me: what if you're right, and he's running the show, controlling Commander Tsang, and working to pin the blame for Sebastian White's murder on Cagnac?"

She nodded, alarmed. "Gellner accompanied Gordon to Carrasco…"

"We need to look into this Major Gellner as a priority."

"I've tried that. There's precious little available, about him or his grandfather, and much of it protected by firewalls."

He dabbed at his lips with a napkin. "I'll get Martin Khalsa on the job. If anyone can uncover anything, it's Martin. Give me a day or two, and I'll get back to you."

She nodded, hesitated, then asked, "Edouard, do you think Gordon's in danger out there?"

He reached out and patted her hand again, the gesture at once patronising and reassuring. Just like Edouard Bryce, she thought. "There's no hard evidence to suggest that," he said, "and if anyone can look after himself in a tight situation, Gordon can."

They finished the meal in silence, Danni maintaining a line of small talk in a bid to avoid the conversation getting back to the topic of *them*.

She was interrupted, to her relief, when Bryce took a call from his office, spoke hurriedly to someone, and said he was on his way. "Duty calls," he said. "I'll be in touch when Martin has anything on Gellner." He stood, hesitating before he left. "It's been nice seeing you again, Danni."

She nodded, unable to bring herself to reciprocate.

"One thing," she said as he made to go. "Could you get Martin to look into the background of my contact at Carstairs Hall, Peter Conway? *Someone* told Tsang I'd been back at the Hall this week. I'd like to know if I can trust him."

Bryce nodded. "I'll do that."

She watched him shamble from the restaurant, then sat back in the booth and considered Commander Tsang's order to drop the Fairleigh-White case.

She selected another coffee, a double espresso this time, then sub-vocced, "Imp, get through to my medic and request a sick-leave pass. I'm feeling lousy."

"*Sending your stats to OmegaHealth now, Danni.*"

"And then forward the pass to Commander Tsang and tell him I'm taking five days' sick leave, starting today, okay?"

"*Yes, Danni,*" her imp said.

"Oh, and block all calls from Tsang for the duration I'm away from the office."

"*Understood.*"

She drank her coffee, and tried not to dwell on the puppy-dog look in Edouard Bryce's eyes as he'd said goodbye and left the restaurant.

16

In With the New

Kemp blinked the command for his imp to start recording, and murmured, "A little present, Danni. Welcome to Carrasco. You asked for a detailed account of my visit – well, what better than if I actually show you? I hope you enjoy this – not that we can see much yet." With communications channels through the wormhole restricted, and controlled by Gellner's security service, Kemp was recording this to pass to Danni in person when he returned to Earth.

Major Gellner led the way down the umbilical from the shuttle, followed by his security team, and Kemp and the others brought up the rear. The material of the umbilical was transparent, and through the membrane Kemp made out a flat expanse of rock, perhaps half a kilometre across, fringed by a margin of vegetation. The mass looked more like a vast sponge than the jungle he'd been expecting. As if that was not alien enough, the sky was an odd shimmering turquoise, with the sun a huge diffuse orange ball high above.

The corridor terminated in a sealed door, and Gellner turned and said, "I think you'll find that we'll be greeted by quite a reception committee. We're something of a novelty, after all – a delegation from the future."

Gellner joined Connery and the two men conferred; Connery nodded to the security detail, and Kemp watched, curious, as the men moved towards the sealed door with a unified sense of purpose. The door irised open with a loud sucking sound, and Gellner gestured for Connery to lead the security men inside. They filed in one by one, and Gellner turned and gestured for Kemp and the others to follow.

Kemp followed the scientists and found himself in a large, domed communal area filled with twenty or thirty individuals, gathered and waiting for the entrance of the new arrivals.

He sub-vocced, "Strange, but you wouldn't think that simple coveralls could be seen as dated, but there's something about the style of the collars, the cuffs, the cut of the tunics... They're all as one with the dome itself, the retro feel of it. It's as if we're on the set of some old science fiction movie, Danni, and that if I break through the scenery I'll find myself in an interactives studio."

He did a quick headcount; there were twenty-seven men and women present, and his imp's facial recognition program informed him that Rima Cagnac was not one of them. Some were sitting at tables and drinking from plastic mugs, or eating from compartmentalised trays; others had been scanning old-fashioned softscreens, abandoned now; their attention was fixed wholly on the visitors. An uneasy silence prevailed.

The security team moved around the dome, addressing the scientists; evidently questioning them. The individuals nodded in response, some gesturing towards their fellows. Connery and his team brought up images – three-dimensional floating heads that clearly startled the scientists, all the more so as half a dozen of the images depicted the specialists themselves.

"What the...?" Kemp said to himself.

He heard Connery snap, "The following will accompany me: Delgardo, Dupré, Greene, Mallory, Muller and Speilmann."

With obvious reluctance, the six moved from where they had been sitting or standing and joined Connery in the centre of the chamber. With a nod to Gellner, the security man led the six from the dome and back along the corridor to the shuttle.

A hatch irised at the far side of the dome and a man strode

in – a tall, imposing figure in a blue uniform, with broad shoulders and an impressive thatch of silver-grey hair. One of the scientists hurried across to him, evidently explaining what had just happened. The uniformed man dismissed the scientist with a quick word, then crossed to Major Gellner.

"Commander Hertzberger," he said to Gellner. "And my deputy, Lieutenant Vignol," he went on, indicating the slim man who had just joined him.

Kemp had expected Hertzberger to protest at the security team's heavy-handed tactics, but the commander merely smiled and nodded as Gellner introduced the new scientists along with Kemp.

"Now, if I could speak to you in private," Gellner said to Hertzberger.

"Of course," Hertzberger said, and turned to his deputy. "Lieutenant Vignol, please show our visitors to their quarters."

The commander and Gellner moved off across the dome and passed down a conjoining umbilical. Vignol gestured. "This way, ladies and gentlemen."

Under the silent, resentful gaze of the scientists, Vignol led them from the dome along a corridor to a smaller sub-dome. Vignol indicated a hatch, and Kemp stepped through into a narrow berth with a low bunk, a storage locker, and a viewing panel looking out over the clearing. A dispenser on the wall issued sanitised wipes: he wondered if this was in lieu of showers; another dispenser proved to be an old-fashioned coffee machine.

As he stood before the viewing panel, a line of scientists in grey biohazard suits made their way past the shuttle and headed off towards the sponge-like mass of vegetation.

"I don't know what you made of that back there, Danni, but it looked to me like a putsch – the new guard replacing the old. I don't know what the six scientists had done to arouse Gellner's displeasure. And Hertzberger seemed... I don't know... oddly acquiescent." He shook his head. "I don't get it, or am I missing something? Those scientists are eighty years out of date, but it can't be merely that they're being replaced by individuals better suited to the job at hand – or all of them would have been replaced. There's a way of going about informing people that they're surplus to requirements, and it's not marching them out as if they're for the firing squad."

He fell silent, staring through the panel at the dark shape of the shuttle.

"Well, all that aside… Here we are, Danni, Carrasco. I must admit I feel the planet itself is a bit… anti-climactic. What was I expecting? I don't know. It's alien enough, but in some way it doesn't feel *real*. I suppose it's alien in a way that all those interactives didn't prepare me for. And odd, because although I'm here on an alien planet, I'm not really feeling it yet. I'm inside, and I only see the world through windows and on screens. In a strange way I don't feel I'm *here* yet." He laughed. "Right, I'm going to freshen up, then go and talk to a few scientists. I'll try to work out what happened back there – if Major Gellner doesn't object, that is. I wonder where Rima Cagnac might be?"

He closed the program for now, stripped down to the waist, and mopped himself with the wipes.

He found a clean coverall in his backpack and changed. Feeling refreshed, and ready to face the massed curiosity of the scientists, he stepped from his berth and made his way back to the main dome.

The woman scientist who had caught his eye earlier was entering the dome before him, and instantly she was surrounded by a small group of men and women who led her across to a table and plied her with questions. Kemp braced himself for a similar assault – he noted one or two individuals ready to make a move – when Major Gellner approached him from across the dome.

"Inspector, I've briefed Commander Hertzberger about your presence. He'd like to see you in his office. This way."

As he fell into step beside the major, Kemp said, "So the reason for the theatricals on arrival, Major?" When Gellner failed to respond, he went on, "Natural wastage? But, if you don't mind me saying, that was a clumsy way of going about it."

Gellner said, "There's no need for you to involve yourself in that, Inspector."

As Kemp struggled to find a fitting response, they moved along an umbilical to a sub-dome. A hatch sighed open, revealing a small office area. Gellner gestured for him to enter, then turned and retraced his steps.

Relieved that his discussion with Hertzberger would be conducted without Gellner, Kemp entered the dome and the hatch slid shut behind him.

Commander Hertzberger, appearing larger for being in such a constricted space, stepped forward and offered his hand. "Welcome to Carrasco, Inspector Kemp. I hope I can make your stay here a productive one." He spoke English with a heavy accent, oddly formal in construction. "Please, sit down."

He indicated a plastic seat, printed with technology long superseded on Earth: it was rough-edged, its surface pebbled. The commander sat behind a similarly printed desk. "A drink? We have a limited supply of processed *baijiu*, for special occasions. Nothing like the real thing, of course."

Kemp accepted and took a sip from the bright red beaker. Much to his surprise, despite a vaguely chemical harshness, the spirit was drinkable.

"I take it Major Gellner smoothed things over with you, regarding...?" Kemp gestured over his shoulder.

He blinked, and the retinal slide appeared in his lower vision. "Regarding, Inspector?"

Uneasy, Kemp gestured towards the main dome. "The security team's heavy-handed tactics back there."

The commander smiled. "A changeover procedure that we knew was happening all along," he said.

Kemp was not in the least surprised to see that the retinal slide indicated Hertzberger was lying.

"Major Gellner informed me why you are here, and he requested my assistance – which I will be more than willing to give, of course."

The slide moved to the left: this time, the commander was telling the truth.

"I appreciate that," Kemp murmured.

Hertzberger took a mouthful of *baijiu*. "You wish to question Rima Cagnac about the death of her husband in Geneva, shortly before the *Strasbourg* left Earth."

"Not question her. My brief is to find her, take her into custody, and return her to London to assist with the investigation."

"My superiors were aware of the case at the time, but decided that Dr Cagnac should proceed with the mission nevertheless. Such a tragic business... Tell me, is Dr Cagnac a suspect?"

Kemp stared at the contents of his beaker, considering his reply. "Certain evidence has been revealed recently which sheds new light on the case, hence the necessity of my presence. At this stage of the investigation, it would be indelicate to say much more. I'm sure you understand."

Hertzberger smiled. "Of course, of course."

"If you could arrange for Dr Cagnac to–"

"At the moment," Hertzberger interrupted, "Dr Cagnac is on a field trip to a base one hundred kilometres west of here. But I'll contact the team leader forthwith and have him return, without of course alerting Dr Cagnac to the reason."

"How long will they take to get back?" Kemp asked.

The commander shrugged his broad shoulders. "I'll contact my team leader now. As we are reluctant to travel during the hours of darkness, they'll set off in the morning – that's approximately fourteen hours from now. It should take them between a day and a day and a half to get back here – the terrain is not exactly conducive to rapid transit. Cagnac should be with us in two days from now: that is, forty-four hours. In the meantime, I will arrange to have someone show you around the various domes – and perhaps you would care to look over the surrounding terrain at some point?"

"I'd like that," Kemp said, thinking of Danni, but also invigorated by the prospect of setting foot on this new world.

"From the little you've seen of the world so far," Hertzberger went on, "you will no doubt have noted that it is unlike anything we as a species have ever experienced. Carrasco has subverted all of our preconceptions. We're confident that the manifold difficulties we are facing at the moment can be overcome." He hesitated. "The atmosphere contains certain pathogens that have proven fatal–"

Kemp leaned forward. "People have died?" He wondered why no one had thought to mention this until now. Cover-up, or a mere avoidance of unpleasant truths?

"My deputy was foolish – she went outside without sufficiently ensuring that her suit was airtight. Others have fallen ill, two with fatal outcomes. Of those still ill, the medics are confident they'll pull through, especially now that we have the latest medical expertise to hand. Not only that, but my specialists are certain we can overcome whatever pathogens are in the air, long-term. I have every confidence we can tame Carrasco and establish a successful colony."

Kemp's retinal slide showed that this was all true.

Hertzberger smiled. "Inspector, the technology extant on Earth when we left, eighty years ago, was deemed sufficient to initiate the terraforming of extra-solar worlds. In the decades that have elapsed, I can only assume that science and technology has come on in leaps and bounds."

"I'd like to think so," Kemp said.

The commander's wristcom pinged – it was a ridiculously cumbersome, antiquated model – and an image hung in the air before him. Hertzberger exchanged a few hurried words with the caller, then killed the image.

"Duty calls, I'm afraid," the commander said. "You've had a long and tiring journey, and Major Gellner mentioned that European time is approaching midnight, so I will keep you no longer. In the morning, perhaps, you would like to accompany one of my scientists on a little excursion, no?"

"I'd like nothing more, Commander."

They stood and shook hands, and Kemp retraced his steps from the office and along the umbilical to the main dome. There, rather than be accosted by scientists eager to bombard him with questions about the Earth he'd recently left, he crossed the dome and ducked into the umbilical leading to his berth.

In its welcome sanctuary, he stood before the viewing panel and stared out.

The bloated orange sun – perhaps five times the size of Sol – hung above the dark green horizon. When he looked at the sun his retinals darkened and he saw a dark speck against the glare – was that the inner planet, Dulcinea, racing on its nine-day orbit around its primary? Danni would know.

He looked away from the sun and surveyed the research base's clearing. Nothing moved out there. The shuttle crouched in silhouette like a predatory insect.

He ordered his imp to record the scene.

"So there you have it, Danni," he sub-vocced. "Rima Cagnac will be back in a couple of days, and in the interim I get to go outside and talk to the scientists. Don't worry, I'll record everything for you."

He paused, then went on, "As for Hertzberger's lies about what Gellner's up to... Well, hopefully I'll find out more, in time."

Soon, with luck, he would arrest Rima Cagnac and make his way back to Earth and the reassuring familiarity of life in twenty-second century London, and the return journey couldn't come soon enough.

"And so to bed."

17

Cold Witness

Kemp awoke to turquoise dawn light slanting through the wall panel and the sound of something dropping into the slot beside his bunk. He sat up and discovered that his breakfast had been delivered in the form of a compartmentalised tray. He pulled a wipe from the dispenser and rubbed his face, then smoothed down his hair. Sitting on his bunk, he ate a simple meal of protein bars, dried fruit and coffee.

He was dialling for another coffee when a tapping sounded on the hatch of his berth. He unlocked the door to find a small, thick-set man in a green coverall standing hesitantly in the corridor.

"Inspector Kemp? Jimmy Ranatunga," his visitor said. "It's a pleasure to meet you. Mijnheer Hertzberger mentioned–"

"Ah, yes – an excursion."

Ranatunga smiled. "Well, I wouldn't call it that – more of a short tour of the area."

"I was just about to…" Kemp indicated his coffee. "Can I get you one?"

"I'd love one, thank you. There's no real hurry."

Kemp dialled for a second cup and they sat on the bunk as they drank. He accessed his lieware program.

Ranatunga said, "I wondered if I'd find you here."

Kemp raised an eyebrow. "Where did you think I'd be?"

"Well…" The young man considered his words. "Last night we drew lots to see who'd show you around–"

"And you lost, right?"

Ranatunga laughed. "Well, as it happens, yes – Jenny Vahota won." He frowned. "But this morning she was seen heading away from the domes, into the jungle. It was assumed you were with her, though my colleague who saw her couldn't say for sure. So I thought I'd check the biohazard suits in the airlock. Only one was taken."

Kemp stopped eating and looked at the young man. "Is that usual – for a colleague to head off alone, unannounced?"

"We usually go out in pairs, but then we're in an unusual situation, Mr Kemp. I mean, after what happened yesterday."

"Ah, you mean with Gellner's men?" he said. "You didn't know about the change-over beforehand?"

"It was news to us, Inspector."

Kemp nodded: Ranatunga was telling the truth. "Yet Commander Hertzberger seemed to be in the know."

Ranatunga shrugged, then said with an appeal in his tone, "Do you know what's going on, Inspector Kemp? You're part of Gellner's team, I take it?"

"I suppose so, technically. But between you and me… Look, there's no love lost between Gellner and myself, and what happened last night – I certainly wasn't informed about it."

"They took six of my colleagues – six good people who'd sacrificed a lot to come on this mission. And it didn't stop there. Last night they rounded up ten members of our security team and locked them in the shuttle with the scientists." Ranatunga shook his head. "We'd just like to know what's going on, is all."

"Have you questioned Commander Hertzberger?"

"Of course, we sent a delegation to see him yesterday evening." Ranatunga shrugged. "He more or less told us to mind our own business."

"The scientists and the security people who Gellner's men took… were they affiliated in some way – politically, ideologically? Has there been any dissent or unrest here?"

The young man shrugged his broad shoulders. "No unrest, and no affiliations that I know of. Politics..." He smiled disarmingly at Kemp. "I like to think we left that fifty lightyears and eight decades behind us. We have more important things to think about, just now."

"Have there been any differences of opinion in the camp? Arguments about protocol, procedure, how to go about surveying the planet?" It was hard to believe that dissent could have grown so rapidly in a research base that had been established for less than three weeks.

"There are always differences of opinion when you get two or more scientists in any one place." He paused, frowning.

"Go on," Kemp prompted.

"I was just thinking about Jenny, going off like that. It doesn't make sense. She was looking forward to meeting you – quizzing you," he said with a smile. "You're in demand, Mr Kemp. We left Earth eighty years ago, and things were pretty bleak back then. The situation between the New California and China, the climate catastrophe..."

Kemp smiled. "Ah, yes, that's what it was called, back then. The Catastrophe."

"And now?"

"We're still living with it, but we get by."

The young man nodded. "Inspector Kemp, I come from Vanuatu. By the time I joined the mission to Carrasco, we'd lost dozens of islands in the archipelago."

He stopped and stared at Kemp, something pleading in his gaze.

Kemp swallowed, unwilling to break the news to Ranatunga until he was one hundred per cent sure. He sub-vocced, "Imp – the status of Vanuatu?"

A split second later his imp replied in its impersonal BBC tones, "*The island chain of Vanuatu was declared a World Disaster Zone in 2150, after sea-level rises and a succession of natural disasters through the 2140s, including super-cyclones and earthquakes, destroyed much of the capital Port-Vila. Much of the island nation's population was evacuated over the succeeding decade, and the surviving parts of the archipelago retain World Natural Heritage status."*

"It could only have got worse, couldn't it?" Ranatunga said in barely a whisper, but with a desperate note of hope.

"Most of the world, particularly around the tropics, has suffered," Kemp told him. "Vanuatu was mostly evacuated." Kemp regretted his choice of words immediately. That *mostly* spoke volumes.

"It was inevitable, really. But I always cherished the hope that something, some miracle..."

"I'm sorry."

"I didn't have much family there. Strong family ties would have made me an unsuitable candidate for the Carrasco venture. But I had friends, memories. Strange to think that the island where I grew up..." He shook his head. "It was a beautiful place, Inspector Kemp."

He finished his coffee. "And New California and China?"

"The power now resides in Europe and China. Most of the old US is chaotic, although New California is still a major player. An uneasy peace exists between Europe and China, with creeping Chinese imperialism and industrial might slowly gaining the upper hand." He laughed without humour. "Some people – nationalists in my country – call London Little Beijing."

Ranatunga looked up and stared through the viewing panel. He was quiet for a time, then said, "And why are you on Carrasco, Inspector Kemp, if you're not with Gellner's team? What's your official position?"

"I'm a detective, based in London–"

Ranatunga smiled. "Way out of your normal beat, then."

"You can say that again." Kemp hesitated. "I'm here to talk to Rima Cagnac."

Ranatunga looked up. "Rima? About... about what happened back on Earth, right, eighty years ago?"

"Did she ever mention it to you?"

"No, never. Rima and I work together. I'm her deputy medical officer, but there's so much to do here..." He shrugged. "But there were rumours–"

"Rumours?"

"That Rima was in some way involved, that she was suspected of the murder for a time." Ranatunga hesitated. "Is she still a suspect?"

"Let's just say that I need to eliminate her from my investigation," Kemp said. "So... she never talked about what happened before she left Earth?"

The young man shook his head. "No, nothing at all. Remember, we were asleep for those eighty years. Events of that time are still fresh. Raw. I like and respect Rima, but we aren't that close. I am not surprised she chose not to talk about what happened, and I respect her enough not to ask. You might do better talking to Jayne Waterford, in ecology. I don't know whether they knew each other on Earth, but they were certainly close here on Carrasco."

Kemp made a mental note of the name. "Thanks. I'll do that."

Ranatunga stood up and gestured towards the hatch. "So how about that tour, Inspector?"

Ranatunga led Kemp through the main dome and along a corridor to a small room with a hatch giving on to an airlock. Half a dozen biohazard suits hung on the walls; complete from head to foot, they looked like deflated skins. Kemp had worn similar suits in disaster-training exercises and simulations over the years, and did not relish the prospect of pulling one on. If it weren't for the prospect of recording his experiences for Danni, he might easily have opted to stay in the dome.

Ranatunga said as they suited up, "You've no doubt been made aware of all the safety protocols. All that I can add is watch your footing when we're in the vegetation itself. You'll find it spongy and a little unstable. Even if you do go over, these suits are pretty tough, but it's best to be on the safe side. You ready?"

Kemp was anything but ready. The suit clung in all the wrong places, and while it had appeared big and clumsy hung on the wall, now that it was about to be his only protection from a hostile, alien environment it felt far too flimsy and insubstantial. He flexed his arms, and felt the suit fabric yield easily. He felt as if he were in fancy dress.

He gave the thumbs up, then blinked to initiate recording.

The first hatch sighed open and the two men stepped into the airlock. The hatch sealed behind them and Ranatunga pressed the control to open the exit.

The hatch opened and Kemp stared out on the alien world.

They were facing a bank of vegetation a couple of hundred metres away, with nothing man-made – no shuttle or dome – between them and the bank of tangled greenery. The contrast between the grey expanse of granite, the verdant vegetation, and the misty turquoise sky was startling – and very, very alien.

Kemp took a step outside and stumbled, almost falling. If anyone said anything he would insist it was due to the subtle difference in gravity, and the unfamiliar grip of the boots, and not at all a nervousness that was verging on panic.

He straightened, and they started to walk.

Despite his earlier somewhat anticlimactic feeling that Carrasco resembled nothing more than an old sci-fi film set, now, as he followed Ranatunga across the rock towards the jungle, the absolute other worldliness of the place overcame him. He was on an alien world fifty lightyears from Earth, and nothing at all in his line of vision, other than the suited figure of the young doctor, was familiar. He thought back to his father, almost obsessively playing the old interactives of the *Strasbourg* disaster. What would he have made of his own son setting foot on another world? Particularly in his later years,

Kemp had not been close to his father, but now, strangely, he felt the tug of family bonds.

In the sky above the vegetation, something swooped, and Kemp made out the stingray shape of a creature. "What the...!" he called out, watching the animal turn and bank in a graceful parabola.

"Your first *bona fide* alien being," Ranatunga laughed.

"I... for once I'm lost for words, Danni," he sub-vocced. "I hope you can sense the atmosphere of the place. This is nothing like Kew Gardens."

He smiled at the lame joke and followed Ranatunga as the young man pointed to the margin of the vegetation where a track, like a rat-run in terrestrial shrubbery only much larger, disappeared into the closely packed sponge-like growth.

They approached the vegetation and entered the tunnel, about two metres in diameter. The fibres gave a little underfoot, making Kemp sway from side to side, and he recalled Ranatunga's earlier injunction to watch his footing.

At one point Kemp called ahead, "What made this tunnel?"

Ranatunga turned and smiled through his faceplate. "This one is man-made, Inspector. Sorry to disappoint you. But other, smaller ones are created by burrowing animals, creatures akin to rats and rabbits. We've discovered some larger tunnels we suspect are just natural features of the growth, like the lateral chambers in loofah sponges."

Twenty metres further on, Ranatunga came to a halt and indicated a tunnel to the left, perhaps a metre wide. Kemp peered at him through the aqueous twilight. "This climbs to the surface of the vegetation, and the view from up there is... spectacular, to say the least."

Ranatunga led the way, climbing ahead of Kemp. The slope angled upwards, and at one point Kemp was forced to move on hands and knees through a gloom that grew steadily lighter as they climbed.

"I hope you're enjoying this, Danni?" he sub-vocced. "Here

I am, on hands and knees on an alien planet. What I go through to capture local colour."

Above him, Ranatunga called out, "We're here." He reached out and took Kemp's arm, hauling him up the last metre onto the summit of a rocky outcrop that emerged from the vegetation. The young man moved away from the aperture and sat down cross-legged a few metres away.

Kemp lowered himself down carefully beside Ranatunga and took in the view.

"You're right," he said. "It is spectacular."

They were perhaps twenty metres above the level of the encampment of conjoined domes, showing like beads of milk against the grey rock, with the shuttle beyond them. What struck Kemp as breathtaking was not the human features of the landscape but the alien aspect of the planet – the endless rolling expanse of green, like a sea made vegetal, the roiling turquoise sky above it, and directly ahead, perhaps ten degrees above the distant horizon, the great swollen hemisphere of Mu Arae, a molten orange semi-circle like nothing Kemp had seen before.

"Beautiful," he said, more to himself than to the young man. "Isn't it?"

The stingray creatures – dozens of them – swooped and banked, and clouds of tiny flies drifted across the sky in great shoals.

Ranatunga reached out and touched his arm. "Look," he said, pointing into the sky.

Kemp looked up, and was about to ask the young man what it was – suspecting some natural feature, the Carrascan equivalent of the Aurora Borealis.

"*The quantum lattice,*" his imp informed him.

"The wormhole!" he said.

Ranatunga nodded. "Opening to allow another shuttle through. I wonder what surprise we're in for this time?"

As they stared up into the sky, the hexagon of light pulsed

light blue against the turquoise backdrop like a gemstone. It was small, perhaps the apparent size of a golf ball held at arm's length, and Kemp found it hard to credit that the simple luminous feature was the result of an incredible technology that connected this sector of space to that above his homeworld.

"A miracle," Ranatunga breathed.

Kemp smiled in agreement as he stared up at the pulsating light show.

Ranatunga said, "It was my life's ambition, Inspector – when I was growing up. To leave Earth, live on another world. I knew that my island home was increasingly vulnerable, and I didn't much like the world beyond the archipelago. When I applied to join the mission, and was accepted, I fully expected never to see Earth again. And do you know something?"

He paused, and Kemp realised that the young man was in the grip of a strong emotion. "To be honest, I don't want to go back. I want to make a go of life on Carrasco, which is ironic, in a way. On one hand I want to remain here – want to be able to remain here – but on the other I don't want humankind doing to Carrasco what we've done to Earth."

"It won't necessarily be so," Kemp said.

Ranatunga went on as if he hadn't heard him. "When I came out of resuscitation and saw Carrasco from orbit... It was odd, but I had the feeling that I was coming home, though it was an alien world. I saw myself staying here for the rest of my life – I certainly didn't want to do my work here, then submit myself to another eighty years in cold sleep and wake up to find myself on an Earth unrecognisable from the planet I left over one hundred and sixty years ago."

Kemp stared at the young man. "But..." He shook his head. "But you wouldn't need to go back into cold sleep."

Ranatunga turned to him, smiling through the visor. "Ah, but I didn't know that immediately on waking up, did I?"

"You didn't?" Kemp said, non-plussed.

"It was only then that Commander Hertzberger sprang the

big surprise – that the ship was carrying the technology, and the engineers, capable of opening up a wormhole back to Earth."

Kemp shook his head. "Are you telling me that you didn't know – that no one aboard the *Strasbourg* knew about the quantum lattice until you were resuscitated?"

"That's right, only Hertzberger and Captain Fernandez."

"But why on earth did they keep it from you?"

"That's what we wanted to know," Ranatunga said. "Hertzberger gave us some spiel about it being for security reasons – they didn't want the Chinese getting wind that we had the quantum lattice tech." He shook his head. "But I don't know… it just didn't sound right."

Kemp grunted. "I'll say."

He sub-vocced. "Danni, I think I need another little chat with Commander Hertzberger."

"So," the young man said, "now planet Earth is just a shuttle ride away, and that's frightening. You see, I still don't want to go back there…" He leaned forward suddenly, then pointed. "Look."

Kemp peered down at the encampment. He made out a file of a dozen figures in biohazard suits moving towards the vegetation below where he and Ranatunga sat. The leading figure gestured towards the jungle, and Kemp had the impression that it was Connery, commanding his men.

Glancing at his wristcom display on the back of his glove, Ranatunga said, "Right, I think it's time I was getting back to work."

He stood and made his way back to the entrance of the tunnel, and Kemp followed.

Kemp made his way down the corridor to the sub-dome where he'd spoken to Commander Hertzberger the night before. He paused before the hatch and blinked. The retinal slide appeared in the bottom-left of his vision.

The hatch irised open, but it was not Hertzberger that Kemp

saw in the cramped office. His deputy, Lieutenant Vignol turned from the viewing panel. "Yes?" He sounded impatient, and his dark eyes flashed at Kemp.

"I was hoping to speak with Commander Hertzberger."

"So was I, but he's out with the security detail."

"I see," Kemp said, then added, "Do you know what they're doing out there?"

Vignol shook his head. "I'm sorry, I don't."

Kemp's retinal slide moved to the right: a lie.

"Do you know how long he might be?" Kemp asked.

"I don't," Vignol said again. "Can I be of assistance?"

Kemp stepped further into the room, facing the slight, dark-haired man. "I wanted to have a word with the commander about the quantum lattice – and specifically about the fact that its existence was sprung on the crew only when they awoke from resuscitation."

Vignol nodded. "That's correct, yes."

"It seems a strange procedure to follow, keeping such a thing from one's colleagues."

"Commander Hertzberger explained that it was an order from high up in ESO," he said. "For security reasons. They didn't want the knowledge of the technology leaking to competitors – China, or any of the Pacific Treaty Group – before the *Strasbourg* set out for Carrasco."

"And you believe that?"

"I have no reason to disbelieve it."

The slide slipped to the left. Vignol was telling the truth.

So either the deception played on the crew of the *Strasbourg* was to subvert the possibility of a security leak, or Hertzberger was keeping the truth from his second-in-command.

Vignol smiled. "If you don't believe me," he said, "you can always talk to Captain Fernandez – he was the only one, beside the commander, in the know about the lattice. I was Fernandez's deputy on the *Strasbourg* and even I was unaware of our surprise cargo."

Kemp nodded. "I'll do that," he said, moving to the door. "Do you know where I'll find him?"

"He spends most of his time in the main dome. If he isn't there, I'm sure someone will know of his whereabouts."

Kemp thanked him and left the office, pondering on the secrecy resulting from the paranoid politics of eighty years ago.

Thirty men and women occupied the main dome, and a silence fell as he stepped through the irising hatch. Kemp could understand the hostile attention; the scientists evidently had him down as one of Gellner's underlings.

His imp said, *"Captain Fernandez – the tall male in the centre of the–"*

"I've studied the case files," Kemp interrupted.

Captain Fernandez was not hard to find: a well-built, swarthy man in his forties, standing with a group at the far side of the dome.

Kemp crossed to him and said, "Captain Fernandez?"

The man turned.

Kemp went on, aware of the stares from the scientists in the captain's company. "If you don't mind, I'd like a word."

"About the conduct of your security team?" Fernandez snapped.

"I assure you that Major Gellner and his men, or their conduct, have nothing to do with me."

Fernandez gestured. "If you'd care to follow me."

He led Kemp from the dome and down a corridor to a narrow berth littered with clothing, discarded cups, and an antiquated softscreen cycling through a series of images depicting what Kemp guessed was rural Spain.

Fernandez turned and leaned against the outer wall, folded his arms and stared at Kemp. "If you're not part of his entourage, Mr Kemp, then I wonder if you could tell me just what Gellner's men are up to?"

Kemp shrugged. "You mean, above and beyond arresting and incarcerating scientists and security personnel? I thought you might be able to tell *me*, Captain."

Fernandez narrowed his eyes. "I've no idea. I don't know who Gellner represents, or what he's doing here."

The retinal slide showed that he was telling the truth.

"As I said, I'm not part of his security team." Kemp hesitated. "I've just seen a contingent of security head into the vegetation..."

"They're searching for Jennifer Vahota. Apparently, she's on their wanted list."

"She found out about it, and she fled?"

"So it would appear."

"But... where would someone flee to on Carrasco? How long would she last out there?"

"Our kit may be primitive by your standards, Mr Kemp, but it's still pretty sophisticated. Our excursion suits are built to last. They recycle bodily waste and fluids, they harvest fresh nutrients and oxygen from the environment. She could last a long time out there."

"She's wanted... for what, exactly?"

"You tell me," Fernandez grunted. "Why not ask Mijnheer Hertzberger? He seems to know what's going on around here."

Kemp stared at the captain. "I thought you and the commander..."

"Yes?"

"I thought you and he would be working more closely together," he said, "considering the fact that only the commander and yourself knew about the quantum lattice."

"That was then," the captain said. "Since we arrived on Carrasco... Let's just say that Hertzberger's been keeping his own council, shall we?"

Kemp nodded, and asked, "Do you know ESO's reasoning behind the decision to keep the crew in the dark?"

"Security, as I understand it. Understandably, they didn't

want knowledge of the quantum lattice leaking to rival powers. Protecting commercial interests was a part of it, I suspect. It was decided to inform the crew when there was no chance of a leak – in orbit around Carrasco."

The slide went to the left; the captain was telling him the truth.

"And you, personally, were informed, when?"

"Hertzberger himself told me just a day before we embarked from L5." Fernandez stared across at Kemp and smiled. "If I may say, for someone who claims they're not part of the security team, you ask a lot of questions. Just what do you want on Carrasco, Mr Kemp?"

"Inspector Kemp," he corrected. "I'm here to talk to Rima Cagnac. I understand that you were acquainted with her, back on Earth?"

Fernandez opened his mouth in a silent "Ah". He moved from before the panel and sat on his bunk. "Rima and I... Yes, Inspector. I knew Rima very well."

Kemp stared at the man, surprised by the sudden change in his demeanour. At the same time, it came to him that he was interrogating someone – a prime witness – from eighty years ago.

He also recalled that his instructions from Tsang had been clear and to the point: find Rima Cagnac and return her to Earth for interrogation. Tsang had told him he was not to question her when he found her, but he had said nothing about interrogating *other* witnesses.

"I understand that you were with her in Geneva at the time of her husband's murder?"

Fernandez held his gaze. "I met her there that day, yes."

He was telling the truth.

"On ESO business?"

Fernandez hesitated. "Yes, but there was more."

"Go on."

"I... Rima is a special woman, Inspector. The truth is that I was a little infatuated with her."

True, again.

"And did she return those sentiments, Captain?"

Fernandez smiled, ruefully. "She was friendly, no more. That day, we met in my hotel suite. I told her my feelings–"

The slider wavered, as if Fernandez was skirting around the truth rather than lying outright.

"What was her reaction?"

"She said she was married – and I recall saying 'Yes, to a man you'll soon be leaving and never seeing again, while we'll be together on Carrasco...'."

This was the truth.

"So let's get this straight," Kemp said. "You were with Rima Cagnac in your suite at the time her husband was being stabbed to death?"

Fernandez looked away. "Yes, that's right."

To Kemp's surprise, the slide moved clearly to the right: Fernandez was lying.

Kemp said, "You met her in your suite, on the 10th of January, 2110?"

Fernandez flashed an angry look. "Yes – as I've told you more than once."

The retinal slide indicated that the captain was telling the truth, and for a few seconds Kemp was mystified.

Then he understood the reason for the ambivalence.

He said, "I believe you when you said that you met Rima in your room on the *day* her husband was murdered, Captain – but you were lying when you claimed you were with her *at the exact time her husband was killed*. Am I right?"

Fernandez stared at him, and the image of a cornered rat came to mind.

"How...?" he said, floundering.

"Am I right?" Kemp pressed.

Fernandez was silent for a time, then murmured, "Yes."

"So... what happened, exactly?"

After a while, staring down at his clasped hands, Fernandez

said, "I met her that morning, the 10th. I told her beforehand it was about the mission, that I had a few questions. We were close – friends, that's all. But... well, I wanted more. That morning, I made it obvious – and she was... she was appalled. She fled." He grinned, ruefully. "She slapped me and ran off. Later... she messaged me with the news that her husband was dead, and that we had to meet. I agreed, of course. When we met, she pleaded for me to lie for her – to say I was with her all that afternoon. It was a little place in the back streets, without surveillance cameras, so with luck her movements wouldn't be traced."

"And you agreed to lie for her?" Kemp asked.

Fernandez stared at the wall. "I would have done so, anyway – I didn't believe she could have killed her husband. But she pressured me–"

"Pressured? How, exactly?"

"She pointed out that the police might suspect that it was *me* who'd killed her husband – prompted by jealousy. Killed him in a jealous rage. So... so I agreed to lie for her, as she would lie for me." He looked up at Kemp. "I swear, Inspector, I'm telling the truth."

Kemp nodded. "I believe you," he said, because the retinal slide confirmed that, all those years ago, Fernandez had agreed to lie for the sake of the woman he loved. He reminded himself that for Fernandez these events were still recent, still raw.

Fernandez looked up at Kemp. "And I have the utmost confidence that Rima didn't kill her husband."

"Even though, after leaving you that morning, she had the time and the opportunity to cross the city and do just that?"

Fernandez hung his head and murmured, "But Rima could kill no one, Inspector."

"What makes you so sure?"

"I know her. She wouldn't do a thing like that... And anyway, there was no surveillance around my hotel, but if she'd returned to her home, cameras or phone signals would have picked her up, wouldn't they? And if there had been such evidence, then your people would have arrested her straight away, not let her leave for another planet."

The captain's argument was a good one, but all it proved was that *if* Rima had murdered her husband, then it was not a spontaneous act – for if she had returned without malice aforethought then, as Fernandez said, there would be evidence. No, all this demonstrated was that if she had returned home then she had chosen her route and method to avoid detection: evidence of cold-blooded murder, rather than a crime of passion.

Kemp thanked the captain and left the berth, making his way to the communal dome where he found Commander Hertzberger holding forth to a group of scientists.

He hovered on the periphery of the crowd until he caught the commander's attention, and gestured that he'd like a quiet word.

Hertzberger finished addressing his audience, then excused himself and moved off to one side with Kemp.

"It's about the quantum lattice," Kemp said. "I understand that you didn't inform the crew until after resuscitation?"

"I was merely following the instructions of my superiors at ESO."

Hertzberger sounded convincing, Kemp thought – but the retinal slide showed he was lying.

"If that will be all, Inspector...?" Hertzberger turned and made his way across the dome.

Kemp watched him go, wondering why Commander Hertzberger had lied to his crew if it was not, as he claimed, on the instructions of his superiors at ESO.

18

Footprints in the Snow

Danni met Bryce two days later, at the South Bank Water Park. She stood on the raised embankment of Queen's Walk, the Thames to her left and the sprawl of Jubilee Marshes to her right. Here, large areas of the land by the Thames had been rewilded as part of a managed retreat from rising sea levels, the land turned to lagoon and marsh as a natural buffer zone against the flooding. Now it was a surreal landscape of wilderness and great concrete buildings like the Sinopec Festival Hall, their lower storeys sealed and reinforced against the surrounding water.

In the marshes, a herd of a dozen or so water buffalo munched on the reeds, crunching the ice with every step. It was, as ever this winter, bitterly cold, and Danni wore only a thin coat, finding the chill an invigorating change from the nausea she was experiencing lately.

Ed Bryce appeared in the mouth of the underwater walkway that passed under the Hungerford Bridge. He saw her, raised a hand, and shrugged his way out of his big camel-hair coat as he approached.

"Here," he said, trying to drape it across her shoulders. "You'll catch your death of–"

"I'm fine," she said with a tight smile, stepping away so that the coat flapped in mid-air. "Put it back on, Ed, you're shivering already."

That was one significant difference between Ed and her father: whereas her father had never been happier than when outdoors, his sleeves rolled up, Ed was a man of the interior, happiest staring at a screen, talking rings around the opposition in a courtroom, or sitting with a frothy beer in the darkest corner of an ancient back-street pub.

"You do realise, don't you," he said, "that if your main concern is privacy, then it's far easier to eavesdrop out in the open than if we had met indoors. A directional mic from the other side of the river would pick up every word we say."

"I do know that, Ed," she said. "I *am* a detective. I just like it here, a wild place in the heart of the capital. I…" She shrugged, unsure what she'd been trying to say.

"Are you okay?" he asked, over-solicitous as ever.

"Why did you want to meet?" she asked. "Have you found something?"

"I've been thinking over what we said before," he said.

They'd spoken of much, last time they had met, both personal and professional. Was this going to be some kind of grand declaration of love? She didn't think she could handle that right now.

"I've had Martin Khalsa looking into our friend Major Gellner," he said, and Danni felt a rush of guilt to feel so relieved that he wanted to talk about professional matters.

"Who is he?" Danni asked.

"Well, that's the thing. Even Martin hasn't been able to find much on him."

Bryce pulled the big coat back on and buttoned it up to the throat. They started to walk, and Danni was grateful for the non-slip walkway – the only surface not rimed in thick ice.

"He does work for European Security, and we pulled his employment file."

"You…?" Danni said no more. Bryce made no secret of crossing all kinds of lines that would get a police officer like her fired and very probably thrown into jail.

"It tells us his name – Mikhail Andreas Gellner – and that he has an apartment in Chelsea, and another in München. We have all his biometric data. We know how he moves and walks, and the precise distances, down to fractions a millimetre, between all his facial recognition loci, but absolutely nothing about who he actually is."

They came to where the walkway dipped to pass under Hungerford Bridge. Here the path was enclosed by walls blown from thick glass, coated green and brown with algae, and the waters of the Thames lapped at waist height. A busker played on a stringed instrument Danni didn't recognise, something Eastern. They let the conversation lapse until they emerged again, the grey bulk of the Sinopec Festival Hall rising to their right.

"What's the connection between the Gellner family and the Whites?" Danni asked.

"We know a little more about Marius Gellner. Born near Augsburg in 2060. Distinguished military service, respected in his community, blah blah blah. Nothing that helps us. We know he was an associate of both Sebastian and Randolph White, and we can assume he was in the family's employ, although personnel records for the White portfolio of companies all that time ago are hard to pin down. We can assume there are bonds of loyalty between the two families, dating back to that time. That would explain why his grandson, our Major Gellner, appears to be in their pay, as well as that of the European Security Agency."

"We're just assuming that, though, aren't we? That it's a grandfather-grandson relationship. Could Martin widen the search, just in case it's a more tenuous link? Great-nephew, or even something more removed. Maybe our search parameters are too tight."

"Maybe, but Martin does think of most things."

"How about that ID data you said Martin copied? Can we run comparisons on Marius and the major? Sometimes physical mapping can be used to establish how closely related two individuals are."

"Not well enough to stand up in court."

"But enough to inform an investigation. Anything that might help us pin down who Gellner is, and why he's pursuing this case in the way he is... That's all I'm asking."

Bryce raised an arm to indicate steps leading up into the Festival Hall. They passed inside, and the glass doors slid shut behind them. Bryce heaved a loud sigh, before reaching to help Danni with her coat. They emerged into a coffee bar that looked busier than it actually was, with faux-customers projected at the tables around the entrance. They took a table by wide windows overlooking the river.

"Any progress with anything else?" Danni asked. The last two days had been full of dead ends for her.

"We still don't really know what's behind it all," Bryce said. "Why dig up a case from eighty years ago? Why send the police fifty lightyears to arrest a suspect?"

"Someone is scared," Danni said. "Of Rima Cagnac, and what she might know, what she might reveal. Perhaps she knows the White family secrets – all the corruption and dirty dealing that a family like that is almost certainly up to its elbows in."

"I wonder... Perhaps she used those secrets to secure her place on the Carrasco mission?" Bryce suggested.

"Then why would that make her someone to silence *now*?"

"Well, if she used those secrets to blackmail her way onto the mission, the Whites might well have helped her, content to send her on her way to the stars – out of sight, out of mind. But now that the prospect of near-instantaneous interstellar travel has opened up, perhaps the heirs to the White fortunes are concerned that she might re-emerge? What corporate threads might she pull that might unravel the White Foundation?"

It was a theory, at least, and better than anything they'd come up with yet.

"We need to look into who's running the Foundation now,"

Danni said. "And see if we can work out what they're so scared of."

"Neither of us has raised the biggest question of all yet," Bryce said. "All our theorising is based on the assumption that they wanted to get Cagnac back so they could control her, stop her from spilling whatever dark family secrets she has. But if that were the case... Why did Commander Tsang send a poorly regarded, dead-end, cold-case detective like Gordon Kemp to make the arrest?"

"But he didn't, did he?" Danni pointed out. "They wanted to send *me*."

Bryce stared at her, as if forcing himself not to answer quickly, measuring his words. "So why couldn't you go?" he finally said.

Danni swallowed. She should tell him. She knew that. But the words wouldn't come.

"You see," Bryce went on, "before Gordon left, we went for a couple of last drinks, and he told me something very interesting. He told me why you couldn't go."

She stared at him. He knew. Which meant he had almost certainly done the arithmetic, and was at least aware of the possibility...

"This is why I called today, Danni. This is why I had to see you." He put a hand on hers, and for once she found it comforting rather than intrusive. "No, not because we really need to talk about this – although, of course, we do. But because of what else I've found out..."

Now Danni was confused. The look on his face. The switch from deeply personal to something else. "What, Ed? What have you found out?"

"You're not going to like this, but hear me out. When I learned of... your news... I asked Martin to check out your imp."

She stared at him, shocked. "You had him snoop on my personal data?"

"Hear me out. It was irresponsible and underhand of me. I just wanted to know... the probabilities. The timings. To know if I might possibly be the father of your baby."

Danni sat there shaking her head, but she said nothing. She would hear him out.

"Martin warned me that every digital intrusion leaves a footprint," he went on, "and he couldn't guarantee that his incursion wouldn't be detected. But then he found *another* footprint: someone else had been snooping on you, Danni. Martin tracked that probe back to source. It was Commander Tsang's office. He's been tracking you, monitoring you. That's how he knew you'd been back to Carstairs Hall–"

"And that was how he knew I was pregnant."

"He knew you were pregnant even *before* he told you that you would be going to Carrasco, Danni."

She shook her head. "He knew I'd be unable to go, even when he told me I was the first choice? So... he planned to send Gordon all along."

"But why send Gordon? As I said before, he's poorly regarded by his superiors. He's a, shall we say, *independent*-minded cop who's willing to bend the rules to get results, and he has a history of over-stepping the mark. It's easy to see him as near retirement with very few shits to give – easy to push around, and perhaps slow-witted and lazy enough to be easily outsmarted."

"What you're saying is, he's expendable," Danni said. "He's been set up, hasn't he?"

Bryce nodded. "And right now, he's fifty lightyears away, completely isolated, and I don't have the faintest idea what we can do to help."

19

Captive

Rima woke encased in vegetation, long tendrils coiled spring-like around her arms and legs. Her mind was a fug, thoughts confused, scrambled. A dark veil lifting slowly, slowly.

She was not encased: she was imprisoned. Those coils were not a natural settling of vegetation, but a deliberate entanglement, too precisely positioned to be a chance configuration: manacles of living, pulsing tissue.

She screamed, the sound deafening within the confines of her helmet. The sound cut off abruptly. As she exhaled with the scream, the tendrils tightened across her chest, and she panicked that she might never be able to breathe in again.

She could see nothing, her visor obscured by growths. She wondered how deeply she lay embedded in the jungle.

Rima forced herself to inhale deeply, relieved that the tendrils across her chest relaxed as she did so. She held the breath, felt her heart rate slowing. Now was not a time for tachycardia and panic.

"Franco? Are you there?"

The comms channel hissed static back at her. Then – thank whatever god there might be – she heard a faint reply: "Rima? You there?" A pause, then he added in tones of awe, "Just how damned fascinating is this?"

If it had not been obvious before, then this response highlighted just how unlike Franco she was.

"Are you okay?"

"Hell, yeah," he said.

"What happened? Did we escape the aliens?" She remembered the vaguely glimpsed grey figures scurrying through the confines of the jungle tunnel.

"Escape? Well I wouldn't exactly say that."

She sensed movement then. Pressure against her body, as if a weight pressed from above, cushioned by the springy vegetation. Then a scrabbling sensation, the tendrils that closed around her being pulled apart.

Light blinded her for a moment, just as she felt a release of pressure and the undergrowth parted from around her.

When her eyes adjusted, she saw a grey face peering down at her, oriented at one-eighty degrees so that for a moment she was reminded of the lack of up and down when she had been in freefall. Then the being was leaning over her.

The face vanished, then a moment later it – or another, different, creature – leaned over from the side. Large almond-shaped eyes studied her, jet black and unblinking.

The face disappeared instantly. These things moved so fast!

She felt more movement, a pulling at the vegetation around her, and at the fabric of her suit.

"No!" She feared they would damage the suit, breaching its protection.

She sat abruptly, triggering a flurry of movement. Grey figures retreating into the shadows of what was a chamber in the jungle growth.

To her left, Franco squatted on his haunches, grinning at her through a green-smeared visor. Tendrils of vegetation twined around his limbs, securing him in place.

"Did you see them?"

He had a knack for asking the blindingly obvious.

"Okay, Franco. Just tell me what's happening, and your assessment of the situation." She remembered Harrie Spier's frustrations with the young exotic sentience specialist on their journey to Base West One – at Franco's awkward manner and his inability to answer a straight question. She needed to learn from that, and do what she could to get him to focus.

"A hitherto uncatalogued species," he said. "Mostly bipedal. Showing indications of social organisation and at least rudimentary action-based symbolic language."

"Sentient?"

"The evidence for that is certainly accumulating."

A shape took form in the gloom, a pattern in the wall of vegetation. The weave parted and a face peered out, staring with those wide, dark eyes. Rima blinked, and it was gone.

A movement to the left of her vision, and now Rima saw an alien from head to foot for the first time. Smaller than her first impression had suggested; no taller than chest-high to Rima. Naked, with skinny limbs and a wiry frame, its arms and legs disproportionately long compared to its torso.

She was staring at an actual, sentient alien.

In all the surveys and studies leading up to the mission there had been no indicator of sentient life, no civilisation or industry on Carrasco. Just as super-telescope studies from Earth-orbit had looked for the kind of atmospheric biochemical homeostasis that would indicate an active biosphere, so too they had searched for radio activity and atmospheric traces that might indicate industry.

The one possibility that remained was that sentience might be at an emergent stage, not yet at a level of development that left a mark on its environment.

The alien moved: a twitch of its body and then a blur of motion and suddenly it stood before Rima, leaning over with its back curved and bending in all the wrong places – to her eyes, as a doctor of human medicine – and its face only centimetres from her helmet's visor.

It reached out and plucked at the fabric of her suit again.

On the edge of barely suppressed panic, Rima wrapped her arms around herself, as if that might offer protection.

Another grey alien appeared, then another, each of them reaching out, pulling at her, pinching fabric and flesh. And in the corner of her vision she saw Franco, still squatting as he studied what was going on.

"Are you going to *do* something?" she cried out.

"Like what?"

Just as quickly as they had started, the aliens stopped, dropped to all fours, and scuttled away to straighten up again on the periphery of the small chamber.

Now that her sight adjusted, Rima wondered if the featureless grey skin was, in fact, some form of body-hugging clothing. And if she was uncertain about something as simple as this, should she then question every reaction she'd had so far? Had those tendrils twined around her actually been an act of imprisonment? Were these creatures hostile and dangerous, or merely curious? After all, she didn't know how to react to them, and she'd been trained. But nothing could have prepared them for this encounter.

"Do you think they're dangerous?" Rima asked Franco, still squatting, still studying.

"Oh yes," he said, matter of factly. "Didn't you hear Abdul Cole scream as they were tearing him apart?"

Nothing had prepared her for this, a kind of sensory overload of panic, waves of fear, but also an element of that sense of wonder that seemed to be Franco's principal response. She was no frontline explorer or scientist, though. She should not be here.

More than anything, she felt powerless and vulnerable. Was this what it had been like for her Senegalese family, displaced by environmental catastrophe, powerless before the gangs and warlords that ran the refugee camps? Not knowing what lay in store for them tomorrow, or the day after that...

She sat with Franco as the Carrascans came and went, with

no apparent pattern to their activities. The legs of her suit had acquired a coating of green slime and she scrubbed at this with gloved hands as they sat.

"How long have we got?" she asked Franco, after they had been sitting for what felt like hours. "Our suits... they can't keep us alive out here forever, can they?"

Franco slapped his chest. "These things are built to last," he said. "The fabric might feel thin, but it's tough, and also, they recycle bodily waste and fluids." It had taken Rima quite some mental adjustment to be able to let go and relieve herself whenever necessary when she was in an excursion suit; it seemed so wrong. "And they harvest and scrub fresh nutrients and oxygen from the environment, so we'll never run out. Don't worry: we could last a long time out here."

"And that's meant to be reassuring?"

She'd transitioned quickly from trying to be understanding about Franco's response to being as irritated by him as Harrie Spier had been. Franco didn't seem to care that they were in danger, or even to truly comprehend the fact. All he could think about was his specialism, this wonderful opportunity to study intelligent alien beings at close quarters. His expertise had crossed over from theoretical to altogether far too hands-on.

The Carrascans brought them food and water.

She was learning to see differences between them as individuals now. The one who brought supplies had a shallow crease running up from between its eyes and over the crown of its head.

Rima smiled through her visor as the being studied her. "Thank you," she said, pressing her hands together namaste-style and bowing slightly forward. Then she pressed a hand to her chest and said, "Rima."

Franco didn't even pretend to disguise the snort of derision at her efforts to communicate. "This isn't a movie," he said. "There's a methodology."

"Which is?"

"Observation. Piecing together the clues as to how they communicate among themselves rather than just blundering in."

The alien – she thought of this individual as Creasey – took this distraction as an opportunity to drop to all fours and scurry away. It had left a bowl crafted from matted tendrils. The bowl looked porous, but it held perhaps a litre of water. Beside the bowl was a doughy lump about the size of a fist, resting on a stack of four circular grey leaves like lily pads.

"Food?" Rima asked. "At least they're trying to feed us."

"Or fatten us up. Or they're making some kind of religious offering. Or maybe this is simply the place where they leave these things at this time every day and we're merely in the way."

"All your years of study... Did it teach you any answers at all about what we're now encountering?"

"No," Franco said, "but it did teach me that there are a lot of questions worth asking." Then, perhaps as if sensing that he was irritating Rima, he went on. "This bowl for instance " he picked it up and casually poured the contents away; they had no means of taking in water, as their suits absorbed moisture directly from the air "–I want to know how they made it, because that will tell me a lot. If they merely break a piece of vegetation away and mould it, then that indicates an understanding of materials, particularly that an apparently porous mass can be water-tight." He broke a lump of vegetation away from the wall and tried, unsuccessfully, to mould it; the tendrils first sprang back out of shape, and then fell apart. "Or do they use tools to craft it? And do they have to treat the surface to render it water-tight, or is that a natural property? Use of tools to make other tools like this bowl is a big step; using processes like glazing or firing is yet another step up, because it indicates an understanding of materials changing state..."

He met her look and came to a halt. "This bowl alone could be a lifetime's study for someone in my field."

Rima indicated the ball of dough. "Is that food?"

"I'd need to analyse it. It could be. Or it could be some kind of poultice, and those leaves a bandage to contain it. They might think we're ill: I'm white, you're black; neither of us a healthy grey."

He was joking, she thought, although it was hard to tell with Franco.

"Why did you say you had to report to Commander Hertzberger?" Rima asked. "That was the first thing you said when you found evidence of intelligent life."

"He told me to," Franco said. "He said any indication of sentient life should be reported to him directly, and no one else."

"Why would he say that?"

"Because he's the commander." Franco was unquestioning: Hertzberger's order simply *was*.

Before Rima had a chance to dig any deeper, there was a commotion in the chamber. Two Carrascans came in on all fours. Normally silent, apart from occasional grunt-like exchanges, these two were jabbering rapidly.

Two more came in behind them, drawing a trailer that ran on sliders like skis rather than the wheels Rima had assumed from the tracks they'd found. She understood that the invention of the wheel was another critical juncture in the development of industrial society. Did this mean these aliens were less sophisticated than she'd thought, or more so, by virtue of their use of the most appropriate technology? These sliders clearly worked well on the matted surface of the tunnel.

Suddenly, grey faces loomed in around her, filling her view. Bony hands grasped her arms and pulled dangerously at her suit, stretching the fabric so far she thought it must tear.

She stood, and the beings started to slap her across thighs, buttocks and back, driving her towards the trailer. Understanding, she climbed on board, and thankfully they stopped.

Moments later, Franco tumbled in beside her. The thing was

a crude half-bucket shape, crafted from hardened vegetation just as the bowl had been.

They started to move, and Rima nearly tipped out. Franco grabbed her, then indicated how he was bracing himself with his back against one side of the sled and his feet hard against the other.

Rima did likewise, and tried not to be too irritated by the grin plastered across Franco's face.

"Isn't it all fascinating?" he said.

And then, just for a moment or two, she allowed herself to be caught up in his excitement. They were riding an organic sled through a tunnel crafted by sentient aliens, deep beneath the surface of a jungle that was fifty lightyears from home. She would allow Franco just one more *fascinating* for that, she decided.

They passed through twisting, turning tunnels, all lit by the eerie bioluminescence of the vegetation itself.

Rima had no sense of time, but her suit told her it was four hours later when they emerged on the surface of the jungle. It was night, a few stars glimmering through the sky's ever-present hazy cloud covering.

"Where are they taking us?" Rima asked, but Franco didn't bother to reply. How would he know?

When they came to a halt a short time later, Rima and Franco were unceremoniously dumped out of their sled as it tipped backwards. They tumbled in a heap on the springy vegetation, and immediately Rima felt tendrils wrapping around her legs. For a heart-stopping moment she feared they were about to be swallowed by the jungle again.

They sat, uncomfortably close, but unable to move, their legs bound fast.

Franco seemed more subdued now. "*Ça va?*" Rima asked. "You okay, Franco?"

"Yes, yes I am. Just tired. Trying to take it all in. I've spent my whole life building up to this point. I don't want to miss a single detail, you know?"

"We haven't even talked about trying to escape."

He laughed at that. Even if they could break out of their bonds, how could they possibly hope to evade sentient beings who knew this territory inside out?

Around them, the Carrascans appeared to have settled for the night, each individual curled up like a dormouse. At her side, Franco did his best to turn away from her, tucked his head into the crook of his arms, and was soon asleep.

Rima couldn't settle. Her mind was buzzing, and she felt as if she'd spent the day on an adrenaline high of fear.

She delved into the belly pouch of her suit and extracted a softscreen. Ever since their capture, her suit had told her there was no signal, but softscreens were robust, built for the field, and could usually get through when the suit's inbuilts struggled. She recalled the difficulty they'd had trying to contact Base West One on their approach – someone had blamed it on the atmospherics, but also she knew that the blue tinge to much of the vegetation and airborne microbial life came from compounds of copper, which played havoc with their comms.

She swiped the softscreen, bringing it to life.

"Jayne?" She couldn't contact her friend directly, but if she recorded a message, the softscreen could be instructed to keep trying to send it until it finally got through. "I don't know when you'll get this message, or if it will even reach you. But all I can do is try, *non*?"

She swallowed. She'd been rehearsing this in her head for much of the journey on the aliens' sled.

"I'm with Gianfranco Marcosi, and… well… we've been taken captive by what appear to be sentient aliens. Yes, *c'est vrai*. I don't know where they're taking us, or what they plan to do with us, and I am more terrified than I've ever been."

Her carefully planned speech was unravelling. It felt so strange to be saying these things out loud.

"I don't know what to do, Jayne, and that is why I am sending this to you and not on some official channel. Because I don't trust Sander Hertzberger. He instructed Franco to report only to him. Now why would he do that? I don't think he has the interests of our mission at heart, or even the greater pursuit of science and knowledge that we're supposed to prize so dearly. No, he has some other agenda. And I don't think he'd do anything to save us if it did not happen to fit with that agenda. So I'm recording this in the hope that it will get through to you, Jayne, and that you will have some better idea of what to do than I have."

She did not say out loud that one of her biggest fears was that it might be weeks or months before the softscreen finally found a signal strong enough for the message to be sent. And by that time, she was sure her fate would have been decided.

Franco's fate, though, had already been decided.

Somehow Rima slept, for when she opened her eyes again an aquamarine light was spreading across the clouds. It was morning.

She sat, one leg pressing uncomfortably against Franco's. He was sitting already, knees drawn up to his chest, arms wrapped around his shins.

He was still subdued, and she wondered if this alternation between manic and flat was normal for him, or simply a form of delayed shock. Then she saw the look on his face.

"Remember what I told you about our suits?" he said. "That they are self-contained survival units, continually recycling and replenishing, capable of keeping us alive for long periods?"

"Franco?"

"Well, that is only the case if their integrity has not been... compromised."

"Oh, Franco." Then she snapped herself into action. "How?" she asked. "Where?"

He lifted his left arm. The perforation in the fabric was small, about the size of her little fingernail.

"I found it in the night: I felt something moving, some bug trying to get inside. I don't think it made the hole; it just found it."

"Cover it. Now!" Her experience with victims of cloud fever back at the main base had taught her that it was a question of probabilities: the surface area of body exposed, the length of the exposure, and the levels of atmospheric contaminant in the immediate vicinity – these combined elements predicted the risk that any exposure incident might result in illness, and whether that illness might turn out to be fatal.

Rima leaned forward and pressed her gloved hand, palm down, against the damaged suit.

"We can repair it," she said. "Pinch the hole together while I check my survival pouch for any kind of patch kit." She was clutching at straws: as Franco had assured her, these suits were tough and they didn't have repair kits, but there must be *something*.

In a moment of uncharacteristic sensitivity, Franco closed his gloved hand over hers.

"No," he said. "It's too late. My head is hurting like hell, my suit tells me my fever has hit thirty-nine, and I have been hallucinating throughout the night. The cloud fever has taken hold, Rima, and I don't know how long I have left."

They travelled for much of the day again, first following a highway incised into the jungle canopy, and then dropping down into the tunnels. Franco lay curled in a ball in the sled, while Rima braced herself across the open rear to stop him tumbling out.

She could do little to help him, she knew, and as a physician that made her feel more powerless than ever.

When they stopped, the alien she called Creasey approached them tentatively, as if aware of Franco's distress. The aliens had stopped bringing Rima and Franco food and water now: it was clear that they were not using it. Rima felt constantly hungry, but she knew her suit's systems were keeping her going at subsistence level.

Now, Creasey placed another stack of grey leaves before them.

"I don't understand," Rima said. She tried to mime her lack of understanding, but of course the alien would not comprehend her shrug and raised eyebrows. "What are these? What do you do with them?" She picked up a leaf, feeling its leathery texture through her gloves.

Creasey shuffled forward and took it from her, then, moving in a sudden blur, swooped in and slapped it against Franco's suit. The leaf adhered, moulding itself to the contours of the material.

"A bandage?" Rima asked. Then, remembering one of Franco's early suggestions: "A poultice? Or are you actually trying to patch Franco's suit?" She took a leaf, gently eased Franco's arm away from his body to expose the small hole, and pressed the grey material against it.

When she looked up, Creasey had left them.

"*Come va?*" she asked Franco, struggling for the little Italian she knew.

"*Sto bene.* I'm okay," he gasped, clearly not. "Although I keep hallucinating that I am back in the... *orfanotrofio*, the... orphanage, is the word? *Scusa*... I..."

Others suffering with cloud fever had struggled for words, too. She remembered Sylvie Wilson, whose English had sounded as if she were a native speaker, reverting to French in her dying hours. This was an indication that the disease had reached Broca's area in the brain's frontal lobe. This, and the hallucinations, did not bode well for Franco.

"Tell me... Tell me what they are doing, Rima."

"There's one particular individual with a groove marking its forehead," she told him. "I call him Creasey. I know: I anthropomorphise by thinking of it as 'he' and giving him a name."

"We need labels," Franco said. "Just not assumptions. So... what is *he* doing?"

She looked across to where Creasey, in a group of a dozen aliens, was squatting beside one of his mates.

"He's with the others, applying a leaf to an individual's torso and pressing it into place. I haven't seen them do this before, but now that I have done it to you, it's as if some kind of line has been crossed, and now they can do this in public, when it was taboo before. Is Creasey a medic, perhaps, tending to lesions? Or a costumier? Or, is he the lowest of the low: a servant or slave, tasked with feeding, watering and repairs?"

"Or... is it simply something they do infrequently... and now is its time, and Creasey does it for reasons we are yet to determine?"

He was still struggling to speak, but his tone was gentle as he corrected her, and suddenly she had the sense that he was almost coaching her in the correct way to study the aliens: note the details but do not make assumptions.

"No," Rima said, her voice tight. "You're not going to die on me now, do you hear? You're the one who studies smart aliens, not me."

"And I am... loving it," he told her.

For a few seconds she struggled to understand, then he added, "Studying these aliens. Building a profile of who they are... how they live... how *they* respond to *us*." He paused, swallowed, struggling to breathe. "Even if I only have this for a day or two – these are the best days of my life."

She looked away. She was a doctor, but after her training she had only infrequently found herself dealing with patients she was unable to help. Dying patients, like Franco.

She didn't know what to do, so she checked her softscreen.

Her message to Jayne still had not been sent. Even when it did get through, though, what would her friend do? Would she be able to do *anything*, if she was right in her assessment that Hertzberger would do whatever it took to suppress news of the discovery of sentient natives? A sense of futility now threatened to overwhelm Rima and, yet again, she felt powerless.

"Sto bruciando."

"Burnt? Burning?" His fever was intense. She could see that through his slime-coated visor even without the confirmation of the reading from his suit that his temperature had topped forty degrees. To be ill with something like cloud fever was bad enough, but to suffer within the confines of a biohazard excursion suit must be some other kind of hell altogether.

They had travelled again for a couple of hours. She wished she knew where they were heading, and why.

It was night, and they were camping out on the jungle canopy. She did not know why they camped in the open. Was it that the airborne toxins were worse during the day, so they retreated into the jungle at such times? A religious impulse, perhaps, to be out beneath the stars?

"It's okay, Franco. Help is on its way." Jayne would do something when she saw that message, whatever Hertzberger might do to stop her. A rescue party would be on its way, she was sure.

Franco reached for his visor and, as she did every time, Rima reached out to stay his hand. But then she stopped herself. What harm would it do? They were well past the time when Franco had moved from the possibility of recovery to the simple need for palliative care.

She watched as he fumbled with the visor release, then she reached out and did it for him.

The visor slid up, his face ghostly pale in the light from her suit and from the canopy's bioluminescent glow.

He breathed deep, and then his eyes fixed on hers. "The air..." he sighed. "It... It really does smell bad."

She helped him free the seals of his helmet, then eased it from his head. Helped him unfasten his suit and roll it down his body to the waist.

"*Grazie. Grazie.*"

He clutched her hand. "And you, Rima? You're okay, aren't you?"

"I am." She knew his concern was not for her, so much as that their observations might stand a chance of making it onto the scientific record.

"*Papà?*"

"No, Franco. It's me, Rima. And this is Creasey – the intelligent alien *you* discovered. You'll go down in history, Franco." She knew that didn't matter at all to Franco; it was knowledge and understanding he relished, not fame. If anything, he would probably prefer that he *didn't* get the acknowledgement and could stay out of the limelight.

Not that any of that mattered now.

She looked down on him, then used one of the leathery leaves Creasey had supplied to mop his brow. The alien squatted with them, its head resting on the point where its legs folded in a U-bend rather than a simple joint – Rima would be fascinated to see what structure lay within, serving the function of knees but in such an elastic way. The Carrascan seemed fascinated by the changes overcoming Franco as he died.

Still stripped to the waist, much of his exposed skin had been taken over by what Rima could only think of as fungal growths: whorls and crusts and scales, in colours ranging from pale grey to deep maroon. Translucent slime glistened from the gaps between the growths – exuded from them or simply another form of Carrascan life moving in to explore this alien body.

For a time, Rima had cleaned him as best she could, but it

was a losing battle against these growths. They did not appear to be harming him, but merely colonising him.

"Franco? Are you still there?"

"*Papà*?"

He'd been flashing back to his childhood, years spent at an orphanage in Puglia, where the children had been worked hard in the drought-ravaged fields.

"Your father isn't here, Franco."

"He left me."

She didn't know his history, but it came as no surprise that he had a troubled one. Not simply orphaned, but abandoned. A lifetime of being the person no one around him knew how to handle or understand. Was that the reason for his interest in the exotic and alien? A strange fellow feeling for those even more alien than he was, himself?

"Franco?"

"Jayne. Are you coming after me now, my guardian angel?"

The softscreen recorded her message, her features illuminated through the visor by the light of another alien dawn.

"I... I'm getting desperate now, Jayne. I don't know how I can survive this alone. Because Franco, he's dead. He's dead and I don't know what to do. We've been travelling on foot for what feels like forever, but I don't know where we are. You have to help me, Jayne. You're all I have left."

20

Locating Vahota

Kemp spent a disturbed second night on Carrasco, woken in the early hours by the dull roar of an approaching engine. He stumbled from bed and stared through the viewing panel. A shuttle was coming in to land, a twenty-second century model which had evidently come through the wormhole directly from Earth.

He lay awake for a while before drifting back to sleep. Then, hours later, he was woken by the sound of people passing back and forth along the corridor outside his berth.

He sat on his bunk and ate breakfast from a compartmentalised tray, contemplating the events of yesterday afternoon. He'd moved around the base, seeking out anyone who'd known Rima Cagnac eighty years ago, only to be met for the most part with cold stares and a blanket silence. When the occasional scientist had deigned to speak to him, they denied any familiarity with the woman, and his lieware confirmed they were telling the truth.

He finished his breakfast, swabbed his face and upper body with a wipe from the dispenser, and changed into a fresh coverall.

He made his way to the main dome and stopped to survey the communal area.

Seeing Jimmy Ranatunga, he went over and said, "Ah, just the man. I was hoping to interview Jayne Waterford this morning." The ecologist was the one person on Carrasco who appeared to have been close to Rima Cagnac.

"She's in the med-bay. She came down with something a few days ago, but she's fine now. In fact she should be returning to work in an hour or two. You're lucky to find her: she's usually out in the wilds working on ecological surveys." He indicated a hatch across the dome. "You'll find the bay down there, the third on the left."

The young man hesitated, then went on, "I wanted a word about something else, Inspector. My colleague Dr Martinez was in the lab when you interviewed the others yesterday. She told me she knew Rima back on Earth" – he nodded across to where a small, dark-haired woman sat at a table, leaning over a softscreen – "and wanted to speak to you."

"Thanks, I'll talk to her now."

Kemp crossed the dome to the seated woman and activated his lieware.

"Dr Martinez?"

She looked up. "Cherie," she said, smiling diffidently.

Kemp introduced himself. "Dr Ranatunga said you knew Rima Cagnac on Earth." He sat down across from her. "He said you wanted a word?"

"That's right," she said, hesitating. "We trained together, and we met socially once or twice."

"Was she a friend?"

"I wouldn't say that, no. Circumstance threw us together."

"How did you get on with her?"

She shrugged. "Cagnac is driven, ambitious. That makes her... Well, she can often be short-tempered, impatient. She can blow up without good reason. Just the other day..." She shrugged again and looked away. "There was an incident in the med-bay – she lost her temper and went for me."

Kemp leaned forward. "Physically?"

Martinez bit her bottom lip. "Well, she started towards me – but no, it was more what she said. And it made me wonder..."

"Go on."

"Look, there were rumours, back then." She bit her lip, considering her words. "I met her and her husband once or twice in Geneva. We had a mutual friend, who wasn't part of the Carrasco mission. And after... after Dr White's murder, she told me something."

Kemp nodded; everything she had said so far was truthful. "About Rima Cagnac?"

"Well, about her husband, Sebastian White," Martinez said. "Apparently, he didn't want her to go on the *Strasbourg*. He wanted her to stay with him... And they argued about it, on and off, for months. Once, my friend was present when they kicked-off, and apparently it got... vindictive. It came to blows."

"Sebastian hit her?"

"No, Inspector," she said. "Cagnac hit him. I told you she had a temper."

Kemp nodded. "Right."

"So... my friend wondered, when she heard about the murder... Well, Cagnac had a motive, you see–"

Kemp interrupted. "Hardly a motive – she would gain nothing by murdering her husband."

"But if they argued, and it escalated, and she grabbed a knife... It might have been a spur of the moment thing."

Kemp thought it through. "So... in your opinion, Rima Cagnac would have been temperamentally capable of killing her husband, in the heat of an argument?"

"Yes, Inspector. That's what I think."

The retinal slide told him that she was telling the truth: she believed what she was saying.

She made to stand and leave the table.

"One more thing," Kemp said. "Did you see Rima Cagnac in Geneva after her husband's death, Dr Martinez? If so, did she appear–?"

She shook her head. "No. No, only much later – here, on Carrasco." She hesitated. "If that will be all, Inspector?"

Martinez stood and hurried from the dome, and Kemp sat back and stared up at the curving wall and the turquoise sky high above.

So on leaving Captain Fernandez's hotel room in the morning, Rima Cagnac had ample time to cross the city and kill her husband, and according to Dr Martinez she was hot-headed and temperamental...

Across the dome, Commander Hertzberger stepped through an irising hatch. He saw Kemp straight away and approached.

"Commander," Kemp said.

Hertzberger remained standing. "Inspector Kemp... I'm afraid there have been developments regarding the return of the team of which Cagnac is a part."

"Developments?"

"A malfunction of their ATV, which has necessitated they remain in the field for at least another night."

Kemp wasn't at all surprised by what the slide was telling him.

"I see," he said. "So do you know when she might be back?"

"They have a mechanic on the team, and he's working on the ATV as we speak," the commander said. "It might be another day, with luck, or two or three days at the outside."

Kemp nodded. "In that case, there's nothing I can do but wait."

"I'm sorry, Inspector. Now, if you'll excuse me..."

He watched the commander's retreating back. Everything he'd told him had been a lie.

Kemp left the communal dome and made his way to the med-bay.

Jayne Waterford was packing a softscreen and some clothing into a backpack when Kemp paused before the open door. "Dr Waterford?"

She looked up. "Ah, the man from the future."

"In the flesh. Gordon Kemp."

"I must say, darling, you don't suit the part."

He raised an eyebrow. "The part being?"

"High-flying detective inspector hand-picked to be the very first cop to go extra-solar and arrest a murder suspect. You'll go down in history, you know?"

"Ah... you mean the gut, the bloodshot eyes, and balding head? You've been participating in too many interactives."

She frowned. "Interactives?"

"Holo-dramas," he amended.

She stared at him, her lips quirking in a smile, and Kemp felt a sudden, odd connection with the woman, despite her attempt at mockery. She was tall, stringy, and attractive in a gawky, awkward way, with a thin face, a hooked nose and long hair in disorganised ringlets.

She finished packing her bag and sat down on the bunk, facing him as he leant against the doorframe.

"So if you're not the dashing hero working for Gellner and his objectionable thugs, my dear – who the hell are you?"

He looked around the small room, found a roughly printed chair, and sat down.

"I'm a washed-up, cold-case has-been pushing sixty who was very happy working in a freezing London before being sent lightyears through space. Against my will, might I add. Also, I'd like to think I'm working independently from Gellner, though he might have other ideas."

"You worked on cold cases?" She laughed. "Well, this one is so cold it's positively cryogenic. For you, at least. But for us..." She stopped and sighed. "She didn't do it, you know?"

"What makes you so certain?"

She hesitated, and Kemp received the impression that she was hiding something. "Rima is a good woman–"

"With a hair-trigger temper," he said. "Her husband didn't want her to go on the mission. He was set against it, apparently. What if they argued, and in anger Rima lashed out?"

Waterford shook her head. "She wouldn't do that. She might be highly strung, maybe even impetuous, but she loved Sebastian."

"She loved him? Yet she was already signed up for the mission and still she married the man. She always knew that one day she'd be leaving him."

She looked at him, her head tipped to one side. "What does that prove, Inspector? They were making the most of the time they had together; nothing lasts, even true love, and they knew that. That she was leaving him to come here was inevitable–"

"But perhaps Sebastian didn't see it that way, and wanted to keep her?"

Waterford gave a frustrated sigh. "Inspector, look... You're asking all the wrong questions."

He leaned back in the fragile printed chair. "So... just what should I be asking?"

"Well, I don't know what's been going on back on Earth that might have brought you blundering in here in your big detective pants, but look around you here. This is only a small research outpost, yet we're surrounded by divisions and questionable loyalties. Shouldn't we all be singing from the same hymn sheet like loyal little ESO boys and girls? But instead, we're being pulled apart in every direction."

"You think it's deliberate? You think it's being orchestrated?"

"I think that free and open scientific discourse is no longer in the interests of those who are running the show. I think there are some big players behind the scenes who are pulling the strings, for reasons of their own – and Christ knows what they might be."

He regarded her for a time. "And Rima Cagnac's part in this?"

She pointed a finger at him. "You're supposed to be the detective, big boy. Get outta here and detect, okay?"

He fell silent, staring at the floor.

Waterford said, "What's wrong? Have I hurt your feelings with a few home truths?"

He looked up and smiled. "As a matter of fact, no. I find your honesty quite refreshing."

"So why the sulks?"

"I was thinking that if this was Earth, and there was a decent bar just around the corner, I'd ask you out for a drink."

She tipped her head and closed one eye. "And if this was Earth, darling, I might just accept."

A figure appeared at the door, interrupting them.

Jimmy Ranatunga said, "Inspector – if you're not too busy, I'd like a word."

"I was just finishing up here," Kemp said, rising and nodding to Waterford. "Another time?"

"I'll look forward to that, Gordon, but you'll have to catch me soon. I'm heading out to my research camp at the first opportunity."

He followed the young man from the med-bay. Ranatunga appeared jumpy, nervous, and when they were out of earshot, he turned to Kemp and said, "Are you up to another excursion?"

"Jimmy – what's wrong?"

Ranatunga licked his lips. "I've heard from Jenny. She's in trouble."

"You've heard from her? Where is she?"

Ranatunga looked quickly up and down the corridor. When he was sure they weren't being observed, he unrolled a softscreen from where it was concealed under his sleeve. He slapped it against the wall and activated the screen.

The image was dark, grainy. Kemp made out a blur of vegetation. Then a young woman's face, scared and tearful, filled the screen. "*Jimmy,*" she said, "*I had to get away. They'll be coming for me. And… and now I'm certain. Do you hear me? I'm certain! Oh…*" The image blanked suddenly.

Kemp stared at Ranatunga. "She's certain," he asked, "about what?"

The young man looked up and down the corridor again,

wide-eyed, then turned back to Kemp. "She's certain her earlier suspicions have been proved correct," he said. "There are sentient aliens on Carrasco."

Kemp followed Jimmy Ranatunga across the communal dome, attempting to appear casual despite what the young doctor had just told him. He was aware of the collective gaze of the assembled scientists, and wished that Ranatunga didn't look so nervous. They passed down a short umbilical to the exit dome.

As they climbed into biohazard suits, Kemp said, "So you know where Jenny is?"

Ranatunga nodded. "Approximately. She messaged me twelve hours ago, but I'd just started a shift and I didn't see that she'd tried to contact me until ten minutes ago. At the start of her message, before the bit you saw – she said she was a kay southwest of here, in a subsidiary tunnel."

Kemp nodded. "That's a start."

"She was scared," Ranatunga said, staring at Kemp.

"And with good reason," Kemp said, sealing the front of his suit. "If she's right, and there are sentients on Carrasco – do you know what the implications might be?"

"We've spent years developing protocols for first contact," Ranatunga said. "Any plans to colonise or exploit Carrasco will have to be abandoned, or at least put on hold for a long, long time."

"Have you tried calling her back?"

"There was no reply."

As they were about to cycle themselves through the airlock, Kemp laid a hand on Ranatunga's arm. "You said she messaged you twelve hours ago?"

"That's right."

"There's always the possibility that Gellner's men intercepted the call – I'm sure they'll be monitoring communications."

The young man stared at him. "So they might have found her already?"

"Or they might still be searching," Kemp finished. "Christ..."

"What?"

"It's nothing."

What if the spyware loaded into his implant had alerted Gellner to Jenny Vahota's communique? For a second, he worried that by going out there he might be leading Gellner straight to the woman. But if Gellner was monitoring the spyware, then it was already too late – and if he and Jimmy could get to Jenny before Gellner's men and warn her...

"Okay, let's go."

He blinked the record facility into activation and sub-vocced "Danni, sorry for throwing you into the action *in media res*, but there have been developments. I'll fill you in later. In the meantime... we're in search of a missing scientist who just might have discovered sentient life on Carrasco."

He followed Ranatunga through the lock and exited the dome. They crossed the grey rock of the plateau, on the opposite side of the main dome to where there was activity around the newly arrived shuttle, and Kemp was grateful that they wouldn't be observed. It was an irrational relief, he told himself, as for all intents and purposes he and the doctor were just another anonymous pair of scientists in biohazard suits embarking on a field trip.

They reached the bank of vegetation and Ranatunga indicated a tunnel like the entrance to an outsized rabbit warren burrowing through the fibroid mass. The young man hurried into its cover and Kemp followed.

The further they burrowed into the mass, the deeper the jade-green twilight became, the only light coming from an eerie glow emanating from the vegetation itself. There was a certain similarity, Kemp thought, to being underwater: the same aqueous gloaming, the sense of being in another realm where a different order of life maintained. Not that he'd ever been underwater, but he'd played the interactives.

Up ahead, Ranatunga paused. "We've gone half a kay," the young man panted, glancing at his wristcom.

Kemp leaned against the tangled weave of the tunnel, taking deep breaths. "Give me a minute, Jimmy."

Ranatunga nodded, looking up and down the tunnel, just as he had done back at the dome. "If they found her..." he began.

Kemp chose his words with care. "My guess is they'll have taken her back to the shuttle, imprisoned her there – as they did with the others on the first day."

Ranatunga swore to himself. "You ready to go on?"

"Lead the way."

Ranatunga set off at a jog and Kemp did his best to keep pace.

From time to time he made out scurrying shadows, rodent-analogues fleeing the advance of two strange creatures. Once or twice something hit his visor and spun away, startling him – flying bugs the size of bees, and some even larger. They hit with a soft squelch, leaving slimy traces that briefly blurred his view.

Up ahead, Ranatunga called out, "Here." He looked up from his wristcom as Kemp caught up with him. "We're a kay from the main dome now. So we're looking for a tributary tunnel off this one. The chances are it'll be small, much smaller – even something you could just squirm through."

"You check that side," Kemp said, moving along the corridor and scanning the curving mass of vegetation to his right.

He sub-vocced, "I'm looking forward to watching this with you, Danni. In your place, with a coffee, and a happy ending to look forward to..." Because right now he was certainly not enjoying the real-time version, particularly the prospect of a tunnel he might just be able to squirm through.

"Here!" Ranatunga called out, ducking to peer up a branching tunnel less than a metre in diameter. "It's the only one in the vicinity, so...?"

"Let's do it," Kemp said, through gritted teeth.

Ranatunga disappeared into the tangled matting, and Kemp bent down and followed him. This tunnel was much more constricted than the first one, and Kemp found himself squeezing through a passage barely wider than his shoulders – progress made all the slower as the tunnel climbed at a gradient of thirty-five degrees. He was hot and sweaty and he paused every few minutes to take great gulps of air.

Ranatunga disappeared from sight around a sharp turn, and for a moment Kemp panicked. When he reached the bend he saw that the tunnel had widened considerably and the young man was standing upright, peering ahead.

"You okay?"

Kemp nodded. "Never better."

Ranatunga set off again.

They had travelled perhaps fifty metres when Kemp saw something projecting from the vegetation to his right. "Stop!"

Ahead, Ranatunga turned and stared at him.

Kemp took a step forward, peering through the half-light at the tunnel wall. He wasn't mistaken: something dark and tubular was embedded in the vegetation. Ranatunga watching him, he reached out and tugged it free of the clutching mass.

"A softscreen," Ranatunga whispered.

Kemp unrolled it and made out the initials JV on the top-right of the dead screen. He passed it to Ranatunga.

"Jenny's," the young man said. "Oh, Christ…"

Kemp peered at the gap in the vegetation where the softscreen had been embedded. He reached in, fearing what he might find, but the gap was sufficient only to contain the screen.

"So why the hell did she…?" Ranatunga began.

"My guess is that security was following her," Kemp said, "and after contacting you, she stuffed the screen in here so they wouldn't find it. It'd make sense."

Ranatunga peered up the tunnel. "And Jenny?"

He called her name, desperation in his tone.

Kemp reached out and gripped his arm. "Don't. If Gellner's men are still around…"

Ranatunga nodded and set off again.

They travelled for a further hundred metres before Ranatunga stopped dead in his tracks and said, "Oh, sweet Jesus Christ…"

Kemp looked past him. Ranatunga was staring at the tunnel wall to his left. The vegetation was scarred, burned. The young man reached out with a gloved hand. "It's been lasered," he said.

Kemp moved past him, staring at the wall a couple of metres further along the tunnel. Another area of vegetation had been burned, but this time in a neat vertical line two metres high. The fibrous mat, he saw, had not yet knit together.

He inserted his hand into the gap.

Behind him, Ranatunga said, "No…"

Kemp's hand touched something. He gripped it and pulled. The mass resisted, wedged as it was in the vegetal growth. He pulled harder, then stepped back with a gasp as a body tumbled out and fell onto the tunnel floor.

Ranatunga dropped to his knees and reached out to touch the young woman's visor, and Kemp caught a quick glimpse of Jenny Vahota's dead, staring eyes.

The woman's biohazard suit was sliced where a laser had cut straight across its chest.

"The bastards!" Ranatunga sobbed, staring at Kemp, then past him to the cut in the tunnel wall. "But why the hell did they–?"

"They didn't want anyone to find her, Jimmy."

"We've got to tell–"

Kemp gripped his shoulder, shook him. "No! We do nothing for now. We tell no one. Understood?"

"But…" The young man stared at the body, tears tracking down his cheeks.

"We've got to be very, very careful. Do you hear me? I want you to understand this, Jimmy: who do you think we should tell? We can't trust anyone, and certainly not Gellner and Hertzberger. So we tell no one. The only way to go about this, the only way we can make sure that Jenny didn't die in vain–"

"What?" Ranatunga said, something like anger in his voice. "What can we do?"

Kemp thought about it, his mind reeling. "If they did this to Jenny to silence her, then no one is safe."

"So what the hell do we do?" Ranatunga cried.

"For the time being, nothing. We go back to the dome, go about our business. I... I'll do my best to find out just who we can trust."

Ranatunga reached out and took Jenny Vahota's gloved hand. "And Jenny? What do we do with...?"

"I'm sorry. We've got to..." He gestured to the rent in the tunnel wall. "It's the only way, okay?"

Ranatunga gathered himself, saw the sense in what Kemp said, and nodded. "Yes, okay. You think they might come back when they decide what to do with her?"

Between them they manhandled the body upright and pushed it, with as much dignity as they could muster, back into the cocoon-like embrace of the fibrous vegetation. Minutes later they stepped back, sweating and panting, and regarded the narrow gap in the wall. In hours, Kemp thought, it would close up, hiding any evidence that there was a body concealed behind the anonymous green tangle.

"I'll find her," Ranatunga promised. "When all this is over, I'll come back and find her, and bury her like she deserves."

"You have the location?" he sub-vocced to his imp.

"*Location saved*," his imp said.

A thought occurred to him, and he said, "Give me your softscreen, Jimmy."

He did so. "What–?"

Kemp sub-vocced, "Imp, you know anything about eighty-year-old softscreen tech?"

"*What do you need to know?*" his imp replied.

Then to Ranatunga, he said, "I'm scrubbing all obvious traces of the message Jenny sent you from your profile. There will be traces deep in the system, but unless they already suspect you, they won't know to look for them and you won't be incriminated."

He passed the screen back to Ranatunga, and they turned and made their way back along the tunnel, following the route they had taken from the dome. They emerged from the mass of vegetation, and the turquoise sky and the orange, bloated sun dazzled after the twilight gloom.

As he hurried after Ranatunga, it came to him that he would be a fool to assume that the spyware had not alerted Gellner to what was going on. Would Gellner be back at the dome, waiting for him, planning to do to him what his men had done to poor Jenny Vahota? Would it be a mistake to return to the dome? He laughed aloud at the alternative: to lose himself somewhere on this inimical alien world...

They crossed the bedrock and approached the airlock, and Kemp stopped Ranatunga with a hand on his arm. "I suggest you go to your berth, get some rest."

The young man nodded. "I have a few hours before I'm due back on duty."

"Fine. And remember, not a word to anyone. I'll do my best to..."

He left Jimmy Ranatunga in the main dome and made his way down the umbilical to his berth.

He sub-vocced, "Well, Danni, wish you were here... as they used to say on old postcards. They're... Oh, to hell with it, I'll explain later. I just wish you were here so we could talk things through."

He cut the recording as he reached his berth and opened the hatch.

He stopped on the threshold, staring.

Jayne Waterford was sitting on his bunk, and she looked up as he stepped into the room and shut the door behind him. She had two biohazard suits and an unrolled softscreen piled on her lap, and some kind of toolkit by her side.

"I don't know what you've done, Gordon, but I overheard Gellner telling Hertzberger that he wants to bring you in for questioning."

So he was right. His spyware had alerted Gellner...

She gave him her cock-eyed, mocking smile. "And I've just had a communiqué from Rima. Hence all this lot..."

"Jayne?"

"We're going to suit up, my darling, and then–" gesturing at the toolkit nonchalantly with one hand "–using this laser rock cutter I've liberated from one of my geologist colleagues, I'm going to cut open the membrane of the wall and we're getting out of here. I've got an ATV ready and waiting–"

She stood up. "It's only a matter of time before Gellner intercepts Rima's message and finds out–"

"Finds out...?" he echoed.

"That Rima's been *taken*, Gordon."

"Don't tell me," Kemp said as he took the proffered biohazard suit. "The aliens, right?"

She winked at him. "So you *have* been doing a bit of detective work, Gordon. Very good. So let's get into these suits and find her, okay?"

21

Breakout

Kemp locked the door of his berth.

"There's multiple redundancy," Jayne told him. "In case of a breach in the outer skins of the dome, inner doors seal themselves immediately to prevent contamination. But just in case…"

From the toolkit she produced a spray gun. Seconds later the doorframe was sealed with a shiny black coating that was foaming and expanding as Kemp watched.

"Airtight," she said. Then she turned the gun on what looked like a small black bulb on the wall and sealed that too, before discarding the spray gun on the bed. "And now your room's atmosphere sensor is isolated, too, so it won't detect any change in levels of methane, sulphur, or hydrogen sulphide. This will hopefully buy us an hour or two."

"You mentioned a breach of the outer skins?"

From the toolkit she produced a hefty-looking power tool and swung it casually towards the wall. "This beauty can carve its way through granite," she told him. "The dome skin won't stand a chance."

She looked through the viewing panel, peering left and right, then nodded. "There's no one out there, Gordon. Here goes."

He watched, his heart thudding, as she took up the power cutter and knelt before the outer wall of the berth.

His first fear – that the tool would create enough noise to alert passers-by – was groundless. It kicked into life with a low electric whirr and made only a slick, slicing sound as Jayne applied the vibrating blade to the composite membrane. A gap opened up, a few centimetres at first, widening as Jayne ran the cutter upwards.

"Stop!" he hissed.

Jayne turned, staring at him. "What the hell–?"

Footsteps sounded in the corridor beyond the door. He braced himself for the knock and an angry voice asking what the hell was going on in there. Or, worse, Gellner's men, who would kick the door in without ceremony and arrest them red-handed.

As he listened, sweating, the footsteps passed down the corridor.

"It's fine," he said. "Go on."

"Don't frighten me again like that, you hear?" Jayne snapped.

She turned to the wall, activated the power cutter again and applied the blade to the membrane. As the gap opened up, Kemp made out the grey expanse of bedrock surrounding the base.

Minutes later, a rent two metres tall gaped in the wall. Jayne turned to him and signalled.

"Follow me, but don't rush," she said. "We don't want to arouse the suspicion of anyone who might be out there." She inserted her helmeted head through the gap, ensuring that the way was clear, then said, "Here we go."

She slipped sideways through the vertical rent in the fabric, and Kemp pushed his way out after her. He peered around. In the distance, to his right, was the tail-end of the shuttle, but there were no suited figures in sight.

Taking a deep breath, he followed Jayne across the bedrock towards the jungle. He felt as if he had a big target stuck to his back. His instinct was to hurry; it felt wrong to be moving so casually when at any second Gellner and his men might emerge and apprehend them. He counselled himself to slow down and follow Jayne's lead. To any casual observer they were just another pair of scientists heading out on routine fieldwork.

They reached the jungle and Jayne signalled ahead to the entrance of a tunnel. He nodded and followed her.

He blinked to start recording as he stepped into the half-light of the tunnel. "Good God, Danni. This brings back memories... This was before we met, perhaps ten years ago. I was following a lead, a homicide involving a Taiwanese triad. I was in Shoreditch, towards dawn, tracking a killer I'd traced to an old warehouse. Only he'd turned the tables with some clever trackware and was coming after me. Well, I'm feeling the same rush of fear and thrill now. Never thought I'd experience it again. Hope you're enjoying the local colour."

He called ahead, "The ATV?"

"Not far now," Jayne answered without turning. "I had to conceal it away from the base, rather than return it to the pool for anyone to use."

"Just how far?" He was sweating in the planet's cloying heat and his visor had slimed up again.

"A few hundred metres."

As he passed down the narrow tunnel, brushing the close weave of the vegetable fibre, he thought of Jenny Vahota entombed in the vegetation a kilometre to the south, and he felt an involuntary surge of pure hatred towards Gellner and his men.

They emerged from the narrow tunnel into a larger one, and in the distance stood a balloon-tyred ATV. Jayne raced ahead, and he gave chase and climbed into the buggy after her.

He took a few calming breaths as Jayne leaned forward and hit the ignition. The vehicle kicked into life and crawled forward.

"Did Cagnac tell you where she is?" he asked, glancing across at the woman.

"Not exactly." She indicated her softscreen attached to the dashboard. "She transmitted a recorded message via her softscreen, said she'd been taken but didn't say where she might be. Oh, she did say that we should not trust Sander Hertzberger." She shook her head. "I don't know how long ago she recorded the communiqué, or where she might be now."

"You can't reach her?"

She shook her head, impatient. "Of course not," she snapped. "Don't you think I've tried?"

He held out a hand. "Give me the softscreen."

"I told you, she didn't say where she was."

"Please, give me the screen."

She peeled the screen from the dash and passed it to him, then glanced at him as he examined it. "What are you doing?"

"Trying to locate Rima Cagnac."

She peered ahead as the ATV trundled down the tunnel. "How can you possibly do that? All she said is that she'd been walking for days…"

Kemp sub-vocced, "Imp, I need some help with that eighty-year-old softscreen tech again…"

"*Happy to assist*," his imp replied.

"Gordon?" Jayne asked.

"Metadata," he explained. "Every message has embedded metadata that tells us all about the message: when it was recorded, what device was used, geographical data… In my line of work we rely on this kind of thing all the time. Just give me a moment."

A few seconds later, his imp had completed its investigations. "Okay," he said. "You received this message a few hours ago, but it looks as if it wasn't sent immediately. It was actually recorded three days earlier. Presumably her softscreen had problems getting a good enough signal to send it."

"Three days?" Jayne said, dismay clear in her tone. "Does that mean we're too late?"

"We can't know what's happened to her in the meantime,

but it's actually a good thing. Assuming she's still alive, of course."

"Good?"

"It means we have two sets of location data: one from when the message was recorded, and one from when it was sent. So, assuming they're taking the most direct route possible to wherever they're going, that means we can extrapolate a route." He closed down the softscreen and replaced it on the dash.

"Is this really happening?" Jayne smiled, but without humour. "I'm an ecologist, Gordon. I'm not accustomed to... to whatever the hell's happening here." She glanced at him. "How did you find out about the aliens?"

He stared ahead at the diminishing tunnel. The vehicle bucked, and they were suddenly heading up an incline of thirty-five degrees.

He chose his words with care, unsure how close Jayne might have been to Jenny Vahota. "Jimmy Ranatunga contacted me this morning. He'd heard from a colleague, Jenny Vahota – she'd fled from the camp."

"Jenny?" She stared at him eyes wide. "Jenny fled?"

"Jenny told Ranatunga that she'd found evidence of sentient aliens. She left a message with him, giving her approximate coordinates, and we made our way through the vegetation." He hesitated, then said, "Did you know Jenny well?"

"Not well. She works in my team. She's a great kid – Gordon? What the...?"

"I'm sorry. We found her... She'd been lasered, her body concealed in a tunnel wall–"

"Lasered? She's dead?"

"We can only presume it was Gellner's men."

"Oh, Christ..."

"So we left her where we found her and returned to the dome. I told Jimmy not to say a damned word – then found you in my berth."

She stared at him. "They don't want it known, Gordon. Sentient aliens. And if they'd kill Jenny to stop word getting out…"

She fell silent, staring ahead as daylight appeared, brightening, in the distance.

She said, "Do you think Gellner knows that Jimmy–?"

"I ran a scrub on Jimmy's softscreen, deleting all trace of Jenny's message from his profile. But if they're monitoring comms then they could easily have intercepted it before I did that…" He shrugged. "Who knows?"

A little later, he said, "You're taking a big risk, you know. Going up against Gellner like this. You could have just laid low…"

"You don't know me, Gordon. I've been picking sides all my life." They drove in silence for a time, then she went on. "And anyway, as far as anyone knows, I'm out at my trapping station. As soon as they released me from quarantine, that's where I said I was going. I spend most of my time out there – 'antisocial Jayne', they call me – so I'm not going to be missed, darling."

She fell silent again as the vehicle emerged from the tunnel into the dazzling turquoise daylight at the top of the world. Ahead, the huge orange ball of the sun hung just above the horizon.

At one point she said, "So… if and when we find Rima?"

He shrugged. "I question her, try to work out what the hell happened back on Earth."

"She didn't kill her husband, Gordon."

"You sound certain."

"I am."

"Did she mention it when you two talked, before she left the base?"

"She didn't say a thing about it." She shrugged. "And I heard the rumours, but…"

"So how come you're so certain she's innocent?"

"I just know, okay?" she said.

Kemp had worried that the lieware might have difficulties reading through Jayne's visor, but it seemed to be performing as efficiently as usual: she was telling the truth.

"Look," she said a little later, "when I said 'if and when we find Rima...', I meant what the hell do we do *then*?"

"All bets are off. The discovery of sentient aliens changes everything. We'll need to play it by ear." He fell silent, aware he was spouting clichés.

"We'll bloody well need to get off the planet," she said, and laughed at the absurdity of her words.

"Ever flown a shuttle before, Jayne?"

"No. You?"

"Not something they trained us in at police academy, unfortunately."

She smiled at him. "So let's just enjoy the ride, and the fact that we're on an alien planet and about to, possibly, come across a few sentients, shall we?"

They were travelling down a long, wide runnel in the vegetation, the track the scientists had created on their way to Base West One. Kemp gestured through the windscreen at the sun hanging above the far horizon. "How long till it sets?"

"Another two hours, roughly."

"We've been travelling for about two hours already," he said, "and we've covered a little over twenty kays. We're still almost eighty from Base West One. Have you tried contacting them?"

"I have my softscreen set to repeat call." She shook her head. "Nothing."

"Why the hell aren't they answering?"

"Bad reception? Perhaps they're buried so deep in this stuff...?"

A while later he was aware of her watching him, her head tipped to one side.

"What?"

She shrugged, smiling to herself.

He said, "You're wondering whether you should trust me, right?"

"A little. But actually I was wondering why *you* trust me. If you do, that is." She paused, then went on, "But on balance, I think you do. You found me in your berth, accepted my story, and came on this wild goose-chase... So you must think I'm on the level?"

He nodded. "I do."

"Are all twenty-second century cops so gullible?"

He shrugged. "Maybe some are, but not me."

"So... you know something, right? You know I'm telling the truth about Rima. You know yourself that she didn't do it."

He shook his head, wishing she'd drop it.

"Come on, what is it? You found something that exonerates her, right, back on Earth. So why the hell come here to arrest her, Gordon?"

"It's not that," he said. "Look, I'm equipped with lieware."

She stared at him. "What?"

"I trust you, Jayne, because I know when you're lying and when you're telling the truth."

"Lieware?" She slowed the ATV and looked at him, her expression suspicious, defensive. "What the hell...?"

"Just what it sounds like: software that detects lies."

"So you... or rather some program you're loaded with...?"

"It can assess the truth of every last thing you say."

She fell silent, scowling.

"What?" he asked at last.

She shrugged, still not looking at him. She began to say something, stopped herself, then fell silent – only to think about it and begin again. "So, Mister Hot-Shot DI, how the hell can you have any kind of relationship with another human being if you rely on software to make sure you're right about them?"

He shrugged. "Hey, I'm a DI, and my default setting is not to trust people, okay?" He was aware of the glibness – and the untruth – of the words as soon as he'd uttered them.

She looked away. "*Shit!*" she said under her breath.

He studied her, considering her choice of words. "And anyway," he said, "what do you mean by 'relationship'? I'm on an investigation here."

She coloured. "I was speaking generally," she said quickly.

He watched her as she turned back to regard the way ahead. "Jayne, I don't use it all the time. I certainly don't use it when I'm *not* on a case – in fact, I haven't had it initiated that long." He was aware that he was trying to excuse himself, win her over.

"And how do I know *you're* telling the truth?" she snapped. "I'm not equipped with lieware, after all."

He raised his hands, exasperated, but unwilling to give in to the degree of apologising.

He must have dozed at some point, because he was awoken later by a touch on his shoulder. When he opened his eyes, he saw Jayne had halted the vehicle. They were still on top of the world; the sun had almost set, laying down molten strata to the west.

"I'm sorry," she said, "perhaps I overreacted – but it isn't every day I come across someone who..." She shrugged. "Anyway, I was thinking about what you said about the lieware. And you know what?"

"Go on."

"I suppose it showed a level of trust, you telling me about the lieware, right?"

He smiled. "Unless I was just stringing you along..."

"I don't need artificial lieware, Gordon. I'm equipped with

my own, natural lie-detector. I'm good at reading people,
okay?"

"You're right. I wasn't stringing you along. I thought it'd
be best if I levelled with you, told you the truth about the
software, okay?"

"I appreciate that." She shrugged. "Anyway, how about you
take a turn at the wheel?"

A short time later, after a crash-course on how to drive an
eighty-year-old ATV, he was steering the vehicle along the
deep, wide groove scored through the vegetation.

"Something I said earlier," she said, "about knowing that
Rima didn't kill her husband. I was telling the truth, so you
must have known that."

"And when I asked how you were so certain, you dodged
the question."

She hesitated, then nodded. She was about to say something
when her softscreen chimed with an incoming call. She
touched the screen and it flared into life, showing the static-
blitzed image of a young woman. Her voice was as corrupted
as the visuals. "Dr Waterford…? Where… can't find you any–"

"Helena, I'm out at my trapping station, okay? Spur of the
moment thing. No need to worry. You hear me?"

The woman's face broke up, reformed again. She was
nodding. "… hell broke loose at this end, Dr Waterford. Major
Gellner…"

She glanced across at Kemp, scowling. "Repeat that, Helena.
You said something about Gellner?"

"He's… his men swarming all over the… And… arrested
Jimmy."

"Oh, Christ," Jayne said under her breath, staring at Kemp.

"Setting off… want to question you. Also, the detective–"

Jayne leaned closer to the screen and said, "Could you
repeat that, Helena? Gellner's setting off? Where to?"

The woman nodded, biting her lip. "… to Base West One,"
she said. "And they… talk to the detective, Kemp. He and

Jimmy… something in the jungle." Her image broke up again as the signal fluctuated.

"Where's Jimmy now? They haven't harmed him?"

"… for questioning. I think… the shuttle… not a nice atmosphere here, Dr Waterford."

The image broke up for the last time and the screen remained blank. Jayne rolled it up and looked at Kemp.

"So it turns out I was right, Gordon. If Gellner is after you, too, then I was right to trust you."

He grunted his thanks. "We have a couple of hours on them, Jayne."

"And after that?"

A silence came between them as they regarded each other. "Is the ATV equipped with weapons?" he asked.

"Laser rifles." She hesitated. "You think we might need them?"

"After what Gellner's bastards did to Jenny Vahota…"

She looked at him. "And then? If we have a shoot-out with Gellner's men, and presuming we win… what then? We're still stranded here with no way out."

He sighed. "Let's worry about that if and when it happens, okay?"

Kemp winced as something occurred to him. Was it a coincidence that Gellner and his security team were heading for Base West One? Could these ATVs be tracked? Or – he thought of the upgrade Tsang had imposed on him before the mission – was it he himself who was being tracked?

"So…" he said, glancing at her, "before we were interrupted, I asked you how you could be so certain that Rima Cagnac didn't kill her husband. Intuition?"

She shook her head. "Intuition had nothing to do with it, darling," she said. "I know for certain she didn't do it."

"How the hell…?"

"Because I know who *did* kill her husband," she said.

22

Fellow Traveller

Franco remained her travelling companion.

Rima sat with him in the back of the aliens' sled, her body braced to stop them rolling out. She'd considered moving aside, letting Franco's bloated, growth-festooned corpse tumble free, but she could not bring herself to do so.

"He's dead," she'd argued, as the aliens had loaded Franco onto the sled. But, of course, they did not understand her words. She wasn't sure they even understood the concept of death, or at least that Franco was dead. Perhaps they thought he had moved into some other state, a deep sleep from which he would emerge.

They were in the tunnels again, and Rima had the sense that they would continue to travel forever. Perhaps this was simply what they did. And perhaps they thought he was still alive because Rima was talking to him.

It was a stupid thing, a macabre comfort thing.

"It's okay, Franco, we're going to get out of this. Jayne is on her way."

"We're going to get through this, Franco."

"Come on, Franco, we're going to be okay."

From there, it became a commentary on what the aliens were doing, just as she'd made his observations for him when he was still alive. "They walk at a pace somewhere between walking and jogging. A canter, like a horse? And their limbs seem to be articulated at multiple points – legs with many knees and ankles – so that their movements are fluid and seamless. They pass time in long silences, then talk in a rapid torrent of grunts that must be words. They are watching us all the time: as soon as one looks away, another turns its gaze on us."

She sipped recycled water from a suit tube, her throat dry from talking to a dead man. She was sure any observer would deem her mad for behaving in this way, but she knew it was just about the only thing that *saved* her from madness right now.

She checked her softscreen, but there was no response from Jayne, and now the device itself appeared to be failing: the screen showed mostly static, and the camera wasn't recording at all. It felt as if her last tenuous connection with the outside world was being stolen from her.

When Franco spoke to her, she thought for a moment that she really was going mad.

She'd lost track of how long they had been travelling when the sled hit a bump and lurched abruptly to one side. Rima braced herself to stop from falling out and then, to her horror, Franco tumbled on top of her.

She experienced the pressure of his weight, the sickening sensation of his bloated body against her through their suits, and then she arched her back, pushing him away. It was nothing more than the movement of the sled tipping his lifeless body, but her panicked reaction was very real, her heart racing, her breath ragged, and a gagging sensation in her throat in response to that bloated touch.

One of the aliens walking behind the sled jabbered something at her, and then, as if in response, she heard Franco's voice: "… moving… falling… fighting…"

She stared at him, fearful that she had hallucinated the whole episode: the tumbling embrace, the words, unmistakable in his Italian accent.

"Franco?" she said tentatively, feeling even more mad merely for addressing him. When she had spoken to him before, she had not expected an answer. "Franco, what's going on?"

And now, she heard more sounds, in Franco's tone, but random, harsh grunts.

The sled came to an abrupt halt, and in a blink the aliens were crowding round, their faces up close.

The silence drew out, and then one of the aliens – Creasey, she saw, who appeared to be the one tasked with looking after her and Franco – spoke in the Carrascan's grunting language.

"... talking... not moving..." Words in Franco's voice again. This time Rima was watching him, though, and she saw that his lips did not move. The voice came from the wristcom he wore on his left arm.

She understood now. Franco must have had a smart algorithm recording and processing the aliens' language, and now it had reached critical mass where it had compiled a lexicon and was capable of at least crude real-time translation. Creasey had said something to the effect that Franco was *talking*, even though he was *not moving*.

"Do you understand me?" she said tentatively.

The wristcom grunted, and immediately the aliens jabbered at each other. Now, though, instead of translating, the wristcom fell silent, perhaps overwhelmed by the sudden confusion of noise.

The aliens lost interest immediately, turning away even when Rima tried again: "Please. Can you tell me where we are? Where are we going?"

As they resumed their journey, Rima eased the wristcom over Franco's hand and onto her own wrist, feeling as if she were robbing the dead.

When they halted a little later, Creasey came to squat on his haunches beside Rima and the lolling Franco. He'd brought another stack of grey leaves.

"Thank you, but there's no need," Rima said into the wristcom. She indicated Franco with a wave of the hand. "He's dead. We don't need to repair his suit."

The wristcom spoke, a jabber of alien sounds.

Creasey tipped his head to one side, delaying for so long that Rima expected no answer, then gave a sequence of soft, almost musical, grunts, and the wristcom started to translate.

"... not moving... animal with words... act of making better..."

Rima reminded herself of Franco's words of caution about the danger of trying too hard to fill in the gaps with assumptions, yet she couldn't help herself trying to make sense of the alien's statement.

Creasey had used the phrase *not moving* before, and she had taken that to be a reference to Franco's state: that, since his death, he had ceased to move.

Animal with words must be a reference to Rima, and the fact that she was suddenly using their language – or at least the wristcom was.

And *act of making better* – healing of some sort? Was Creasey telling her he thought he could heal Franco?

"No," she said. "My friend is dead. You cannot heal the dead."

The wristcom gave a sequence of grunts, and Creasey paused again, perhaps carrying out the same process Rima had of trying to piece together the meaning of an incomplete and crude translation.

Then Creasey took one of the leaves and proffered it.

"... not moving... moving still..."

Creasey leaned forward and held the leaf as if to press it against Rima's thigh, then paused.

Franco was the *not moving* one, and therefore Rima must be *moving still*.

She looked down and saw a line about two centimetres long on her thigh, a mark on the fabric of her suit. Not a mark... and not quite a tear, but still a flaw in the material, an indication of damage.

Her suit had been breached. She did not know how long ago it had occurred, or how serious the damage.

When she'd realised Franco's suit was damaged, she'd thought through the computation of risk: extent of exposure multiplied by duration of that exposure, all multiplied by the ultimate unknown – the level of toxic pathogens in the surrounding environment at the time the body was exposed.

Such a tiny flaw... It might have gone unnoticed for days, or it might have occurred in that moment when Franco had tumbled onto her earlier today. And the rent was tiny, not a complete tear at all.

Surely her risk factors were low, almost negligible? She would be fine.

She took the leaf from Creasey, pressed it to her thigh and felt the leathery material moulding itself to her form, tactile and strangely alive.

"Thank you," she said, and the wristcom grunted her words in alien syllables.

Creasey studied her blankly. She could translate some of his words, but not yet his expressions.

And she could not escape the bitter irony of her position: that the first time she sat down to actually talk with an alien it was for that alien to point out to her that she might well be dying.

It was an old truism that doctors made the worst patients. They understood the symptoms, and they understood the range of risks resulting from any condition.

Cloud fever might affect some people only mildly – they had not experienced enough cases, or established reliable enough testing, to assess whether some people exposed to the airborne pathogens might even be infected but symptom-free.

At the other end of the scale, of course... Franco lay beside her under the cloud-veiled stars, carefully laid out by Creasey and another of the Carrascans. Rima was still unsure whether they had any real understanding that he was dead.

She had a headache, and a sore throat she had put down to talking too much and not drinking enough on her suit's subsistence rations. She felt deeply fatigued, so that every movement required conscious effort. She struggled to concentrate, and in particular to order her memories of the past few days: these existed as images and recalled conversations, and even though her memories of Franco being alive must have come before those where he lay bloated and lifeless beside her, she still struggled to put them in sequence. When she slept, she dreamed of Geneva, and this worried her more than anything, for these memories had been suppressed – both consciously and chemically – and she knew that cloud fever patients often regressed in their hallucinations and rambling monologues.

All of these things were potentially symptoms that fit a diagnosis of cloud fever.

But also, she reminded herself, they tallied with the reactions, physical and mental, of someone subjected to the unprecedented stresses of abduction by sentient aliens.

She woke to the sensation of something smooth and cool pressing against her fevered brow.

Her visor was gone… Her helmet removed.

Panicking, she pushed herself into a sitting position and saw Creasey squatting before her, one of the grey leaves in his hands.

Had she removed her helmet, or had the alien, having seen her do the same for Franco?

It did not matter. She felt as if she were burning up, and now memories of a night of tortured fever and pain came flooding back.

There could be no doubt now. She was suffering from cloud fever. That nick in the thigh of her biohazard suit was all it had taken.

She reached for the leaf, took it and pressed it to her forehead.

It seemed to draw the heat from her, and for a moment she
was able to gather her thoughts. Her head throbbed painfully,
and every joint in her body felt as if stabbed by hot needles.
Her chest ached with every breath. Every time she moved she
felt vertiginous. And, somewhat bizarrely, through all the pain
and disorientation, she found herself intensely aware of the
sulphurous stink of the air she breathed.

She lay back, and her head felt as if she were still moving
long after she came to rest.

Again, she felt coolness pressed to her forehead as Creasey
tended to her.

"You..." she gasped. "You're a... a... *un médecin*?" Words
were evading her. Had it reached her frontal lobe already?
Surely the illness was progressing too rapidly? Unless, of
course, she had been harbouring the fever for longer than she
had thought. When had she started to feel so fatigued? When
had she first experienced that raw pain in her throat?

Alien grunts emanated from her belly pouch, the wristcom
translating her garbled words into Creasey's language.

"... everyone... act of caring..."

"Every man a healer be." Was that a quote from somewhere,
or just words that made sense to her in her addled state? Again,
the wristcom grunted its translation, but this time Creasey did
not respond. Did the alien understand that she was becoming
delirious? She wondered what repercussions this would have
for the relationship between humans and Carrascans, if the
aliens' first communication with humankind was with her as
she became increasingly incoherent.

"You should know," she said. "My kind can be dangerous
and untrustworthy, but on the whole... well, we do our best
to be *good*."

The effort of talking exhausted her and she struggled for
breath as the wristcom translated.

"*Je meurs*. I... I think I'm dying."

Creasey pressed a fresh leaf to her head. Its cool embrace

was just about the best thing she had ever experienced, and then she felt darkness closing over her.

Sebastian. Oh, Sebastian. Standing here in one of those white suits he so loved to wear. "You should cover up, *mon cher*. The air... it is not good."

The translator grunted, although her husband had no need of alien monosyllables.

"Why do you not trust me, Sebastian? Why do you not tell me what is troubling you?" Because troubled he most certainly was, these past few weeks. At first, she had put it down to her approaching departure on the *Strasbourg*, and they had rowed about this, because he had always known the day would come and she would not change her mind now.

But there was more than that. Something else.

"You have secrets, but you will not tell me, *mon chère*. Troubles."

"I am not sure, my dear. I'm waiting for certain answers. I must tread with the utmost discretion."

"Discretion? You will not tell me, but you talk to your brother, *non*? You tell him everything."

He pursed his lips in that way of his that said he would not shift.

"Sebastian? Oh, Sebastian..."

She opened her eyes, saw a grey face with large, dark eyes close to hers.

"Sebastian?"

Coolness against her forehead again. Delicious coolness.

She was hallucinating. She knew that.

Her husband was dead. Had been dead for eighty years.

He'd always gone to Randolph, before he had gone to her. Right until the end.

And so, she knew that if anyone had known what had really happened to Sebastian, then it had been his brother.

Oh, Sebastian.

She was dying, and she would do so without ever knowing what had happened.

But at least she had him, for these last few moments of her life.

Sebastian had been the love of her life, even though they both knew from the outset that it was love on a finite timescale. She knew, though, that those few years with Sebastian had packed in more than a lifetime of love for others.

The white-suited figure blurred now, and she felt a flash of anger that he was leaving prematurely once again. Fading away.

The jungle canopy spread all around, and a small grey alien squatted nearby, studying her.

Her biohazard suit was pulled down around her waist, her body a patchwork of grey leaves and the fractal patterns of alien growths: crusts and polyps and scales, clinging to her skin, pressing against her and into her.

Her pulse had slowed, her breathing become shallow. Even the raging fever appeared to have abated a little, although she knew that was from a growing sense of detachment rather than any kind of improvement of her condition.

She was dying. Barely clinging to the last few vestiges of life.

Sebastian?

Was that white glimmer before her a ghostly image of his suit, or was it the ethereal light some reported in the last moments of life? A beacon, drawing her away. An ending point, to a life with so many unresolved questions.

Sebastian. Oh... Sebastian.

"Where are we going?"

They'd loaded her unceremoniously into the cart once again, crammed up against Franco's decaying corpse.

She didn't want this. Every bump, every movement, sent jolts of pain coursing through her body. She just wanted to *stop*.

A grey face loomed over her: Creasey, clinging to the side of the sled.

"Where are you taking me?" she sighed, and Franco's wristcom grunted its translation from her belly pouch.

Creasey grunted in response, and seconds later the wristcom translated into Franco's soft tones: "The place of death," it said. "And... the place of life."

23

Outside, Looking In

Danni stood in her pyjamas in the middle of the lounge, staring at the three screens surrounding her in the air. The first showed an aerial shot of a luxurious greensward and a distant villa, the second a grainy close-up of a woman against a background of shrubbery. The third screen was text, the big file containing the case notes from the 2110 investigation of Sebastian White's murder.

The lack of progress was getting her down.

Added to that, she was hungry, and when she was hungry she was always tetchy.

She should really take a break, call out for some food, and spend the evening participating in some mindless old interactive. She'd been reading through the case notes all day, and if she didn't stop soon she'd suffer later with a debilitating migraine.

"*Incoming, Danni,*" her imp said.

"Who is it?"

"*Edouard Bryce.*"

She sighed. He'd called three times yesterday, each time leaving messages saying that he'd like to apologise, make it up to her in some way. Danni had ignored the calls. She still felt angry at how he'd got Martin to delve into her private medical records, and she was in no mood to forgive him any time soon.

She swore to herself, then said, "Put him through."

Instantly a fourth screen expanded in the air, showing Bryce's head and shoulders in what looked like a car. He smiled out at her, warily. "Danni? Why no visuals?"

"I'm not decent," she said.

"I was wondering... Look I'm sorry about–"

"You tried to apologise yesterday – three times, or was it four?"

"I'd like to see you, Danni. In person."

"I'm busy."

"Just an hour," he said.

She sighed, relented. "Okay," she said wearily, "how about tomorrow?"

He shifted, easing his bulk from side to side. "Actually, I'm outside. I hired a car. I know a nice little Gujerati place in Lewisham."

The bastard... He knew she couldn't resist Indian food.

"So," he went on, "are you hungry?"

She hesitated, thinking it through. "First," she said, "seeing as you're here, could you come up? I want to show you something."

"And then dinner?"

"Just get your backside up those stairs, Bryce," she snapped.

He must have shifted himself at double-quick time, for twenty seconds later her door chime sounded. She waved a command to let him in, then called out, "In here."

He appeared in the doorway, looking hesitant, and something in his cowed body language forced her to smile.

"Danni, look... I'm so sorry."

She wasn't going to let him off that easily. "Come here and look at these," she ordered, waving him over.

He shrugged off his camel-hair coat and stepped into the triangle formed by the three screens, squinting at the images. "What are they?"

She waved aside the case notes, and the screen shrank. She swiped one of the other screens and the shot of the greensward expanded.

"Randolph White's place in Geneva on the Saturday morning of his murder. These are all the files from Europol's investigation into the killing back then."

"Does Tsang know you've downloaded them?"

She shrugged. "They're readily accessible from my office. I don't know if he's got anyone monitoring what I'm doing. I haven't seen him for three days, and I'm blocking his calls."

"That will put him in a fine mood."

"As if I give a shit," she said. "I've taken a few days off. I called in sick the other day."

"You're okay?"

"As fine as I'll ever be, thank you," she said stiffly.

He nodded, glancing at her. "So, you've found something?"

"I don't know. It doesn't make sense."

"Show me."

She nodded towards the expanded screen. "This is White's place a few minutes before he was murdered at eleven fifty that morning. Now, look there…"

He peered. "I don't see – ah, what's that?"

She waved, commanding the screen to expand even further and home in on a patch of shrubbery in the top left corner.

It showed a faint figure, crouching behind a stand of pampas grass. "She's there for the next four minutes or so, staring at the villa. Then she gets up suddenly and hurries away, back towards the perimeter wall."

"'She'?"

Danni turned to the other screen and waved. The pixelated image of a woman's face filled a metre of air before them, nothing more than a coffee-coloured blur. "Even with image enhancement, that's the best I could get, which is a fat lot of good. She moved off towards the wall and climbed over."

"So was this before White was killed?"

"She was in the bushes, watching the villa, at the exact time forensics say White was stabbed to death."

"Can you get a closer image of the villa?"

"I tried, but this is interesting." She waved again, calling up another screen. "This one shows the front of the residence and the driveway, an hour before the murder. And then, look..."

The image was hit by a hail of static, flickered and turned black.

"That was the only surveillance camera operating at the time – quite a coincidence that it should malfunction just before he was killed, don't you think?"

"Surely there were other cameras? Audio? Motion detectors?"

"There should have been, but according to the police reports, the security system was undergoing an overhaul at the time, and the only camera operating was the one covering the drive and the greensward. But that's the other strange thing – there's no mention at all in the detectives' case notes of anyone following up the figure lurking in the shrubbery."

He stared at the grainy image of the woman. "Okay, so maybe they overlooked it, and only your enhancement picked her up."

Danni pursed her lips. "I wondered that – for about five seconds. It might've been eighty years ago, but the tech back then wasn't that primitive. Any cop with half a brain would have detected the woman. So that failure, combined with the very coincidental downtime of the other security cams, *and* the malfunction of the camera covering the driveway, would lead you to suspect a cover up. But that's as far as I've got. It's so damned frustrating. The case notes get me nowhere, and the image of the woman is so compromised I can't even begin to make an identification."

He looked at her, nodding towards the image. "She's black, medium build – that much is obvious. You don't think...?"

"What?"

"Could it be Rima Cagnac?"

Danni pressed two fingers against her right temple. "If so, and if she witnessed the killing of her husband, then why didn't she say anything to the investigating officers before she left aboard the *Strasbourg*?"

Bryce stared at the pixelated image, shaking his head. "We really need to identify the woman," he said. "Can you send me these files? I'll forward them to Martin and see if he can find anything. Chances are, at the rate he works, he'll have something for us by the time we drop by on our way to Lewisham."

She gasped, staring at him. "The presumption of the man!"

"I know you love Indian food," he said, "and the meal will be on me…"

"You patronising–!"

"So that's a yes, I take it?" he said, smiling.

"I should really tell you to fuck off and don't come back, but luckily for you I'm hungry."

She instructed her imp to send the files to Bryce, then moved to her bedroom and changed into a navy-blue trouser suit and matching beret.

Five minutes later, Bryce was making inconsequential small talk that she wasn't listening to, as his car steered through the neon-lit streets of south London. She could tell he was nervous, perhaps wondering if her acquiescence to join him for the meal indicated she had forgiven him. He should be so lucky… It would take more than a dall makhani to win her round.

They pulled up before a shuttered fruit and vegetable shop, and Bryce led the way up a murky staircase and rapped on a steel door.

Martin Khalsa was pacing back and forth when they entered, cracking his knuckles as he moved from screen to screen, gesturing with quick flicks of his long, bony fingers and muttering to himself. Views of the Geneva greensward, and the compromised image of the woman, hung in the air beside others – screens full of scrolling texts, surveillance footage from around the world, and old black and white movies. Among them was a stilled image Danni recognised as that of

Marius Gellner, from the photograph she'd recorded in Alastair
Fairleigh-White's room at Carstairs Hall.

Danni leaned against the steel door, taking a deep breath of
fetid air. It was like a greenhouse in the room and already she
was sweating.

"Interesting," Martin said, peering at the image of the
woman, "almost antique. And it's running on a system
I haven't come across for a decade."

Bryce indicated the woman. "Do you think you can identify
her?"

"Eventually," Martin said. "And you said you wanted to
know what might've compromised the security surveillance
system at the villa?"

"You can do that?" Danni asked.

"I can look into whether it was a legitimate system
overhaul," he said. "If it wasn't, I might be able to tell how it
was compromised – it all depends on how expertly whoever
did it covered their tracks. Give me an hour, and by then
I should have something."

"Good work," Bryce said. He gestured at the image of Marius
Gellner. "Any luck there?"

Martin cracked his knuckles and swore. "There's very little in
any archives about Marius Gellner after 2100, when he joined
the White Foundation. It's as if he vanished – the Foundation
did a good job of scrubbing his traces."

"Have you managed to work out his relation to Major
Gellner?" Bryce asked.

Martin sighed. "You've given me very little to work on.
I have a poor-quality image of Major Gellner outside the police
HQ, and nothing else. And he has virtually no online footprint.
The problem is that there simply isn't enough good-quality
footage of the major to use for comparisons."

"He visited Carstairs Hall last week," Danni said. "How about
you scour surveillance cams in the area, or could you get into
the security system of the hall itself?"

"I was about to try that when Edouard dumped the latest files on me." Martin smiled. "So what do you want first? Gen on the mystery woman, or on the Gellners?"

Bryce said, "How about you concentrate on the woman, Martin, and then turn your attention to the Gellners?"

"Will do. Oh, one thing, before you go," Martin went on as Danni moved towards the door. "You wanted me to check on Peter Conway, the secretary at Carstairs Hall."

"What have you found?" she asked.

"He's been with the Foundation just three months. Before that he worked for a tech fund based in London. He's twenty-eight, a keen sportsman, with no criminal record or known sexual deviancy."

Danni looked at him. Martin held up a hand. "It's something I thought it best to look into," he said.

"So I can trust him?"

"I see no reason why you shouldn't."

Danni thanked him and led the way from the sweltering room. It was a relief to hit the freezing air of the street. As they drove away, she considered Martin Khalsa and smiled.

"What?" Bryce asked, glancing at her.

"Martin. Does he ever leave that room?"

"I've never seen him outside. I suspect he's agoraphobic."

"It's a wonder he can breathe in there."

"It's his world," Bryce said, "or rather the datasphere is."

They fell silent as Bryce's car steered through the city streets towards Lewisham. At one point he said, "About the other day, what I did—"

But Danni interrupted with, "I haven't eaten since breakfast. Once I started going through those files, the time just flashed by..."

Bryce got the message and said nothing for the rest of the journey.

The Agra was a converted carpet warehouse on the high street. The ceiling on the second floor had been converted into a transparent dome through which they could watch, if they so wished, the floating megascreens dispensing world news and sporting events.

Danni kept the conversation inconsequential as she ordered mushroom bhaji starters, palak paneer, and a jug of sweet lassi. Bryce said he rarely ate Indian food, asked her advice, then ordered onion bhajis, murgh masala and a beer. Even his condescending bow to her culinary knowledge, Danni suspected, was a bid to win her over. Or was she being hard on this big, lonely, but well-meaning man?

Their starters arrived and Danni bit into the succulent spiced mushrooms. She poured two glasses of lassi and sat back, staring up through the dome. "It's a pity we can't see the stars."

"I didn't have you down as an astronomer."

"I've always been interested in space. And now that Gordon's out there…"

Bryce reached out, but Danni moved her hand away.

"Gordon will be fine," Bryce said. "He can look after himself."

She nodded, unconvinced.

"Are you close to him?"

She shrugged. "I first met him almost ten years ago, and we've worked together for three, so yes, you could say that. I know him pretty well, and I like him."

He sipped his lassi and regarded her. "Do you know something? I've known Gordon for going on six years, and he never told me what happened."

"What happened?"

Their main courses arrived, interrupting the conversation. Danni spooned creamy spinach and cheese onto her plate, scooped up a mouthful of spinach with a chapatti and chewed. She sighed. "God, that's good."

"So," Bryce said, "five years ago Gordon was working in the homicide squad, a high-flying inspector with good promotion prospects. He might even have made it as commander. I didn't really know him at the time, but I knew him by reputation.

I came up against him in court early that year, and he made a big impression. Then just a few months later I heard he'd been dumped in cold cases – the morgue, as he calls it – and I never could find out why..."

"He doesn't like talking about it." She ate a little more, then went on. "It was before I started working with him, but I've seen the case files. He'd been working on a rape case, and it became increasingly clear the culprit was going to get off on a technicality. In the cells, before his release... Well, the guy started taunting Gordon, and it was more than he could take. He only hit him once, but the guy fell, landed badly, hitting his head. That one punch almost killed the bastard. Gordon was lucky he wasn't fired there and then – or worse. Our commanding officer at the time knew Gordon was one of the good guys. She pulled a few strings and saved his neck, though he was demoted to cold case investigations. It changed him, Ed. He'd lived for his work, and suddenly he was shuffling old crimes he had little chance of solving, with no resources to back him up, and little support from the brass."

"I met him when I heard he'd moved to cold cases," Bryce said. "You're right, there were no resources, but at last at least there was someone of quality there. Someone who might get results. I had a case, an eighteen-year-old who had been missing for ten years–"

"Sophie Holding."

"That's right. I could see Gordon had hit rock-bottom. I had too: it was around the time Kat died. We never found out what had happened to Sophie, but in a strange way that case rescued a pair of middle-aged has-beens who'd lost direction, not that that was any comfort to the girl's mother... I tried then to find out what had happened for Gordon to be shunted over to cold cases, but even when we'd had a few beers, he wouldn't open up."

"Well, now you know." She pointed to her meal and changed the subject. "This is excellent. Thanks for suggesting the place."

"No problem. We should do it more often. Look–"

"You've apologised," she cut in, "so let's just forget about it."

He nodded. "I just wanted to say... About us. Look, later... when the baby's born... I'd like to be around for you, for–"

"Her," she said. "It's a girl."

He smiled. "I'd like to see her from time to time, help out." He held up both hands. "That's all. I know where I stand vis-a-vis me and you, so it's not about that. But I'd like to be there for you both, okay?"

She stared across the table at him, then smiled and nodded. "Okay, Ed. Okay, that'll be fine."

He matched her smile, and she could see that he was relieved. As if in celebration, he ordered another beer.

They were finishing the meal when Bryce's wristcom pinged.

"It's Martin," he said. He looked at his watch. "Less than an hour – that's not bad going."

He accepted the call and Martin's image expanded at the end of the table, half a metre tall. He peered out at them, surrounded by his floating screens. "Edouard... Safe to talk?"

Bryce nodded. "Go on."

"I've made an ID match on the image of the woman in Geneva," Martin said.

Danni leaned forward. She knew what he was going to say: that the woman skulking in the shrubbery was Rima Cagnac.

Martin surprised her. "Facial recognition was hopeless on such degraded imagery, but I ran skeletal and gait analysis against databases of the time and I've made a high-confidence match. The woman is Jayne Waterford, a journalist turned ecologist who shipped out aboard the *Strasbourg* six days later."

"What the hell was she doing near the villa that morning?" Bryce said.

"Search me," Martin said. "But there's more. I've found footage showing a street not far from Sebastian White's villa. It shows Waterford climbing into a car and being driven away. I did some digging and traced the owner of the car. Selma

Betancourt, an investigative journalist: quite a big name, back then. It was Betancourt who blew the lid on the Chinese backing of the Saudi invasion of Iran a few years earlier."

"Good work, Martin."

The young man held up a hand. "It doesn't end there. Just two weeks after Sebastian White's murder, Selma Betancourt was also murdered – a single shot in the back of the head while walking in Epping Forest. Her killer was never found."

"Did you look into the security failure at Sebastian White's villa that morning?" Danni asked.

"On first impression, it looks as if it was a real-time failure, but it's pretty clear to me that it was retroactive."

"Meaning?"

"Someone got into the security system and wiped it *after* White was killed. Someone was covering their tracks."

A little later, Bryce thanked Martin and cut the connection. They sat for a time, staring at each other.

"I wonder..." Danni began. "Could it have been Jayne Waterford who murdered Sebastian White?"

Bryce considered the question. "But the footage shows her *outside* the villa, looking in, at the time White was stabbed to death. It's more likely that she and Selma were investigating the White family's shady dealings – especially as, two weeks after Sebastian White's murder, Betancourt herself was killed."

Danni sighed. "Martin said Jayne Waterford shipped out on the *Strasbourg*. I wonder if Gordon has come across her? Do you think we'll ever work out what happened all those years ago?"

Bryce reached across the table and took her hand, and this time she didn't pull it away.

24

Last Days on Earth

"I wasn't always an ecologist," Jayne told him as they drove over the roof of the world. "I studied journalism and politics at university, and in my early twenties worked for PanEuro, stationed in the Far East as an investigative journalist. I found myself covering corruption at high level, corporate and governmental." She shook her head, her thoughts far away. "I thought I was cynical and hard-bitten when I began, but what I saw during the course of those years – graft that didn't just line the pockets of tycoons and politicians but undermined aid projects and environmental programs – well, it wore me down. What I'd learned in that time about ecological infrastructure projects gave me an interest in the subject, so I went back to university to retrain. After graduating, I worked on various schemes in Africa and the Indian sub-continent."

She stopped, staring down at the water bulb in her hand.

Kemp kept his eyes on the furrow along which their ATV was travelling. "Don't tell me, you came across graft there, too?"

"On a grand scale. I must admit, Gordon, it rocked me. There I was, trying to do my little bit to make the world a better place, and corrupt politicians were..." She waved. "So call me naive, idealistic. Perhaps I was... Anyway, that was about the time the Carrasco mission was recruiting a whole raft of specialists, amongst them ecologists. I didn't think twice about applying. I was pissed with the world and just wanted to get off – so I applied, and what do you know?" She smiled across at him.

"So how does all this lead to knowing who killed Rima Cagnac's husband?"

"I'm getting there, darling. Bear with me. So… three years into the project, I'm all trained up, mission briefed and ready to say goodbye to planet Earth – which I wouldn't see again for around a hundred and seventy years. Which didn't bother me in the slightest. I reckoned I'd either come back to a world by some miracle rejuvenated, or devastated – and my money was on the latter. Anyway, a few months before we were due to leave aboard the *Strasbourg*, I was contacted by an old friend, Selma Betancourt, a colleague based in London who worked for PanEuro. She said she'd come across something big, but needed my help. To cut a long story short, she suspected some… cabal was the word she used, a dodgy consortium of businessmen… of syphoning monies from government grants and private donations. This money was intended for materials for power plants, factories, hospitals, etcetera, to reconstruct climate-damaged nations in the tropics. But the infrastructure never materialised at its supposed destination. She wanted me to do some digging in Switzerland, where I was based at the time. She'd done her detective work, traced leads back to a group of businessmen in Geneva and Lucerne and headed by someone who carefully guarded his identity."

"So who was he?"

She cocked an eye at him. "Come on, you're supposed to be the detective here…"

"Randolph White?"

"Right. But Selma suspected there was more to it than just syphoning off funds meant for reconstruction. There was something else going on, something connected to the European government. Randolph White had his fingers in a lot of pies –

he was active in the pan-European alliance, working to shape it to his own needs. He had politicians in his pocket."

"So what did Selma suspect him of?"

"That's just it. She didn't know, exactly. That's where I came in. She knew I was on the Carrasco project, as was Rima Cagnac – we'd met during training and hit it off. Rima was married to Sebastian White, Randolph's brother. Selma wanted me to get to know Rima's husband, do some digging."

"And you agreed to this?"

"I was torn. I didn't want to jeopardise my place on the mission, but at the same time I was intrigued. I wanted to know what was going on. So I set up a meeting with Rima in Geneva." She gestured. "She cancelled a couple of meetings at short notice, so I decided to call round at her place uninvited, maybe talk to her husband. They lived in a big house in extensive grounds in the exclusive district of Eaux-Vives, overlooking the lake. It wasn't that difficult to bluff my way in at the gate. I had a story prepared, that I was a friend of Rima Cagnac's and wanted to talk about aspects of the mission – all genuine, by the way. I was approaching the house when..." She paused, biting her lip. "I was pretty close to a window, perhaps a few metres away, when I saw two men in the kitchen, arguing, pushing each other about... I ducked out of sight then, when I looked again, one of them was lying face up on the floor, covered in blood. And the other, a man in his fifties, was reaching for a towel, his hands bloody. I hid in some shrubbery and made damn sure he didn't see me as he walked from the house." She smiled across at Kemp. "So you see, it can't have been Rima Cagnac who killed her husband, Gordon... So, am I telling the truth?"

He nodded. "The whole truth and nothing but," he said. "But this man, the killer – did you recognise him?"

"Yes, I did," she said. "It was Sebastian's brother, Randolph White."

* * *

"I got out of there pretty damn quick, I can tell you. Through the shrubbery and over a wall. I was scared sick they'd trace me. I knew from years as an investigative journalist that I wouldn't stand a chance up against the might of Randolph White and his empire. Selma was waiting for me that day, and I told her what I'd seen. She agreed with my assessment and persuaded me to depart on the *Strasbourg* as planned, leaving her to continue with her work, compiling a dossier of evidence on the White family's activities. So I did exactly that."

She grinned across at him. "Imagine my reaction when I learned that a detective inspector had come all the way from Earth, investigating Sebastian's murder. For a time back there, I thought you'd come for me." She took a drink of water. "I learned from one of the scientists who came through the wormhole with you that Randolph White died in 2114 while holidaying in Bermuda, four years after he murdered his brother. So the bastard never paid for the crime..."

Kemp smiled. "The super-rich never do, do they? Randolph White was powerful enough to pay people to cover his tracks, provide him with an alibi. There was no forensic evidence at the scene at all – he clearly paid for a clean-up. He wasn't even a suspect." He thought about it. "So okay, you saw him arguing with his brother... I wonder why, and why he resorted to killing him?"

Jayne shrugged. "If you want my guess, and that's all it is, I reckon it was a spur of the moment thing. They had a heated confrontation, pushed each other about a bit, and Randolph sees red, snatches up a knife and lashes out in rage..."

"And your friend, this Selma Betancourt, she claimed that the person responsible for all the corrupt money-moving was Randolph White?"

"That's what she said."

"So maybe that was what the fracas was about, that day?

Sebastian had discovered that his brother was up to something shady, confronted him about it... and paid the price."

Jayne rocked her head. "Who knows? A lot of time has passed since then. Let's face it, we might never discover the truth."

He considered her. "Unless Rima Cagnac knows something, of course."

He sat in silence for a while as they drove along the grooved track.

He pointed at her. "I wonder..."

"Go on."

"Randolph's shady dealings that Betancourt was looking into, his syphoning off of vast funds... Might it be possible that it was to subsidize the quantum lattice project, which he ordered ESO to keep secret until you all emerged from cold sleep? And maybe *that* was the reason for the secrecy until then – because he didn't want anyone investigating the illegal diversion of resources into the lattice project until he was dead and gone."

"Maybe, Gordon – but it's all speculation. The truth died along with Randolph White over seventy-five years ago."

"It's the cold-case detective in me," he laughed, "wanting resolution after all this time."

25

The Line of Descent

It had taken Danni two days of intermittent trawling through the datasphere – between bouts of fatigue and frustration – to come up with anything of interest concerning the investigative journalist, Selma Betancourt.

She found lots of the woman's crusading journalism highlighting the Chinese involvement in Middle Eastern affairs, and some routine articles on the climate crisis, but little else. As might be expected, Betancourt had made efforts to keep her personal life out of the public sphere – or, at least, that was Danni's first impression. But somehow it didn't ring true... A journalist like Betancourt would understand the importance of limiting her personal digital footprint more than most, but even so, the records Danni did find seemed anodyne... *curated*. Put that together with the fact that Betancourt had been murdered in what looked like a very professional manner, and it seemed that the journalist's very existence had been purposefully cleaned up.

That morning, she'd turned her attention to ancient marketing databases and local government records. She discovered that although Betancourt had been born in London and had lived there until the age of forty, she'd then moved to a separatist community on the Isle of Ely. There, eighty-five years ago, she'd given birth to a daughter, EmilieJane.

Danni sat back and placed a hand on her stomach. She felt

an odd connection with the murdered investigative journalist. Her daughter would have been just five years old at the time of her death, and would have grown up without knowing the love and care of a mother; despite herself, Danni found that she was weeping.

She dried her eyes, swore at herself, and laughed.

Would it be too much to hope that EmilieJane might still be alive – more, might still live on the Isle of Ely?

She searched the records for any details for EmilieJane Betancourt, but came up with nothing.

She'd seen something a while back about the Isle. She recalled that over the years the tiny island had attracted counter-culture anarchists, radical environmentalists, and those disaffected with the modern world – and hadn't there been something about the community attempting to declare the island independent from the rest of England fifty years ago?

She called up a screen and ran a search, and for the next ten minutes read about the disparate group of anarcho-Greens who wanted nothing to do with the ultra-technological world of 22nd Century Europe. For its part, the rest of the world was content to ignore the island and its odd inhabitants, despite the occasional rant in parliament from right-wing politicians complaining about the commune's Luddite leeches and parasites.

The community was still in existence, but it proved difficult to contact. There appeared to be no local leadership or commercial infrastructure, and the community had no datasphere presence. Which, considering their anti-technology stance, wasn't at all surprising.

However, she did find an archaic contact tag listed for a body calling itself the Isle of Ely Independence Committee.

Danni instructed her imp to place a call with the tag, then sat back and waited.

A minute later a gruff male voice sounded in her ear. "Who's

that?" The call screen hanging in the air before Danni remained
dark; she didn't know if this was because the committee chose
not to show themselves to the world, or simply did not have
the technology.

"Danni Bellini, I–"

"What do you want?"

Rather than admit to being a police officer – which she
thought might not win any favours – she had a lie ready and
waiting. "I'm a journalist, covering ecological movements, and
I'd very much like do a piece about the Isle."

A hesitation, then: "Who do you work for?"

"I'm an independent," she said, adding, "and I have a contact
from quite a few years ago, EmilieJane Betancourt–"

"Oh, I see." The man's tone became instantly less hostile.
"Well, I'm sorry… Em died just a few months ago."

"My word…" Danni feigned shock. "She was a wonderful
woman. I'm so sorry…" She thought fast, and went on, "Didn't
she have a child–?"

"That'd be Kiri," the man said.

"Kiri, of course. I wonder if I could have a word with Kiri,
offer my condolences?"

He hesitated again. "She's out in the field. I could call her."

"If you would, I'd be grateful."

"Hold on a minute." She heard a door opening, then the
man's voice bellowing, "Kiri!"

She waited, considering what she would tell the woman.

"Hello?" A light, pleasant, middle-aged voice sounded in her
ear. "Jethro said you're a journalist?"

"That's right. An indie." Danni gave her name. "I knew your
mother, and I was shocked to hear of her passing. I wanted to
do a story on the community, and" – she ventured – "a piece
about your grandmother."

The woman sounded surprised. "Selma?"

"That's right. You see…" Danni winced, anticipating a negative
reaction, "… I'm investigating the circumstances of her death."

"You want to talk to me about Nan Selma?"

"That's right. I could come across and we could talk. I'm very interested in your nan's work, and the mystery surrounding her–"

"It was no mystery," the woman interrupted, "she was assassinated."

Danni echoed the last word.

"That's right, and…" The woman hesitated, and Danni wondered if she were considering the wisdom of what she said next. "And I know who did it."

Danni swallowed. "You do?"

A silence ensued, and for a second or two Danni feared that the woman had cut the connection.

Then she went on in a quiet voice, "Not over the line, okay? You never know who's listening in."

"I understand. I could come up–"

"I'm working for the next couple of days."

"I could come up at the weekend, on Saturday."

"Do that. You'll find me at Hackley Farm. It'll be good to talk. I never knew Nan, but Mum said she was a good woman, the best, and what those bastards did to her…"

"I'm sorry," Danni said, choking up at the emotion in the woman's voice.

"I'll see you Saturday," Kiri Betancourt said, and then she did cut the connection.

Danni sat back and closed her eyes, considering what the woman had said. Did she really know the identity of her grandmother's killer, or was it merely hearsay passed down from her grieving mother?

She moved to the kitchen and put a plate of three samosas into the heater, poured herself a tall glass of mango lassi, and returned to the lounge. She was finishing the second samosa when her imp said, "Incoming. Edouard Bryce."

"Put him through."

Bryce was in the back of a car, swaying back and forth. "Danni, Martin's come up with something. He said it was important, though he was reluctant to say much more until I got there."

"Important?"

"It's about our friend, Major Gellner. I'm on my way to see Martin now. I'll be passing your place in two minutes if you want to come."

Danni nodded. "I'll see you then."

She gulped down the last of her lassi, held the third samosa between her teeth while she pulled on a coat, then hurried from her apartment and down the stairs.

A heavy fall of snow had coated the street to a depth of ten centimetres, and more blew into her face as she stamped her feet against the arctic wind. A cab puttered around the corner and drew up in the street, and Bryce gestured at her from the back seat.

She climbed in beside him, chewing the last of her samosa.

Bryce stared at her. "Are you addicted to those things?" he asked as they set off.

"I think I am." She wiped crumbs from the front of her coat. "Martin didn't say anything else about Gellner?"

He shook his head. "Watch this, and tell me what you think."

He waved, and a small screen opened before them showing a miniaturised Martin Khalsa staring out in some agitation. "*Edouard... Get over here, now, okay? We need to talk.*"

"*What is it, Martin?*" Bryce had said.

"*I... I've found something on Gellner. But... look, I need to show you, okay?*"

"*What?*"

"*Just get over here, okay!*"

The connection died.

Danni said, "He looked terrified."

Bryce nodded. "I wonder what the hell he's discovered?"

Five minutes later they pulled up before the fruit and veg shop and climbed the stairs to Martin's bedsit. Martin snatched open the door and slammed it behind them, then strode back and forth, interlacing his fingers and bending them back until they cracked.

"Martin, calm down. What is it?" Bryce shot a concerned glance at Danni, and placed a hand on the young man's shoulder. "Look, just sit down and tell us all about it."

Martin nodded, slumped into the only armchair, then instantly jumped up and resumed his pacing.

"I don't like it," he muttered.

Danni said, "Martin, what is it?"

Still pacing, he shot out, "I did what you asked, hacked into a surveillance system in the road outside Carstairs Hall. I tried the hall itself, but no go. Their security is high-grade, government-level stuff."

"What did you find, Martin?" Bryce said softly.

Martin nodded. He looked frantic. "Gellner. Major Gellner. He was in a car, being driven to the hall a week or so ago. I managed to lift some clean footage of him, good enough to run an ID comparison. Christ…" He fell silent, pacing manically.

"Martin?" Danni said.

"As you'd expect for a security operative, I didn't get any matches on public systems, so I ran comparisons with Marius Gellner, the guy you suspected was the major's grandfather. Looking for familial traits, indications of lineage, relational proximity. If Marius was the major's grandfather, those tests would confirm it."

"And?" Bryce said.

Martin stopped dead in his tracks and stared from Danni to Bryce. "And I found out who Major Gellner is."

Bryce nodded. "Very well… So? Who is he?"

Martin smiled, nervously. "I ran, and re-ran, all kinds of tests – mannerism, gait, skeletal structure, facial ID, I even ran eyeball-tracking to establish how he moved his eyes! What

I found was that Major Gellner, the guy in the car, just two weeks ago… he's *Marius* Gellner, from eighty years ago."

Silence filled the small room.

Danni swallowed, overcome with a sudden sensation of light-headedness.

Bryce laughed. "Impossible!"

"That's what I thought." Martin nodded. "No way, I thought. I've got it wrong. The system's glitched, the software's compromised. So I checked, and checked again, ran a few alternative tests. Ran the same tests on *other* people, just to be sure they worked." He shook his head, cracked his knuckles. "I wasn't wrong. The software wasn't lying. They're the same person. Christ, what have we got ourselves into…?"

He started pacing again, but Bryce placed his bulk before the young man, stopping him. "Listen to me, Martin. What you're saying… it can't be possible. It's a mistake. They can't be one and the same. Listen to me," he said, grabbing Martin's shoulder as the young man tried to resume his compulsive pacing. "I said, listen! Run the tests again, check the analyses. The telomerase rejuvenation procedure isn't that advanced – it can't keep a fifty-year-old man at the same age for eighty years. Look at what it did to people like Fairleigh-White, for chrissake!"

"Then how the hell do you explain it?" Martin said, tears in his eyes.

Bryce confronted him, red in the face. "As I said, it's a mistake. The system's made an error. *You* made a mistake!"

Martin faced him, shaking. "I don't make mistakes like that!" he screamed, spittle flying from his mouth.

"Christ, I need a drink!" Bryce said, turning and striding from the bedsit.

Danni made to follow him, then stopped and turned to the sobbing young man.

She took a step forward. "Come here," she said, and took him in her arms.

"I... I don't make mistakes like that," he sniffed, "and he...
he of *all* people... should know that."

"I know," she soothed. "I know you don't, Martin."

She made for the door, then turned. "I'll be in touch."

Slumped in the armchair now, staring down at his knuckles,
Martin nodded.

Danni hurried down the stairs and joined Bryce in the
freezing street.

26

Base West One

Kemp awoke and struggled into a sitting position. The sun was rising on the far horizon, flooding the top of the world with its cerise light.

Jayne glanced over her shoulder from the driving seat. "You're awake at last."

"How long have I been out?" Grabbing handholds, he made his way to the passenger seat and slumped down.

"Eight hours, just over."

He took two water bulbs from the cooler and passed one to Jayne.

"And you've driven all that time?"

She nodded. "Popped a couple of pills," she said.

He peered out at the ceaseless monotony of the plain. The only feature was the furrow along which they travelled, arrow-straight to the horizon. "How far away are we from the camp?"

"An hour, maybe a little more."

He considered the message Rima Cagnac had sent Jayne, then said, "So the sentients took Cagnac and Marcosi... why just those two? What became of the rest?"

Jayne shrugged. "Maybe they just grabbed the pair when they were away from the others. We'll find out when we get there, perhaps."

"And why the hell were they taken?"

She gave him an odd glance. "Is that your detective mentality working overtime, asking questions when they're redundant?"

He bridled. "Redundant?"

"Gordon, we're dealing here with aliens, not with your run-of-the-mill criminal humans. Who can second-guess the motivations of sentients evolved in an environment totally unlike anything we've experienced, primed by behavioural drives we can't even guess at?"

He slumped in his seat, lost in thought. "When we get close to the camp," he said, "I wonder if we could conceal the ATV somewhere and go the rest of the way on foot?"

She grunted and gestured around them. "In this terrain? Look around you, Gordon. You see anywhere to hide an ATV?"

"That's what I feared," he said. He shrugged. "I'd just like to know if Gellner is following the ATV."

"That's a good bet, seeing as it's odds on they know we're heading in this direction."

But there was always the possibility, he knew, that they were tracking not the vehicle, but him – or rather, his imp.

But he wasn't ready to tell Jayne that, yet.

"You said the ATV had a cache of weapons?" he said a little later.

"In the silver locker under the back seat." She looked at him as he stood unsteadily. "The aliens or Gellner's men?" she asked.

"I was thinking more of Gellner, but if the sentients turn out to be hostile, then we'll need to defend ourselves. They have taken two humans captive, after all."

A little later, she said, "So what's our story when we reach the base?"

He shrugged. "The truth. We've come to find Cagnac. They might have seen the aliens take her, might be able to give us directions." He stopped and smiled at her.

"What?"

"Here I am, talking about aliens... A few days ago, aliens meant illegal refugees from North America."

"Surprising how rapidly the once unfamiliar becomes the norm," she said.

She peered at her softscreen unrolled and adhered to the dash. The image of a crude route map showed a flashing light denoting Base West One, and a small one designating their ATV.

Minutes later, Jayne slowed down and pointed straight ahead. Half a dozen irregularities showed on the plane: a couple of ATVs and a few domes. They were minutes away from the base.

Kemp turned in his seat and looked back across the roof of the world, as if expecting Gellner and his men to show themselves on the horizon. With an involuntary shiver, despite the heat in his biohazard suit, he told himself not to be so paranoid.

"I wonder what we'll find?" he asked. "A bunch of men and women spooked by first contact?"

She glanced at him. "I don't want to alarm you, Gordon, but while you were asleep I tried to contact the team."

"And?"

She shook her head. "No reply."

They approached the camp and Jayne slowed down, then braked.

At last she said, "Oh no ..."

Kemp climbed from the buggy and approached the camp, then halted beside the first dome with Jayne at his side.

At first, he found it hard to take in the reality of what his vision was relaying: he'd never seen anything like it, and for a few stunned seconds he failed to make visual sense of the sectioned remains of what once had been human beings, the scattered arms and legs, the occasional head and bloody torso.

Beside him, Jayne was weeping.

He turned, stumbling as he hurried back to the ATV and pulled two lasers from the storage unit under the back seat.

He rejoined Jayne and passed her a weapon. Directly behind the second ATV, twenty metres away, he made out a dark depression in the ground, evidently the mouth of a tunnel leading beneath the surface. Ten metres to its right was a second.

He turned to Jayne. "How many were there?"

She was still stunned. "What?"

"The scientists? How many?"

She shook her head. "Perhaps a dozen. I don't know... What happened to them?"

He ignored the question. "Keep an eye on the tunnel mouths, okay? I'll see if there are survivors."

She nodded and lifted her laser.

He moved across the camp, picking his way through the body parts. He stopped and knelt, examining a severed leg. At first he'd entertained the notion that one of the researchers might have gone berserk, turned a laser on his fellows – but the evidence of the sectioned limb indicated otherwise. The wound showed no signs of laser burns; it was made by something sharp, a blade, perhaps, or maybe even claws...

He moved on, stopping from time to time to examine random body parts, only to find that all of them exhibited the same clean wounds.

Just when he was doubting that he'd find anyone left alive, he heard a faint groaning to his right.

He hurried across to the second ATV and made out, half concealed beneath the vehicle, a young woman in a ripped biohazard suit. She lay on her side, curled into a protective foetal position, the front of her suit split open across the stomach. Her facemask had come off – perhaps in the struggle with whatever had attacked her – and she stared at him with wide, stunned eyes. "Help me..."

He climbed into the ATV, found the medical storage unit and fumbled through vials and containers until he found a cylinder of sedative and a hypoject. He returned to the woman and knelt, trying to avoid her spilled entrails as he did so. He applied the hypoject to the exposed skin of her neck and gave her a 10cc dose. She gasped, smiling up at him in relief.

He found her hand and squeezed.

From across the camp, Jayne called out, "Gordon..."

He looked up. She was unrolling her softscreen.

He turned back to the dying woman as she tried to say something.

"They..." she began.

He leaned closer to catch her faint words.

He squeezed again. "What happened?"

"Aliens..."

He swallowed, his pulse throbbing. This massacre would have huge implications for human activities on Carrasco, he knew. Hostile, sentient aliens changed everything.

She took a breath, gasped. "We had an SOS from Cole..." she began.

He looked up, startled by a sudden movement. Jayne had joined them. "Abdul Cole, a security guard," she said. "He was with them in the tunnels."

She knelt and gently stroked a strand of wet hair from the scientist's cheek.

"Cole..." the woman said, "he told us... he said he'd killed some of the aliens already, but they were coming for him..."

He nodded, squeezed her hand, willing her to hang on.

"Then they came and..." She fell silent, her eyes staring into the turquoise sky.

Kemp said to the woman, "So you heard from Cole... and then they came here?"

"The aliens," she gasped.

She smiled, her eyes losing focus. At least, he thought, the sedative had begun to take effect. She would die without pain.

"Rima Cagnac?" he asked. "Did the aliens take her?"

But why, he asked himself, would the aliens have slaughtered the scientists and taken Cagnac?

The woman whispered, "Cagnac, Marcosi, Cole... they went off earlier."

"How long ago?"

The scientist shook her head minimally.

"We'll get help," Kemp said. "You'll be back at base in no time..." He stopped.

The woman was staring up at him, her expression oddly immobile, no longer imbued with life.

Jayne reached out and closed the scientist's eyes.

She stood and indicated her softscreen. "That was Rima," she said. "Another recorded message. She's desperate. She said Gianfranco Marcosi's dead..."

"Give me the screen, and keep an eye on the tunnels. We don't want to be caught napping if the aliens pay a return visit."

He instructed his imp to parse the metadata from Cagnac's last communique, and fifteen seconds later the voice in his head said, "*The signal originated to the south-west of present location, at a distance of three kilometres, sent two days ago.*"

He relayed the imp's data.

Jayne stared at him, fear on her face. "What now?"

"How long before Gellner's men get here?" he said. "A couple of hours? Less? Considering what they did to Jenny, I don't think they'd think twice about killing us and laying the blame on the aliens."

"So...?"

"There's only one thing we can do, Jayne – press on, find Cagnac–"

"But..." She waved a hand to indicate the carnage surrounding them. "Or we... we could always get the hell out of here and head back to base."

"What if it's the ATV that Gellner's men have a trace on?"

He felt bad as he posed the question. What if the trace was embedded in whatever Tsang had downloaded into *him*, back on Earth?

He pressed his advantage. "You want to find Rima, don't you?"

She looked at him through her faceplate. "You know I do. But..."

"We don't know what happened here, Jayne. We're just trying to fill in the gaps. But we *do* know that Rima has been taken by the aliens and there's a chance we could save her."

He indicated the scientists' second ATV and the tunnel mouth beyond. "And Cole was with Rima and Gianfranco down in the tunnels when first contact was made, so we can assume that's the best place to start looking. So how about we take the ATV and try to find Rima?"

She nodded.

They hurried across to the ATV and climbed aboard. Kemp gunned the engine, and they set off towards the tunnel entrance.

27

The Amphitheatre
of Life and Death

Although she understood on some level that the aliens' treatment of her was indifferent to her suffering, to Rima it was little more than torture. They travelled, wedging her back in the sled with Franco's festering remains, continuing on the journey that she now believed would never end: this was how they existed.

Every jolt of the cart over rut or bump, every snag on vegetation, jarred through her fevered body. Her joints were on fire. Every breath rasped painfully. She just wanted it to be over.

The coolness of fresh leaves pressed against her body was almost as delicious a relief as simply coming to a halt, yet even so, she resented Creasey's ministrations, for they merely prolonged the agony.

Night-time. Cloud-veiled stars overhead. Creasey pressing leaves to her until she was encased, smothered. It was then that the fever became intense, the leaves trapping her body's heat. She felt as if she were about to explode.

And then, at some point, she began to feel better. She felt the release as Creasey peeled the leaves away, felt the coolness of the air.

This repeated wrapping and unwrapping brought to mind the flyer nest Jayne had shown her on one of her first excursions from the main base. So far, theories about cloud fever had focused on the prevalence of dangerous pathogens in the atmosphere. But what if there were also *good* pathogens, ones which conferred some kind of protection? Or what if a sufficiently low dose, even of the otherwise deadly pathogens, might confer some kind of immunity, akin to inoculation? That might explain the flyer nest, and why periodically an adult would return and bury itself deep, exposing the young to controlled doses of pathogens. Was that what Creasey had been doing for her? Protecting her, but also periodically exposing her by peeling away the layers of leaves...

She was a scientist, and she reminded herself of Franco's warning not to jump to conclusions: it was an intriguing hypothesis, but no more than that. But for now, all she knew was that, in her thoroughly unscientific sample of one, she'd been subjected to Creasey's ministrations and, miraculously, she appeared to be recovering.

Sebastian had once taken her to the opera at Verona. They had sat at one of the street cafes in the Piazza Bra, eating finger food and drinking Aperol, and then they had crossed the piazza, bypassing the queues – the White family always bypassed queues – and sat in one of the private boxes in the centre of the space, the limestone ranks of the amphitheatre rising up all around them.

Why was she dreaming of this now? Of Sebastian, in that white suit of his, of their friends, Cassie and Ibrahim, the four of them sharing a box large enough for many times their number and Sebastian opening another bottle of Bollinger.

She opened her eyes and saw that she was at the centre of an amphitheatre not of pale-pink limestone, but of thick tangles of vegetation. The bowl of the amphitheatre was perhaps half a kilometre across, and the same high, its rim framing a perfect circle of turquoise sky. At the centre of this space, a great tree, or group of trees, their trunks twisting together, towered above them, as if reaching for that sky.

The place had an atmosphere unlike anywhere else Rima had encountered on Carrasco. The sense of space she recalled from the Arena di Verona, but also that sense of anticipation as the crowds had filed in – for now, as she peered around, she saw that the place was filling with aliens, far more than had been in the group she had travelled with.

Had these others – perhaps a hundred of them – been here already, waiting for them, or had they all converged on this place at the same time?

Rima forced herself into a sitting position, her movement now encumbered not so much by the pain of her illness, now receding, but by the thick layers of leaves and bulbous encrustations that covered her body.

Creasey appeared as if from nowhere, in that way he had, and squatted before her, his limbs bending where no joints should be. He grunted at her, and moments later words in Franco's voice came from the wristcom, muffled now by the layers of growths on her arm.

"... stars... not us, from sky..."

Rima and Franco were *not us*, and this was the first indication that perhaps the aliens understood they had come from the sky, from the stars. She followed the direction of Creasey's gaze, skywards. The first stars were breaking through the gloom.

"Yes," she said. "We do come from the stars."

This whole arena... It was as if it had been constructed to frame the night sky, and now she understood that this was no amphitheatre: it was a cathedral.

Franco had passed the bloating stage now. He lay slumped at her side, and it was as if his skeleton was somehow receding within his body. His skin hung loose, his eye sockets hollow and the eyes themselves like raisins.

"It's okay, Franco," she said. "I'll get you out of here." She didn't know if her madness was the result of the cloud fever, or if she had lost her grip on reality some time before falling ill.

She fumbled in her suit, bunched now around her waist. Everything was covered in polyps, layers of slime, but she had long passed the stage where this made her retch. She found her softscreen, unrolled it and wiped its surface clean of growths, and held it up as if to show Franco. *Et voila.*

She expected no answer when she tapped Jayne's avatar. Her first message had taken days to get through, after all, and the softscreen had shown no signs of life for at least a couple of days. So when her friend's face expanded to fill the screen she had to do a double-take before she understood that a comms channel had opened up.

"Jayne...?"

"Rima! My darling, we're on our way. We're almost with you."

There was a man with Jayne, loose jowls and thinning grey hair, leaning in from the side of the screen. "Where are you?" he asked, almost aggressively, she thought.

She tried to explain that she was deep underground, that she was in a cathedral and what a wondrous place it was, but they seemed confused. She knew she was rambling. Within seconds, the signal broke up, the exchange over.

And when she turned to Franco and saw him staring back at her with sunken raisin eyes, she wondered if the exchange had taken place at all.

No, she had been wrong about this place. It was more than a mere cathedral. It was a celebration of all that it was to be of Creasey's kind.

Rima still drifted in and out of consciousness – not cured, as she had hoped, but still in the process of *being* cured. So when she saw the grey aliens appearing to merge with the vegetation – one moment there, and then melting into the tangled growth – she thought at first that she was dreaming, or hallucinating.

"… make more…"

She didn't understand Creasey's grunted explanation, if that was what it was.

She made herself stand, take a staggering step. She caught herself, an arm across what were, for want of a better anatomical label, Creasey's shoulders. Had she touched him before? She did not recall, but the feel of his body under her arm, the seeming lack of skeletal structure, merely emphasised his otherness.

They did not melt into the vegetation: on closer inspection she saw that the aliens were enclosed within vesicles or sacs within the thick growth of the surrounding walls. Were they ill? Being cured, as she had been cured?

Some time later, she saw the first emerge, and this appeared to confirm her suspicion that they were suffering some kind of ailment. When the aliens had given themselves to the strange vesicles, they had been indistinguishable from all the others of their kind, but now, as they tore their way free and emerged, crawling on all fours, they were mere husks of the beings they had been.

Others emerged in similar poor condition.

"Why?" she asked Creasey, who squatted placidly at her side.

"… make more…" The same translation of his grunts as before.

She staggered across to the nearest cleft in the vegetation. Through its slit opening – drawing closed even as she looked on – she saw skinny grey limbs, a head, and then another. *Make more…* This was some kind of hatching ground.

"And them?" she waved a hand to indicate two wasted aliens dragging themselves away.

"… not moving… soon…" *Not moving* was the term Creasey

had used to describe Franco. After giving birth, the aliens would die.

Rima looked around the arena, and saw dozens of etiolated aliens crawling in the same direction, away to the place where they would die. This was no cathedral, then: it was a birthing area, and also a dying place, a burial ground, perhaps.

This place represented the full circle of life for Creasey's people: birth, death, the cosmos up above.

And yes, she knew she was doing what Franco would have chastised her for – filling in the gaps and no doubt getting most of it wrong – but the story she was constructing was helping her to get some kind of grasp of who these beings were, at least.

28

Betrayal

Kemp drove for six hours, and then Jayne relieved him at the controls while he slept. He woke some time later as the ATV they had taken from Base West One jounced along the tunnel, lit by an eerie bioluminescent glow from the walls. "How long have I been out?"

"Eight hours. Do you know you snore?"

"I have been told," he grunted. He moved from the rear of the vehicle and dropped into the passenger seat beside her.

"This is madness," Jayne said. "What the aliens did back there at Base West One... And here we are in hot pursuit."

"We don't know what they did," Kemp reminded her. "We know what we saw, but we don't know the story of what happened. Whatever the explanation may be, it's going to have huge consequences for the human presence on Carrasco – and perhaps Rima Cagnac is our best chance of getting that explanation."

He'd been trying to convince himself of this argument all the time he'd been driving, and he still wasn't sure.

"How far are we from Cagnac?"

Jayne indicated the softscreen on the dash. "If we extrapolate their rate of travel from the coordinates in the messages' metadata, about fifteen kay."

He nodded and fell silent, overcome by a sudden wave of despair. He could envisage no realistic positive outcome: Jenny

Vahota's murder had signalled the intent of Gellner's men, and perhaps the object of the mission in general: to make Carrasco habitable for humankind at any cost – even if that meant the murder of individuals whose opposition at a later date might prove problematic to the colonisation program.

But where did that leave him regarding his mission to bring Rima Cagnac back to Earth for questioning? He smiled to himself: as if Gellner would consider that a priority now that the exploration of Carrasco faced bigger issues.

Jayne glanced at him. "Gordon? You okay?"

He voiced his concerns. "So even if we find Cagnac – assuming she's still alive – what then?"

She gripped the wheel and stared ahead. "We take her back to base, as planned–"

He was relentless. "And what *then*?"

"Then we inform my colleagues – those I can trust – about what we found. The aliens…" She looked at him. "If enough of us know what's happening here, then surely Gellner's men…" She trailed off.

"Vahota's murder changed all that, Jayne. Gellner will stop at nothing. You've got to realise that the lives of a few scientists are nothing beside what his masters stand to gain here. This is about possession of an entire world."

She nodded and fell silent.

"And we might not even make it back to base," he went on, "if Gellner's men catch up with us."

She glanced at him. "My, you are pessimistic today. Chances are that we've shaken them off, okay? They might have traced us to Base West One because they were tracking the old ATV, but I reckon we're clear of them now."

He closed his eyes. He wanted to come clean and tell her that it might be *him* they were tracking, but he couldn't bring himself to make the admission.

They travelled in silence for a time, and the sameness of the tunnel walls burrowing through the sponge-like vegetation set up a maddening monotony. He found himself wishing for some sign of variation in the encompassing mass, a differentiating growth to at least give the illusion that they were getting somewhere.

"So if we do make it to Cagnac and somehow free her from the aliens without being caught," he asked, "what then?"

She thought about it. "How many men does Gellner have under him?"

"There were the dozen who came with him originally, and then the back-up that came later from Earth." He shrugged. "Twenty, a couple of dozen?"

"Assuming he left a few men back at base... they'll still outnumber us."

He nodded towards the lasers in the footwell. "And we have these damned useless antiques while Gellner's squad is equipped with..." He swore. "And they're trained killers, Jayne. It doesn't bear thinking about."

Behind her faceplate, she bit her lip as she regarded him. "Maybe you're being overly pessimistic."

"So tell me, please, where I'm going wrong."

She nodded. "Okay. Two things. You were sent here to get Rima Cagnac, yes?"

"I don't see–"

"Hear me out. You have a mission to accomplish. You were tasked with taking Rima back to Earth. There's no reason to assume that Gellner is set against you accomplishing that."

"There's every damned reason, Jayne. The fact that we know about the aliens, for starters."

"But do they necessarily know that we know?"

"On the balance of probabilities, yes they do. The way we quit the dome is a glaring indication that we're onto something. As is the fact that they'll know we saw the carnage at Base West One – and before you say they might not know we've been there, consider the fact that this ATV has been taken. That's a big giveaway, isn't it?" He waved, despairing. "And even if they weren't a hundred per cent certain we knew anything, do you think they'd take the chance and let any witnesses live, or simply hedge their bets and kill us?"

"Put like that..." she said, staring ahead.

A little later, she asked, "So what do we do?"

"We just hope we're still well enough ahead of them so that we can find Cagnac, free her, and head back to base before they catch up with us."

"And then?"

"Let's worry about that when we get there."

His wristcom pinged, alarming him. He stared at the screen, and his heart lurched. "For Chrissake... it's Gellner."

"Ignore it!" Jayne said.

Kemp thought about it. "No, if I can find out where he is, how far away... Stop the buggy."

Jayne eased the ATV to a halt and Kemp relayed the call to the softscreen on the dash. Gellner's head and shoulders showed; he was evidently somewhere in the tunnels, as his features were illuminated by the verdant luminescence.

"Gellner?"

Careful to remain out of view, Jayne stared at the major, wide-eyed.

"Inspector Kemp, just where are you?"

He controlled his breathing and replied, "I'm not at all sure this place has a name, Major. Where are you?"

Gellner's face broke up, reformed. The connection crackled. "... just found the remains... Base West One. You're in danger, Kemp... Are you alone?"

"Of course—"

"Waterford isn't with you?"

Kemp feigned mystification. "Who?"

"The ecologist, Jayne Waterford... I assumed—"

Kemp shook his head. "I'm on my own, Major."

"Just..." Gellner's face broke up again, "... back here, okay? You're in danger."

"And where is here, Major?"

"Base West One."

Kemp swallowed, nodded. "You're breaking up, Major...
I'm losing you..."

He cut the connection and stared at Jayne. "He was lying,"
he said. "He was in a tunnel – coming after me." He swore,
then went on. "On the plus side, he doesn't know you're with
me. Okay, let's get the hell out of here."

She nodded and gunned the engine into life, and they
bounced off along the tunnel.

Kemp sat back in his seat, wanting to shout out in rage. If he
needed any convincing that it was *him* – something embedded
in the hardware that his body had become – that Gellner was
tracking, then the major's call was sufficient.

"Imp," he sub-vocced, "how far away is Gellner?"

"Major Gellner's location data is currently unavailable."

He found himself reaching for one of the lasers in the
footwell and cradling it in his lap.

"How far away is Rima now?" he asked a little later.

"A little under five kay."

She accelerated, the ATV swinging from side to side down
the concave track like a toboggan.

He said, "Jayne..."

She glanced at him.

"What we said earlier, way back... before we came to Base
West One. About trust."

"I have a feeling I'm not going to like this."

"Christ... Look, they're following *me*, okay. Gellner's lackeys.
I didn't know earlier, I just suspected."

"Following you? How the hell...?"

"My implant." He slapped the side of his head. "The one
that's loaded with lieware. Back on Earth, my bosses upgraded
that implant and I don't fully understand what they put in
there. *That's* how Gellner's following me."

She stared at him. "Why the hell didn't you tell me this before?"

"I didn't know for certain, and as we assumed they'd be able to trace the original ATV…" He shrugged. "It didn't seem to matter that much either way."

"Jesus, Gordon, if the odds weren't bad enough–"

She was interrupted by the chime of her softscreen.

The image was impossible to make out: a flash of turquoise light, a smear of green, and something bloated behind it.

"Jayne…?"

"Rima!" Jayne cried. "My darling, we're on our way. We're almost with you."

Kemp leaned towards the screen, staring at the blurred image. "Where are you? On the surface? That light…?"

They heard her distant chuckle. "Far underground… in a cathedral."

Kemp exchanged a glance with Jayne.

"A *cathedral*?" Jayne echoed.

"It's… numinous, exalting…"

"Cagnac," Kemp snapped, "listen to me. Where are the aliens? We've just come from Base West One. The aliens… they slaughtered everyone there. You're in danger if–"

"But the aliens are peaceable… They saved me, brought me back to life."

"We're on our way," Jayne said. "Five minutes, ten at most."

"… want you to see this, Jayne. It's wondrous. And the aliens…"

The image swung, as if Cagnac was waving her softscreen to give them a panoramic view of where she was – but all Kemp could see was an impressionistic rush of turquoise and jade green.

Then the image blanked and he said, "She sounded delirious. And a cathedral?" He shook his head. "And what she said about the aliens… she's empathising with them. I suppose that makes sense, if they took her a week ago."

As Jayne accelerated, Kemp wondered how far away Gellner might be. The possibility that the major was just minutes behind them filled him with dread. At least that brief exchange had given them an accurate fix on Rima's location now.

"Look," Jayne said, nodding ahead.

He peered down the tunnel and made out, perhaps a hundred metres away, a lightening of the gloaming: the circular disc of the tunnel had turned a shade of turquoise, as if they were suddenly emerging onto the surface – which was surely impossible.

Jayne slowed the ATV, looking to her right and left.

"Jayne?"

"There must be a tributary tunnel around here. I saw a few further back. It makes sense to hide the ATV from Gellner. There!"

As she spoke, she slewed the vehicle to the right and they bounced down a narrow tunnel. She killed the engine and jumped out. "The rest of the way is on foot," she said.

Kemp passed her a laser and cradled his own, then followed her down the tunnel and turned towards the light.

"I hope you're appreciating this, Danni," Kemp sub-vocced, initiating the record facility.

They came to the end of the tunnel and stared down into what Kemp thought at first was a vast cavern. Beside him, Jayne swore beneath her breath, then reached out and gripped his gloved hand. As his senses slowly took in what lay before them, he realised that it wasn't a cavern: it was a great well or hollow in the vegetation, like an amphitheatre – perhaps half a kilometre across, and rising as far again to the surface of the planet. Far above was a vast circular opening, and he stared up at the rapidly falling twilight and the scatter of stars laid out across the indigo dusk.

Jayne murmured, "Now I see why Rima called it a cathedral..."

He could only nod in silent assent.

In the centre of the well was a tree, though he realised that in fact it was nothing like a tree. It was an alien growth, trunk-like, but made up of a dozen thick cords that wound about each other and rose spiralling towards the distant opening. Far above, it ended in a single pointed tentacle that waved slowly from side to side in the surface breeze.

But more amazing even than the amphitheatre itself, or the central spiralling growth, was what was being enacted at its base, and who was taking part in this... what? Dance? Religious ceremony?

Rima Cagnac's insistence that the aliens were peaceable puzzled him, given what he'd seen, and he reminded himself to reserve judgement on that. But in the meantime, recalling the fate of those at Base West One, he was acutely conscious of the comfort afforded by the laser he gripped in his right hand.

Perhaps a hundred small, grey aliens were gathered in a great semi-circle around the upthrust trunk, their backs to Kemp and Jayne. They moved as one, shoal-like, flowing towards the trunk and then rapidly away, then timorously edging forward again – and then away; when they reached the trunk they rose en masse on two feet, but when they retreated they quickly dropped onto all fours as they scampered away – and it was this quicksilver transformation from humanoid to animal that Kemp found so disconcerting.

At first, he thought the object towards which they were directing their 'dance' was the trunk itself – then realised that he was mistaken. The aliens were approaching and retreating from another alien, but one almost unrecognisable as such. It was a slumped, bloated mass propped against the trunk, humanoid in form but pustulant with boils and scabs.

Only then did he make out, leaning against the trunk some metres away, a human figure wearing the lower half of a biohazard suit.

He pointed to the suit and whispered to Jayne, "Cagnac?"

She turned to face him. "No, Gordon, that's Franco."

"Then...?"

She released his hand and pointed. "*That's* Rima," she said.

"No!"

He stared, disbelieving. How could something so... so grotesque, so *alien*, be a human being?

It moved, lifting a hand, and Kemp saw that Jayne was right: it was human – it was Rima Cagnac, but transformed.

At the sudden movement, the aliens fell on to all fours again and moved away as one, drawn from the trunk like iron filings following the attraction of a magnet.

And then they halted suddenly, freezing, and turned to stare up the slope to where he and Jayne stood, looking down.

Kemp found himself gripping his laser and raising it involuntarily. Beside him, Jayne stayed the movement with a hand on his arm.

Alerted, the aliens moved, flowing away from Kemp and Jayne and crossing the amphitheatre towards the walls. There they seemed to be absorbed into the sponge-like vegetation. Kemp stared at the aliens closer to him as they melted into the walls, and he made out hundreds, perhaps thousands, of small follicles or sacs in the fabric of the vegetation, and it was into these that the aliens retreated. He was aware of the large eyes of those closest to him, peering out through the close-knitted weave.

He exchanged a glance with Jayne, and she nodded.

Side by side, they left the opening and advanced down the gently sloping incline towards the central trunk and Rima Cagnac. Kemp scanned right and left as he went, very conscious that he and Jayne were now surrounded by the same creatures that, just hours ago, had massacred the scientists at Base West One.

As they neared Cagnac, she stirred herself, shuffling into a more comfortable sitting position against the trunk and raising her head to stare at them. She was more recognisably human, now, with her head no longer slumped forward. The pustules had cleared from the right side of her face, leaving bloody cicatrices and scabs, and her halved smile of greeting seemed oddly out of place on a face so ravaged.

Three metres away, Kemp saw that the figure in the biohazard suit was clearly dead: the limbs had stiffened, and the man's torso and face were a mass of boils that had burst and flowed with blood and sulphurous pus.

"Wondered when you'd turn up, Jayne," Cagnac said.

"I…" Jayne said, her voice catching, "I came as fast as…" Then she laughed through her tears at the incongruity of her words.

Kemp gestured towards the corpse. "Franco…? But how – I mean, how have you–?"

"Survived?" Cagnac said. "I told you, they saved me, nurtured me."

"But they killed Cole and…" He gestured feebly over his shoulder.

"They're not animals," Cagnac said. "They're not wild, atavistic creatures who kill by instinct. They were… provoked. Abdul Cole – he shot three aliens back there. Only then did…" She turned a hand in an eloquent gesture. "Think about it," she went on, "suddenly, from nowhere, strange creatures descend on their world, and one of the first acts these invaders commit is murder. Is it any wonder that the aliens retaliated? You could say that they were protecting themselves, their young."

"Their young?" Jayne said.

Cagnac gave her grotesque half smile again. "At first, when they brought me here, I thought this place was some kind of… of cathedral. The atmosphere of… sanctity, the attitude of the aliens when they reached this place, like penitents…" She laughed. "I should have recalled what Franco told me, not to ascribe anthropocentric reasoning to things wholly alien. I realised, after a while, that it wasn't a cathedral, but a hatchery."

Kemp echoed the word.

"The walls, the thousands of cells in the vegetation... This is where the aliens come to give birth and attend to their young for the first months of their lives. And it is also where they bury their dead–" she pointed across the gradually shelving ground on every side "–in shallow graves cut into the vegetation." Her eyes sparkled with what might have been delight. "So, sorry, Franco, I might have been right first time, perhaps? Maybe this place *is* some kind of holy place."

Jayne leaned forward and took the woman's arm. "Can you stand? We need to get away from here."

"I can stand, but... You need not fear the aliens, Jayne. I've become close to them. They are... altruistic creatures. They mean us no harm."

"Rima, Gellner's men are on their way."

Cagnac gave a half frown, as if struggling to recall the name. "Gellner?"

"Head of security," Jayne said. "Long story, darling. We might not have reason to fear the aliens, but we have every reason to be terrified of Gellner. No arguing. Come on."

"But... the aliens, my friends, Creasey..."

"Creasey?"

"He saved me," Cagnac said as Jayne assisted her to her feet.

"Come on. We have an ATV."

Cagnac raised her wristcom to her lips and spoke the alien's name again. To Kemp's surprise, the speaker issued a two-syllable grunt.

He saw movement to his right, and turned quickly as a small alien, perhaps the size of a large dog, approached warily on all fours, staring up at them with massive dark eyes.

Cagnac said, "We can speak, Creasey and I... What I've discovered here, a race of peaceable fellow sentients... We need to get this news back to Earth, Jayne, tell the world."

"I don't think Gellner will allow that," Jayne said as if speaking to a child.

The alien was within a couple of metres of the trio now, and

Kemp felt a sudden wave of nausea rush over him. He stepped back, staring at the extraterrestrial.

"Creasey," Cagnac said, "these people are my friends. They want to help me."

A series of grunts issued from the speaker, and the alien replied in kind, turning its oval head from Cagnac to Jayne and Kemp. It spoke, and a human voice sounded from Cagnac's wristcom. "Friends...?"

"But there are bad humans too. Like the one who killed your people."

"Bad...?"

Kemp backed away. He felt light-headed, suddenly sick. He experienced a sudden compulsion to turn and run, to put as much distance between himself and the group as possible. He thought, at first, that it was his proximity to the alien being that was causing this revulsion. Only later did it come to him that the compulsion to flee was not provoked by any desire for self-preservation.

It was as if an inner voice were compelling him to act against his will. He wanted to raise his laser and aim it not towards the alien, but at Rima Cagnac. He fought the urge, sweating and trembling.

His arm moved, lifting the weapon.

He fought to control it, lower the laser. It was as if he were fighting against an invisible foe, battling for control of his very body. Only then, belatedly, did he realise what was happening, what had control of him.

Commander Tsang's download...

The others were turning to him now, alerted by his odd, spasmodic movements.

He was fighting the overwhelming urge to lift his laser and shoot Rima Cagnac dead.

"Kemp," purred the smooth tones of the imp in his head, *"you know what you must do. Turn the gun on Cagnac and fire..."*

"No!" he said between gritted teeth.

"Kemp, do it..."

Weeping, the muscles of his arm spasming as he fought to stay his actions, he raised the laser and aimed at Rima Cagnac's head.

29

Deadly Passenger

Rima watched the man raise his laser and direct it at her head. Behind his visor, his features were pale, his skin sheened with sweat. The hands holding the laser shook, and she was struck with the incongruous observation that he was not a professional assassin – he had not done this before. Not that that made this situation any better...

Beside her, Creasey gave a brief series of grunts, which her wristcom translated as, "... friend?... bad?"

"Very bad," Rima gasped.

Creasey moved in a blur, in that way the aliens could switch from almost statue-like motionlessness to sudden action in the blink of an eye.

She heard a guttural male cry, saw a blue needle-line swing skywards, and then, when the scene froze again, Creasey squatted on the fallen man's chest, poised with one hand drawn high, a rapier-like claw emerging from what would have been a wrist.

"... friend?... bad?" Creasey grunted again.

Rima exchanged a look with Jayne. This whole exchange had taken barely a second. There was something in her friend's expression – confusion, and perhaps fear, although Rima realised it was a fear *for* her male companion.

"Friend," Rima said to Creasey. "Maybe."

Creasey eased back, letting his arm drop as the claw retracted.

The man stared up at them, his gaze moving from Rima to Jayne. "Open my suit," he said.

Jayne stood over him, the laser poised. "What?"

"Open my suit!" he said again, his words almost a plea. As Rima watched, his right arm moved with effort, reaching up and pulling at the fastening on his helmet. "I... I can't do this myself..."

"In my pouch," he called out, staring at Jayne with desperation in his eyes. "A datapin... insert it in... in my wristcom... Do as I say!"

Jayne hesitated, looked from the man to Rima.

"Jayne," he pleaded, "the download, back on Earth. I was installed with... with the command to kill Cagnac. My imp has taken over my body. Christ...!" His features twisted as he fought to force out the words. "The datapin might counteract... Do as I say!"

Jayne made a decision and passed her laser to Rima. "Cover us."

As Rima stood over them uncertainly, Jayne knelt and pulled off the man's helmet. He drew a breath, gagging on the atmosphere in the amphitheatre. "Now, in my pouch... the datapin."

Jayne found the pin, then removed the man's right glove. His hand flailed, jerking itself away from Jayne – impelled by whatever had taken control of his body – even as he fought to keep still. Jayne grabbed his arm, then knelt on his hand to keep it in place and stabbed the data-pin into the port of his wristcom.

The effect was instant and startling. The man screamed, and his body arched from the ground as if electrocuted. He slammed back down, spasming, his breath coming in great gasps.

"What happened?" Rima gasped.

"I..." Jayne knelt beside him, pressing down on his torso as if in an attempt to quell the involuntary spasms that racked his body.

"Who is he?"

"Gordon Kemp... a detective investigating the death of your husband. He came to arrest you, but I persuaded him otherwise."

"Arrest, or kill?"

"It wasn't like that. You heard what he said. He was taken over. Hacked."

Rima squatted beside Kemp. Her encrusted hands made it hard to check, but he appeared to have a carotid pulse, albeit weak and irregular.

Then Creasey was squatting at her side, a hand on her arm. He was staring across the amphitheatre, past the great tree. She turned, and as she did so she heard the first faint sound of an engine.

Jayne heard it too. "Gellner's men. We need to hide," she said.

Rima looked around her, then pointed to the nearest tunnel, perhaps fifty metres away. "There?"

Jayne indicated Kemp. His spasming had ceased now, but his breathing was stertorous, irregular. "We're taking him, okay?"

Rima hesitated, then nodded. The sound of Gellner's ATV increased, funnelled along the tunnel as it approached the cavern.

Together, Rima and Jayne knelt and tried to raise him. Kemp must have weighed well in excess of a hundred kilos, though, and even if she had not been recovering from a major illness, Rima would have struggled.

Between them, they sat him up, took hold of an arm each, and started to drag Kemp in the direction of the tunnel. One thing in their favour was the nature of the vegetal surface: just as when the aliens had hauled their sled, it seemed to lubricate the passage, and so it was easier to drag the man than it might otherwise have been.

Still, their progress was slow, and at any moment Rima expected the security squad to emerge from the opposite tunnel.

They had covered just twenty metres before Rima allowed herself to glance back. She made out the faint illumination of an ATV's headlights.

She put all the strength she had into hauling Kemp, trying not to wonder why she even bothered. Without his dead weight, she and Jayne would have reached the tunnel already.

But Jayne's explanation... How could a human being be hacked? There was so much about this that Rima still did not understand, but she trusted Jayne, and she knew there was no way her friend would have abandoned the detective.

She had to stop then, doubled over, coughing and wheezing. She watched as Creasey stood up on two legs and stared back towards the far tunnel, grunting rapidly.

Her wristcom translated. "... friends... good... stars..."

No. He was forgetting her words of caution. Not all humans were good, or friends...

"Come on," Jayne urged her.

They laboured on towards the tunnel. She felt dizzy with the effort, and her vision was blurring, darkening around the edges. Every muscle ached, every joint was on fire again, as if the cloud fever was sweeping over her once more.

She focused on each step. Didn't let herself look up, or back.

Jayne said, "We won't make it..."

Rima looked up. The tunnel entrance was still some twenty metres distant.

She heard a grunt from nearby, and her wristcom spluttered into life with a hiss of static, and then: "... bad... hide..." Had Creasey picked up on their fear, their need to flee?

She looked up. The alien was at her side, loping along jointlessly on all fours. "Creasey?"

Again: "... hide."

"Where? How?" They would never reach the nearest tunnel before the ATV arrived at the cavern. She and Jayne could not drag the man that far.

"... hide."

She felt soft pressure on one shoulder – Creasey's hand. Slowing her. Stopping her.

"... hide."

She halted, overcome with exhaustion.

The detective sagged, as Jayne, too, slumped to the ground.

Creasey was doing something... pointing at a groove in the tangled vegetation of the wall, just five metres away.

The breeding vesicles!

"... hide."

Gently, Creasey guided Rima, Jayne and Kemp across to the vegetal wall and a gaping vesicle, and then nudged her until she allowed herself to roll inside. Moments later, she felt the dead weight of the detective thud down into the small chamber beside her. Then came Jayne, and finally Creasey.

As he settled in beside her, with a soft sigh, Creasey said, "... hide... give life..."

She interpreted that as something like *Hide if you want to stay alive*.

The vegetation began to seal itself after them, tendrils twining around them, separating them off from each other within the vesicle. Rima felt a sudden wave of claustrophobia threaten to overcome her, but she fought it down. She had experienced far worse in the last few days.

Soon she was cocooned in the vegetal mass, only just able to see her companions through the green curtain surrounding her. She found herself unable to move, and only then did she wonder if they would ever be able to extricate themselves.

Beside her, Kemp began to struggle. At first, Rima thought he was attempting to claw his way from the vesicle and return to the cavern, and she struggled too against the enclosing vegetation in an effort to reach across and restrain him. Then the big man paused, pressing his face to the close weave of the vegetation and staring out.

Rima followed his gaze.

Across the amphitheatre, the first ATV appeared at the

distant tunnel entrance, followed by a second. They ground to a halt and twenty security personnel climbed out, staring in silent wonder at the cavern before them.

And then, from their hiding places in the walls of the amphitheatre all around, the aliens emerged, slowly at first, in ones and twos – and then in a great flowing rush across the amphitheatre and around the great tree at its centre.

They came to a halt as one, staring up the gently shelving slope to the humans.

For a moment it resembled a scene from a movie, the fabled first encounter. But no…

She'd warned them. Warned Creasey. Humans can be bad as well as good.

The suited figures carried weapons, and as Rima looked on, a figure in a jet-black biohazard suit lifted a hand and the men under his command aimed their lasers.

And then the slaughter began.

30

Selma's Isle

As she waited for the ferry to arrive, Danni stood at the end of the timber jetty and stared across the strait towards the Isle of Ely. A bitter east wind cut across the fens, driving the wind farms that occupied the shore of the island. Beyond the furiously turning turbines, the towering bulk of Ely cathedral dominated the skyline. The low island was dotted with villages and farmsteads, with patchwork fields in between. There was not a single megascreen or Big-5 display to be seen. Danni suspected that little had changed here in over a century, and wondered just what kind of subsistence living Kiri Betancourt eked from the land.

The tiny ferry butted up against the serried tyres at the side of the jetty, and the dozen foot-passengers climbed aboard. They were all locals, garbed in greatcoats, scarves and knitted hats. She hung back and was the last to step onto the timber deck. In keeping with the island's low-tech policy, the ferry was hand-cranked: a chain connected the ferry to a jetty a hundred metres away on the island, and two men turned a handle on the ratchet mechanism that laboriously drew the flat-decked vessel across the icy waters.

Danni stood a little apart from the other passengers, who cast her the occasional suspicious glance and murmured amongst themselves. In her long black coat and blue beret, she was conspicuously well-dressed and clearly not a local.

She turned her collar up against the wind and dug her hands into her coat pockets as the ferry approached the jetty a few minutes later. The ferry bumped against worn timber and the passengers disembarked, assisted by the ferrymen. A queue of horse-drawn carts awaited the locals, and a skinny boy called down to her, "Ely, ma'am?"

"Hackley Farm."

"It's on the way. Hop aboard."

She did so, joined by a scrawny man and a big, red-faced woman. As they set off, Danni smiling at the novelty of riding on such a primitive mode of transportation, the woman said, "You'll be the reporter, then? Kiri mentioned you were coming."

"That's right."

"Doing something about Selma, right?"

Danni smiled and nodded.

"She was a good woman, Selma."

Danni stared at the red-faced woman. She was old, but surely not *that* old. "You can't have known her?"

The woman laughed. "Not personally, but everyone on the island knows *of* her. She was one of the Founders, see? A hundred years ago. She put up the money to buy some of the land, along with a few others. She wanted independence, even back then. She saw the way the world was going. Didn't like the Chinese, she didn't." She hesitated, then went on, "It was them that got her in the end."

Surprised, Danni said, "It was?"

The woman nodded, emphatic. "Stands to reason, all those reports she did on the Chinese. They didn't like that, so they had her silenced." She peered at Danni. "You're not sympathetic to the Chinese, are you?"

Danni smiled. "Certainly not."

The cart halted in the middle of nowhere, and the skinny boy pointed down a rutted track to a collection of farm buildings a hundred metres away. "Hackley Farm," he said. "That'll be two bits, ma'am."

Danni stared at him. "Bits?"

The old woman laughed. "Local scrip." She said to the boy, "I'll see you right, Will," and to Danni, "On you go."

Danni thanked her and jumped from the back of the cart, staring at the farm as the horse plodded away. She set off along the track between fields of cabbage.

A woman appeared at the door of a thatched cottage that stood beside the main farm building.

"I'm looking for Kiri Betancourt," Danni called.

"You've found her. You look frozen. Tea?"

Danni smiled as she approached the low front door. "Thank you."

Kiri Betancourt was a big woman in soiled dungarees, her iron-grey hair tied back in dreadlocks. She looked to be in her fifties, her face and hands roughened by the elements and years of working the land.

She led Danni into an incredibly primitive front room with bulging whitewashed walls and low, blackened oak beams. A wood-burning stove belted out heat in palpable waves and a big kettle rattled on the hot-plate. Danni stared around in wonder, then realised she must appear rude and took a proffered seat before the stove.

The woman poured some kind of herbal tea into two chipped mugs, and Danni wrapped her hands around hers in gratitude.

Betancourt sat in a rocking chair across from Danni and sipped her tea.

Old-fashioned photos in bamboo frames hung above the hearth, and in many of them a round-faced woman gazed out, smiling. She appeared to be in her forties, and looked like a younger version of Kiri.

Danni sipped her tea, hot and redolent of fennel and camomile. She indicated the closest picture. "Your mother?"

"No, that's Selma," Betancourt said.

Danni mentioned the old woman in the cart, who'd told

her that Selma had been a founding member of the island community.

"That, and a lot more besides," Betancourt said, nodding. "She was a writer. I have some of her books, over there" – she pointed to a bookcase in the corner – "real printed books, mind. She worked for papers and magazines and wrote hundreds of articles on the internet too. She was an activist, protester, a bloody aggravating thorn in the side of the powers-that-be..."

"The old woman on the cart," Danni said, "thought that your grandmother was killed by the Chinese."

Betancourt hesitated, staring at Danni for perhaps ten seconds. Then she said, surprising Danni, "Just what do you want here, Ms Bellini?"

Danni swallowed, said, "As I mentioned the other day–"

"I had someone check," the woman interrupted. "Sent a lad to the mainland to look you up on the Net, or whatever they call it these days. He couldn't find one single article or what-not with the by-line of Danni Bellini, or variations thereof. So... who are you, and what do you want?"

Danni nodded. "I'm Danni Bellini, and I'm a police officer overseeing the cold case department of the Greater London police force."

She waved, and her accreditation hung in the air before the woman. Betancourt sat back, surprised by the shimmering image.

Danni went on, "I'm investigating the murder of your grandmother."

Betancourt sipped her tea, watching Danni over the rim of the mug. "The police. They're hand in glove with the authorities, the Chinese."

"Not me. I'm... you could say I'm working on this case independently. Look, you'll have to take what I tell you on trust. Nothing I can say will convince you, but I'd really like to know more about your grandmother and what happened to her."

"She was murdered, assassinated, by a cold-blooded killer," Betancourt said with ill-concealed bitterness. "She was abducted from her bedsit in Hackney in the early hours – according to neighbours – then taken to Epping Forest and shot, here," she placed a finger on the back of her head, "and her body left for walkers to find."

"The woman I spoke to on the cart, she seemed to think the Chinese were behind it."

Betancourt smiled, without humour. "That's what my mother encouraged the locals to think, and I don't say anything otherwise. It's safer that way."

"Safer?"

"Safer than *them* getting to know I know, if you see what I mean?"

Danni leaned forward. "And who is 'them'?" she asked.

The woman licked her lips. "My mother told me this when I was in my early twenties," she said. "She told me I wasn't to believe that it was the Chinese that killed my grandmother – not that she had any love for that lot. She said that the man behind the murder, the man who ordered it – he was too high up to get his own hands bloodied – was the business tycoon, Randolph White."

Danni looked up from her cup, nodding as she took this in. "Right. Okay... I don't suppose your mother had any hard evidence, anything that might implicate–?"

Betancourt said, "Just something that Nan Selma told her, a week before she was killed. She said she was investigating a man called Randolph White, who was involved in some vast conspiracy or fraud or something. And that if anything ever happened to her, then it would be White who was behind it. And then her body was found in Epping Forest..."

"Do you know if your mother went to the authorities with the information?"

Betancourt laughed. "As if! She was too frightened to do that. You might have noticed we don't trust the authorities, here on the island. And anyway, how would she have proven what Nan claimed?"

"Did Selma leave your mother anything, any papers or computer files, about her investigation into Randolph White?"

"I think Nan didn't want to endanger my mother," Betancourt said. "The only thing she did leave Mum, other than a bit of cash, was this."

The woman pulled a pendant from around her neck and passed it across to Danni. It hung on a fine gold chain, a white-metal anarchist symbol, chunky and quite ugly.

"Nan wore it all the time," Betancourt said. "You can see where it's been rubbed away with her constant handling..." Her voice caught and she went on, "You've finished your tea? How about a refill?"

Danni nodded and stared down at the pendant, at the slight indentations on either side where a thumb and a forefinger had rubbed the metal over the years.

Betancourt stood, took the kettle from the stove and crossed to the ancient ceramic sink to refill it.

Danni took the pendant in both hands and twisted, first one way, then the other. It clicked. She looked up. The woman had her back to her, filling the kettle. Danni pulled apart the two pieces and stared at the antiquated storage-pin. She withdrew it from its mounting in the metal, slipped it into her pocket, and snapped the two halves of the pendant back together.

Betancourt returned and poured two cups of herb tea.

Danni passed her the pendant.

"A cold-case detective?" Betancourt smiled. "Well, it would be nice if you could discover the truth after all these years, wouldn't it?"

Danni smiled and promised that she would do her very best.

She recalled Kiri Betancourt's words as she pulled up outside the fruit and vegetable shop in Southwark two hours later. She

felt it her duty to learn the truth of who really did kill Selma
Betancourt back in 2110, not that it would do anything to
bring the culprit to justice. At least a service would be paid to
the investigative journalist's memory, and her granddaughter
might gain a little satisfaction. It might also help them unravel
why Kemp had been sent on what must surely be a futile
mission to Mu Arae.

It was just after six o'clock, and twilight was descending on
the city. Big flakes of snow sifted down, covering the quiet
road with a scintillating patina under the streetlamps.

She left the car and hurried up the staircase to Martin's
bedsit.

He was a long time answering her knock, and Danni
wondered if he might have gone out, before recalling what
Bryce had told her. Martin *never* left his cluttered, over-heated
Faraday cage.

She was about to command her imp to call Martin when
the door opened a grudging hand's width. The young man
peered out.

"Edouard isn't with you?" he asked.

"Not this time." She entered the room and sat down in the
armchair. "You two still not talking?"

Martin pulled a face. "He's tried calling, but I blanked him."
He cracked his knuckles. "How can I help?"

She pulled the old storage pin from her pocket and held it
up before Martin. "Ever seen one of these?"

He took it for a closer inspection. "Old Sony memory pin.
What, ninety, a hundred years old?"

"Do you think you can access it?"

"I'm sure I can," he muttered. "I'm not entirely useless."

He strode across the room and rooted amongst a pile of
hardware that looked to Danni like so much discarded junk,
ancient cables, adaptors and softscreens. He pulled out an old
crystal stack and tinkered with it for a while.

She recalled something he'd said at their last meeting.

"Martin?"

"Mmm?" Absorbed in plugging half a dozen leads into the stack, he didn't look up. "When you and Edouard were arguing the other day—"

"You mean when he was calling me incompetent?"

"Whatever." She hesitated. "You said that Edouard, of *all* people, should know you didn't make mistakes. What did you mean by 'of *all* people'?"

He hesitated fractionally, shook his head and ignored her.

"Martin?" she persisted.

From his cross-legged position on the floor, he stopped what he was doing and looked up at her. "You know, don't you?"

"I guessed. Am I right?"

"Not that he's ever acknowledged it to me. But then again, I've never asked him. I know he kept a watchful eye on me while I was growing up, but we don't talk about these things."

"So he is your father?" she said. "Does he know that you know?"

He grunted. "Of course not. He's never realised I know, and I've never told him. Edouard doesn't open up like that. He doesn't do emotion." He shrugged. "That suits me fine."

"How did you find out?"

He gestured around him at the floating screens. "Give you one guess," he said. He looked at her, then went on, "He and my mother lived together for a year, back in '65. They had me, and a few months later she was killed in the Henley monorail crash."

He shrugged again, and sorted among a spaghetti of black leads on the dirty carpet.

She asked, "So Edouard brought you up alone?"

"No, he had a breakdown. He was institutionalised for a year or so."

She shook her head. "I never knew..."

"It affected him pretty badly, losing someone he loved like that. I was raised in a social care facility, and by the time

Edouard got his head together… Well, he had other things to occupy him. I saw him from time to time – but he just said he was a friend of my mother, nothing more. I know he paid to get me through college – I've seen the files – and he brings me work now. He's always been there in the background when I need him."

"He never told me."

Martin shrugged. "He doesn't talk about his past – you must have noticed that."

She had, but she still thought it odd that Edouard had never publicly acknowledged his son. She wondered if Gordon was aware of any of this, though she thought not. Like Edouard Bryce and his son, Gordon didn't do emotion.

Martin slotted the storage stick into a crystal's port, then hunched forward over a softscreen.

"Any luck?" she said after a minute.

"It might take a while," he muttered. "I might even have to do a bit of coding. Where did you get it, anyway?"

Danni told him. "How long before you have anything?"

"Hard to say. Why don't you go home and I'll give you a call when I crack it?"

She nodded and rose from the armchair. At the door she hesitated. "Look, if I were you, I'd talk to Edouard, okay? What he said, it was a heat of the moment thing. He was tired, frustrated. I'm sure if you talk, he'll apologise."

Without looking up, he nodded abstractedly.

She let herself out and hurried down to her car.

She was halfway through an Indian take-away three hours later when her imp said, *"Incoming, Danni. Martin Khalsa."*

"Put him through."

A screen expanded before her and Martin peered out. "Danni, I wrote an open sesame program and ran it on the storage-stick."

"Any luck?"

He nodded, grinning. "Cracked it wide open."

"You star," she said with a laugh. "What was it?"

He shrugged. "A journalist's files from eighty years ago. Scads of text, information about the White Foundation, what they were up to. A few photos. I'll send it across to you, but I thought it best to encrypt it, keyed to your imp's ID."

"Thanks, Martin. I owe you one."

"Glad to be of service – to someone who appreciates it," he muttered.

"Martin... Have you called him?"

"What do you think?"

"I think you should do so, or at least unblock his calls, okay?"

"I'll think about it," he said grudgingly, then cut the connection.

"Imp," she sub-vocced, "send a message to Edouard Bryce: 'Call your son'."

"*Done*," her imp said.

She sat back, smiling, and finished her aloo gobi.

Minutes later her imp informed her that Martin Khalsa was sending an encrypted file.

"Open the file," she commanded, and there was a delay of a few seconds while her imp's unique handshake engaged with the file's encryption, then a screen flared before her, showing a block of text.

For the next hour she read through the notes Selma Betancourt had made detailing her investigations into the White Foundation, and specifically into the far from legal practices of its CEO, Randolph White. Along with documentation of long-running payments to senior European politicians, Betancourt had uncovered evidence that White had appropriated and funnelled trillions of euros into a mysterious, and very private, personal project. The journalist had been looking further into this, Danni judged, when she was murdered in Epping Forest.

The text was accompanied by half a dozen photographs

showing Randolph White in meetings with several prominent politicians.

She homed in on White and expanded a head-and-shoulders image of the tycoon, a tall man in his late fifties, thin-faced and hollow-cheeked, with long grey hair tied in a ponytail that must have been the fashion at the time.

Eighty years ago, Selma Betancourt had ended the text with a note to herself: *I don't know what the hell they're hiding down at Carstairs Hall, but let's try to get in there, shall we?*

Danni closed down the files and killed the screens. She felt like a beer, and fetched an ice-cold Belgian lager from the kitchen.

Back in the lounge, she sat before the window and stared out at the falling snow. A megascreen hove into sight above the streets of central London, exhorting citizens to try their luck on the billion-euro daily lottery.

"Imp," she sub-vocced, "put me through to Edouard Bryce."

Seconds later a miniaturised image of the solicitor hung in the air, staring out at her.

She said, "I was just wondering if you and your son were on speaking terms yet?"

Edouard pursed his lips. "How did you find out–?"

"Oh, come on, Ed," she said. "It didn't need a detective to work out that you two were close, and shared certain... ah, characteristics."

He nodded. "To answer your question, yes, I did call him."

"And?"

"I apologised–"

"Good. Your son knows his stuff." She told him about the old file he'd cracked. "Selma Betancourt was investigating Randolph White, and she seemed to think he was hiding something at Carstairs Hall. So I'm going to call Conway now and sweet-talk my way in there."

"Tonight?"

"That's the plan."

KEITH BROOKE & ERIC BROWN

"Look, don't do anything risky, okay?"

She sighed. "I can look after myself, Ed. I'll be in touch if I find anything. Bye."

She cut the connection, then instructed her imp to put a call through to Peter Conway at Carstairs Hall.

31

Bearing Witness

Pain blitzed through Kemp as he pressed his face against the vegetal weave and stared out. He felt as if he'd suffered a stroke, or some other neurological dysfunction. He had difficulty in moving the left side of his body, and a synaptic firestorm raged in his head, throbbing like a migraine multiplied a hundredfold. The pain was nothing, though, compared to the anguish he experienced as he watched what was happening in the cavern.

He slumped against the vegetation, relying on it to keep him upright so he could keep watching and record the atrocity unfolding before him.

"So it's come to this, Danni..." he sub-vocced. "If we were in any doubt as to why they might have murdered Jenny Vahota..."

The first sweep of lasers from Gellner's men had killed perhaps fifty aliens. The grey creatures had gathered innocently before the humans, staring up at them like children. Kemp had seen Gellner raise a hand and give the command, and he'd looked on with a terrible sense of inevitability as Gellner's men aimed their lasers and fired.

Beside Kemp in the vesicle, Rima Cagnac wept and Jayne held her close.

The first sweep had caught the aliens by surprise and sliced through those at the head of the gathering, killing some outright, while maiming others. In a split second, the aliens attempted to flee, dropping onto all fours and dispersing, and it was this desperate attempt to save themselves that Kemp found so profoundly sickening. As they fell, the aliens gave off a heart-rending cacophony of cackling grunts – the most alien sound Kemp had ever heard. Many of the fleeing aliens were terribly injured, some with lacerated torsos and others missing limbs, and even the partially injured aliens at the rear of the gathering stood little chance as Gellner's men waded through strewn body parts and despatched stragglers with dispassionate efficiency. Kemp was heartened to see that a few aliens did manage to gain the sanctuary of the tunnels on the far side of the amphitheatre, rapidly pursued by humans.

He looked on as Gellner himself stepped forward, picking out those aliens still living amidst the carnage and dispatching them with short, bright blue bursts of laser fire.

It was only a matter of time, he realised, before Gellner brought his attention to bear on his own whereabouts...

Beside him, Jayne made a despairing sound and struggled to lift her laser, constrained by the clinging vegetation.

His glance stopped her movement. "Not yet," he managed, forcing the words out despite the pain.

Through tangles of green, he saw Cagnac force her hands up to her blistered face as she wept, and Jayne could only murmur futile words of consolation.

Kemp looked at the alien on the far side of Rima Cagnac. The tiny creature appeared to be comatose, its big eyes closed and its slit mouth open. He wondered if the sight of the slaughter had brought this on, or fear of what might lie ahead: his inevitable death at the hands of the invaders from the stars.

Noise had accompanied the genocide: the shouted commands, the crackle of lasers and the awful grunting cacophony of dying aliens. Now an eerie silence fell over the amphitheatre as Kemp stared through the weave, his heartbeat pounding in his ears.

with six others. As Kemp looked on, fearful, they moved across
the cavern to within a few metres of the vesicle.

The seven were spread out. Jayne lifted the laser again,
but Kemp shook his head minimally; there was no way that
she might account for seven trained killers before one of their
number returned fire. Yet he knew with absolute certainty that
Gellner would find him: he had tracked him this far through
the jungle, after all.

Kemp struggled; if he were to free himself from the vesicle,
confront Gellner and attempt to reason with the man...

He turned his head to Jayne and whispered, "Cover me. I'm
going to force my way free of this stuff and get their attention.
They'll approach me... When they're together, I'll drop – and
then you fire, okay?"

Jayne gave a slight nod, fear in her eyes.

Cagnac forced a hand through the undergrowth and gripped
his arm. "No!" she hissed. "That's crazy. We should remain in
hiding – they don't know we're here–"

He stared at her blistered, peeling face. "They know very
well," he said. It was only a matter of time before Gellner
discovered their hiding place

He tried to struggle upright, but the vegetation pinned him
back and pain lanced down the left side of his body, making
movement difficult.

Jayne said, "I could fire anyway. I'd get a few of the bastards –
and Gellner. You never know, I might get lucky and–"

She stopped.

Gellner turned to the nearest of his men and said, "You
three, that tunnel. The rest of you, follow me."

Kemp swallowed, wondering at the reprieve – if reprieve it

was. Gellner moved closer to where they cowered, but he was heading for the tunnel to the left.

"We're looking for Kemp," Gellner said. "The last signal had him somewhere around here."

"If he's dead...?" another man began.

"The signal would still be viable," Gellner snapped.

"And Cagnac?"

Kemp could hear the satisfaction in his voice as Gellner replied. "By now, *she* will be dead."

Jayne reached out and clutched Kemp's hand.

Hardly daring to hope, Kemp watched as Gellner led his men past the vesicle and approached the tunnel to the left. They passed from sight, and Jayne increased the pressure on his hand.

"Imp?" he sub-vocced.

There was no reply.

"Imp, run a health status check."

His imp should have responded with, "*Initiating,*" but once again only a profound interior silence greeted his command.

"How the hell...?" Jayne said.

"The datapin," he said. "I was warned it was a last-ditch thing to do. I... I think it wiped everything, including the tracker."

Cagnac gave a sob. With difficulty, Kemp raised his head and stared at her, his vision swimming with pain. The woman was reaching out, stroking the alien's face. Creasey lay very still, cocooned in green – his small body stiff, eyes closed, slit mouth open.

Jayne said, "Rima...?"

"He's dead," she said. "He's... *not moving.*" She said that phrase as if it held some kind of special meaning for her. As she spoke these words, her wristcom repeated them in the aliens' grunting language, still translating for the dead Carrascan. She fumbled with the device, silencing it.

Kemp stared out into the cavern; there was no sign of

Gellner's men now, only the bloody evidence of their recent presence.

"What happened to...?" Kemp was still unsure how he felt about Rima Cagnac, but her reaction to the alien's death touched something deep inside him.

"Before all this," Rima said, "I watched them, or at least some of them. They enclosed themselves in these vesicles in the vegetation, and while they were inside something happened... a transformation, almost a metamorphosis. They gave birth, and when they re-emerged, leaving their offspring behind, they were empty shells – emaciated and dying."

"But... I don't see any babies." Kemp knew his words sounded brusque and uncaring, but he didn't understand.

"He knew this would happen. I think there must be something about the vesicles – secretions or something in the air, something that acts like hormones and triggers the birthing process. I think Creasey went through all that, and his body was transformed even though he wasn't pregnant, and the process was too much for him."

She choked back a sob. "He knew this would happen, but he did it to protect us."

Kemp looked from Cagnac to the dead alien, and then at Jayne. "We should get out of here."

Cagnac stared at the dead alien, weeping.

"We have to leave, Rima," Jayne said gently.

Cagnac swallowed and nodded. "How?"

"We came in an ATV," Jayne said. "I concealed it in one of the tunnels."

Jayne hacked through the vegetation with the butt of her laser, widening the gap and pushing herself through. Cagnac followed her, and Kemp struggled after them. He had difficulty moving his left leg and winced in pain as Jayne and Cagnac took his arms and dragged him out. He staggered upright, gasping, as lancing agony raced down his left leg. He looked around the amphitheatre, panning his vision left and right, taking in the aftermath of the carnage, a hundred dead bodies, severed limbs.

At last, he blinked to terminate the recording.

He staggered forward, the women still holding him upright. He tried to shake them off, but Jayne snapped, "Don't be so bloody stubborn, Gordon! If you walk unaided, you'd only slow us down, okay?"

He gave in, allowing himself to be half-carried across the amphitheatre towards the far tunnel.

They took a zigzag course, avoiding the worst of the slaughter, the areas where alien blood spread in slicks across the vegetation, already soaking into the ground. He wondered how long it might be before the surviving aliens dared to return to this holy area – if Rima Cagnac's assumption as to its purpose was correct – and inter their dead.

He limped on, gritting his teeth against the pain, and staring not at the slaughter but the darkened tunnel entrance ahead. He feared hearing the return of Gellner and his men at any second, feared the blue flash of their lasers...

With relief, they gained the tunnel.

Cagnac wriggled free from Kemp and said, "Let me get something. This is important." And with that she hurried back across the amphitheatre.

Kemp watched her, confused again and angry at his own powerlessness to stop her from putting them all at risk. When she reached the central tree, she knelt and gathered something up in her arms, and a short time later she was back with them.

"What the hell...?" Kemp said, indicating what looked like a bundle of leathery grey fabric in her arms.

"Some kind of poultice the Carrascans use," she told him.

He snapped, "A poultice? Couldn't you have waited to gather samples?"

Both women stared at him, as if waiting for him to understand. "Not for me," Cagnac told him. "These are not medical samples for me to study. They're for *you*. You've been exposed to unknown pathogens in the air. The aliens use these poultices to protect and heal. I think it is what saved me from the cloud fever, and it could well be the only thing that saves *you.*"

Chastened, Kemp turned away, and in silence the three set off down the tunnel.

It seemed a long time before Jayne located the side branch where she had concealed the ATV, and they turned right. "Almost there."

They rounded another bend and there was the vehicle, and Kemp had never been so grateful to see an ATV in his life. He wasn't sure his pained body could have carried him any farther.

They hauled him aboard and he lay in a rear seat as Jayne gunned the engine and the vehicle surged into life.

"We're taking the overground route, right?" Jayne said a little later. "The other option, working our way blindly through the tunnels, would take God knows how long. We want to get back to base before Gellner and his troops."

"That makes sense," Cagnac said.

Jayne gripped the wheel and peered at the tunnel sloping towards the surface of the world. The walls passed on either side, close to the windows. She accelerated, and Kemp thought of Gellner back there, looking for him. With luck, the fruitless search would continue long enough to allow them to make it back to base, though after that... The near future was imponderable: the only option, as far as he could see, was to make it known to the scientists what atrocities Gellner's men had committed on behalf of humanity. Surely even Gellner would baulk at taking the lives of over ninety innocent men and women?

He felt dog-tired and wanted to lie back and sleep. He resisted the impulse: if the physiological side effects of the datapin's blitz was analogous to a stroke, then he would be wise to stay awake and keep his left arm and leg moving. He sat up, flexing his left leg painfully back and forth, while attempting to rotate his arm and restore some semblance of life.

Rima Cagnac turned in her seat and stared at him for a time.

"So..." she said, "you were sent all the way out here to arrest me."

"That's what I was told. Arrest you for the murder of your husband and bring you back to Earth to stand trial. Of course, that was a cover. I was expendable, and they installed me with a command to kill you – software in my head. They wanted you dead, all along."

She stared at him. "I didn't kill Sebastian," she said.

Kemp smiled. "I know you didn't," he said, and he didn't need the lieware to tell him that she was telling the truth.

"So," she said, "who wanted me dead?"

He glanced at Jayne, then back to Cagnac. "Whoever's behind all this – behind Major Gellner and my commander – those pulling the strings on Carrasco to set it up as some kind of colony world, whatever obstacles lie in their way. The same people who framed you as your husband's killer, all those years ago."

"But why would someone frame me? It doesn't make sense–"

"It does," Jayne interrupted. "They needed someone to take the fall, and you fitted the bill."

"'They'?" Cagnac said.

"The person who *did* kill Sebastian," Jayne said.

Cagnac stared from Kemp to Jayne, then said, "You sound as if you know very well who that might have been."

Jayne nodded, and looked at Kemp. He said, "It was Sebastian's brother, Randolph."

"Randolph?" Cagnac shook her head, incredulous. "But..."

"I saw it," Jayne said. "I was there that morning. I saw them arguing, saw Randolph leave the villa covered in blood."

"And you tell me none of this until now?"

Jayne looked away, and Cagnac pressed her fingers to her temples as she tried to take in Jayne's words.

"I suspect your husband discovered what Randolph was doing," Kemp said, "what he was planning. He was diverting funds away from projects intended to help the world cope with the environmental crises and directing them towards the Carrasco mission, and towards the research and development of the quantum lattice."

"Randolph White was playing a long-term game," Jayne said, "with Carrasco as the ultimate prize for his political heirs to inherit."

"So when your husband found out about his brother's plans, about the lattice," Kemp went on, "he confronted Randolph at his villa that day. They argued and..." He shrugged.

Shock evident in her dark eyes, Cagnac looked from Kemp to Jayne and back again, before saying, "No..."

"I'm sorry, darling," Jayne murmured.

"No, I mean..." Cagnac lifted a hand, let it fall. "I mean, Sebastian didn't know about the lattice. He *couldn't* have. He would have mentioned it to me, no? I was going on the mission – he would most certainly have told me about the lattice, had he known. No," she went on, "there was something else that he knew, that he disagreed with Randolph about. He told me about *that*... Good God!" she said, almost sobbing. "That *must* be it. And it would explain..."

Jayne reached out and took the woman's gloved hand. "Rima?"

"A few days before he... before my husband died... he came home late one evening after a meeting with his brother. Sebastian was shaken. Increasingly he and Randolph had not seen eye to eye, as you say, politically. They had their rows, and they could be heated. This time, I could see that it had been worse than usual. Sebastian refused to talk. I demanded that he tell me... At first, I thought it must be just another ideological disagreement, but I was so wrong." She fell silent, staring into space. "It explains everything," she said at last in a murmur.

"Rima?" Jayne coaxed.

"My husband first heard about it from a mutual acquaintance of his and Randolph. This man, he worked in the administrative department of the company manufacturing the suspension pods for the mission. He told Sebastian that agents working on behalf of a billionaire had made enquiries about the purchase and private use of a number of suspension pods." Cagnac paused, looking from Kemp to Jayne. "This was illegal, of course – my husband himself had been instrumental in drafting a bill that was passed through the UN council to the effect that the use of suspension technology should be proscribed; he foresaw it as a potential tool for the rich and powerful to employ in pursuit of long-term power... His contact told him that agents had made enquiries, and the person suspected of hiring the agents was Randolph White. That day when Sebastian came home in a state of shock, he told me he'd confronted his brother with the accusation, and Randolph had admitted that he wanted to use the technology. He said that as he was the major private benefactor of the Carrasco mission – that as it was his billions that had made the venture viable – then he should be around to see it come to fruition."

"Randolph died back in 2114," Kemp said, "but his body was never discovered. He was reported missing in a boating accident off Bermuda..." He stopped suddenly.

"Jesus Christ," Jayne said.

"You're right," Kemp said, staring at Cagnac. "It does make sense – it explains everything. Randolph's diverting funds for the mission, his secrecy about the quantum lattice – and the actions of Gellner's men back there. Randolph was planning for the long-term – but not for the benefit of his political heirs. He used the suspension technology for *himself* – he's still alive, back on Earth, directing events from afar."

The image of a malign spider sitting in the centre of a vast web sprang to mind, and Kemp felt suddenly sick.

Light appeared up ahead, and the ATV trundled over the last hundred metres towards the surface. They emerged into a deepening turquoise twilight, with the vast sphere of Mu Arae setting to their left in a brilliant spread of crimson strata. Kemp stared blindly at the scene, too shocked by the turn of events to appreciate the beauty of the extrasolar sunset.

"How long before we reach base?" he asked, sitting back and massaging his left arm. He thought the pain was lessening, becoming almost tolerable, and the pounding in his head was certainly easing.

"At a safe pace," Jayne said, "I'd say we're a little over two days' travel from the main base."

"If Gellner realises we've given him the slip, he's hardly going to follow at a safe pace," Kemp pointed out.

Jayne met his look, and he knew she was up for the challenge. "Well let's not do it at a safe pace, then," she said. With that, she gunned the engine, and with an almighty lurch the ATV accelerated.

He must have given in to exhaustion at some point, as he came awake with a start to hear the women arguing.

The ATV had come to a halt, after a day of travelling at breakneck speed, and they were no longer on top of the world, but once again surrounded by thick jungle vegetation. Walls loomed close all around, and Kemp felt a strange recapitulation of the fear he'd felt in the amphitheatre following Gellner's slaughter of the aliens.

"I'm coming with you," Jayne said. "You can't go into the domes in your condition. Christ, not only is it a contamination issue–"

"Okay, you're right. I..." Cagnac gave a sheepish smile and

gestured to her face. "I've been like this for so long, I think I forgot how grotesque I must look."

"Not exactly grotesque, darling... Let's just say frightening, okay?"

Cagnac nodded. "And, as you say, it is a contamination issue. I should think of that – I'm a doctor, after all. But it is some time since I have had to think in terms of biohazard..."

Kemp leaned forward. "Would someone please tell me where the hell we are, and what's happening? And what is all *this*?" His face and bare arm, where they had been exposed to the air of Carrasco, were plastered with those leathery grey leaves Cagnac had taken from the amphitheatre.

"The poultices could well be what's keeping you alive," Jayne said. "We're a few minutes from base, by foot. And Rima here has a hare-brained scheme to get you back to Earth."

Had he really slept through the entire journey? He remembered snatches of wakefulness, almost like dreams. He hoped, at least, that his body was starting to recover from the onslaught of the datapin's blitz.

"I'm going in there to find Xavier Fernandez," Cagnac said. "You're staying here, because you can barely walk and security will be looking out for you. Don't worry, we're well concealed – Gellner won't find the ATV."

Before Kemp could frame another question, Rima Cagnac jumped from the vehicle, and Jayne turned to him. "Get some rest, Gordon. If all goes well, you'll soon be away from here."

He leaned forward. "And you?"

But she had turned from the ATV and was hurrying along the tunnel to catch up with Cagnac.

Cursing, Kemp lay back on the seat and closed his eyes.

32

Negotiations

As she made her way with Jayne towards the main dome, Rima considered the last words that Franco's wristcom had translated for Creasey.

Hide… give life…

At the time, Rima had taken them to mean that they should hide if they wished to remain alive, but no: Creasey had been telling her he was giving his life in order to save theirs.

He had known that sealing himself in the vesicle with them would trigger the birthing process, the vesicle leaching him of all – what? Nutrients? All vitality. Draining him of his essence even though there were no offspring to pass it on to.

As much as she tried to blank it out, the image of Creasey's motionless body kept coming back to her. His withered, emaciated frame; the life gone from those big eyes.

In the same way, she tried not to think of the scene that had unfolded before them at the amphitheatre. Major Gellner's security squad slaughtering the Carrascans with a methodical efficiency that was almost as horrific as the act itself.

She was in shock, she realised, as they all were.

The detective's response to shock was to lie on the seat at the back of the ATV, drifting in and out of consciousness. She didn't think he'd been aware of much of the journey – which was just as well, for they had driven at reckless speed, almost losing control of the vehicle several times.

It was not just the shock that the detective had had to deal with, of course, but also whatever it was that had happened inside his head: being taken over – being *hacked* – in order to kill her, and then having those overriding commands wiped by the datapin. She didn't really understand: these people from her future had hardware in their head, implants, and now the datapin had subjected that implant – and perhaps any surrounding brain tissue that interfaced with it – to some kind of memetic cleansing. She was a highly experienced doctor, but this was eighty years and an entire field of cybernetics away from any of her specialisms, and it was beyond her.

She had tried not to think. Instead, she'd focused on tending to him, the detective who had come first to arrest her, and then to kill her. Throughout the journey, when she was not taking her turn driving, Rima had plied him with the grey healing leaves, plastering them to his brow and his exposed arm.

He had no fever, but his delirium had concerned her. "Talk to me," she said, whenever he returned to awareness, for losing his speech would be a sure sign that the cloud fever had got to him. "Do you have pains? Do you have any unusual symptoms?"

"How will I know," he asked her one time, "if it is cloud fever and not just being generally fucked up by the datapin?"

"You will know," she assured him. "Oh, *monsieur*, you will know."

As they reached the main dome, Rima sealed her biohazard suit and turned to Jayne. "I thought I knew you," she said. "I thought you were my friend."

"I'm sorry. But I–"

"You could have said something. You knew who killed Sebastian, and yet you said nothing."

"I was scared," Jayne told her. "In over my head. I'd gone to your house as a favour for a friend, an investigative journalist.

And I saw one of the most powerful men in the world coming out, covered in blood. Not long after, it emerged that your husband had been murdered. I was only too grateful to dump it all back on my friend and leave for Carrasco a few days later. I knew you from training, but I didn't really *know* you, and I didn't know what was going on, or who I could trust."

"And now?"

"I know you, Rima, and I trust you more than anyone. But by the time I got to know you properly, the untruths and not telling were cast."

Rima turned away. So much had happened in the past few weeks, but the death of Sebastian was still raw to her, still so fresh.

"You can't go in," Jayne insisted. "Out here you're just like anyone else in a biohazard suit, but in there… I can go in on my own, though. Trust me, darling, and stay here. Can you just do that?"

Rima stared at her. Until she'd found out that Jayne had been keeping secrets from her, that would have been easy, but now?

"They're not looking for *me*," Jayne went on. "As far as anyone here is concerned, I've been out at my trapping camp all this time – antisocial Jayne, just getting on with her research. I can go anywhere quite freely still."

They paused outside one of the airlocks to the rear of the dome, and finally Rima said, "Okay, I'll trust you." Because in a strange way, Jayne telling her she had lied – or avoided sharing the truth – made her seem even more trustworthy than before: she had exposed her guilty secret now.

But still, as Rima watched her friend step into the airlock and cycle it shut, she wondered if she would ever see her again.

* * *

A mere ten minutes later, Rima saw figures step into the lock from within the dome. She scrambled back into the cover of a storage shed and waited as the lock cycled and the outer door peeled open.

The figures emerged: Jayne, in her jungle-stained suit, and a tall figure in a pristine suit – he turned, and Rima saw the features of Xavier Fernandez behind the visor.

She stepped out into the open.

"What the hell...?" Fernandez snapped, clearly frustrated. "You said–"

"I don't know what Jayne said," Rima interrupted. "But she could not have told you the truth – that I am here – because we are being hunted by Major Gellner's security squad, and they want us dead."

That stopped him in his tracks. He stared at her, then at Jayne, and then back at Rima.

"Rima?" he said. "I thought..."

"That I was dead?" Had this been an enormous mistake, and even Fernandez was in on the plot to have her put to death?

"I didn't know what to think," he told her. "Commander Hertzberger told us you were missing from Base West One, but the rumours... People were saying you'd been abducted by aliens."

So he wasn't in on the plot to kill her, and word of sentient aliens had already circulated back here at the base. Both of those factors must weigh in their favour.

"And, Rima, why..." He gestured at her helmet. "Why is your visor mirrored?"

She hesitated. Like it or not, of all the people on Carrasco, Xavier Fernandez knew her the best. And now she felt strangely exposed before him.

She spoke the command, and her visor de-opaqued.

"Rima... *Joder!* What has happened to you?"

She knew how she must look to him: the pustules and scabs,

the dry, scarred skin on the right of her face where the growths had fallen away.

"Oh, Rima." He stepped towards her and, before she had time to react, was hugging her clumsily, suit to suit.

Rima stepped back, confused at his reaction. She'd expected horror, revulsion, not... *sympathy*.

"We need your help, Xavier," she said into the growing silence.

"Anything," he said. "Just tell me what you need."

"No. I won't do it," Fernandez said. "There are so many reasons why this is a bad idea."

Rima and Jayne had led him back to the concealed ATV, and now they stood beside the vehicle, with Kemp stretched out on the rear seat.

"Look at him." Fernandez gestured, his movements exaggerated by stress. "He is uncovered. Exposed." Kemp was in his biohazard suit, but the helmet was still removed and one sleeve rolled up. "He is *sick*."

"He is," Rima agreed, "but it is not the cloud fever. He is the victim of an attack by Gellner and his associates – a cybernetic assault on a device implanted in his brain. I've been treating him against airborne infection with a technique shown to me by the aliens and he's remained entirely symptom-free."

"The *aliens?*" Fernandez turned away, holding his head.

"There's more."

"Of *course* there is more."

"What's your impression of Major Gellner?" Rima asked.

The look that flashed across Fernandez's face was answer enough. "I don't know what he is doing here, but he rides roughshod over all that we have established." And then, as if it was a judgement to trump all others, he added, "The man has no class."

Kemp tried to struggle into a sitting position. "He's here to ensure that the human presence on Carrasco serves the aims of his pay-masters," he said. "And he won't let anything get in the way of that."

"What do you mean?"

"Watch this." Kemp tapped at his wristcom and an image sprung up on the ATV's viewscreen: the view across the amphitheatre, a frozen image showing men in biohazard suits, their weapons raised, bolts of blue lancing across the arena to where a few surviving aliens stood amongst their fallen comrades. Small grey figures, looking like nothing so much as small children, cowering from the slaughter.

The image unfroze, and those bolts of blue cut across, slicing the last few aliens through the middle. Arms fell, detached, and one figure toppled in two pieces, cut neatly in half at the waist.

Kemp skipped the footage forward. Now the screen showed four armed men, one of them – even though Rima had never met the man, he was clearly in charge – the figure of Major Gellner.

"We're looking for Kemp," Gellner said. "The last signal had him somewhere around here."

"If he's dead...?"

"The signal would still be viable."

"And Cagnac?"

"By now, she will be dead."

Fernandez turned to stare at Rima. "He really wanted you dead?"

"And the only thing that saves me right now," Rima told him, "is that he thinks I must already be dead."

"He's still searching for me, though," Kemp said.

"And that's why you want me to smuggle him up to the wormhole in one of the shuttles," Fernandez said.

"It is," Rima said. "If he can get back to Earth, get word out about the atrocities being committed here..."

Kemp stared at Rima, and then at Jayne. "He?" he said. "No,

we need you to get us *all* out, Captain Fernandez, not just me."

Jayne put a hand on his arm. "No," she told him. "Just you, Gordon. The chances of getting one person out are far greater than if all three of us tried."

"But–"

"Look at me," said Rima. "How do you think someone looking like this would ever get onto a shuttle, through the wormhole, and through security back on Earth?"

"But... Jayne?"

"I'm not just abandoning my friend to her fate," Jayne said. "I let her down once: I could never do so again. If you know me at all by now, then you know that much about me."

"But..."

Jayne leaned in and hugged him. "Go," she said, so softly that Rima could barely make out her words. "Go and save this new world, Gordon. Go and do your duty."

"What now?" Rima said.

Fernandez had led Kemp towards one of the domes, and Rima stood with Jayne beside the ATV. She felt exhausted, as if she had been holding everything together just to reach this point and now might easily unravel.

"Now?" Jayne asked. She put a hand on Rima's arm, reassuring and steadying.

Rima really did feel close to collapse.

"Now we take another of the ATVs from the hangar," Jayne told her. "We have to leave this one here, as they'll be looking for it – they know Kemp took this one from Base West One. We'll go out to my trapping station, and hope no one comes visiting. As far as anyone here is concerned, that's where I've been all along, focusing on my ecological mapping and oblivious to anything that's gone on here."

Rima nodded.

"If we're lucky, Gellner will have convinced himself Kemp

must have killed you out in the wilderness, so he's not looking for you. We should be okay until all this sorts itself out."

"And if we're not so lucky?"

"I know the terrain around that trapping station better than anyone," Jayne said. "And I reckon you've learned a thing or two about how to survive in the wilds of Carrasco. I think we have a better chance than most of hiding out and surviving, don't you, darling?"

And with that, Jayne looped an arm around Rima's waist and led her across to the hangar where the researchers kept their vehicles.

33

Return Trip

"I fly shuttles. It's what I do."

There was a defiant pride in Fernandez's words. Once the captain of the first manned starship to leave the solar system, now he flew shuttles from orbit to the surface of Carrasco and back, but he was clearly proud of that and saw it as no demotion: he was one of the vital cogs that kept the research base functioning.

"And you can get me out of here?"

"I can get you off Carrasco, Inspector Kemp. And I can smooth-talk you past the wormhole technicians and on your way back to Earth. But beyond that…? You're on your own, I'm afraid. There's nothing more I can do."

The two emerged from an umbilical, stripped of their excursion suits and now wearing casual grey one-pieces – practical clothing for the research base, but an outfit that still made Kemp feel like some over-sized toddler at kindergarten. As they walked, he scratched at his face, convinced there was still residue from the grey healing leaves.

He felt fine, considering his brain had been nearly wiped two days before. He was able to walk, albeit with a limp. His left arm had regained some strength, although he didn't know if he'd ever be able to raise it above shoulder-level again. And his thoughts were about as coherent as they had ever been.

A figure appeared in a doorway and Kemp looked down. Had word got back to apprehend him?

"Xavier, all good?"

"Everything's fine, Henri. Is the shuttle ready?"

Just one of the mechanics, evidently. No alarms. No arrest squad swooping in to seize Kemp.

"I've rescheduled a shuttle run that had been due to head out this evening. You'll be in orbit within the hour."

They passed across an open area where a couple of women stood at a window looking out, and then entered another umbilical. This one branched away from the main dome, its skin transparent, so that it was almost as if they were walking unprotected across the cleared land around the base. Kemp felt exposed. At any moment one of Gellner's security detail might pass by outside and see them.

They reached one of the smaller domes. This was where the vehicles from the shuttles docked: sealed trucks that connected directly with the dome's airlocks, so personnel could move between them and load or unload without the need for suits.

Fernandez led Kemp through to one of these locks, and immediately the door irised open.

When the interior of the truck was revealed, Kemp saw three armed security guards standing there, weapons poised.

A man at the driving seat twisted to face them. Luis Vignol – Sander Hertzberger's deputy. "Inspector Kemp," he said, a slight smile tugging at his features.

Kemp turned to Fernandez. He had nowhere to go, no chance of outrunning these armed men – even with the full use of his left leg, he would not have stood a chance.

"It's okay," Fernandez said. "Come on. Take a seat. Luis, here, was my deputy on the *Strasbourg*. We go back many years together, eh, Luis? And neither of us is a fan of Mijnheer Hertzberger."

"And these gentlemen?" Kemp indicated the armed escort of three.

"Protection," Vignol said, turning back to face the front. "Come on. We don't have long. Gellner and his men are not far away."

Kemp and Fernandez entered the truck and stood, hanging onto ceiling straps as the door slid shut.

"Just how far?" Kemp asked, as Vignol swung the truck clear of the dome and headed out across the stripped bedrock. Ahead of them the squat shape of a shuttle lay in wait.

"We've been tracking him," Vignol said. "He'll be reaching the main dome about now."

So close behind them!

Kemp swallowed. The simple act of walking through the domes and tunnels had been harder work than he'd anticipated; holding himself upright as the truck trundled over uneven ground was almost too much.

"He'll see us leaving," Kemp said. "Won't he stop us?"

"There is a fire in the room you stayed in," Vignol said. "And reports that you were seen there, recovering your possessions before fleeing into the jungle."

That small room had certainly seen a lot of damage in Kemp's short time on this planet. He glanced through a viewscreen. "There's no smoke."

"My man hasn't started it yet," Vignol said.

They reached the shuttle minutes later. Kemp kept watch out of the viewscreen, but saw nothing. No smoke, no men rushing about. But also, no trucks coming in pursuit.

He hoped, desperately, that Rima and Jayne had made their escape before Gellner's return. He still couldn't work out quite what had happened with Jayne. He'd been convinced she would come with him – to the extent that he hadn't even considered the alternative – and when she said she was staying with Rima, he had felt… Not exactly loss, but certainly a sense of lost potential.

They came to a halt by the shuttle, and waited as the docking tunnel made good its seal.

A short time later, Fernandez, Kemp and their guards were seated on the shuttle – Kemp sitting up front beside the captain as he prepared for take-off. Vignol remained behind to face whatever chaos Gellner was causing back at the base.

"What will you do?" Fernandez asked Kemp, as the engines cycled up.

"I'll get through security, somehow," Kemp told him. "And then I'll get together with a couple of friends in London and work out how the hell we're going to spread word of what's happening here. And then I'm going to bring the bastards to book. Every last one of them, for every single crime that has been committed here – even the crimes against laws that haven't been written yet, because there's no precedent in law for the things Gellner has done."

"You do realise you won't be able to... bullshit your way through security, don't you?"

"No?"

"There will be strict quarantine, even if you're not arrested the moment you set foot on Earth. You're returning from an extrasolar planet, carrying unknown pathogens. You'll go through decontamination protocols so strict you'll feel as if they've scrubbed every cell of your body. Even worse, you show signs of bad health – even though we know that is from the cybernetic assault on you, they do not know this. So they'll be even more strict with you. You'll be kept in quarantine and isolation for at least a month, I'd say."

He'd not allowed for any of this. Not just the delay of a month, but the simple calculation that for every minute he spent in quarantine, Gellner was more likely to get word back and have him detained. Or worse.

"There must be a way around that," Kemp said. "An accelerated route for the likes of Gellner – he would never sit for a month in quarantine. Can't you pull some magic and get me through on the fast track?"

Fernandez laughed. "My friend," he said. "It is eighty years since I knew how things worked back on Earth, and you're talking about entry protocols that have been established for a transport technology that's only just entered use for the first time…"

Kemp peered through the viewscreen. There was still no sign of anything happening at the base. He hated not knowing, even as he understood that was better than seeing signs of actual disturbance.

Lift-off was easy, almost imperceptible. Rising vertically, so slowly at first that Kemp could not be sure they were moving.

The shuttle hung in the air, about a hundred metres up, and that was when he looked down and saw a plume of dark smoke emerging from the rear of the main dome. He wondered how much resistance Gellner might meet among the original contingent of researchers, particularly as his first act had been to weed out and isolate those scientists who might be aware of what he was doing here. The active rebellion of Hertzberger's own deputy suggested the resistance might be significant, and for the first time in ages Kemp felt a surge of hope.

Then the acceleration kicked in as the shuttle arrowed away from the base, angling upwards at about forty-five degrees. Kemp felt his face pulled back, his eyeballs bulging, felt the most disturbing shifting of the bulk around his waist, and now he wished that Fernandez had offered him the relief of sedation.

The wormhole technician on board the *Strasbourg*, now used as an orbital transfer station, didn't bat an eyelid when Fernandez showed up with Kemp and said, "Inspector Kemp, returning to London. Could you just get him through, and do the admin later?"

The tech nodded. "Sure, Captain. No problem."

Fernandez turned to Kemp and held out a hand. "This is as far as I go. Good luck, Inspector."

"You will keep an eye out for them, won't you?" Kemp said. "Do your best to ensure they're safe."

"Rima and Jayne? Yes, of course."

"You care about Rima, don't you? Behind all the bravado and bullshit."

Fernandez looked away. "Back in Geneva... I was foolish. She was married, about to leave the planet. I saw only opportunity – and I rushed in. Until Rima, I'd always been successful with women, you know? Now, are you ready?"

"I am. But tell me: I know you can't fast-track me through quarantine at the other end. But do you know how I might at least get a message out from the spaceport? There must be a way."

Fernandez grinned. "There's always a way, Inspector." He nodded towards the tech, who was now waving her hands through data-streams hanging in the air, preparing the portal for Kemp's departure. "There's always someone you can bribe, isn't there?"

Minutes later, Kemp was seated on the shuttle that would take him through the wormhole, and within another fifteen minutes the shuttle was in Earth orbit, preparing for descent. He still couldn't quite get his head around the fact that the most arduous part of the journey was the ascent and descent from orbit, while the actual jump of fifty lightyears took place in the blink of an eye.

He closed his eyes as the shuttle fell towards Europe.

Thames Spaceport was an artificial island constructed off the eastern tip of Canvey Island. Until recently it had only ever impinged on Kemp's existence as the source of occasional light-trails across the night sky of arrivals and departures. Kemp didn't like the idea of it being his home for the next twenty-eight days.

"Twenty-eight days *minimum*, Inspector Kemp," the official

reiterated. "We have strict decontamination protocols, and even after the official quarantine period you will need to present with a clean bill of health before release will be considered."

"I haven't been able to present with a clean bill of health since I hit my mid-twenties," Kemp said. At least he hadn't been arrested on sight, or spirited away into some top-security European Intelligence interrogation centre.

But he couldn't hang around here. Vignol's diversion back on Carrasco would not hold up for long. Soon Gellner would report back and warn security to be on the look-out for Kemp.

"Sir," Kemp said, leaning his elbows on the man's counter in what he hoped appeared a friendly manner – as if they were standing at a bar together, sharing a beer or two. "Can I at least make a call?"

"Not until we're finished with processing your return, Inspector. This was not scheduled in, and there are anomalies in your authorisations."

Kemp considered Fernandez's advice to try bribery, then dismissed it. He was an officer of the law. Intimidation was far more likely to work.

"Listen, this is important. I'm a senior police officer working on a case that involves, quite literally, hundreds, if not thousands, of offences, ranging from the trivial to what would be regarded as war crimes. If you don't want to be considered an accessory to that veritable treasure chest of offences, then just authorise that call, would you? I'm tired, and I'm in a bad mood, and my imp has been disabled, so I simply need a private room with a smart wall: is that too much to ask?"

The man stared at him, his mouth slightly open, his dark face noticeably paler than it had been a minute before.

A short time later, Kemp sat alone in an interview room. "Call Bryce," he said, and the wall found the lawyer from Kemp's contacts and made the call.

A second later, Bryce's face filled the wall. "Gordon?" he

said. "My god, Gordon. What have they done to you? You
need a beer, and fast."

"Ed? A beer would be magnificent. But in the meantime…
I think I need some help."

All that stood between Kemp and a safe ride back to London,
now, was Thames Spaceport security.

He limped across the brightly lit concourse, conscious of
armed security guards stationed at intervals around the vast
chamber. His heart set up a laboured pounding and he was
sure the perspiration on his face was a giveaway. Ahead of
him, a dozen travellers breezed through the security check,
and he envied their nonchalance, the way they didn't even
acknowledge the armed guard as they passed him by.

He approached the barrier, knowing that every step he
took was being recorded, measured, analysed. Sensors would
be reading his body shape and the way he moved, checking
the way he held himself. They would even be assessing the
new limp and the way he held his weakened left arm, and
extrapolating these as fitting the subset of how he would
carry himself after injury. They would capture every little
mannerism, and measure the bones in his face, the layering of
his musculature.

The security AI would collate all of these and come up with
a confirmed ID that measured on the scale of trillions to one
that it was him, unmistakably DI Gordon Kemp.

At any moment, he expected a tap on the shoulder, a
command to stop. Gellner might not have sent word to seize
him just yet, but there was no way they would let him pass
through spaceport security within hours of his arrival from an
extrasolar planet.

It was impossible.

Impossible, at least, unless you had a friend like Ed Bryce,
and unless that friend had a friend like Martin Khalsa.

At the barrier, the armed guard stepped out, and he knew they were onto him.

The man dipped his head briefly, then, as the spaceport's security systems fed information direct to his imp.

"Sir," the man said, nodding to Kemp and stepping back. "Welcome back to London, Major Gellner. Please come through. Your clearance is all in order."

Kemp nodded, thankful that the guard had never met the real Major Gellner in the flesh. He walked through the sliding door and stood beneath the star-flecked night sky of home, taking deep breaths of the icy air.

A car waited outside the terminal building, Martin Khalsa in the back and Ed Bryce behind the wheel, leaning over to push the passenger door open. "Gordon," Bryce said. "Hop in before they cotton on, there's a good chap."

34

Carstairs Hall

It was almost eight by the time Danni pulled up before the tall iron gates of Carstairs Hall. She called ahead to tell Conway that she'd arrived, and the gates swung slowly open. Her car drove up the curving drive and braked before the steps leading up to the porticoed entrance.

She climbed out, hurried up the steps, and raised a hand to the sensor. Seconds later Conway pulled open the door.

"Are you always on duty?" he laughed.

"It seems like it these days," she said. "That's the thing with cold cases – we're always making up for lost time." It was a cliché she'd used many times before. "As I said, I'd like to question Mr Fairleigh-White on a certain matter, if he's up to it."

"He's had a good day," Conway said, "reminiscing about his past, apparently."

"And afterwards..." she said, "I've heard there's a decent bar in the village."

The way his face lit up at this made her feel guilty at the way she was manipulating his obvious attraction. It went with the territory, though: the moment a detective let such feelings interfere with getting the job done was the moment they should start thinking about a career change.

"There is, and they stock a very good British wine."

She masked her disdain and smiled. "Just let me talk to the old man first..."

He gestured to the left of the hall. "This way."

They walked side by side down the corridor. "Will you be in your office?"

He shook his head. "In my apartment upstairs, but I'll meet you in the hall at nine, okay?"

"How many people work here?" she asked as they walked, hoping the question came over as casual curiosity.

"Along with serving staff, cleaners and the like, about a dozen. Only four of us live here, though: Dr Radzinski, myself, the hall manager and his deputy. We occupy the upper floor. The ground floor is given over to offices and the like. Here we are. I'll see you at nine."

She thanked him and slipped through the door into Fairleigh-White's room.

To her surprise, the old man was conscious and staring directly at her.

"My, what a surprise. Inspector Bellini, isn't it?" His lips moved, but as ever his voice was computer-assisted.

"You remember me?"

"And why shouldn't I? It isn't every day I'm visited by such a vision of beauty."

She smiled as she approached his life-support pod. She wondered at the hell his life must be, incarcerated in machinery, unable to move, with only imminent death in prospect.

"You're looking well, Sir Alastair," she said. It wasn't a lie: his eyes were bright, and his usually white cheeks held a little colour.

"I'm feeling on top of the world, Inspector. Far better than last week, at any rate. I thought I was on the way out. Oh, I'm under no illusion: I could shuffle off at any moment. I'm glad you're here. Far better if you're the last thing I see than *him*..."

"Him?"

"Gellner. I never liked him. Always was a bastard."

She asked, "Always?"

He looked momentarily confused. "He was forever ordering everyone around."

She asked, "When was this?"

"Oh, I don't know!" Fairleigh-White said tetchily. "How should I know that? I don't even know what year it is now."

Danni hesitated, then took the plunge. "So you've never liked Marius Gellner? And you don't like seeing him now?"

"That's what I said, isn't it? Eh?" He licked his lips feebly. "Anyway, why are you here?"

"I came to say hello," she said, "and then I thought I'd take a look around the hall."

He chuckled. "Enjoy! It's a beautiful building. Or it was, before the damned Foundation had its way."

She leaned forward. "What did they do?"

"Gutted the library, for one thing. Turned it into... into, I don't know. Put all those contraptions in there. I don't pretend to understand all this modern technology."

"When was this?"

He blinked, recollecting. "Oh, many years ago. I was much younger. I came here in my holidays to stay with my uncle."

"Randolph?"

"That is correct, Inspector. It was he who made the changes. He should have known better – the hall had been in the family for generations."

"Tell me, where will I find the library?"

"Find it? I don't now... Where am I now?" He looked confused. "The library? It's... somewhere to the right of the hall as you enter. At the rear, near the ballroom, as far as I recall. But if you really want to admire something, it's the ballroom that you should take a look at."

She smiled. "I'll do that," she said. She glanced at her watch. She'd been here almost ten minutes. "I must be going... It's been nice talking. I'll drop in again at some point."

"Do that, young lady. It's always nice to see..."

Leaving him singing her praises, she slipped out of the room and hesitated, her heart thumping. Sir Alastair was talking of things that had happened decades ago: surely there would be nothing to see now? Even so...

She would head back to the hallway, make her way to the rear of the building, and take a look at the ballroom. If anyone apprehended her, she would say she was taking up Fairleigh-White's suggestion to admire the room. If she made it that far without being accosted, she'd try to locate the library. Not that she would have a hope of entering it, she knew: it would most likely be locked, accessible only to a select few. Perhaps if she were to exit via the rear of the building and attempt to look in through library window, or even gain entry that way...

She crossed the entrance hall and turned towards the back of the house.

The carpet was mauve, luxurious, the walls a pale green and hung with a series of Sung dynasty pen-and-ink landscapes.

The chances were that the interior of the hall was under surveillance, and that it was only a matter of time before her presence alerted the security smartware. Her one opportunity of going undetected was if there was no one on duty to respond to a security alert, but she knew the possibility of that would be slim indeed.

She came to a pair of double doors, reached out and turned the handle. She stepped into a vast ballroom with a sprung dancefloor, a high vaulted ceiling and a pair of French windows at the far end. The silence was eerie, in contrast to the hundreds of instances down the years when the cavernous room would have resounded to the sound of music and laughter.

She withdrew and carefully pulled the doors closed behind her.

Opposite the ballroom were doors giving on to other rooms. She moved to one, and to her surprise it opened. A storeroom: shelves of plastic cartons and cleaning equipment, mops and buckets.

She moved to the door next to the storeroom.

This one, unsurprisingly, was locked.

She debated what to do next. Return to the entrance hall and wait for her date, or continue searching through the rooms on the ground floor?

In the event, the decision was taken out of her hands.

The sound of soft footsteps on the carpet caught her by surprise, and a voice said, "I think you'll find that that one's locked, Danni," Peter Conway said.

She turned. His smile gave nothing away. In a split second she debated: make a run for it, or play the innocent?

"Sir Alastair told me I should take a look at..." She gestured towards the ballroom.

"It's quite something, isn't it? I never tire of the place, and thank my blessings that I work here."

Her heart resumed its usual rhythm: had she got away with it?

He said, gesturing towards the locked door, "But would you like to look inside?"

She tried to match his smile, falteringly "Why not?"

He stepped past her and raised his palm to the sensor beside the door. She could run now, she thought; cut her losses and get out of here.

Something about his studiedly casual manner should have alerted her – but she only realised this later, looking back.

The door opened and he ushered her inside.

She stepped into the room ahead of him, and he followed her. The door clicked shut behind them.

She swallowed, feeling sick. She should have taken the chance when she had it...

In contrast to the corridor and the ballroom, this room belonged unequivocally to the twenty-second century. Its walls were stark white, aseptic, the floor tiled the same colour.

It was not the walls or the floor, however, that held her attention, but what occupied the room.

Conway was smiling at her, amused by her reaction.

Six jade-green pods stood against the far wall, and it took Danni perhaps two seconds to realise where she'd seen images of these before.

In publicity shots of the *Strasbourg* mission to Carrasco...

They were suspension pods.

Conway crossed the room and laid a hand on a pod's sleek, curving lid.

"Is this what you've been looking for all along, Danni?"

She wondered what it was that persuaded her to stay in character, and not admit defeat: the forlorn hope that she could bluff her way to freedom, convince Conway that she really was an *ingénue*, interested in sixteenth century interior architecture? She wondered how long he'd suspected her – from her second visit, or from monitoring her surreptitious movements just now?

She tried to smile. "What are they?"

He feigned surprise. "Oh, I'm sure you know that."

"Suspension pods, right? But whatever are they doing here?"

He laughed. "Can't you guess?"

She swallowed. "Gellner?" she said.

"Clever girl."

"Marius Gellner and Major Gellner... They're the same–?"

Before he could come up with some patronising reply, the door opened and a short, thick-set man slipped into the room. He wore a harness over a black sweater, with a handgun lodged under his left armpit.

Conway said, "Come with us, Danni. There's someone I'd like you to meet."

The security guard gripped her upper arm, and between the two men she was escorted from the room and into the ballroom.

They walked her to the middle of the dance floor. The guard released his grip on her arm and walked to the far end of the room, turning before the French windows and standing with his legs planted astride, arms crossed. Beyond him, Danni could see a snow-covered lawn and a line of shadowy woodland beneath a dark sky.

Conway moved back to the door, and Danni turned to watch him. He stood with his head on one side, evidently conducting a sub-vocced conversation with someone.

"Imp," she sub-vocced in turn, "get through to Edouard Bryce. Tell him where I am and that I'm in danger."

"*Impossible,*" her imp replied.

"What?"

"*All outgoing communications are blocked.*"

"Okay, right. Very well, record everything in this room from now, okay?"

"*Initiating...*"

Conway finished his call, leaned back against the door and smiled at her.

She said, "I take it the drink in the village is on hold?"

"Well, *I'll* certainly be enjoying a drink a little later. I don't know about you."

She wondered if she could charge Conway, barge him aside and get through the door before the guard at the far end of the room had time to draw his handgun and fire. She judged that she had an even chance of escaping. She was bracing herself to run when the door opened and someone stepped into the ballroom.

She swore under her breath as a second guard, identical to the first one right down to the harness and handgun, nodded to Conway and stationed himself beside the door.

"So... what's happening here?" she asked.

"As I said, we're waiting for someone. I'm sure you'll be delighted to meet him. After all, it's what your investigations over the past week have all been about."

"Who..." her voice caught. "Who is it?"

Conway gave a short laugh. "Come on, you're a bright girl,

Danni. Can't you guess? The suspension pods back there were the giveaway."

The door opened behind him, and his smile widened as he saw her reaction.

A tall man strode into the room, impeccably attired in a sharp grey suit. His face was long, hollow-cheeked, and he still wore his hair in a ponytail. The sight of it made Danni want to laugh: nerves, she thought. There was nothing inherently funny about the ponytail, just anachronistic.

She had expected him to be arrogant, playing up to the part of a clichéd villain in the last act of a bad interactive, gloating at the fate of a captive. Randolph White, however, appeared to be distracted, as if annoyed at being called away from important business to deal with something beneath his concern.

He looked at Danni and snapped at Conway, "Who's this?"

"The detective who Commander Tsang told you about, sir."

"Oh, yes. Her." He paused. "Well?"

Conway shifted uncomfortably. "What do you want us to do with her, sir?"

Danni said, "Mr White…"

Randolph White turned from Conway and walked towards her, halting a couple of metres from Danni. Beside the door, the security guard took a pace forward, going for his handgun.

She stared at the man who, eighty years ago had killed his own brother – who, a week or two later, had ordered the murder of Selma Betancourt. The man who had illegally used the suspension pods to deny the passage of time and emerge towards the end of the century to oversee his corrupt business empire once more, just as it established a presence on a distant planet.

She swallowed, gathered her thoughts, and said, "My colleagues know I'm here, and they know exactly what you've done."

He nodded, biting his bottom lip. The way he listened to her, as if hearing out the report of a boardroom associate, made him appear almost reasonable. "And what is that, Ms Bellini?"

"The murder of Sebastian White," she said, "and the shooting of Selma Betancourt. We have evidence–"

"Evidence?"

Conway stepped forward. "Sir, Commander Tsang has everything under control."

White nodded. "I have every confidence in Tsang, Mr Conway. Very well," he went on, "you've wasted enough of my time." He gestured to the guard near the door and said with dispassion, "Take Ms Bellini out and dispose of her."

The guard stepped forward and gripped her upper arm. Danni fought her panic. She'd wait till they were outside, then attack the thug, go for his handgun...

As the guard pushed her forward, a white light filled the room. Danni's first thought was that a searchlight had been directed through the French windows. Then, as everyone turned and stared, through the windows she saw a vast megascreen move with the majestic grace of all colossal objects over the distant trees and come to a halt above the snow-covered lawn.

The huge screen was blank, showing merely a hail of silver-grey static.

Randolph White moved slowly towards the French windows and past the guard. He opened the glass door and paused on the threshold, staring up at the megascreen.

Beside her, the guard drew his gun and held its cold muzzle against her temple.

35

Welcome Home

Kemp sat back and closed his eyes as the car sped away from the terminal building. Perhaps it was some physiological reaction to the stress he'd recently undergone, but he felt even worse now than he had when fleeing Gellner's men in the ATV. His left arm and leg ached like hell and his skull felt as if it were about to split in two.

He tried to shut out the images that played in his mind's eye, the slaughter that had occurred fifty lightyears away, but the nightmare would not be banished.

He opened his eyes and massaged his arm. They were on the outer orbital around London. Nose to tail juggernaut convoys thundered to their left and right, walls of hurtling metal marked with company sigils and Big-5 script.

Bryce turned in his seat to look at Martin Khalsa. "Anything?"

"Not a thing," Martin replied.

"Ed," Kemp said again. "Where the hell are we going–?"

Bryce stared at him, his intent gaze silencing Kemp. "Danni called a little while back. She was approaching Carstairs Hall. We haven't heard from her since, despite repeatedly trying to reach her." He looked at Martin. "No digital footprint at all? No signal trail?"

"Nothing since she called," the young man said.

Bryce licked his lips. "If they'd killed her–?"

"Then I'd still be able to read her imp, just like the other day," Martin interrupted. "I'd be able to trace her. Wherever she is, no signals are getting through."

"Carstairs Hall?" Kemp said. "Why is she at the nursing home?"

"Long story," Martin said. "Danni was investigating some journalist from eighty years ago who was onto Randolph White. She traced her granddaughter, who had an old storage-pin that held an archive of the journalist's case notes. They suggested that White had been hiding something at the hall."

"Selma Betancourt," Kemp said.

Bryce stared at him. "How do you know of her?"

"I got to know an ecologist on Carrasco, Jayne Waterford. Before she left on the *Strasbourg*, Jayne worked with Betancourt, investigating Randolph White."

"It's likely that White had Betancourt killed eighty years ago. Perhaps she discovered something, and White was worried she was about to expose his undercover dealings. Anyway, Danni thinks the White Foundation was behind sending you to Carrasco to arrest Rima Cagnac."

"It was Randolph White himself," Kemp said.

Bryce stared at him. "What do you mean?"

Kemp rubbed his eyes, suddenly exhausted. "Randolph White is behind everything the Foundation is doing."

Bryce reached out and gripped Kemp's arm. "Gordon, White died around seventy-five years ago."

"That's what I thought. That's what everyone thought – what we were led to believe. Listen, I had this from Rima Cagnac herself..." He went on to tell Bryce about Randolph White's scheme to use the suspension pods, and his brother's objections which had resulted in his murder.

Bryce looked shocked. "So... you're telling me that Randolph White is still alive?"

"And directing the mission to Carrasco. I suspect he's indirectly responsible for the massacre there."

"Whoa, hold on there! The massacre?"

Kemp took a deep breath. He'd had the last day or so to get his head around all they'd discovered and now he was dumping it on Bryce in a rush. It was a lot to take in.

"White wants Carrasco for himself," Kemp explained. "If nothing else, it's prime real estate, but it's also somewhere a lot more attractive to establish a stronghold than the mess we've made of our own planet. It's a blank canvas for a megalomaniac like Randolph White. But he thought without the presence of sentient aliens."

Bryce shook his head. "Aliens...? Is there anything else you're not telling me, Gordon?"

"White's militia, led by Major Gellner, massacred an entire tribe of sentient aliens."

Bryce swore.

Kemp closed his eyes again, trying to still his thoughts, but all he saw was a random montage of images from the slaughter. He knew the importance of this moment. How the events of the next few hours played out was largely in his hands.

He gestured and a small screen opened in the air above the dashboard, showing images he'd been recalling with closed eyes only moments before. Kemp was back on Carrasco, secreted in the vesicle, staring out at Gellner's men as they systematically lasered the aliens to death. The massacre played out now in miniature, the sound muted.

The three men watched in silence.

At last Kemp said, "I've got to get this out there. We have to let the world know what the White Foundation is up to."

"Gordon," Martin said, leaning forward between the front seats and staring at Kemp, "can you send me the file?"

"You have contacts we can use?"

"Better than that."

Kemp sent the file, and Martin sat back in his seat, muttering to himself; the car lit up with multiple small screens and the young man waved his hands in frantic agitation.

They were heading away from London now. The night was

dark, illuminated by roadside advertisements and Big-5 signs. A megascreen hung over a satellite town, relaying a football match, the emerald-green pitch and the dazzling floodlights. Kemp thought about what he'd left, a world that knew none of this, a world without industry, technology, a world unspoilt. The perfect prize for a man like Randolph White.

He thought of Jayne and Rima back on Carrasco, and Gellner's men...

Bryce had resumed control of the vehicle, perhaps in a bid to give himself something to do, and was hunched over the controls, staring intently ahead.

"Danni?" Kemp asked.

"She's been working on the case while you've been away," Bryce said. "Tsang ordered her off it, so she took a few days' sick leave so she could pursue the investigation off the books. It's safe to say that if Tsang isn't up to his neck in all this with Randolph White, he's at the very least succumbing to pressure from those who are."

Kemp smiled, without the slightest trace of humour. "I worked that out for myself." He told them about the assassination command Tsang had had installed in his imp. "They sent me there to kill Cagnac, and they selected me to do it because it would be easy to portray me afterwards as a rogue copper with a track record of taking the law into my own hands... That reminds me, Martin, you saved my life, and you saved Cagnac's too."

"The Buddha pin?"

Kemp smiled at the young man. "Left me feeling a little rough, but it wiped my imp before it could force me to kill Cagnac."

Martin nodded, but for some reason he looked downcast. He said, "I feel guilty, Gordon."

"Hey, thanks to you, me and Rima Cagnac are still alive–"

"About Danni," Martin went on.

Apprehensive, Kemp said, "Why's that?"

"Danni asked me to run some background checks on Peter Conway and I told her she could trust him." He shrugged. "He came up clean. He'd only worked for the White Foundation for a few months. I had no reason to believe he was anything but a minor administrator." He hesitated.

"But?"

"Then... when I couldn't get through to Danni, I dug deeper."

"What did you find?"

"Conway was head-hunted from college by a technology investment company based in Hong Kong. I should have realised... You see, I recognised the name of the company... It was part of a portfolio of shell companies used by Randolph White eighty years ago. He was using them to illicitly channel funds into the Carrasco project."

Bryce said, "You did your best, Martin. Do you hear me? You heard what Gordon said – what you did saved his life, and that of Cagnac. And anyway, Danni can look after herself."

"Against the White Foundation?" the young man murmured, and turned back to his screens.

Bryce flicked a glance at Kemp and gestured at the dashboard. "Open the dash unit."

Kemp did so and found two automatic pistols. He took them out.

"For emergencies," Bryce said.

Kemp glanced over his shoulder. Martin was muttering and busying himself with his screens, flicking his fingers and gesturing in mid-air, a latter-day alchemist effecting miracles that Kemp had no hope of comprehending. "I'm editing the footage you sent," he explained, "selecting and sequencing clips, constructing a running order and highlighting effective close-ups and freezeframes."

He fell silent, working in a semi-darkness illuminated by the half a dozen small screens that flickered around him. His head turned from one to the other, his lips in constant movement as he talked to himself or issued instructions.

Kemp turned to Bryce and murmured, "When we get to the hall...?"

"*You're* the one trained in these things," Bryce said. "But I suggest we play it by ear. Keep the weapons concealed, and go in there low-key: we're just enquiring after a colleague. Martin has worked up a search warrant that might fool whoever's in charge for a few minutes, if they won't let us in..." He waved in the air and the warrant appeared on a floating screen; it looked genuine enough to Kemp.

"The fact that we can't reach her..." Kemp began, feeling sick.

"Left turn ahead," the car interrupted them.

They left the roar of the highway in their wake and cruised down a country road between looming olive trees. There was little traffic now, and the headlights sliced white cones through the darkness, illuminating the falling snow.

"Five kilometres to Carstairs Hall," Bryce said. "How's it going, Martin?"

The young man swore. "I need to concentrate..." he muttered.

Bryce glanced at Kemp. "How are you feeling?"

"Christ... I don't know. I just want to see Danni safe."

Bryce slowed the car, then turned along a winding lane. Minutes later, the perimeter wall of the hall came into view, and in due course he braked before a pair of high wrought-iron gates.

"The last time we were here," Kemp said, "we had to call through to be allowed in."

"We've thought of that," Bryce said. "Or at least Martin has. Martin?"

In the back, Martin gestured, snapping his fingers. "Open sesame!" And as if by magic the gates swung slowly open.

Bryce eased the car forward and they rolled up the gravel

drive and around a stand of rhododendrons. He braked, and
they stared at the big Georgian building, and the glow of a
megascreen that hung high in the air behind the hall showing
nothing other than a screen of black and white static.

"Don't tell me White has his own private megascreen?"
Kemp said.

"I uncoupled it from its moorings above Milton Keynes
twenty minutes ago," Martin said. He stopped. "Hey! I have
something... Danni! She's at the back of the building, outside."

Bryce was already steering the car towards the house, the
headlights switched off now. They passed the front of the
building and turned the corner.

Kemp reached out and laid a restraining hand on Bryce's
arm. "Stop here. We'll go the rest of the way on foot. Martin,
hang back. And don't slam the doors when you get out,
okay?"

Bryce braked and they climbed out. After the heat of the car,
the freezing cold was a surprising assault. Kemp clutched his
handgun, moving stealthily along the side of the house, still
limping. He glanced over his shoulder. Bryce was close behind,
followed at a distance by Martin, trailed by half a dozen small,
bright screens. It was hardly the most reassuring-looking
rescue squad he could have imagined...

Kemp came to the corner, pressed himself against the
brickwork, and peered round.

He saw light spilling from a pair of French windows, twenty
metres along the back of the house. A tall man was staring up
at the megascreen, and beyond him two figures stood close
together. One of them was Danni.

"Put the gun away, Ed, and follow me."

Slipping his own handgun under his jacket, he moved
around the corner, his heart thudding.

He crunched over the gravel, approaching the French
windows. The tall man turned and stared at the interlopers.
Kemp recognised Randolph White. He was much thinner than

he'd expected, and wore his grey hair in a ponytail. He looked more like a European intellectual from a hundred years ago than a fat-cat business tycoon.

Beyond White, a squat man clutched Danni's upper arm, pressing a gun to the side of her head. She saw him, winced a smile, and Kemp gave her a reassuring nod to intimate that all would be well.

Kemp came to a halt five metres before Randolph White. Behind the tycoon was another bodyguard, his weapon drawn and levelled at Kemp. Beside the guard was the blond young man Kemp recognised as Peter Conway.

White said, "And you are?"

"Inspector Kemp." He nodded towards Danni. "Tell your man to release her, White."

Randolph White smiled. "Kemp... Kemp... The name is familiar. Won't you enlighten me?"

"I'm the poor dupe Commander Tsang sent to Carrasco, on your orders, to kill Rima Cagnac. I'm happy to report that she's alive and well, and prepared to testify."

He drew his handgun but left it pointing at the ground, forefinger resting lightly on the trigger guard. "So do the sensible thing and order your man to release Inspector Bellini."

Kemp glanced at Bryce. He stood a few metres away, nervously fingering his handgun. Beyond him, Martin Khalsa twitched, clicking his fingers and muttering, his attention on the screens flying around his head.

White smiled. "I'll do nothing of the kind."

For a terrible second, Kemp wondered if he was about to order the guard to shoot Danni. He said, impulsively, "Did you give Gellner *carte blanche* to do what he did on Carrasco?"

White smiled, covering his surprise. "I beg your pardon?"

Kemp swallowed, struggling with the sudden emotion that welled up as he came to articulate Gellner's crimes. "Gellner and his men... they slaughtered fifty defenceless Carrascans, maybe more. I take it you authorised his actions – it wouldn't do to have the UN impose restrictions on the planet, would it, after all the work you'd done to ensure the place was in the grip of your Foundation?"

To his credit, White maintained an impeccable élan as he smiled at Kemp. "You're lying, Kemp. My men wouldn't–"

"No? You have a track record. You had Selma Betancourt killed, and you yourself murdered your own brother. What's the death of a few aliens to you, to get what you want, what you'd planned for more than eighty years…?" He took a breath. "Do the sensible thing, White – tell your man to release Danni. It's over now."

"You're making a lot of unfounded accusations, Kemp."

For the first time, Bryce spoke. "Not unfounded, White. We have evidence."

The second bodyguard moved to White's side, his handgun trained on Kemp. He murmured something inaudible to his boss. White heard him out, his head cocked.

White said, smiling, "I'm reliably informed that back-up is on the way. You'll soon be outnumbered, Kemp. Now *you* do the sensible thing," he went on, mimicking Kemp's own earlier instruction, "and drop your weapons."

Kemp saw movement to his left, and then to his right. Fifty metres away, a line of troopers emerged from the trees and approached the rear of the hall. He guessed there were perhaps thirty of them, garbed head-to-foot in black and advancing carefully. Their uniforms reminded him of those worn by Gellner's men, and he felt sick.

They stopped twenty metres away, their weapons levelled on the silent tableau at the rear of the hall. He should have known someone like White would have heavy security on hand.

"You might possess all manner of evidence," White said, "for all the good it will do you…"

Bryce called across to Martin Khalsa, "Do it!"

Martin waved a hand, and high above them the floating

megascreen flickered, flooding the lawn with its polychromatic illumination.

Kemp looked up, staring at a horribly familiar sight.

The screen displayed a still image of the aliens' holy amphitheatre, with Gellner's men in the background and the slight forms of the Carrascans gathered before the invaders like a supplicant congregation.

Martin waved again, and the stilled image sprang into motion.

Gellner's men moved forward, hosing the hapless aliens with their merciless laser fire. The aliens fell, limbs severed, bodies sliced in two... attempting to flee but slipping and falling in their own spilled life blood. The frozen air behind Carstairs Hall was filled with the haunting, grunting cacophony of dying aliens and the occasional shouted commands of Major Gellner.

The sequence lasted just a minute and finished with the slow-motion close-up shot – selected and enhanced by Martin – of Gellner striding forward and finishing off those aliens not yet dead.

Then Martin stilled the image, and a sudden and terrible silence reigned.

"There..." Kemp found his voice at last, "... is the evidence."

He was surprised, and revolted, by Randolph White's reaction. The man smiled. "I don't have the slightest idea what you hope to achieve by showing me this out here in the middle of nowhere, Kemp. Blackmail – is that it? Go on, then, name your price. What do you want? A million euros each? More? Is that what this is all about?"

Kemp stepped forward, and for the first time raised his handgun and directed it at the tycoon's chest. "Release Inspector Bellini!" he said.

White laughed. "As if I'd be stupid enough to allow her to have her freedom – to allow any of you to get out of here alive."

Beyond Danni, he saw the line of armed militia, and he had a terrible presentiment of how this was going to end.

Bryce moved to Martin Khalsa's side, his voice shaking as he said, "He's asked for it, Martin. Go ahead!"

Martin waved.

The screen above their heads flickered again. The image changed. The scene was no longer one of carnage on a distant alien world. Now the giant screen showed a crowd in Trafalgar Square, staring up at a floating megascreen in stunned silence. The scene shifted again, this time showing Times Square, New York, and yet another crowd gazing in appalled fascination at what was playing on the huge screen above their heads; then St Peter's Square, Rome, the quayside in Sydney, Cinelândia Square in Rio de Janeiro, and even Beijing's Tiananmen Square... And while the scene of extraterrestrial slaughter played out all around the world, a commentator's voice-over boomed from the megascreen's speakers: "... from Anchorage to Melbourne, Oslo to Manila, the same footage showing humanity's first ever contact with alien beings... Oh, my God..."

Bryce called out to White, "We've pushed it to every network and every social dataspace in the world, and it's showing on every single megascreen."

The tycoon turned to Conway, and for the first time Kemp saw his composure beginning to slip. "It's a fake, Peter! Tell me that it's a mock-up..."

The young man shook his head, transfixed, staring up at the looping slaughter in stunned silence.

"The footage is genuine," Kemp said. "It will stand up to the deepest levels of digital scrutiny and verification. Do you think the networks would be picking it up and reshowing it if they weren't convinced?"

On the megascreen, the scene changed again. They stared at a close-up of Randolph White standing before the French windows, saying, *"I don't have the slightest idea what you hope to achieve by showing me this out here in the middle of nowhere, Kemp. Blackmail – is that it? Go on, then – name your price: what do you want? A million euros each? More? Is that what all this is about?"*

The commentator cut in, "And... we're reliably informed that the image you're watching *is* indeed that of Randolph White, presumed dead seventy-six years ago... alive and well somewhere in southern England..."

Overhead, the giant image of White said, *"As if I'd be stupid enough to allow her to have her freedom – to allow any of you to get out of here alive."*

The flesh-and-blood Randolph White, shaking visibly now, swung towards Kemp. "As if this will get you anywhere, Kemp! Do I need to remind you that you're surrounded?"

Kemp turned, resigned, and stared at the semi-circle of troopers, weapons trained unflinchingly. He felt like making a last, desperate quip that they weren't exactly surrounded, but the words died on his lips. All he felt, then, was a crushing despair that it had cost so much to bring the tycoon to his knees.

Bryce moved to his side, smiling. "Don't worry, Gordon..."

Kemp assumed he was about to make some last-minute, heroic speech about dying in pursuit of a noble cause, but before his friend could finish what he was about to say, one of the black-clad militia stepped forward and called out, "White! Order your men to get to their knees and drop their weapons, now!"

Kemp stared at the troopers, hardly daring to hope.

Randolph White raised a hand in a beseeching gesture, mouthing, "But...!"

"I said *now*!" the guard yelled.

Beside White, the bodyguard needed no second telling. He knelt, tossed his weapon away across the gravel.

The trooper turned his weapon towards White and Conway. "Now you two – on the ground!"

Hands in the air, Randolph White and Peter Conway knelt, and then lay face down on the gravel.

Kemp looked across at Danni. The man at her side knelt and

tossed his weapon away, then lay face down, his hands at the back of his head. Danni crossed to the gun and snatched it up. Then she produced restraint-ties from a pocket and bent over the supine guard to secure his wrists and ankles.

Moments later, she stood facing Kemp, all four prisoners lying in the dirt.

Kemp couldn't quite work out the look on her face. Was he missing something?

"Can't you see, Gordon? The troopers – they're not real. They're projections, just like the *faux* customers you get in every bar in London. Martin must have spoofed a message from White's head of security to tell him to expect reinforcements, so he wouldn't call for anything else, but there were none. White was so concerned about your footage being faked that he didn't see what was right in front of him – or *wasn't*..."

Martin Khalsa gestured, lifted a hand, and the semi-circle of black-clad militia winked out of existence in an instant. Then he glanced towards Bryce, and the older man simply nodded and mouthed, "Well done, son."

As Kemp watched, Bryce crossed to Danni and took her in his arms.

Danni smiled across at Kemp and said, "Welcome home, Gordon."

They looked up at the megascreen in silence.

The loop had begun again, showing the world the work of Randolph White's men on Carrasco, Mu Arae II.

Epilogue

In the aftermath of the slaughter, Rima spent two days holed up with Jayne at her trapping station, living in constant fear of arrest. Then word came through that Gellner and his thugs had been rounded up and arrested, and now Luis Vignol was running the base, with the aid of reinforcements from Earth.

They returned to the base, and tried to fit in, but after all Rima had been through, it was hard. She felt like a freak, always on display – not a person to interact with, but a novelty. The woman who had lived with the aliens and now bore the scars.

"I'm not sure I can do this any more," she told Xavier Fernandez.

"I'm a pilot," he told her. "I fly shuttles. I do what I do. You, Rima, must do what *you* do."

"But I don't know what that is…"

She did though; she was just shying away from it. She asked Jimmy Ranatunga to assume the role of chief medical officer while she took what he insisted on calling her sabbatical. She spoke to Luis Vignol about her intentions but he didn't want to know, preferring to turn a blind eye to her plan to venture out alone, against all protocols.

And Jayne… Her betrayer and her saviour – she still had not fully forgiven her friend for not telling her the truth of what had happened to Sebastian, but in those two days holed up at the trapping station, finally she had started to see Jayne as a friend she had truly come to know.

"What will you do, Jayne?" she asked, as the two stood outside the main dome, Rima preparing to leave.

"I don't know," Jayne told her. "There's a whole new world here, just waiting to be studied and understood. My life has led me to this point. But also, there's the world we left behind…"

And so Rima set out from the base, still not really sure what she hoped to achieve. She'd been the first woman awake in orbit around another star, and one of the last to land. And now she felt an air of fate to what she was doing: the first human to truly start the journey of becoming a Carrascan.

Rima left her ATV in a side tunnel a short distance from the amphitheatre and proceeded the rest of the way on foot. It seemed disrespectful to do otherwise, given the actions of the last humans to enter this arena by motorised vehicle.

She wore boots, shorts and t-shirt, having dispensed with the biohazard suit shortly after leaving the main base two days before.

She had slept out for two nights under the stars, so that now the yielding embrace of the jungle canopy held no horrors for her. She knew how to shrug her way free of the tendrils that crept over her in the night, how to ease the polyps from any exposed skin; since surviving cloud fever with the aid of Creasey's ministrations, she seemed resistant to any recurrence. She truly felt more at home here than she ever had on Earth.

The amphitheatre had been the obvious place to come to, a site of huge significance to the Carrascans. She was mindful of Franco's warning not to over-interpret and anthropomorphise the aliens' story, but she knew she was right. This was the place of life and death, where the aliens came to give birth, and to die. If she was to find them anywhere, she would find them here.

It might not be the only such place, of course. For all she knew there might be a thousand amphitheatres on this continent alone, but she had to start somewhere.

She came to the mouth of a tunnel and paused, almost overcome by the rush of emotion. The memories of the awful events that had unfolded here a week before.

There was no sign of the slaughter. No sundered limbs or broken bodies. No smears of dark blood. Even the breeding vesicles were sealed, hidden from the eye.

Had the surviving Carrascans returned to clear up, or was this a natural process, the planet's high-octane biological processes healing and concealing?

Whatever the explanation, it was as if the massacre had never taken place.

Days passed with no sign of the aliens. It wouldn't surprise Rima if they had abandoned this amphitheatre altogether, regardless of its significance to them.

She started to explore the tunnels, venturing ever farther from the arena, but still she found no sign of sentient activity.

She would leave here, she decided. It could not be long before Vignol sent a team to study the place and assess the damage Gellner had done.

She headed deeper into the tunnels, sleeping where tiredness took her, losing track of day and night. Until, finally, she heard sounds – the soft grunt of alien voices. At first she was convinced she was hallucinating, perhaps succumbing to a new variant of cloud fever, but no... she could definitely hear them.

She walked faster, but heard nothing more. She *had* been hallucinating.

She rounded another corner and the tunnel opened out. She saw movement – a blur of grey – and then felt a tight grip on her arms and ankles. Tendrils, twining around her, binding her tightly and dragging her down until she lay on her back.

Another grey blur, and a figure loomed over her. Big eyes, and the flash of a sharp talon, close to her face.

"Friends," she gasped. "I'm here in peace." Her wristcom translated, but the alien did not respond. If this individual was not from Creasey's original group, did it even speak the same language?

"I've come to make amends," she said. "I have come from the place of life and death, and now I seek a place of understanding and enlightenment." Because she was starting to understand that far from being a simple language of grunts, the aliens spoke on many levels, and there had been deeper layers when Creasey had spoken of the place of life and death – it was a sentiment, or perhaps a metaphor, as well as a physical place.

"My people are from the stars," she said, buying time if nothing else. "Some of us are good, some bad. The bad ones... they're no longer here. I am called Rima."

Still the alien showed no response, and Rima wondered if she had only seconds to live. And then, slowly, the being retracted its talons into its wrists.

"Rima," it grunted.

Did this mean it knew of her, perhaps through word of mouth from Creasey's original group before the slaughter? Or was it merely repeating what she had said?

In a flowing movement, the alien stood and backed away. Rima felt the tendrils loosening around her, and managed to ease herself free, first to sit and then stand.

The alien grunted, and her wristcom translated: "Walk."

Was this an invitation, or an instruction?

The alien turned and started to walk, and Rima fell into step at its side. This must mean something, she thought. Acceptance, or at least curiosity. It was not exactly a welcome, but was still far better than she had anticipated.

They walked for almost an hour, but Rima had lost all sense of direction and her wristcom's mapping tools were hopeless this deep in the jungle. She didn't know if they had been walking away from the amphitheatre or back towards it.

They rounded a corner and she saw the grey light of the tunnel mouth ahead. Had they come back to the arena, then?

"Walk." It was impossible to read emotion into the translated word, but the alien's instruction seemed more urgent now.

When they came close to the tunnel mouth, Rima paused. Her heart was pounding, her throat dry. She could hear noises ahead, a low murmur punctuated by the unmistakable grunt of the Carrascans.

She felt a sharp prod between her shoulder blades.

"*Walk.*"

Stubborn, she braced against the push and held her ground, but the next prod sent her stumbling forwards.

Her foot caught in a tendril and she fell face first, catching herself on hands and knees.

Kneeling, she peered up.

All around her, massed ranks of aliens lined the amphitheatre, their big eyes studying her, and all Rima could think was had they brought her here to be accepted among them, or had they brought her to be judged?

Kemp left the police HQ and took a rickshaw to the *Cockerel*.

Two weeks had elapsed since his return from Carrasco, and today he'd been called in to meet his new commanding officer. For that long he and Danni had been granted leave, with no word of when they might resume their duties.

It had taken him a while to acclimatise himself to being back on Earth, to the freezing weather and the press of people in London. His memories were of Carrasco and what he'd experienced there. His thoughts were so focused on the recent past that he hadn't for a second considered his future.

Until now.

His audience with Commander Khan today had been brief,

and he was still reeling from what she'd told him. He needed a drink, and to talk things over with Danni.

He came to the *Cockerel*, paid off the driver and stood outside in the weak winter sunlight, wondering at his reluctance to enter the pub. Danni was in there with Ed Bryce, and Kemp wasn't sure if he wanted to know what exactly was going on between them. A part of him was curious; another part didn't really want his suspicions confirmed: that, while he'd been away, something had happened to bring Danni and Bryce together, however improbable that might seem.

He told himself that he should be happy for his friends, not jealous.

He pushed into the warmth of the crowded pub and eased his way to the bar. Through the press of bodies, he saw Danni and Bryce in the corner, hands linked across the table.

She saw him and quickly removed her hand from Bryce's, smiling across at him and shaking her head as he mimed a drink. He saw that Bryce's glass was almost empty, and ordered two Fuller's-Tsing-Tao.

He carried the drinks across to the table and sat down.

Bryce nodded his thanks and lifted the glass to his lips.

Kemp lifted his own glass, tried to think of an appropriate toast, but failed.

Instead he said, "No Martin?"

"He promised he'd be along later," Bryce said.

"You're joking?" Kemp laughed. "We're honoured."

"I've just had to relocate him for the third time since the events at Carstairs Hall," Bryce said. "He's understandably paranoid about the media intrusion."

"Where is he now?" Kemp asked.

Bryce looked around uneasily. "If you don't mind, I'd rather not say…"

Kemp nodded. "Understood."

He looked up, distracted by something on the wallscreen above the table. Rolling news was rehashing recent events on

Carrasco. A head-and-shoulders shot of Major Gellner showed briefly, accompanied by a voiceover saying the security chief was in detention in Paris, awaiting trial.

Danni tapped his arm. "So," she asked, "how was the meeting?"

"They haven't contacted you?"

"I'm due to meet someone called Commander Khan tomorrow. What's she like?"

"In her fifties, worked her way up through the ranks, superficially friendly." He took another drink and thought about the meeting. "I asked what had happened to Tsang, and she simply told me he'd been 'relieved of his duties pending an investigation'. Then she dropped a bombshell."

Danni leaned forward. "Go on."

"She offered me my old job back. I'd be working in Homicide again, with a new, small team of detectives based here in London."

Bryce raised his glass. "Congratulations, Gordon."

Danni smiled, reached out and squeezed his hand.

Kemp said, "I declined the job."

The silence stretched. Danni stared at him. "You did what?"

He stared at Bryce, then Danni. "I'm past it. After what happened on Carrasco... Five years ago I might have jumped at the offer, but I'm no longer ambitious. And also... Well, you know me, Danni. I'm a bloody-minded, bolshy old sod. I'm not going to do something because some high-up tells me to do it. And also..."

"Go on," Bryce said.

Kemp shrugged. "All this publicity – the media bombarding us for interviews and 'guest appearances'... A part of me wonders if Commander Khan is taking the opportunity to up the profile of the department by having me back in the team. If so, I don't want any part of it – and anyway, I have work to do in missing persons. I promised Ma Holding I'd find her daughter's killer, and I intend to do just that, even if it takes me another ten years to do so."

Danni shook her head. "Are you quite sure?"

"Quite," he said. He smiled at Danni. "And a head's-up... When I said I was happy in the morgue, Khan told me in strictest confidence that the new Homicide team would be headed by you. I think she was hoping to win me over."

She stared at him, and he could see the conflict in her expression: delight at the prospect of promotion battling with disappointment at his refusal to work under her.

She said, "But she failed to win you over, Gordon?"

He nodded. "Like I said–"

"We make a good team," she interrupted. "Why not tell Khan you'll think it over, at least?"

"I have thought it over, and I'm happy at the morgue."

She glanced at Bryce, biting her lip, then said, "Is all this because... because of me and Ed? Is that why you don't want to work with me?"

He smiled, relieved that it was at last out in the open. "So you two *are*–?"

Bryce said, "We'll see how things pan out. It's early days. Whatever happens, I'll be there for Danni and the baby."

He nodded, smiling. "That's good to know," he said, and hoisted his glass. "And no," he went on to Danni, "my decision has nothing to do with you and Ed, okay?"

Bryce raised a hand to his ear as his imp relayed something, and a second later a screen opened in the air before them.

Bryce smiled. "Told you Martin would be along, Gordon."

On the screen, Martin Khalsa looked wired, fidgeting like a marionette and cracking his knuckles as he paced back and forth. Without so much as a hello, he said, "You've heard the latest? They've found the bastard! He was in a container ship in the channel with a cadre of his diehards..."

"Slow down," Bryce said. "First of all, they've found who?"

"Who else? Randolph White."

Kemp sat back, relieved. Two weeks ago, just hours after Martin Khalsa had revealed to the world the extent of Randolph

White's criminal activities, six armed men had attacked the police convoy taking White into custody in London, killing three armed guards and spiriting White away to an unknown destination.

"Look," Martin said, and waved. His image vanished, replaced by a drone's eye view of a container ship in the channel, a helicopter in the air above and an assault team swarming over the deck. The scene cut to a brief and bloody firefight, and then a shot of a tall, harassed-looking, handcuffed Randolph White being escorted between two security personnel.

"... the arrest and detention of Randolph White," the anchor was saying, "charged with the deaths of over two hundred native Carrascans, as well as a long list of other crimes..."

Martin reappeared. "This happened two hours ago," he said. "He's now in a high-security detention centre somewhere in the south of England."

"When he got away," Danni said, "I really thought he'd won. Okay, so he might not have got everything he'd wanted – an entire damned world! – but I thought he'd escaped punishment."

Martin said, "They'll have to invent a new category of crime to cover what he ordered, out there on Carrasco."

Bryce grunted, "How about Mass Extraterrestrial Homicide?"

Kemp's imp pinged in his ear. *"Incoming... From Jayne Waterford."*

He sat back, more than a little surprised. "Accept..." he subvocced, "but give me fifteen seconds."

He excused himself, edged from the table, and found an unoccupied room beyond the bar. "Okay," he said.

A screen opened in the air, showing the thin, tousle-haired woman smiling out at him. He was surprised at his reaction of delight he felt at the sight of her. "Jayne..."

"The man himself. You look..." she leaned forward, frowning out at him, "you look shocked, darling."

He laughed, uneasy. "Just... surprised," he said. "Where are you?"

"Thames detention centre," she said, "but I get out of here in two weeks."

"But I thought... That is, I didn't think you were planning to come back."

She shrugged. "I had plenty of time to think about the future, Gordon. Work out just what I wanted. Was I cut out to spend the next few years on Carrasco, like Rima, or...?"

"Or?"

"Or take time out on Earth, and really think about what I wanted from life."

He nodded, tempted to ask her what that might be. Instead he said, "And Rima?"

"You haven't heard?"

"There's been a news embargo on all things Carrascan here on Earth," he said, "until the investigation of the slaughter is completed... Is Rima okay?"

"She's more than just okay," Jayne said, "she's fine. She... Well, I suppose you could say she's been accepted as an honorary Carrascan. She's working as a liaison officer between the UN delegation newly arrived on the planet, and the aliens. The last time I saw her – just a few hours ago – she was full of what she'd learned about the little critters."

He said, "And you?"

"I'm okay," she said, nodding. "And I was wondering... just as soon as I get out of this place, how about that drink you promised me?"

"I'd like that," he said.

She smiled. "See you then, Gordon," she said, and cut the connection.

Kemp moved to the bar and bought another round of drinks – in celebration, he decided. He looked across the room at Danni, Bryce, and the image of Martin hanging in the air above the table. Behind them, the wallscreen relayed images from the massacre on Carrasco, intercut with expert analysis from scientists and political pundits.

As Danni's laughter rang out at something Bryce had said, Kemp picked up the drinks and rejoined his friends at the corner table.

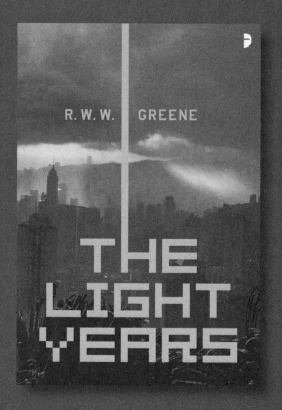

Adem

Versailles City, Oct 14, 3235

Maybe God will make it better.

The thought escaped Adem's throat in barely remembered Arabic. Years before, his grandmother had given him the words as a talisman against specters like the one he faced now. A crusted sore sealed its right eye into a squint, protein starvation bloated its belly, and its arms were thin as sticks. The little boy smiled and presented the bowl again. The blessing might have worked better in French. The Almighty always had a soft spot for Europeans and their descendants, the EuroD.

Adem reached into the belly pocket of his utilisuit and sorted through his supply of coins by touch.

"That bowl is an antique," he said. The technology used to produce them had been lost to Gaul a century before. Sealed in its bottom, an animated 3D image of a once-popular cartoon character offered a cheerful thumbs up in recognition of cereal well eaten. "You should take it to an–"

Adem finished the sentence in his head. An antiquities dealer would most likely swindle the boy, and he would come away little better off and in need of a new bowl. There wasn't much justice available to people like him. There were work programs and shelters for state-approved orphans, so the boy had to be an *illicite*: an illegal birth. His parents had abandoned him in fear of punishment or lost him to the streets when they went to prison.

Adem covered the cartoon's grinning face with triangular coins, enough for a month's worth of food. He dug into his supply of New Portuguese, a simplified language adopted by Gaul's civil service and foisted on the planet's refugee population, hoping to be better understood. "Keep it for yourself. Don't give it to any–"

The boy dashed away, the bowl tight against his narrow chest. Adem cursed. The money would likely end up in the hands of whatever kidsman gave the child his daily meal and a corner to sleep in. Adem pulled up his hood and resumed his walk.

The russet afternoon light turned the roadway's cracked pavement the color of dried blood. The area had devolved since Adem's last visit, the people becoming poorer, more desperate. Rows of refugee shanties and hovels pressed up against the elevator depot. In a taxi he could have blocked them out completely by darkening the vehicle's windows and watching a news or entertainment vid. But when he was on-planet, Adem walked where he could, curious to see what had changed. Once, his simple clothing helped him blend in with the locals but now his sturdy utilisuit made him a target.

A woman beckoned him from the next corner. She was standing in front of a crumbling building that had been a thriving noodle shop half a standard century before. She ran her hands down her short dress and raised its hem to reveal her scrawny thighs. "You look lonely, spaceman!"

"Bad luck," Adem said. "I'm getting a wife today." Talking to another child might have broken his heart, but he had thicker skin where adults were concerned.

"I'll give you my bachelor discount." She stepped closer. The smell of her sweat allied with the chemical tang of whatever drug she favored and the cheap ginja on her breath. Her tight dress was grimy, hugging bone more than curve. Her hair was dry and limp.

"Last time I was here this was a nice place," Adem said.

The woman shifted position, her malnutrition not quite eliciting the desired response. "How long ago was that?"

"Two and a half years relative. About fifty years your time."

She rubbed her lower lip with the stump of her missing left thumb. "I have a friend across the street. Maybe you'd like him better. Maybe you want both of us."

"I'm all set." Adem reached in his pocket for more coins. "Take a couple of days off. My treat. Call it a wedding present."

She limped away with the money. Rationed, it might keep her off the streets for a couple of weeks, but more likely she'd head to a tea shop and spend it on Bliss or whatever people like her were inhaling these days. If she forgot to save a few of the coins for her pimp, she might lose the other thumb.

Adem pushed his hands into his pockets. Nearly three standard centuries ago, during his first visit to Gaul, Adem had offered a woman named Tamara his virginity and four coins from his pocket. She had relieved him of both with algorithmic efficiency, and he'd been back on the street in fifteen minutes. Tamara had long been dust, but once she had been beautiful enough to attract well-heeled customers. The one-thumbed woman might be dead the next time Adem came this way, and her daughter or son, or even a grandchild, might be working the corner where the noodle shop used to be.

Four grim-faced men in cheap armor manned a checkpoint on the next block, slowing the creep into midtown. There hadn't been a checkpoint fifty years before, and the line between the central city slums – *La Merde*, as locals called them – and everywhere else had not been so sharply drawn. Adem brushed at the front of his utilisuit. A block prior it had made him desirable; at the border it made the authorities wonder why he was afoot.

"What's your business?" The guard was a big man, and his ceramic armor strained to cover the vulnerable parts of his body.

Adem kept his hands in sight. "I'm just down the elevator. Got an appointment with a matchmaker." He offered the address.

The guard inserted Adem's ID stick into his reader. Adem held his breath. There had been a couple of dust-ups when he was a kid. No one alive had anything to complain about, but the law could get complicated when relativity was involved.

The guard grunted and handed back the stick. "You crew?"

Adem shook his head. "Family. Part owner."

"You paying for gene work, then? Give her a big smile and no brains?" The guard's face darkened. "A nice little splice to keep you happy up there in space?"

Adem forced himself not to take a step back. "Nothing like that. Just a standard contract."

The guard sneered. "Lost my little sister that way. She married a Trader, too. Standard contract. Won't see her again until I've got gray in my hair."

"What ship?" Adem said. "Maybe I can get a message to her."

"Doesn't matter. She's gone. I tell Ma that she's got to move on with it." The guard gestured with his stun club back down the street. "Still better than that. Her contract got us out, but the shit keeps coming. Next time you're here checkpoint's liable to be a mile further up and all these pretty offices turned to squats." He spat on the sidewalk. "She's better off up there. She might as well be dead to us, and she's better off." He waved Adem on. "Go meet your wife."

Past the checkpoint, the midtown business district assembled along well-groomed streets. There was a green park to Adem's left, complete with a statue of Audric Haussman, a long dead city planner who had claimed descendance from the First Baron Architect of Paris. Adem double-timed the next two blocks with his head down, hoping to avoid anyone else who might want to flag him down for the novelty of a conversation with a spaceman. Too many times it turned hostile. No matter how far *La Merde* spread, no matter how many ad-hoc refugee settlements sprang up around the elevator, Traders like him could stay above it all. Take the ship up to 99.999 percent of light speed, and decades of standard time might erase the stain by the time it came back into port.

Adem held his ID stick up to the door scanner of a nondescript office building and walked through the airlock into the climate-controlled lobby beyond. He nodded to the robot secretary. "Adem Sadiq. I have an appointment with the matchmaker."

The repurposed robot stared blankly at him as it accessed the information. It was a bulky thing, nearly immobile behind the desk and built for construction or mining, but it seemed comfortable with its reprogramming. It gestured toward the waiting room.

Adem paced up and down the small room until the matchmaker came to fetch him.

"Monsieur Sadiq?" The small woman held out her hand as she advanced on him. Adem accepted it clumsily, unsure whether to shake it or offer it a kiss. "I am Madam Toulouse. You look younger than I expected." She spoke Trader Esperanto clearly but with a thick accent.

Adem touched his cheeks. In his rush to make the elevator he'd forgotten to shave. "We don't get a lot of solar exposure on board. Gives us baby faces."

The matchmaker smiled. "Your bride is lucky to have you." She had vetted Adem's application and verified his mother's credit, but that was as far as her knowledge of him went.

Madam Toulouse's heels clicked like a half-interested radiation detector as she led Adem into the lift and down a long hallway. "Are you nervous?" she said.

Adem stuffed his hands in his pockets. "Some."

"You'll just answer a few questions and sign some documents." She fiddled with Adem's collar. "Are these the best clothes you have? No, never mind." She studied his face.

Adem half-expected her to lick her thumb to scrub at some smudge or other he had missed. "What happened to your hair?"

Adem brushed his hand across the left side of his face and head. The skin graft had taken nicely – his father did good work – but his hair hadn't grown back out all the way. "Conduit fire."

The matchmaker sighed. "You're pretty enough. She might not notice." She pointed to an alcove. "Get in there, and smile when the computer tells you. We'll get a picture for your future wife."

Adem had never found it easy to smile on command but felt he may have managed a friendly grimace by the time the computer had taken half a dozen shots. Madam Toulouse frowned at the test strip the computer printed out for her. "These will do." She propelled Adem by the arm farther down the hallway. "Let me do most of the talking. I know what your family is looking for and how much they are willing to pay."

The lighting in the interview room was warm and subdued. The chairs were well-stuffed, and the table in the middle of it all was an antique made of honey-colored fauxwood. Adem took a seat, interlacing his fingers on the tabletop. The matchmaker frowned, shaking her head an inch in either direction. Adem got the hint, slid his hands off the table, and rested them on the reinforced knees of his utilisuit.

The door swished open. A pear-shaped man in an old-style suit walked in first, trailed by Adem's future in-laws: a man and a woman in their early twenties. They walked closely together, and their clothes fit like they had been purchased for larger people. Adem experimented with a charming smile, but it felt phony. He looked at the table instead.

The matchmaker stood and discreetly touched Adem's shoulder. Adem lurched to his feet and, again not sure what to do with them, put his hands in his pockets.

Madam Toulouse smiled at the newcomers. "This is Adem

Sadiq, son of Captain Maneera Sadiq. He is part-owner of the *Hajj*." She put her hand on Adem's elbow. "Adem, this is Joao and Hadiya Sasaki."

The Sasakis offered Adem a formal bow. He returned it clumsily, hands still in his pockets. The pear-shaped man ignored him completely. "I am representing the Sasaki family," he said. "They do not understand the Trader's language."

"Of course," Madam Toulouse said. "Won't you sit down?" She gestured to the chairs on the other side of the table.

The Sasakis sat close together with their attorney taking up more than half the table to their left. He tented his fingers. The cuffs of his shirt were worn. "Captain Sadiq wants the bride to study United Americas physics and engineering," he said.

Madam Toulouse looked at Adem expectantly.

"Yeah," he said. "I mean, yes. That's what we want."

"Not much use on a Trader vessel."

Adem had wondered about that, too, but his mother hadn't seen fit to enlighten him. "I'm sure we'll find a way to put her to use."

The attorney's eyes widened. "I'm sure. Are there any other skills and interests you would like her to acquire? Cooking? Materials recycling, perhaps? BDSM?"

Adem rubbed the back of his neck. "Maybe she could learn to play an instrument."

"Will children be required?"

"If it happens, it happens, but I don't want anything like that in the contract."

The representative whispered with his clients and turned back to Adem's matchmaker. "My clients have no objection," he said. "Does the Sadiq family want naming rights? It will cost extra."

"Her parents can pick a name. That's their business."

"We want a contingency fund for genetic alteration in case the fetus does not have the math and science traits. If it is not used, it will revert back to Captain Sadiq."

"We are prepared for that," Madam Toulouse said. "There will be enough in the fund to get the work done on Versailles Station."

"Fine." The representative rolled his shoulders and adjusted the cuffs of his shirt. "Let's get down to it."

Adem tuned out. Madam Toulouse had a reputation for being fair and having a soft spot for the families of the brides she was placing. Both families were in good hands. Besides, he had a lot to think about, not least of which was turning his bachelor quarters into something a woman might like.

The matchmaker stood abruptly and offered her hand to the Sasakis' representative. "We have a deal."

Adem scrambled to his feet in time to see his future in-laws headed for the door. Hadiya Sasaki was crying. Her husband put his arms around her and pressed his mouth to her ear. She wiped her eyes on her too-long sleeves. Before Adem could say goodbye, they were gone.

"Congratulations," Madam Toulouse said. "You have a bride."

Adem looked at the door the Sasakis had gone through. "Will they be alright?"

The matchmaker's mouth twisted. "Their representative kept as much as he could for himself, but they will be far better off than they were."

"Thank you for that." Adem forced a smile. Marriage was supposed to be a happy thing, but what he felt was more akin to shame or embarrassment. "I should get back to my ship."

Madam Toulouse showed Adem where to sign his name and press his thumb. "Your mother has already transferred the funds to my account. Everything, minus our commissions, will go to your bride's rearing and education."

Preparations for departure were underway when Adem came aboard the *Hajj* and climbed to the environmental-control deck. He winked at the engineer in charge, a slim AfriD man named Sarat. "Everything all set in here?"

"We are breathing, and we have hot water to spare." Sarat turned from his workstation. "And you're married."

"Betrothed. I'll be married in a year." Adem's eagerness to see Sarat faltered. Making environmental-control his first stop had been a mistake. "Let's not talk about this now. We're about to leave orbit, and you know how my mother gets."

"Your sister can handle it."

"She's the pilot. I'm the one who makes sure the ship moves when she tells it to."

They both knew he was dodging.

"Let's have dinner tonight," Adem said. "My cabin."

Sarat nodded and turned back to his work.

Adem skimmed through the cargo manifest as he rode the lift to the command-and-control section in the bow. They'd invested heavily in food stuffs and building materials, an odd choice considering their next scheduled stop was Freedom, where entertainment and luxury items were in demand. Adem put his reader away as the lift slowed. Mother knew best. The *Hajj* hadn't ended a trip in the red since she'd taken over the bridge.

Adem took the five steps between the lift door and the entrance to the bridge and crossed to the command chair to kiss the captain on the cheek. "*Marhabaan 'ami.*"

She nodded, not taking her eyes off her display screens. "How did it go?"

"You have a daughter-in-law full of useless knowledge on the way."

"Nice family?"

"They didn't say much, and they left right after we shook on it."

"Probably afraid they'd back out." The captain rotated her chair to face the helm, where Adem's sister Lucy reclined in the piloting chair. While linked, she saw through the ship's cameras and sensors.

Lucy spoke through the bridge intercom. "Hello, little brother. How is Sarat?"

Adem refused to take the bait. "Did you get enough shopping done on the station?"

Lucy's sigh was amplified and dehumanized by the intercom's processors. "Can I ever? And it will be out of style by the time we come back."

"The time after that it will all be vintage and in high demand," Adem said. "You can sell it back at a profit."

"True. Did you buy me a new little sister?"

"A future math and science genius. Most likely spliced. Her parents are smart enough, but they don't have the genes for it. You'll have a lot to talk about when we pick her up."

Lucy had spent her teens and early twenties on Versailles Station to get the modifications necessary for piloting the *Hajj*. She'd had a wonderful time and never let anyone forget it.

"How close are we to leaving?" the captain said.

"Ten minutes, Mother, dear. Right on schedule."

Adem yawned. "I'll go back to the engineering section to keep an eye on things."

"There's a leak in the plumbing you might want to sniff out," Lucy said. "Wouldn't want our profits to go toward replacing water volume."

"I don't suppose you'd tell me where it is." Linked to the *Hajj*, Lucy could probably feel the leak.

"That wouldn't be nearly as fun as making you crawl through all the conduits," she said.

"I'm on it." Adem nodded to his mother. "Captain."

His mother waved, her eyes fixed on her readouts. There was nothing she could see that her daughter could not, but she was protective of the old ship. Her own mother had been captain before her, and her grandmother before that. She had spent years as ship's pilot before upgrades made her obsolete. Adolescent brains adapted better to the modifications.

"Say hello to Sarat for me," Lucy called after him.

Adem stopped by his quarters to leave his bag. The bottle of bourbon he'd purchased with Sarat in mind clunked against his bed as he set the bag on the floor. The continuous vibration he felt in his feet shifted in frequency as his sister moved the big ship out of orbit.

The ship's mass-grav system made a million calculations every second as it struggled to cope with the velocity changes. The vibration increased until Adem felt it in his teeth and the roots of his hair.

Adem's great-grandmother declared her family had left God behind when they fled to the stars. What God, after all, would have allowed His creation to be so utterly destroyed? Even so, the old woman would mutter to herself in Arabic at the start of every trip: "In the name of Allah, the merciful, the compassionate..." Adem heard the words in his head now, and knew that, on the bridge, his mother was hearing them, too.

Adem swayed as natural physics warred with ancient Earth science. Science won once again, and the *Hajj* slipped away from Gaul back into space.

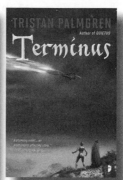

We are Angry Robot

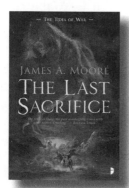

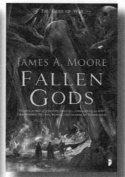

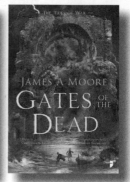

angryrobotbooks.com

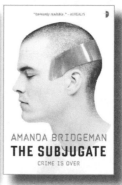

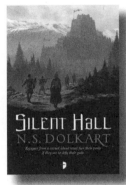

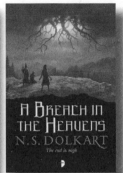

SILENT HALL
N.S. DOLKART

AMONG THE FALLEN
N.S. DOLKART

A BREACH IN THE HEAVENS
N.S. DOLKART

Science Fiction, Fantasy and WTF?!

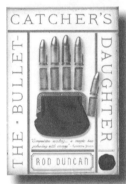

THE BULLET-CATCHER'S DAUGHTER
ROD DUNCAN

UNSEEMLY SCIENCE
ROD DUNCAN

THE CUSTODIAN OF MARVELS
ROD DUNCAN

@angryrobotbooks

PAIGE ORWIN
THE INTERMINABLES

MOONSHINE
JASMINE GOWER

AN OATH OF DOGS
WENDY N WAGNER

We are Angry Robot

angryrobotbooks.com

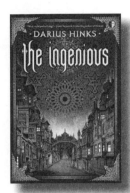
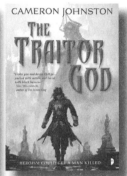

We are Angry Robot

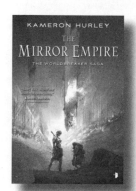

angryrobotbooks.com

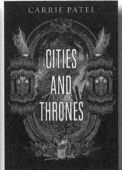

We are Angry Robot

angryrobotbooks.com